EVERYTHING LEFT UNSAID

The Hamilton Series

Everything we Lost

Everything for Love

Never Let You Fall

Everything left Unsaid

Everything we Dream

Everything we Promised

EVERYTHING LEFT UNSAID

KATE SMITH

Paperback ISBN: 978-0-9953487-7-6
E-book ISBN-13: 978-0-9953487-6-9

Anyone who truly touches and enriches your life must forever remain part of it ...

Kate Smith

CHAPTER 1

Savannah

SAVANNAH GAZED THROUGH THE WINDOW, shifting in her seat as the engines roared and their plane touched down. The aircraft slowed, the murmur of voices filling the cabin, along with the bleats of cell phones as the aircraft turned for the short taxi to Logan International Airport terminal.

She closed her eyes and drew in a deep breath, holding onto the vivid memories of long sunny days at sea. It had required some serious sweet talk, along with major support and encouragement from her Uncle Tom, but Savannah coerced her dad into allowing her adventure. Tom's endorsement had filled her with confidence. *Savannah is a mature young woman, Aiden. She's seventeen. You spent years away from your family, starting at a much younger age, and you managed just fine.*

Not that her dad worried needlessly. He had solid reasons for concern, but he'd understood her longing to experience life and become self-reliant, and after some discussion, they'd reached a happy compromise.

She'd never regret the three months away from home. As part of a small, but tight-knit sailboat crew, she'd shared the on-board duties in addition to studying Greek history, mythology, marine biology, and earning valuable sailing certifications. All with one of her best friends at her side.

A smile touched Savannah's lips as she studied the handsome young man who'd risen to retrieve their backpacks from the overhead bin.

"I'm sad we're home," Justin said in a deep low voice, a dimple appearing as he rewarded her with a heart-stopping grin. He'd morphed from the cute teenage boy Savannah had dated at fifteen into an attractive fully grown man. "It's great your dad is allowing me to stay in Boston for a few days."

"Thanks, sweetie." She accepted her bag. "You do realize it's your reward for taking care of me while we were overseas. If you hadn't come, I swear he would've said no. Like he doesn't trust me to take care of myself."

Fresh air rushed into the cabin as a crew member opened the outer door. They joined the crowd of eager passengers traipsing through the jet-way.

"It wasn't about trust." Justin frowned. "You've had several rough years, and he didn't want you to be alone, halfway around the world. With the panic att—"

"Don't remind me." She smacked his arm. "Besides, I kept it all under control."

"You did great." Justin nodded, his expression remaining serious. "I've noticed a huge change in how you handle things."

Savannah entwined their fingers, giving his a light squeeze. No doubt his words were sincere. During their three months abroad, she'd nurtured her inner strength, focusing on each new experience, refusing to waste a moment of the unique opportunity she'd been granted. Personal growth, her therapist would call it. For Savannah, it equaled a new perspective and appreciation of everything and everyone in her life.

Justin pulled her aside as they stepped onto the main concourse. "I meant every word, Savannah. I respect your dad for taking care of you. When you left Portland to live with a virtual stranger on the opposite side of the country, I worried."

"You didn't need to. Aiden's amazing." She cupped his cheek in her palm, rewarding him a gentle smile and a light kiss. "Thank you for caring."

"Always. I will never forget our summer together." He linked his fingers with hers. "I bet your dad's waiting. Let's get out of here."

Savannah's smile widened as she tugged Justin toward the baggage claim. She dodged other passengers while searching the endless sea of faces. "Dad." She hurried forward, pulling from Justin's grasp.

"Vanna." Aiden opened his arms, hugging her tight before he lifted her and swung her around. "Have I missed you." He planted a kiss on her cheek before setting her on her feet. "You look great. How was it?"

"Amazing. The places we visited were incredible, and I have a zillion new pictures." Savannah patted her bag, reassured by the solid feel of the case that protected the high-end camera her dad and stepmother, Emily, had given her last Christmas. "I missed you so much." She glanced around, seeking the other two faces she longed to see after her extended absence. A few stolen minutes here and there for a video chat wasn't the same as seeing her family daily. "Where are Emily and Kellan?"

"They wanted to come, but it's a constant challenge to keep up with our little man these days. Neither of us felt like playing hide and seek with a toddler in a crowded airport, so they're waiting at home."

"He's running now?" Tears sprang to her eyes as she pictured the little brother who'd only managed a few wobbly steps before she'd left for her trip. "I can't wait to see him."

"He's missed his big sister." He slid an arm around her waist and guided her to where the younger man waited by the baggage carousel. "Justin. How are you?"

"Great, sir. The trip was incredible. Thank you, for everything." Justin grinned. "I've never flown in seats where you can be comfortable and sleep."

"We couldn't have you banished to economy while Vanna lounged in first class." Vanna's dad gave the boy a warm smile. "And none of that sir stuff. You're making me feel old. It's Aiden."

"Right, Aiden." Justin shook the offered hand.

"Bags are coming down." Aiden pressed another kiss to his daughter's temple. "I'm glad you enjoyed the trip."

"Thank you for sending me, Dad," she said. "I may never have the chance to do that kind of trip again. In a week, I start at Harvard. Can you believe it?"

"Nope. Having a seventeen-year-old daughter still freaks me out." He laughed as he grabbed her bag from the carousel and took her hand in his. "Let's go home."

⌇

Vanna settled onto the couch beside Justin and patted his knee. "The last of the preparations are done for the barbecue, and the caterers arrived to take over." She rested her head against his shoulder. "I can't believe the summer is over, and you go home tomorrow. I'll miss you."

He entwined their fingers. "We knew this couldn't last forever. I start Stanford in less than a week, and you'll be at Harvard, which is crazy."

"Yeah, my underachieving self got in." She laughed. "I can't believe it, either."

"You're brilliant, and you know it. I'm so proud of you." He gave her one of his crooked, adorable grins.

"There's my girl." Tom appeared. "I heard you were back. How was your trip?"

Vanna bounced to her feet and threw her arms around him. "Wonderful and completely amazing. I'll show you my pictures when we have time. Uncle Tom, this is my friend Justin, from Portland."

"Right. You joined Vanna for the summer." Tom shook Justin's hand. "And you're off to Stanford soon for undergrad?"

"I am. I would've liked to attend Harvard or Yale, but ..." Justin shrugged.

3

"Stanford is a great school. Our good friend Ryan went there and loved it. I've been after Vanna," he said as he gave her an affectionate squeeze, "to apply at Yale once she's finished her undergrad. You could do the same."

"It would be amazing to be near Savannah again." Justin's expression softened. "We've missed her."

A group appeared on the well-appointed rooftop patio.

"That's Piper Nelson, our newest intern." Tom waved and beckoned to a petite young woman with auburn hair. "Piper, come meet Savannah and her friend Justin. You and Vanna will be working together once school starts, and you may be in some classes together at Harvard."

Piper grinned. "Hi, Savannah."

"I should greet the rest of the guests." Tom patted Vanna's shoulder. "Glad to have you home." He strode across the patio to join Vanna's dad, who was talking with a woman she didn't recognize.

"It's nice they invited us. I just moved from Montana to attend school," Piper said. "This is some place. I heard it belongs to one of the partners, but I haven't met him yet. Tom hired me."

Savannah nodded, and sipped her drink.

Piper glanced toward the bar where Tom, Aiden, and Joel chatted and poured drinks. "Wonder who that is with Tom and Joel." The girl's eyes skimmed over Aiden. "Wish he worked at the office. We could have a hot lawyer trifecta."

Justin snorted and a laugh erupted.

"What?" Piper stared at him.

"That's Aiden Hamilton." Savannah raised a brow at Piper. "The silent partner. He's a doctor, not a lawyer." She bit back the sigh that begged to escape. "He's my dad."

"No way. He looks barely thirty." Piper giggled. "You're teasing. How old are you?"

"Eighteen in January." She studied Piper. "My dad's thirty-three."

"You're not kidding?" Piper looked between her and Justin, her cheeks flaming as she peered out of the corner of her eye at Aiden.

"It makes me uncomfortable when girls my age get gushy over him. And he's married."

"Sorry. I didn't know, but I understand. Girls get that way about my stepbrother. He's twenty-three, and my friends think he's super hot. They get weird and flirtatious around him."

"Exactly." Savannah threw her hands in the air. "I get tons of messed up comments. One time we attended a parent-teacher conference, and the Dean told Aiden she wanted a parent, not a sibling." She giggled. "You should have seen her face when he told her he was my dad. And then, when she realized he was single, she slipped him her phone number. Like I wouldn't notice?"

"Ewwwww." Piper laughed but then gave her a serious look. "This might be nosy, but your mom and dad had you when they were pretty young. Like fifteen? What's your mom like?"

"She's never been part of my life. Emily"—Savannah pointed to her stepmother—"has been like a mother to me. She's amazing." She fell silent for a moment, her thoughts straying to her other parents. She missed Ross and Jayde, though every day got easier.

"So no wicked stepmother for you. Lucky. Mine's a troll. She looked positively thrilled when I announced I'd be moving all the way across the country to attend Harvard. I'm living in the residences, and I hope to stay in Boston next summer. I never want to live with that woman again."

"What about your mom?"

"She died." Piper looked away, brushing at her tears. "Sorry, I'm getting weepy."

"Don't apologize for missing your mom." Vanna shook her head. "How did it happen?"

"Cancer. Our lives were spent in the hospital for about two years. My mom died five years ago, and Dad married the troll two years later."

"I'm sorry. It's hard to lose someone so special." She couldn't hold back her own sniffle.

"Oh, don't cry. I'm sorry. I shouldn't tell sad stories."

"It's okay, but it makes me think of people I've lost." Vanna blotted at her eyes.

Justin wrapped an arm around her shoulders. "How about we get some drinks?"

"Thanks." Savannah smiled at him.

Piper nodded. "Sounds good. People will wonder about us, standing here weeping."

"Do you have any other siblings? Or just your stepbrother?" Justin asked as they moved toward the bar.

"I wish it were only him. I have a stepsister, and she's a nightmare. She's fifteen, and we hated each other on sight." Piper rolled her eyes. "My stepmother is always *Mia this* and *Mia that* like the girl's a damn princess. At least Brandon is cool, and we get along." She smiled. "I hope we have some classes together, Savannah."

"Me too."

I can do this. Savannah gazed at her reflection, taking a long breath and pushing it out slowly, hoping to still the flitting butterflies. She pushed her shoulders back and straightened, drawing on the newfound confidence in herself, hoping it wouldn't desert her.

Savannah grabbed her snacks and a water bottle from the fridge and patted down her bag one more time, taking a mental inventory. Laptop. *Check.* Charger. *Check.* Ample supply of pens and her notebook. *Check, and check.*

"Morning." Aiden wandered into the kitchen, rubbing a hand through his hair.

"Hey, Dad. You just get home?" She stretched to kiss his cheek. "You look tired."

"We have a whole new batch of medical students to keep tabs on, and the ER was crazy busy last night. Every kid in Boston came in needing emergency medical care. So much for them enjoying their last day of freedom." He kissed her in return. "You ready for your first day?"

"I'm excited. I still can't believe it." She smiled. "Wish me luck."

"I can't believe it, either. The last year flew by, and here you are, starting undergrad. And you don't need luck, Vanna, you'll be great."

"Papa." Kellan charged into the room, his tiny feet pounding across the floor as he careened toward his dad. He threw his arms around Aiden's legs before stretching his arms. "Uppeeeeee."

Aiden tossed him into the air, making the boy giggle. "Morning, little man." He planted a kiss on his son's cheek before tucking Kellan on his hip.

"Manna." Kellan pointed at Savannah, before stuffing his fingers into his mouth.

"That's right. Vvvanna," Aiden said.

Emily wandered in moments later, her dark hair piled in a messy bun. "Good morning. The gang's all here." She accepted a kiss from her husband before relieving him of his armful of squirming toddler. "Let's have breakfast, Kellan. I bet Papa needs sleep."

"Bekfas, Mama?" He clapped his hands and pointed to the bowl of fruit on the gleaming counter. "Nana."

"Oh, banana, yum." Savannah grinned. Her baby brother always brought a ray of sun into her day. Her grin widened as Aiden brushed a hand over his son's dark hair, absolute joy reflecting in his eyes. Savannah had wondered many times what it would have been like growing up with him. Would Aiden have been as great a dad at fifteen as he was at thirty-three?

"Can I drive you, Vanna?" Aiden scrubbed a hand over his rough stubble.

"Thanks, but you were on shift all night. Go to bed. The subway only takes twenty minutes." She stopped to give Kellan a kiss and waved. "Bye-bye."

"Bye, Manna." Kellan fluttered his chubby hand in her direction.

Emily and Aiden's goodbyes echoed after her. She enjoyed family time, but she didn't want to be late on the first day.

⌒≼

She spotted Piper chatting with a group of other students, who she assumed to be some of their classmates. After the barbecue, they'd compared schedules and found they were in many of the same classes.

"Hi, Savannah. Nervous?"

"A little, but I'm sure it'll be fine." Savannah smiled at Piper. "Did you get your room setup?"

"Yup. We have limited space, so I couldn't bring much." Piper beckoned to the nearby group. "Hey everyone, this is Savannah." Piper pointed around the circle. "This is Rochelle, Jackson, Pete, and Gray."

Savannah waved. "Call me Vanna."

"So, we're planning to form a study group. You interested?" The boy who'd been introduced as Gray swept a hand through his blondish hair, studying her with intense blue eyes framed by long dark lashes.

Savannah's heart flipped as a grin lit his face. "Sure. Maybe." She noted the wide-eyed look Piper threw her way. "Yes?"

Piper giggled. "She's in, Gray. And trust me, you want her in our group." She nudged Savannah with her elbow.

"Oh?" Rochelle gave Vanna a long cool look. "Why's that?"

Savannah looked her straight in the eye. "I'm planning to work hard."

The girl gave her an assessing look. "We'll see."

"Don't mind her." Jackson casually slung an arm around her shoulder. "You're in."

"Thanks." Savannah tried to relax as the handsome young man gave her a light squeeze. He reminded her of a younger version of Shemar Moore.

"Time for orientation." Pete tapped his watch.

Shouldering her pack, Savannah joined the group as they wound their way through the open courtyards to their orientation.

By the end of the day, she'd met most of her new classmates and had started to feel comfortable on campus.

"We're going for pizza to celebrate our first day." Piper motioned her over to join the group loitering in the common area. "You in?"

"Of course." As she fell into step beside Piper and Rochelle, her phone buzzed and a text popped up from Justin.

How was it?

As they walked, she typed her reply.

Great. How was your first day?

Incredible. Wish you were here, or I was there.

Vanna grinned as they shot texts back and forth.

Piper eyed her. "What has you so happy?"

"Justin. He started at Stanford today."

"Ohhhhh, right." Piper smirked. "He's a cutie, that one. How long have you been dating?"

"We're not dating." Savannah shrugged. "Not now, anyway. We used to when I lived in Portland, and we reconnected over the summer, but it's nothing serious. He's in California, and I'm here, so we agreed we'd date other people."

"Reconnected, huh?" Rochelle smothered a laugh. "You have pictures?"

Savannah pulled up a favorite photo from over the summer and held out her phone. "This is Justin."

"He's not a cutie. He's a hottie." Rochelle snickered. "You're letting that boy go?"

"He's thousands of miles away, and I love him, but I'm not in love with him."

"Smart choice." Piper nodded. "Long distance never works, and you get to keep your options open." She tilted her head toward the group of boys ahead of them who were immersed in loud discussion and lowered her voice. "Gray's had his eye on you all day."

"He has not." Heat rose in Savannah's cheeks. "Anyway, it's too soon to be dating someone else."

"Ahh, so you're still a little hung up on hottie Justin," Rochelle said.

Savannah rolled her eyes but smiled at the teasing of her new friends. Her angst over the first day seemed unwarranted.

As they reached the pizzeria, she paused to allow Rochelle and Piper to precede her inside. Her cheeks flushed hot as Gray held the door, their hands brushing as she passed.

The corners of his mouth twitched and he winked in an exaggerated fashion, wiggling his eyebrows.

Damn. This guy was going to be trouble.

Chapter 2

Tiffany

THE LAST OF THE GUESTS disappeared through the door. Isla locked it behind them, giving Tiffany a thumbs up before beginning the task of sorting paperwork at the front counter.

Tiffany scanned the gallery, noting the rapid and efficient dismantling of the catering set-up. Her practiced eye assessed each art installment in turn. Satisfied all was in order, she retreated to her office and sank into the plush leather chair, kicking off the high heels and wiggling her toes. She loved these shoes, but they were murder on her feet by the end of a busy evening. She'd barely had a chance to sit since her brief lunch break, and it was now after ten.

"It went well," her assistant said as she strolled into the office and dropped a thick folder onto the pile on Tiffany's desk. She picked up the stack of invoices, flipping through them. "Leave me a note on which works you want for permanent display. I'll hang them tomorrow and ship the sold pieces."

"Perfect." Tiffany leaned back and stretched her arms high above her head while she attempted to contain the yawn. "Thanks for the good work. I couldn't have done it without you."

"You're welcome." Her assistant gave her a warm though tired smile. "Anything else?"

"You look exhausted. I'll organize the invoices while the caterers finish." Tiffany waved toward the door. "Head home. We have a lot to accomplish tomorrow."

"Which is amazing. It's great to see that appointment book filling with names." Isla paused in the doorway. "You sure you don't want me to wait? We could go for a drink to celebrate our success."

"No, I'm beat." Tiffany wrinkled her nose. "I'd probably fall asleep in my drink. Rain check?"

"Deal. Night, Boss." Her assistant disappeared into her own office.

Tiffany closed her weary eyes, sighing in contentment. *Boss.* That word had a magical ring. She'd opened this gallery in downtown Chicago four years ago, and it had been a labor of love. Now, at long last, her hard work was paying off. The profits were slim, but she persevered. Every time she stepped through the door, a sense of pride filled her at all that had been accomplished.

Forty-five minutes later, Tiffany pulled on her comfortable walking shoes, set the alarm, and locked the front door, taking a moment to enjoy the light summer breeze fluttering through her long hair. It felt refreshing after hours of being cooped up indoors.

The sidewalks were quieter at this time of the evening, but the traffic never seemed to cease. She enjoyed the beat of the city and the bright lights as she strolled toward home.

A mix of emotions overtook her as she crossed the lobby and rode the elevator to the tenth floor, letting herself inside the dark and quiet apartment. She'd fallen in love with the cozy space and purchased it only a year before she'd opened her gallery. Though small, it was the first place she could call her very own.

In the months since the broken engagement to Harrison Taylor, she'd led a solitary existence. Some days were lonely, and she longed for someone to come home to, but … none of her relationships worked out as planned. Men asked her out on occasion, but this past year had been rough.

Life had become complicated, so she embraced the advice from her therapist, Liz. *Take your time and learn to be alone. It's not healthy to need a man in your life every moment of every day. Don't rush into anything. Deal with your immediate issues first.*

It tested her resolve. Tiffany hated being alone—something she'd discovered at the tender age of thirteen.

She padded through the dim and silent apartment, pausing at the bank of floor to ceiling windows. The full moon hung low over the lake, but the stars were obliterated by the glow of city lights.

Tiffany closed her eyes, picturing the Milky Way as seen from the beach in the Vineyard, remembering those precious nights she'd spent with Aiden. Nights when she hadn't had to vie for his attention. Hours when she'd become the center of his universe. Incredible nights when the rest of the world ceased to exist, and she felt safe and loved and needed, cocooned in his arms, talking, watching the stars appear, or making love in front of the fire.

She wrapped her arms around herself and wished she could transport back in time and recapture the pure happiness that now eluded her.

There had been a time when her involvement with Aiden seemed anything but certain. She had only been at the boarding school a few months and far too shy to approach the larger-than-life Aiden or engage in the shameless and endless flirtation bestowed on him by other girls. Instead, she'd coveted him from afar.

How could an awkward girl compete with the bevy of lovely teenage girls who surrounded him daily? Envy filled her as she witnessed the comfortable, easy friendship her roommate Alexis Carr shared with Aiden. She longed to be part of their tight-knit group.

Then, during those last months of school before the summer break, Alex had intervened, tired of Tiffany's inability to act on the mad crazy crush she'd been nurturing on the adorable, dark-haired, brown-eyed teenage boy. An invitation to join them on one of their escapades, along with a little finagling from Alex to allow her time alone with Aiden, changed everything.

That one night had caused a cascade of events that altered the course of her life. She'd blossomed under his attention. Aiden became the man she loved beyond measure, the man she'd marry then betray, the man she'd long for during many endless and lonely nights.

Her cheeks grew damp, and she dabbed at them as she continued her journey through to the bathroom. She avoided the mirror as she washed her face. As she donned soft pajamas and crawled into bed, she left the lights off, unable to bear looking at what she'd become.

She lay in the dark for some time before she turned on the bedside lamp.

The ornate silver double picture frame on her nightstand brought back memories. Aiden had intended for it to be one of Tiffany's gifts for their second Christmas as a married couple, but things hadn't gone as planned.

As painful as the memories were, she'd never had the heart to dispose of the frame. It seemed fitting it now held a picture of a red-faced baby bundled in a pink blanket, her dark, serious eyes staring out at the world. A photo of a teenage girl occupied the second spot. Tiffany traced a fingertip over her daughter's face. Savannah's long blonde hair whipped in the breeze as the girl gazed down the beach.

It had been irresistible. Tiffany's artistic eye framed the picture in her viewfinder, snapping it without thinking, shocked when she found she'd gone through an entire roll of film. She'd tucked them away, not knowing quite what to do with them. She couldn't display them, nor could she admit to anyone that she'd lurked on the outskirts, spying on Aiden's happy family.

Sadness squeezed her heart. That day her own eye had been drawn to where Emily cuddled Aiden's tiny precious son in her arms, the man looking on both with complete adoration, his arm looped around the woman's waist. The couple looked so content and fulfilled, the perfect family Tiffany had dreamed of but never had. Perhaps the elusive wish would forever remain out of her grasp.

She brushed the heartbreaking memories aside and concentrated on the girl. Apart from those deep brown eyes that reminded her of Aiden, it could be Tiffany herself standing on that beach. The resemblance and the reality that her daughter had grown up without her caused a pang deep inside her chest.

A tear trickled down her cheek. Her daughter's final rejection had torn something loose. The girl refused to give her a chance to make amends, and even worse, Aiden allowed it to happen.

He hadn't fought for her. The familiar rush of anger flooded through, but she pushed it down and flicked off the light, settling against her pillow and closing her eyes.

Tiffany tossed and turned, unable to sleep while the tangled emotions ran rampant, crushing her under their weight. In such times, her mind refused to shut down, constantly seeking the answer to the never-ending question; how to make things right?

Tiffany looked up from her perch on the edge of the chair as the door opened.

Liz beckoned. "Come in, Tiffany."

She set the magazine onto the table, rising to follow the dark-haired woman into the inner sanctum, a space dominated by overstuffed chairs and a comfortable sofa decorated with bright throw pillows.

A flowering plant with vibrant fuchsia blooms, long graceful stems, and lush green leaves sat in the middle of the coffee table. Tiffany wondered if this token effort cheered up the numerous depressed individuals who filtered through this office daily.

As she lowered herself onto the couch, she straightened her back and clasped her hands in her lap.

Liz folded her own hands on top of her notebook, her keen eyes scrutinizing every movement Tiffany made. Finally, her therapist broke the silence. "You're on edge today, and you look tired."

"I didn't sleep well last night." Tiffany shrugged. "It was a busy evening."

"How did the art show go?"

"I'm thrilled with the results." She forced a smile. "Not all shows have such an amazing turnout."

"Uh-huh." Liz gave her a searching look. "But you're unhappy."

"It's been a year since she refused to see me." Tiffany tucked her feet beneath her and curled into a ball. "I'm stupid to obsess over it."

The other woman tilted her head. "Why do you think it's stupid?"

"Why would she want to know me? I'm nothing to her. She has Emily, the fantastic mommy replacement, and Aiden didn't help my case. My daughter doesn't need me. She never has."

"Tell me how you feel about that."

Tiffany met the woman's gaze. "We've been over it so many times."

"And yet you're still holding it all inside. At some point, you need to forgive yourself … and him."

Tiffany bowed her head, shaking it as she traced the floral design on one of the pillows with a manicured fingertip. "How can I?" she whispered. "I let them take her away and never even had the opportunity to see her again until she was almost fifteen."

"You were only fifteen when they took your baby away."

"Yes." Tiffany hugged the soft pillow to her chest. "I know what you're going to say. We were too young. We were immature. It's all for the best. Her adoptive family gave her everything we couldn't."

"I wasn't planning to say that." The slight shake and tilt of her head relayed exasperation, but Liz's expression softened quickly. "Having a child is a personal choice only you could have made. I want to help you find peace with the events that transpired. You've lived with an enormous burden of anger, guilt, and shame for years. There's nothing shameful in having a child or in giving that child to a good and loving home."

"Tell that to my family and all the other people who stared, and shook their heads, and talked behind my back. They judged me to be an irresponsible slut for having a baby when I was fifteen."

"No one said it was fair that society is hard on women while giving men a free pass for the exact same behaviors. Anyway, it doesn't matter. You experienced a devastating loss at a young age regardless of what anyone believes. Other people's opinions change nothing. You have to accept it, make peace with it, and forgive yourself."

After her grueling counseling session, Tiffany dragged herself to her car and negotiated the crowded roads. She clenched the steering wheel, her palms growing clammier with each mile. Finally, she drew up in front of the house with its expanse of manicured lawn. She eyed the vine-covered trellis and beds filled with the fading blooms of summer.

Tiffany took her time trudging up the front steps and through the door. "Anybody home?" She hung her coat and padded through to the kitchen at the back of the spacious house.

"Tiffany. Good, you're here." Her mother smiled and moved in for a hug. "I've made us lunch."

"Where's Father?" She glanced around. Soft strains of music flowed through the air, but otherwise, the house remained silent.

"He won't be home until dinnertime. Did you need to speak with him?"

"No." Tiffany avoided her mother's gaze. "Just curious."

"Uh-huh." Michelle sipped her wine, motioning to the half-empty bottle. "Would you like some?"

"Please." Tiffany sank onto one of the stools.

Her mother poured her a glass of the rich red liquid and set it in front of her. "Your show went well?"

"We received several orders." She swirled the burgundy liquid before tasting it. "This is a nice one."

"How's everything else?"

Tiffany shrugged, staring over the backyard, watching the leaves fluttering in the wind.

"No news to share?" Her mother placed a sandwich in front of her. "You're not seeing anyone new?"

"Nope." She took a bite, chasing her first mouthful with a liberal dose of wine.

"Have you seen her?" Michelle asked.

"Don't call, don't write, and most certainly do not visit. That's what Aiden said, Mother. He refuses to allow me anywhere near him or Savannah. He wishes to have nothing to do with the Baxter family. End of story." Tiffany shoved her half-eaten sandwich across the shiny counter.

"You're wasting away." Her mother edged the plate closer to Tiffany. "You need to eat."

"I'm not a child. I'm fully capable of deciding if I'm hungry, Mother." Tiffany gulped her wine, the crystal ringing as she smacked the glass onto the quartz counter. She extended her index finger, poking at the plate and sliding it away as she curled her lip. "What did you want to talk about?"

"I wanted to see my daughter." Michelle snatched up the plates, making a show of depositing the remains of their lunch in the trash. "You never visit and rarely call. We've gone back to your days as a surly teenager. Don't think I haven't noticed you're avoiding any meal where your father might be present."

"I'm busy with the gallery." Tiffany rolled her eyes. "Running a business isn't easy."

"No, but surely you could spare some time for your mother." Michelle planted her flattened palms against the counter, taking several breaths. "Perhaps you'd allow me to treat you to some pampering at the spa on Saturday, with a little shopping in the afternoon."

Fighting it would be futile. When her mother gave her that disappointed look, Tiffany didn't have the heart to refuse. "Fine. Saturday."

"Wonderful. You won't regret it." Michelle patted her knee. "So, how are things with Alex and Jenna?"

⌒≺

"Aren't you supposed to be somewhere in about … ten minutes?" Isla tapped her watch.

"Don't remind me. An afternoon of torture with my mother. Like lunch on Monday wasn't bad enough." Tiffany forced a fake cough. "Maybe I'm coming down with something."

"Up." Isla pulled her from the chair. "Go for lunch with your mother. Some daughter you are."

"You didn't grow up with her." Tiffany sighed as she retrieved her handbag from her desk drawer. "Now she acts like she's been nominated for mother of the year."

"Have you ever told her how you feel?" Isla lifted a brow.

"What's the point? She never listens, yet she always knows what's right for me. Monday I got lectured about not eating enough. I thought she'd threaten to withhold dessert if I didn't finish my sandwich."

"I can't say I disagree about the eating." Isla eyed her. "How much weight have you lost over the past few months?"

"Not you too." Tiffany threw her an annoyed look. "It's not only that. She droned on about my ex-friends and my ex-husband, and then we played twenty questions about my non-existent dating life. Can you imagine? She insists I settle down, like I've never been married or engaged. Look how great those relationships turned out. Though in her mind the wedding to Aiden didn't count. That was my young and stupid phase, and hey, I proved them right and totally fucked it up."

Isla squinted at her.

Tiffany hung her head. "I'm ranting again."

"It's fine. But now you're late." Her assistant shoved an elegantly wrapped parcel into her hands. "Don't forget the peace offering." Isla steered her toward the door.

"I'm going." She glowered at the other woman as she snagged her handbag.

A few minutes later, Tiffany arrived at the spa. Though she usually loved pampering, the mere thought of an afternoon with her mother had Tiffany's blood pressure rising and her tiny appetite melting away.

"I was worried you'd forgotten." Michelle rose from her chair, drawing Tiffany in for a hug.

"Sorry. I got busy—"

"At the gallery. Yes, I know. Always too busy for anything but work." Her mother waved down one of the attendants.

Tiffany sighed gratefully as she sank into the chair several feet away from her mother's. Her luck held out during her manicure, but she wasn't so fortunate when they were placed side by side at the foot baths.

"You've been carrying around that fancy parcel like it contains a treasure. Aren't you going to open it? Who's it from? A new man?"

Tiffany fought the urge to either throw the box in her mother's face or rush out the door, but instead, she handed the present to her mother. "It's for you."

"For me?" Her mother beamed before she tugged on the lavender satin ribbon, taking her time unwrapping the box. When she opened the lid, she emitted a small gasp. "Is this …?" Michelle stared at the photo. "It's her?"

"You don't have to take it." Tiffany extended her fingers, anxious to reclaim the gift box.

"Why wouldn't I want it?" Michelle lifted the frame and pressed it to her chest, directly over her heart. "She's my granddaughter. I'm speechless. How could you ever think I wouldn't want a picture of my only grandchild? I've never even seen her."

Tiffany frowned as she noted the shimmering blue eyes. If she didn't know better, she'd think her mother was about to burst into tears. "You've never wanted to see her."

"Oh, honey." Michelle bowed her head. "This is an incredibly special gift. Thank you."

"You like it?" Tears burned her eyes at her mother's obvious pleasure at receiving the photo.

"I love it. She's so beautiful, and despite your assumptions, I'd love to meet her. One day, perhaps my wish will come true."

The rest of the afternoon progressed smoothly—or at least as smoothly as a visit ever did with her mother. After their spa visit, they spent another two hours shopping. A little of Michelle Baxter went a long way, so Tiffany pleaded exhaustion to avoid dinner and returned to the gallery.

"I won't even ask how it went." Isla studied her face before handing over a vellum envelope. "Did she at least like the gift?"

"She said she did, but who ever knows with that woman. For all I know she'll show it to Father, and he'll toss it in the fireplace." Tiffany inserted a nail under the flap and plucked out an invitation, skimming it before handing the embossed card to Isla.

"This show looks amazing," Isla said. "You might find some new artists to represent. I'll book tickets and a hotel for you."

"Let me look at my calendar." Her stomach twisted. Things were tight, but as much as she wanted to go, it would mean groveling for extra funds from her father. He'd provided most of the financing, her own funds had disappeared long ago during her struggle to get the gallery operable.

Isla raised a brow. "We need more artists."

"Right. Book it." Tiffany sighed. She'd swallow her pride and do what needed to be done to survive.

CHAPTER 3

Savannah

THE COLORFUL AUTUMN LEAVES AND bright sunshine brought a smile to Savannah's face. A few weeks into college and her life seemed almost normal.

"Vanna. Wait up." Piper's footsteps and cheerful voice carried across the square. "Wow, you look happy today."

"I feel great."

"You finish that assignment?" Her friend tossed her rich auburn hair over her shoulder. The sunlight caught it, turning the highlights to blazing fire as the girl regarded her with serious gray eyes.

"Yup." Vanna smothered a giggle. "Math, ugh."

"I'm thankful Tom saw us struggling with it and explained. I can't believe he took time out of his busy schedule to help two lowly interns with homework." Piper puffed out a breath, blowing a stray strand of hair out of her face.

"Tom's amazing." Savannah adjusted her bag on her shoulder. "And he's family. You'd think he and my dad were actual brothers. Besides, Tom wants me to apply to Yale when it comes time for law school, so he has a vested interested in my GPA."

"Isn't that where he went?" Piper smirked. "Bet you get in."

"We'll see. It would mean moving." Savannah twirled a lock of hair around her finger. "It might sound strange, but I'd miss my little brother. And …" She grinned. "I hope Aiden and Emily have another baby. I'd love a sister."

"Careful what you wish for." Piper shuddered. "I have one of those, and she's a nightmare."

"You have a stepsister, and she's a teenager. This would be a tiny little baby sister. It's totally different."

"True." Piper adjusted her bag across her shoulder. "Why do you call him Aiden when he's your dad?"

"I was adopted as a baby. When I first met Aiden, who is my biological father, my adoptive dad was still alive. It would have been weird to call both of them Dad. Plus, I barely knew Aiden. I found him when I was almost fifteen."

"I can't imagine what that would be like."

"Strange and awkward at first, but then …" Savannah shuffled her feet along the ground. "When my other dad, Ross, became ill, Aiden flew to Portland to take care of me. We grew close during that time. When I moved to Boston, it finally felt right to call him Dad."

"Wow, I'm sorry. That had to be tough. What about your mom?"

"My mom died in a car accident a couple of years before I lost my dad. I never see the woman who gave birth to me."

"You understand about my mom, don't you?"

Savannah nodded. "All too well." She waved at the tall dark-haired girl striding across the square toward them. "There's Ro."

"Hey, you two." Rochelle joined them. "Ready to start that project this weekend? We have to decide where to meet and let the guys know."

Piper motioned her head toward Savannah. "Vanna has an incredible rooftop deck. Maybe we could work there?"

"Sure." Vanna gave her friend a sassy eye roll. "No problem."

Her friend grinned. "I'm serious. The rest of us live in the dorms, and we spend every minute of the day on campus. Would your parents mind?"

"I'm sure it wouldn't be an issue."

"Oh, that would be amazing." Rochelle sighed as they located seats in the auditorium. "Campus is great, but I miss the comforts of home sometimes."

Savannah smiled as she took her seat. Living on campus sounded like fun, but it seemed like her life had only become normal. She loved having a dad and a mom, and a little brother. Even more, she loved that she blended in, and her new friends referred to Aiden and Emily as her parents. "Yeah, I'd miss home too."

⌒≼

Savannah arrived in the foyer just as the doors slid open to reveal her five classmates, who were loaded down with bags and laptops.

Gray stepped out first, his eyes widening as he looked around. "Great digs."

"Thanks. It's warm today, so I thought we'd use the rooftop patio." Savannah waved them all inside, the elevator closing behind them.

"Sweet." Jackson said. "I'm down. We could catch a few rays while we work."

"Yeah, I'm down too." Gray flashed his perfect white teeth.

"Let's go." Vanna grabbed her own books and laptop before leading them up the short flight of stairs onto the patio.

"Awesome." Gray took in the view before he stripped off his t-shirt and grinned. "Might as well take advantage of the last few days of sunshine before the long dark Boston winter."

Savannah couldn't help herself. Her eyes were drawn to his smooth and well-toned chest and his washboard abs. As her gaze traveled up, she met his vivid blue eyes, a blush rising as she realized everyone had noticed her inspection.

"Drinks. We need some …" She hurried to the small fridge tucked under the stone counter, ducking her head to hide her mortification.

"Here, let me help." Piper appeared behind her. "Practically drool-worthy, isn't he?" she said under her breath.

"Not that anyone noticed." Savannah let out a nervous laugh.

"Nope, nobody noticed anything." Her friend snickered before they returned to the group who were now all lounging on the luxurious patio set. "Alright, slackers. Let's get to work."

$\sim$

"Anyone need anything?" Several hours into the study session, Savannah stood and stretched, then began collecting the empty soda cans and bags littering the tabletop. "Hungry? Should we order pizza? We need more than chips to keep our brains functioning at full capacity."

"I'm starving." Pete looked up from his laptop. "I'm down for pizza."

"Let me give you a hand with those." Gray jumped from the couch, scooping up some of the cans and following Vanna down the stairs.

"Thanks. They go there." Savannah pointed to the recycling container just outside the doors. She stepped through the door and wandered into the kitchen to dig in a drawer for the takeout menu.

"I'll take up a collection for the pizza," Gray said.

"Don't bother. My dad left money."

"Won't he mind buying us all pizza? The six of us eat a lot."

"Nope. He told me to order in if our session went long." She shrugged. "He remembers what it's like to be buried in assignments. Remember, he's an M.D. so …"

"Oh, right, he knows how intense it is, and how being a broke student feels."

Savannah wrinkled her nose but said nothing. Intense, sure, but broke? She held back the snicker as she scanned the menu. "Which ones."

They choose several options and she picked up the phone to order.

Gray wandered around the living room. "You have a lot of photos." He scanned the frames on the mantel. "Who's the little kid? He's cute."

"My little brother, Kellan. My dad is a camera junkie and always taking pictures."

"Ahh, parents. When my younger brother and I were little, mine did the same thing. Not so much now, though. Guess we're past that cutesy stage where they document every single move we make." He picked up another photo from the mantel. "Is this your older brother? Your little brother looks just like him."

"I only have one brother. That's my dad and stepmother, Emily."

Gray squinted at the picture and set it in its place. "Huh."

She met his blue eyes, heat rising in her cheeks, but the connection broke when she heard voices in the entrance. "Oh, my dad's home."

Kellan rounded the corner into the kitchen, reaching for his sister. "Mannnaaa."

Savannah noted the odd look from Gray as she scooped up the little boy. "Hi, Kellan. Did you have fun at the park?" She heard more little feet and Adrianna toddled into the kitchen, followed by Aiden and Tom.

"Hey, Vanna, how's the project going?" Aiden spotted Gray leaning on the counter. "Hi. I'm Aiden." He introduced Tom, and then he helped the toddlers wash their hands and got them seated while Tom sliced fruit. "You're on the patio?"

She nodded. "We've taken over. Is that okay?"

"We've been out all morning." Tom arranged slices of strawberries and bananas on small plates and placed them in front of the kids. "If we're lucky, these live wires will nap and we can catch the game. Let us know if you need help with anything."

"We will." She headed toward the foyer to meet the pizza deliveryman.

Gray followed, accepting the boxes as she handed over the cash, making sure to add a decent tip.

"There's lots if you want some, Dad. I know Emily is at work."

"Thanks, sweetie." Aiden peeked into the box. "We'll take a few slices off of your hands."

"Enjoy." She kissed his cheek before she and Gray carried the boxes upstairs.

Savannah gathered plates, napkins, and cold drinks from the outdoor kitchen. "Dig in."

Gray studied at her as everyone snagged slices of their favorites.

"Why are you staring at me?"

"Who, me?" Gray lifted a brow. "No reason."

"Yeah, right." Savannah gave him a disbelieving look. "You've been giving me funny looks ever since you met my dad and little brother."

"He looks too young to be your dad." Gray shrugged.

"Oh." Vanna controlled the urge to roll her eyes. "I get that all the time."

"He seems chill," Gray said. "How old is he?"

"Thirty-three." Vanna savored the spicy chicken on her pizza. "What?"

"Your dad's thirty-three?" Jackson chuckled. "I wish mine were young and cool."

This time Vanna did roll her eyes. She'd always wished for younger parents, as people had often assumed Ross was her grandfather. Now she had to contend with people thinking Aiden was her brother, or worse. "I get looks all the time when I'm out with Aiden and Kellan, especially when Emily isn't there. Sometimes people make rude comments like Aiden's a cradle robber or something."

"Seriously?" Rochelle's eyes widened.

"Yup. And I get strange looks when I take Kellan to the park, but I ignore them."

"It doesn't bother you that people think you have a kid?" Jackson asked.

"Nope." She looked around at the group. "I've had to deal with it ever since Kellan was born. I babysit him or Adrianna, and people make assumptions, but I don't feel the need to apologize or explain my life to judgmental people."

"Nor should you." Rochelle's head bobbed in agreement.

"Should we get this project finished?" Piper pointed at her laptop. "And we can quit grilling poor Vanna on her family?"

Savannah bestowed a grateful smile on her friend.

～◆

Savannah tucked her laptop into her bag after the professor dismissed them.

Piper tapped Vanna's shoulder. "You two ready to meet everyone for lunch? We have two hours before our next class, and we planned to review our notes before the exam."

Rochelle stuffed her books into her bag. "I'm so nervous."

"You'll do great. You're ready." Piper draped her satchel across her shoulder. "Vanna, can I ask you something?"

"Sure." Vanna freed her hair from under the strap of her pack.

"Are you interested in Gray?"

"What?" Savannah giggled. "Why?"

"Call it a hunch." Piper waggled her brows. "You two have chemistry."

"Like the way you couldn't peel your eyes away when he removed his shirt," Rochelle said. "He followed you around like a puppy this past weekend."

"You think he's interested? He's cute and all, but ..." A flush crept into Vanna's cheeks.

"I don't think. I know." Piper gave her a look. "He's nuts about you. Give him a little encouragement, and I guarantee he'll ask you out."

"He's not just cute, he's downright mouthwatering." Rochelle smirked. "Like you didn't enjoy him shirtless on the patio."

"Well, he's fairly attractive." Since the time she'd met Gray, there'd been an undercurrent flowing between them. No point in denying her interest.

"Have you heard from Justin?" Rochelle asked. "I bet he wouldn't be happy to hear you think Gray is attractive."

"I'm not dating Justin. We're friends."

Piper scoffed and gave her a knowing look. "Friends with benefits, you mean?"

"Oh, stop." Savannah's cheeks flamed as Rochelle snickered. "We had a thing over the summer while we were on our trip, but I already told you, we've agreed to date other people. We live on opposite sides of the country."

They strolled across the square in silence.

"A friend of mine gave me tickets to an art exhibit. You two should come with, and I'll invite the guys." Piper's mouth twitched into a wicked smile. "If I tell Gray you're going, I bet he'd be on board."

A grin spread across Vanna's face. "Let me know the deets, and I'll see if I can borrow the car. Hey, what are you doing for Thanksgiving? You two plan on traveling home?"

"Nope. Brandon can't go, and he's the only one in my family I can stand being around for more than a day." Piper grinned. "Hard to believe he's related to them, he's so great. And my stepmonster and her daughter are so … not. Anyway, I won't go home until Christmas. My dad can only afford to fly me home twice."

Rochelle sighed. "My parents are away on business, so I'm not going home, either. I'll be hanging around campus."

"I should ask my dad if you can come with us to the Vineyard."

"Seriously?" Rochelle's eyes lit up, then the light faded. "I wish. I doubt I could afford it."

"Me, either." Piper sighed. "How would we even get there? My dad would never agree to pay for it, and my internship income has to cover other things … like food."

"And your coffee addiction," Rochelle said.

"It wouldn't cost much. We sometimes drive, but this trip we're taking the company jet. We have a large group, and my dad wants to fly my Gramma and Abuela to Chicago at the end of the weekend." She twirled a lock of her hair around her finger. "We have a house with tons of room."

"Ohhhh." Piper giggled. "We'd get a trip on the private plane?"

"That would be fun." Rochelle tilted her head. "Do you think your dad would allow it?"

"I'll ask. Why stay on campus when you can come with us? It'll be quiet now the summer is over, but it's pretty. We all get together and have this incredible turkey dinner. And one night, Abuela Nina will cook a traditional Spanish feast. Her food is amazing." Vanna pulled out her phone and tapped in a text to Aiden. "There. I might not hear back for a while. Aiden's at work."

"He's a doctor, right?" Rochelle shifted her backpack to the opposite shoulder.

"He and Emily both work in the ER. I don't know how they deal with it, but they take most of the majors that come in, like those gruesome accident and gunshot victims."

"Yuck, but Brandon is in medical school and talks about that stuff. He doesn't get all grossed out either." Piper shuddered. "Hey, there's the guys." She shook a finger at her friends. "No more blood and guts talk, or I'll lose my appetite."

⌒≼

Savannah took a last look in the mirror and added a touch of gloss to her lips. Her simple burgundy dress fell above the knee and emphasized her waist and was paired with gold high-heeled shoes, and she'd arranged her hair to cascade in waves down her exposed back. She adjusted the gold chain and diamond heart pendant Aiden had given her on her fifteenth birthday.

"Whoa." Aiden raised his brows as she entered the kitchen. "Who are you going out with again?"

"Rochelle, Piper, Gray, and Jackson." Savannah tilted her head, taking in the expression on his face. "You've met them all, Dad. It's an art show."

"Gray, huh?" His eyes narrowed.

"Why the look?" She frowned.

"Maybe because that guy will be too busy staring at you to even notice the artwork. Be careful with that one."

"Dad …" Savannah huffed out a breath as she rolled her eyes upward.

He pressed kiss to her temple. "You look so beautiful."

"Thank you." She smiled and spun to show him the back. "It's not too much?"

"If I said yes, would you change into something else?" His brows lifted, a smirk appearing.

"Ha-ha, and no chance. Emily helped me pick this, you know."

"Did she? Well, she has an eye for clothing, and you look amazing. My little girl, all grown up." Aiden held out a set of keys to the brand new SUV. "Be careful. No drinking, and pay attention to the road."

"You worry too much." Wearing the heels, she didn't even have to stretch on tiptoes to plant a kiss on his cheek and claim the offered keys.

"I worry the right amount. Dad thing, remember?"

"I appreciate it, you know." She rubbed his arm. "Thanks for agreeing to let Rochelle and Piper come with us to the Vineyard. I'm excited."

"Glad to have your friends join us." Aiden's phone buzzed. "That's the concierge. Your friends are here. Have fun … but not too much fun."

"Thanks, Daddy." Savannah gave him a final kiss before donning her coat and taking the elevator to the lobby.

Her friends waited by the elevator bank, and she beckoned them in for the short ride to the parking level.

"Whoa." Gray halted, eyeing the sleek black Maserati parked beside the Range Rover. "Sick car." He skirted it and then peered in each window, as did Jackson. "Gotta meet the neighbor who owns this baby. Maybe they'll take me for a ride sometime."

Vanna hit the remote, sliding into the leather seat of the Range Rover. "That would be my dad."

"No way." Gray claimed the front passenger seat and stared out the window at the sports car. "Have you ever driven it?"

"Are you kidding? That would be a big N-O. It's too powerful of a car for a new driver." She giggled. "Aiden would never let me behind the wheel, but we did a road trip in it two summers ago."

"Huh, I bet it's fast."

She focused on the road, listening to the conversation as Gray and Jackson compared trivia on the best and fastest sports cars. Piper and Rochelle bounced in their seats and sang along to the music flowing through the high-end speakers.

Everyone was in high spirits by the time they parked and headed across the lot toward the museum.

Piper nudged her before skipping ahead to catch up with Jackson and Rochelle.

Gray laughed. "She's sooooo subtle."

"Sorry." Heat rose in Vanna's cheeks, and she avoided his gaze. "Not my idea."

"Yeah, I know." He rubbed her arm. "She's not wrong, Vanna. I know we're in the same study group, and I don't want it to get awkward, but I'd like to take you out sometime. You're not seeing anyone, are you?"

"No, I'm not. I'd like that." The smile twitched the corner of her lips. "Maybe we could catch a movie sometime."

"That would be great." He grasped her hand. "At the risk of sounding overeager, would you be up for a movie tomorrow night?" He looked at her steadily. "I bet you're busy."

"My big plans these days revolve around studying, hanging out with Rochelle and Piper, working at the law firm, and babysitting. I'd love a break." She smiled and shrugged. "Sad life, right?"

"No. I get it. Mine isn't much different. You moved to Boston from Portland, right?"

"We moved here a couple of years ago." She stared at him in surprise. "How did you know I'm from Portland?"

"I listen when you girls talk." Gray looked away, then back. "Sorry, does that sound stalkerish? I don't mean to be, but us guys are around, even if you don't notice."

Savannah blushed. *Nope. I noticed.*

They were now at the entrance and funneled into the museum, Piper presenting the invitations.

Gray pointed to the bar after they'd checked their coats. "Can I get you a soda?"

"That would be nice, thanks."

After he walked away, Piper leaned in and said in a voice low, "We'll leave you two alone. Have fun." She waved and joined Rochelle and Jackson.

Savannah admired a painting while waiting for Gray to return with drinks. She stepped back and tilted her head, studying the smooth lines and the way the colors blended, creating a mood.

"You like this one?" Gray appeared beside her, handing her a glass.

"I do. It's joyful."

"Mmmhmm."

She peeked at him from the corner of her eye. "You're not even looking."

"Oh, yeah, I am." His gaze traveled over her, lingering. "The painting's nice, but you …"

Savannah rolled her eyes. "That's so cliché." She led him to the next piece.

Over the next hour, they moved around the room. Gray stayed by her side and threw in the odd comment, but she sensed he didn't appreciate the art the way she did.

"Look at this." Savannah pointed at yet another photograph. "It's amazing."

"You have an incredible eye." A woman's soft voice came from beside her. "I heard some of your comments on the pieces. Do you paint?"

"Sometimes, and I love to draw and take photos. My dad …" Vanna's smile faded as she turned toward the woman. She collided with Gray as she stepped back, and he placed his hands on her shoulders to steady her. "What—why are you here?" Vanna stared into the woman's crystal blue eyes, her breath catching in her chest. The sight of this woman and hearing that voice brought it all back. That awful day when Savannah's heart had broken, her dreams crushed by her mother's rejection.

"I'm here to view work by a new artist. I saw you, and I ..." Tiffany took a step forward. "I own a gallery in Chicago. Your dad never told you?"

Vanna shook her head as tears burned behind her eyes. There were no words, the lump in her throat preventing her from forming a single sound. *After this woman who gave birth to me rejected me, what was left to say?*

"You look wonderful. You're so ..." Tiffany extended a hand toward her daughter. "I'd love it if we could talk, Savannah. Please?"

"No. *No!*" Savanna spun and rushed toward the entrance without looking back.

"Vanna." Gray chased her as she charged toward the doors. "Hey, who was that? What's wrong?"

She shook her head as tears streamed down her face and stumbled down the steps, fumbling in her bag for her car keys.

"Hey, hey." Gray wrapped an arm around her. "Wait."

"I need to go home." She buried her face against his shoulder. "Just let me go."

"Shh, relax. You can't drive while you're so upset." Gray held her, stroking her back as she wept. "Who was that?"

"M-my mother. She shouldn't be here. I don't want to see her. I want to leave." Sobs wracked her body. "P-p-please?"

"Let me grab our coats, and I'll take you home." He rubbed her arm.

Savannah's phone vibrated, and she fumbled it out. Swiping at her face, she hit the answer button. "Dad."

"Are you okay, Vanna?" His warm voice carried down the line.

"I-I ..." She choked, her chest hitching.

"Do you need me to come get you?"

"What?" She sniffled. "How did you ...?"

"She called me." His voice remained calm and even. "Vanna?"

"I'm okay, Daddy. Gray said he'd drive me home."

"You're sure?"

"Yes." She shivered, but Gray hugged her closer and rubbed her back. "I can't believe she called you. Why can't she leave us alone?"

It didn't seem fair that Tiffany kept showing up, expecting something Vanna couldn't give after that woman had rejected her.

"I can deal with her," he said. "I'm glad she called. She realized she upset you. We can talk when you get home."

"Thanks, Dad."

Gray squeezed her tight as she said goodbye and hung up. "Do you want me to drive?"

Savannah nodded as exhaustion overwhelmed her. "Please."

Gray retrieved their coats and led her to the car, settling her into the passenger seat. Soon they were heading toward downtown Boston.

She stared out the window, barely registering the passing scenery. "I'm sorry for ruining our night. I'm a mess."

"No problem." He hummed to the music, shooting the occasional glance her way. "Do you want to talk about it?" he asked after a while.

She shook her head. "I'd rather forget about it, though I'm sure my dad will have a few things to say."

"Will he be mad that you wouldn't talk to your mother?"

"No." Savannah leaned her forehead against to cool glass of the window. "He knows how I feel about Tiffany, but he worries. It's a long story."

Her dad would be loving and supportive, and it would be easier to talk to him than explain the convoluted mess to Gray. Aiden understood how she felt, and what she'd been through. "You must think I'm a raving lunatic. It's so attractive when a girl cries all over you." She dabbed at her eyes. "We didn't even see the entire exhibit."

"No worries." Gray reached across the console and took her hand in his. "I'm not disappointed we didn't get to see it all, and anyway, that's what friends are for."

"Thanks," she whispered, pulling out a tissue to wipe away the fresh round of tears. "Why did you come to the show if you hate art?"

"I like art." Gray glanced at her. "But I came tonight because you'd be there."

They pulled into the garage and Gray parked the SUV before helping her out, wrapping an arm around her shoulders.

"Do you want to come up? We could watch a movie or something?" She pressed her fob against the panel of the elevator.

"Will it be okay with your dad?"

"He'll be glad I'm not in my room, moping alone." With forced levity in her tone, she pasted on a smile and brushed at the streak of mascara on the soft wool of his coat. "I smeared makeup all over you. Sorry."

"Don't worry about it." He winked. "I love being there for a damsel in distress."

The elevator swished open, and Aiden appeared.

"Hey." He hugged her for several seconds before drawing back and studying her. "Glad you're home. Gray, thanks for driving her."

"No problem, Dr. Hamilton."

"Call me Aiden, please." Her dad led them through to the kitchen. "You two need anything?"

"We might make popcorn and watch a movie," Savannah said.

"You're good then?"

"I am now I'm home. Can we not talk about it right now?"

"Okay." Aiden kissed her cheek. "I'm off to bed. Don't stay up too late." He sighed as his phone rang. "I should get this."

"Night, Dad."

He retreated down the hallway, lifting the phone to his ear as he walked. The expression on his face told her everything she needed to know about the caller. Tiffany. Again.

CHAPTER 4

TIFFANY PACED BACK AND FORTH in front of the large window of her hotel room, hoping Aiden would answer. By now, he may have her number blocked.

"Twice in one night. I'm so honored."

"Liar," she muttered. "You'd like to drown me in Boston Harbor."

"Ahh, you know me so well. Haven't you done enough damage for one evening?"

"Is she there?" Tiffany sank onto the bed. "Did she make it home safely?"

"Why are you so concerned about her welfare?"

"She's my daughter, Aiden. Believe it or not, I care a great deal. I regret turning her away, and I wish she'd give me a chance to explain," she said softly. "But, that's not my choice, right?"

"It's not mine, either," he said. "You agreed to abide by her decision. I wish you'd respect that agreement. Why are you even in Boston?"

"I flew in for an art exhibit. I never expected her to be there." She combed her fingers through her hair. "I didn't mean to upset her, but I couldn't resist talking to her."

"Why? You demanded we leave you alone. We did. Now you won't leave us alone. Go back to Chicago."

"Aiden." She rubbed her chest, wishing the dull ache would subside. The way he talked to her, dismissed her even, grieved her in an unexpected way.

She longed for those days when he couldn't wait to see her and hold her in his arms. Now he couldn't wait for her to leave the state.

"What?"

"It's been over a year. Things have changed since Savannah appeared. I've changed."

"Huh. Right. Sure you have." His scoff carried down the line. "How can I trust anything you say? One minute you're sweet as pie and making inappropriate offers and the next you're ready to shred me into tiny pieces. You are not even close to being the girl I knew in high school. What do you want from me?"

"But I am her. I never stopped being her." She dragged in a deep breath. "I'm seeing a therapist and dealing with my issues. Can you meet me for a coffee and listen to what I have to say?"

Aiden should be the one who understood why she'd sought counseling. He'd never been the poster boy for a happy family life with his domineering grandfather and distant relationship with his parents. He had his own pile of issues and must understand how difficult this admission was for her.

"What could you possibly say that would be of any interest to me? Haven't we taken enough from each other? Had too many fights, and disagreements and …"

A vivid picture formed in her mind of his shoulder lifting in a small shrug. "Everything I've said and done has been wrong, but I need this. Please? Even if I can't see Savannah, could you at least spare me fifteen minutes of your precious time?"

"Why would you want to spend any time with your worst nightmare?"

Her anger rose. The man knew how to push each and every one of her buttons and cornered the market on stubborn and infuriating. It seemed to give him great pleasure to taunt her with the many failures and misspoken words in their relationship.

Intent on keeping control, she locked down her swirling emotions. As Liz constantly reminded her, losing her temper wouldn't win him over.

"I'm sorry I said it. I never meant …" She rose from the bed and stared out the window, hoping the view of the serene waterfront would calm her. "I took out my own failings on you. It wasn't fair for me to blame you or to vent my anger at you. I won't ask for anything, ever again, if you'll just talk to me. Please?"

"I don't know if I can." His softened tone gave her reason to hope. "What is this, a twelve-step program or something?"

"Not exactly. I have a lot of apologies to make and it's fitting that I start with you. It is part of my therapy and long overdue. I'd hoped you'd understand, Aiden. Do you remember what we went through?"

"Like I'll ever forget?"

"Well, neither will I." Tears brimmed her eyes, blurring the lights below. "I carry it with me, every single day."

"You're serious."

"Please? It doesn't have to be long." She crossed her fingers, holding her breath as she awaited his answer. "I promise it's not a trick."

"We can meet in the morning. Where are you staying?"

"Thank you, Aiden," she said once they'd agreed to meet in the restaurant of her hotel. "I appreciate this more than I can express."

"It's coffee. Nothing else."

"I know, but still …" She bit her lip. "Would you relay my apologies to Savannah? I didn't intend to ruin her evening."

He sighed. "Good night, Tiffany."

The phone line went dead. Perhaps she'd pushed too far with that last request, but at least he'd agreed to talk. One tiny baby step at a time. It was all she could do.

⤚≺

Tiffany awoke early the next morning feeling like she hadn't slept at all. An examination of her face showed the toll numerous sleepless nights had taken on her. A small part of her wondered if Aiden seeing her this way, as less than the perfect self she strived to portray in public, might help her case. She could only hope.

Still, she took care dressing and applying her makeup as she always had. After collecting her handbag, she threw one last glance at her reflection. As he pointed out, the girl he'd dated at the age of fifteen had disappeared, along with the girl he'd married. She'd protested his observation, yet the truth stared back at her. Recapturing the past was impossible.

She leaned against the wall of the elevator, musing about that long-lost teenage girl, and the Fourth of July that had changed everything. Their friends had decided to hang out, enjoy the barbecue at Tom's house, and then sail to Edgartown later in the afternoon on Aiden's boat to enjoy the celebrations and watch the fireworks.

She'd gone to Aiden's house mid-morning to help him organize the boat. Thomas and Grace Hamilton had already left for the barbecue at the Grayson's home.

It had taken an hour to stow the supplies on the boat and check the gear, and by the time they were done, they were both hot and tired. They'd returned to the air conditioned house for cold drinks and ended up in his bedroom while he selected clean clothes.

A smile twitched her lips as she pictured him, the firm tanned chest, and the youthful six-pack and biceps which had already developed due to his active lifestyle. All of the sailing, rowing, skiing, swimming, and multiple other sports he participated in had done him justice.

"Come join me." She patted the bed.

"We should go before they eat all the food." Despite his words, he stretched out beside her, tucking an arm behind his head as he twirled a strand of her hair around his fingertip.

"Like they won't have enough to feed half of the island." She giggled, but when she met his deep, soulful eyes, it died on her lips. How could she resist running her fingertips over his tight abs, savoring the heat of his smooth skin before plucking at the strings on his swim shorts? She rose up and leaned in to kiss him, winding her fingers into his soft thick hair.

Their kisses became deeper and more urgent until Aiden pulled back. He rested his forehead against hers, letting out a long slow breath as he tangled his fingers in her hair. "You're so amazing, but we should stop while we still can."

"What if I don't want to?" She brushed her lips over his before dropping gentle kisses across his cheek.

He cradled her face in his palms, staring into her eyes. "Are you sure you want to do this? I can wait."

"I'm ready," she whispered. "I want to share this with you."

Aiden had been sweet and gentle, every touch and kiss tender and loving. Afterward, as she cuddled in his arms, a deep contentment stole over her. She felt loved and treasured, and without a single regret. Many would lead her to believe that boys were only after one thing, but she hadn't even considered that to be true of Aiden.

Their shared intimacy drew them closer, made them inseparable, and after that day, she spent every waking moment with him. The sultry summer days were filled with swimming, sailing, and enjoying the many pleasures of laid-back island life. By the end of August, he'd captured her heart. The complete and total love she felt intensified, a love so deep she couldn't bear for them to be parted.

That autumn when they'd returned to school, their relationship grew and flourished along with the bonds of friendship within their group. Her every wish had come true. She'd belonged, she loved, and Aiden loved her in return.

Her eyes fluttered as the elevator bell dinged and the doors slid open.

Tiffany straightened, drawing in several long breaths before she entered the restaurant, spotting him at a table by the wall of large windows.

Damn, he looked good enough to eat. A flush rose in her cheeks as lustful and lascivious thoughts ran rampant through her mind. Once upon a time, this man had been hers. This man had loved her with a fiery, intense passion that threatened to consume them both with its heat. But no longer. She fought the urge to fan herself as a rush of memories surfaced, while her inner voice chanted … *Married. Off-limits.*

His platinum wedding band glinted and mocked her as he swept a hand through that thick silky hair and motioned to the seat across from him.

The waitress appeared the moment she'd slid into the booth, providing a glass of water. Tiffany gulped back a mouthful. "Have you eaten breakfast?" As she crossed her fingers, she wished for his answer to be *no* so she could have more than fifteen minutes of his undivided attention.

"Not yet." He tilted his head. "You?"

She shook her head. "Do you mind if I eat while we talk?"

"Not at all." He perused the menu the waitress had left on the edge of the table for a few seconds before he closed it.

"Nothing for you?" Her heart sank.

"I already know what I want."

"Ahh." She studied him for a moment "I'll have the same."

He raised a brow, but waved the waitress down and ordered their meals. "Are you happy with the selection?"

"Yes, but I knew I would be. How many times—" She clamped down on her lip as she bowed her head. It would be so easy to be drawn off course. "Well, you're probably wondering why I wanted to see you."

"I figured you'd circle around to it. You never were one to jump to the point." He spun his cup, staring into the depths, apparently more interested in his coffee than her.

"You know me too well."

"Danger of visiting the ex. We have a lot of history." He finally looked up and contemplated her with dark serious eyes. "I'm sure you know me better than I care to admit. Why don't you tell me what it is you need … or want … or whatever?"

"You're not planning on making this easy, are you?" She issued a small nervous laugh.

"Just tell me. You seem to think there are things to be said. No time like the present."

"Because it's my last chance, isn't it?"

"Your last chance happened some time ago, but you never noticed. You wonder why I don't greet you with open arms? Welcome you into our lives? Think about how we broke up, all the shit you pulled back then, and all the crap you've piled on since. We had something once, but it's long gone. Broken beyond repair."

"You hate me." She met his eyes.

"Not true. I hate pretty much everything you've done, but I never waste my energy hating *you*."

An uneasy silence fell over them as the waitress reappeared to fill their cups.

"Is there a difference?" She twirled a strand of hair, concentrating on his left hand as he stirred his coffee. *What had he done with my ring? The one I picked for him. The gold band I'd chosen with such care and slid onto his finger while promising to love and cherish this man forever.* "Isn't it the same thing?"

"It's not. Your actions have been reprehensible, but I don't wish bad things for you. Your antics annoy me, but otherwise, I rarely give it much thought."

She almost doubled over from the heart-wrenching blow. Worse than hatred was the bitter absence of emotion. Complete dismissal. The knowledge of being unwanted. Unneeded.

The passionate love affair, so steamy and intense, bound in its not-so-tidy package, had evaporated. She craved its sweet messiness. Longed for it. Wished to rescind the careless abandonment that allowed his love to slip away. Mourned that rare, precious, and fiery passion she'd lacked with every man since him.

"Huh." She clutched her cup. "It's painful that you don't give a damn about me or what we had." She bowed her head as the server arrived to deliver their breakfast and refill their coffee.

The woman's perfect timing allowed a brief reprieve before Tiffany had to wade back into this onerous discussion. Too soon the waitress left to check on her other tables.

"What do you expect me to say?" Aiden picked up his fork.

Tiffany concentrated on her plate and managed a few bites before she set her utensils aside. "Why even bother?" She peeked at him.

"Bother with what?" A deep frown marred his features. "Is any of this a surprise? Not like you have any great love for me. You off-loaded me from your life a long time ago. Why do you even care what I think?"

"Because you own a piece of me, Aiden. You were my first … in every way that counts. You're the father of my child, no matter if I'm part of her life or not." She gulped another mouthful of water, desperate to soothe the ache in her throat. "So much of my life has been ruled by our relationship. But I wasn't your first, was I?"

"That doesn't mean what we had meant nothing." He scrubbed his jaw. "You were the first girl I loved. Or thought I loved, or … yeah, whatever. You get it."

"Did you? Love me?" Tiffany longed to hear his answer, to know if she'd been imagining it all.

"Why else would I put myself through that? Most guys would've encouraged you to terminate, and they sure the hell wouldn't have stuck around or come back for further abuse. What happened wasn't because I didn't care. I'm not one who ch—"

"Stop!" She shuddered, her heart thudding as the pictures of that day rose in her mind.

He rubbed his temples, trailing his fingertips over his closed eyes, pausing for only a moment before resting his hand on the table.

"I loved you so much," she whispered. "Here is where it gets difficult."

A tiny scoff escaped him.

"I have all these emotions I've denied to myself for so long. They're so tangled, I can't tell real from imagined." She pulled a tissue from her purse, dabbing the tears streaking down her face. "I'm sorry."

"Fuck. Don't cry," he said in a low voice. "I'm so over it."

"I'm *not*." Tiffany snuffled, dragging air into her lungs. The ache grew. Oh, to return to those days when he cradled her in his arms and kissed away her hurts. "I … have never been gotten closure. You owe me nothing, but I have to ask." She implored him with her eyes, still sniffling.

"Umm, yeah, not following." He shook his head. "What could I possibly do, ten years later? It's bygones, and it's impossible to take any of it back."

"You could …" She heaved out a breath and allowed the words to rush from her mouth. "Come to a therapy session with me." Her fingers trembled as she twisted her napkin and bowed her head.

Dead silence hung over them, and she wondered if he'd left. She peered across the table. *Nope. Still there.* Facing abandonment might have been preferable, given his stormy expression.

Aiden leaned back in his chair, arms crossed, his breakfast forgotten. "Say what?" One brow rose. "You want me to go to counseling?" The dark but quizzical look made her quake. "With you? Why the hell …?"

Heat rose and she longed to crawl underneath the table and hide. Why in the hell would he ever agree? She'd been a horrible bitch, and now she asked him to … do what? Assuage her guilt and make her feel better? Her heart sank straight to her toes as she shifted, clenching the edge of the table with bone-white fingertips, forcing herself to stay seated.

"Tiffany?"

"Sorry," she whispered. "My therapist thinks we need to sort out our issues. You walked out and never came back, and there was so much I never got to say."

"We're going there?" He scoffed again. "Who needs to be told? Your actions showed your feelings."

Tiffany drew in her shoulders and hunched lower.

"You screwed what's-his-name in our bed."

Derrick. This would forever circle around to that unfortunate error in judgment. The unforgiven and unforgivable incident that shredded their marriage.

"You were done with me before our second anniversary. Yet, in your mind, or this therapist's mind, or whoever is running this never-ending shit show, it's fine to dredge it all up again for your benefit?" He yanked out his wallet and tossed several bills on the table. "Absolutely no fucking chance. Not interested."

"Please, please let me explain."

"I don't want to hear it."

Desperation ran through her. She needed to make him understand, but would he listen? He hadn't back then. She'd endured one of those looks he'd perfected over the years. The one that made her feel like an unsavory mess scraped from the bottom of his expensive leather shoes.

The aftermath of her betrayal included his week-long disappearance, long sleepless nights—at least on her part—topped off by a curt request from Tom that she make herself scarce while he gathered her soon-to-be-ex-husband's belongings.

By the time Aiden deigned to speak to her, irreparable and irreversible damage had been done. "Aiden, please."

"Are you completely insane? You expect me to inform my wife I'm attending therapy with my *ex-wife* so she can sort out her damn feelings and make herself feel better about destroying our marriage? Bloody hell. Does this idiot therapist know I'm married?"

She cringed, avoiding the glares of the other diners, some of whom were now throwing *shut-the-fuck-up-I'm-trying-to-eat* looks their way.

"It's not couples therapy. It's so we can work out our issues and be better parents."

"Last I checked the only person who needed to work on their parenting skills was you."

"Shhh. Everyone is—"

"Oh, wait. You don't have any children. Savannah is not your daughter. You had the chance to be part of her life, but told your worst nightmare to get lost. Forget it. Go home, and stay out of our lives." He flung his napkin onto his plate and stalked through the exit without another word.

Déjà vu.

Tiffany remained immobile for several minutes, barely managing an embarrassed grimace as the server took away their half-finished meals. The woman's curious looks and the stares from the other diners confirmed what a terrible idea this had been.

If that's how Aiden reacted, then she might as well call it quits now. Jenna and Alex wouldn't be any easier to approach. She forced herself to her feet, keeping her head bowed as she shuffled out the door.

Once in her room, she tossed her clothes into her suitcase while booking the first flight home. The sooner she left Boston, the better.

CHAPTER 5

Savannah

GRAY WRAPPED HIS ARMS AROUND Savannah, pulling her down into the tangle of sheets. "Stay."

"It's late. I should go home."

"My roommate is at his girlfriend's place. Anyway, the subway stopped running an hour ago."

"Zane must hate me. I'm always here, so he never even sleeps in his own bed. Anyway, I call a cab or a car service when I have to travel late at night. My dad worries about me on the subway."

"With good reason." Gray cuddled her against his chest.

"I'll call now. I don't have clean clothes for tomorrow, and I've barely been home." She grabbed her phone from the nightstand. "Oh, I missed a text from Justin." *And several calls from my dad.*

"That guy again? He texts far too often."

"He's my friend." Savannah waved a hand and then typed a reply.

"You used to date him, though, and you spent all summer with him on a sailboat. Tell me nothing happened."

Vanna ignored the comment and focused on her conversation with Justin.

"Huh, nothing to say?"

"What do you want to hear?"

"You dated him when you were what? Fifteen? Did you two … you know?" Gray waggled his brows. "Who was the first guy you had sex with?"

"None of your business, that's who."

"It was him. That pretty boy claimed your V-card. So, a little"—he clicked his tongue—"reunion happened over the summer?"

"I hate it when people call it a V-card, like you handed over some sort of damn prize to the guy. When a boy has sex for the first time, it's high fives all around, but when a girl does it …" Savannah rolled her eyes and pushed away his hands. "Damn double-standards." She slid from the bed and dressed as she gathered each item of clothing from the floor. "Anyway, what do you want me to say? I'm a grown woman, not a little girl." She yanked on a boot. "You never complain when we're in bed together."

Gray held up his hands. "I surrender. You are a beautiful and sexy woman." He wrapped an arm around her as she picked her phone off of the bed. "Don't be mad, baby. See you tomorrow?" Pulling her closer, he kissed her.

She sank against him, enjoying his luscious lips on hers. The guy could kiss, no arguments or disappointment on that front.

Gray grasped her face between his hands. "It's you and me, right? You aren't still seeing him, are you?"

"He lives in California."

"Yeah, but we're exclusive, right?" Gray wound a lock of her hair around his finger.

Savannah nodded. "I only date one guy at a time. It's just you and me."

When she arrived home, the penthouse was dead quiet. She tiptoed into the kitchen, intending to get a glass of water.

"Vanna."

"Dad." She pressed a hand to her chest to calm her thudding heart. "You scared me."

"It's two in the morning. Where the hell have you been?" He crossed his arms.

"Sorry, I should've texted. We lost track of the time."

"Didn't you get any of my messages?" He sighed. "I worry, even though you're almost grown up and all. These past few weeks you've been coming home at all hours, and you're not acting like you. Do I need to be concerned? Is there something more going on that we need to talk about?"

"You're worrying too much. I'm fine, and I promise I'm keeping up with school." She yanked open the fridge and retrieved a carton of juice. "You think it has to do with her, don't you?" As she leaned against the counter, she met his gaze in the dim light. "Maybe I'm the one who should worry. You've been a total grouch ever since that night. What did she say to you?"

"The usual, but," he said as he pointed his index finger at her, "we aren't talking about me. Don't change the subject."

She sighed. Her dad rarely allowed her to play the game of misdirection. But what could she say? No way would she reveal the reason for her recent late hours. She picked at a nail and avoided looking at him.

"Be careful, Savannah," he said. "How's Gray?"

"Fine." She popped her head up. "How did you know I was with Gray?"

"Aha. Gotcha." His brow went up. "Don't get in too deep, too fast. You barely know the kid. Concentrate on school, the course load won't get any lighter."

Damn, damn, damn. He'd sucked her into confessing without even trying. She often thought he'd missed his calling. He would have made an excellent lawyer. "I'm almost eighteen, not a little girl. I can take care of myself." She lifted her chin.

"Don't remind me." His theatrical shudder had her rolling her eyes.

"Ha-ha, funny."

Aiden moved closer, looping an arm around her shoulders. "Are you really okay? You haven't said much about what happened with Tiffany."

"I'm fine, Dad. But you're not. Are you?" Ever since her birth mother had rolled through town, her dad had been the one acting strange. "Is she bugging you about seeing me again?"

"Nope. Worse."

"What could be worse?"

"Never mind. It's not important. Time for bed. Now you're home safe, we can both get some sleep." He kissed her temple. "Come talk to me if you need. I'm here. I love you, Vanna."

"I love you, too." She wrapped her arms around him. "I'll be careful. That's a promise."

⌐≺

Saturday morning, Savannah rose early, hoping to get through her reading and finish the pending assignments. That would leave her evening free to spend with Gray.

She wandered into the kitchen. "Morning, Emily."

Her stepmother leaned against the counter, sipping from a glass of water. "Vanna." The faint smile didn't quite reach Emily's eyes as she took a deep breath.

"You okay?" Savannah frowned as she slapped a pan onto the top of the gas range and dug out a carton of eggs. She beat the raw eggs in a bowl and pouring them into the hot pan. They sizzled and Vanna tipped the pan, letting the mixture spread evenly.

Emily emitted a small choked sound, her face ashen as she pressed a hand to her mouth and dashed down the hallway toward the bedroom.

Savannah switched off the burner before following and peeking into the master bedroom. The sound of retching coming from the bathroom made her grimace. "Emily?" She padded through, tapping on the frame of the open door. This scene seemed familiar. "Are you feeling okay? Can I get you anything?"

"I'm fine." Emily rinsed her mouth and splashed water on her face. "Bad sushi or something."

"Sushi. That's your story?" Savannah smothered a laugh but caught a glimpse of the woman's reflection. Emily looked miserable, her face chalky and damp. Vanna leaned in the doorway, a grin spreading across her face. "Oh wow. You're pregnant, aren't you?" Excitement built at the thought of having another sibling. "Are you?"

"Well, no fooling you."

"I'm right? This is so exciting. Does Dad know?"

"Does Dad know what?" His voice came from behind her.

"Stop doing that." She spun. "You'll give me heart failure."

"Sorry. Didn't realize my presence was so unexpected, considering I live here and this is our bedroom." He slipped an arm around Vanna's waist, bouncing Kellan on his hip. "Sooooo. Why are we all gathered in the bathroom?" He exchanged looks with Emily.

"Vanna's figured it out." Emily smiled faintly. "I confessed our secret."

"Ahh." He looked at Vanna. "How do you feel about a new baby in the house?"

"It's amazing." Savannah extricated herself and took Kellan from her dad. "Hear that, Kellan? We're going to have a little brother or sister."

"Yes, another June baby." Emily's cheeks flushed and her eyes sparkled as she looped an arm around Aiden's waist.

"So Kellan will be two." Savannah bounced her brother, noting how happy her dad and stepmom looked at this moment.

"And you'll be eighteen." Aiden reached out to squeeze her hand. "Can you keep this to yourself for now?"

"I won't say a word." She ran her fingers across her lips as if zipping them.

"Good. It's too early for big announcements. Ready for some breakfast?" He peered at Emily. "If you are, I'll make you some pancakes."

"Waffles?" Emily lifted a brow. "With fruit sauce."

"Your wish is my command." Aiden grinned.

Two weeks later, Savannah unpacked her bag in the Vineyard. Her friends bounced around laughing and chattering about the flight and the amazing scenery.

"Lucky girl." Rochelle stared through the window. "You live in a fancy Penthouse in Boston, have a house in the Vineyard, and your dad owns a place in Chicago. Is your dad paying for university?"

"Well, no. My great-grandmother is." She dropped onto the bed. "My life hasn't always been like this, you know. I lived in Portland until I turned fifteen. It's new to me, in many ways." Though she had to admit, she'd become used to the lifestyle.

"You girls interested in a trip into town?" Aiden said as he peeked through the open door. "I need to pick up a couple of things if you want to come with. Emily is losing her mind because she forgot the key ingredients for Nina to make her traditional dessert."

"Sounds like fun." Piper leaped off the bed.

"Sure." Vanna nodded.

Soon Aiden, Kellan, and the three girls were in the SUV on their way toward town. Kellan chattered non-stop at the two young women flanking him in the back seat. Vanna peeked at Aiden, who seemed to be amused at how her friends lavished attention on the adorable toddler.

Aiden parked the car on one of the quiet streets. "You girls hungry?"

"Starving." Piper giggled.

"You're always hungry. Like that's news." Vanna accepted the cash Aiden dug from his wallet and stretched to kiss his cheek. "Thanks, Dad. I'll take Kellan and feed him lunch." She suspected part of the reason he'd brought them all into town was to take some pressure off of Emily, but she figured he needed a break too.

"You sure?"

"He'll be happier with us than being dragged around the market. Take your time." Vanna scooped the small boy into her arms, and the girls wandered into the diner.

They ordered and it wasn't long until they were devouring burgers, fries, and milkshakes. Vanna cut Kellan's grilled cheese sandwich into small triangles and added a dab of ketchup to his plate so he could dip his own tiny stack of French fries.

"Tank you, Manna." Kellan crammed a fry into his mouth.

"Don't look now, but that lady is watching you," Rochelle muttered. "She hasn't stopped staring since we sat down."

Vanna rolled her eyes and gave her friends a conspiratorial smile. She'd seen the woman when they'd arrived but had learned to ignore the looks she received when she cared for Kellan. A mere glance at the other table caused the woman to look away.

"Ignore the judgmental old lady." Savannah kept her voice low. "People stare at me all the time, remember? I'm over it." She shrugged it off and bit into her burger.

"How do you tolerate it?" Piper twirled a fry through her ketchup before popping it into her mouth.

"I have no choice." She sneaked a look at the occupant of the other table. As she suspected, the woman had resumed her vigil on their group, but this time, her gaze didn't falter. "Some people will decide who they think I am on appearances, but I can't let them get to me. It's like Aiden says—he's either assumed to be a cradle robber or irresponsible for having a kid at fifteen. Those who think that way will always find a way to criticize, no matter what you do." She lifted her chin, daring this stranger to say something.

The silver-haired woman rose and approached their table. "He's beautiful. Kellan takes after his dad."

Vanna's eyes widened. "What?"

"Sweet boy." The lady brushed a hand over his hair. "You have Aiden's eyes, Savannah."

"You know Aiden? Have we …?"

"You and I have never met, but I've known Aiden since he was young." The woman smiled. "I'm Michelle from Chicago."

"Michelle." Savannah met the woman's blue eyes. Something about this stranger seemed familiar, but she couldn't place why. "These are my friends, Piper and Rochelle."

"It's wonderful to meet you." She pointed at the extra chair. "Do you mind?"

Vanna motioned for Michelle to sit, not wanting to be rude to someone who knew her dad. Besides, she wanted to know more.

Kellan reached out, almost spilling his small tumbler of milk, kicking his feet and squirming.

"Here. Let me." Michelle rose and unclipped the highchair's safety belt, tucking the little boy onto her lap as she sat. "You finish eating, Savannah." The woman helped Kellan take a sip of milk, and she pulled his plate closer so he could reach his grilled cheese.

"Do you have children?" Piper asked.

"A daughter, but she's grown now." Michelle smiled sadly. "Tell me, Savannah, how do you like Harvard?"

"It's … good."

"What a wonderful opportunity to attend such a highly regarded school. Do you have any hobbies?"

Savannah answered the stream of questions as best she could, noting how at ease Michelle seemed with her brother, and how the boy responded with a toothy grin as the woman dabbed ketchup from his cheek.

When the waitress came by to clear plates and present the bill, Michelle waved Savannah's hand away. "I'll take care of it." She slid a credit card into the small black folder and handed it to the server.

"Thank you, but you don't have to buy our lunch. My dad gave me money."

"It's my pleasure, Savannah. It was so lovely to meet you."

The bell over the door tinkled as Aiden stepped through. He froze for a split second as concern fleeted across his face. A small frown knit his brow.

"Aiden." The woman rose and covered the few steps between them, hugging him while balancing his son on her hip.

Aiden stiffened and pulled away, reaching for his son. "Come here, bud." He cuddled Kellan against his chest. "What are you doing here?"

"I'm visiting a friend for the holidays." Michelle looked toward the table. "My daughter is joining us tomorrow. She has some big event happening back home this afternoon." After another glance at the table, the woman lowered her voice, becoming inaudible.

The two conversed for several minutes before Aiden finally allowed Michelle to tap something into his phone.

Michelle returned to the table and collected her coat and purse. "I'm glad to have met you all." She squeezed Savannah's shoulder. "I should run as I'm expected for dinner. You have a beautiful family, Aiden." Michelle touched his arm and stroked Kellan's hair before she disappeared through the door.

"Well, that was interesting," Piper said. "She bought us lunch."

"Did she?" Aiden said. "That was nice of her."

His smile seemed forced, but the other two girls chatted on like nothing out of the ordinary had happened.

For Vanna, things had shifted ever so slightly, but she wasn't sure how or why.

"Did you ladies want more time in town? I know there's not much open this time of year."

"Yes, let's stay longer." Vanna looked at her two friends. "We ate, but didn't have time to visit anywhere else."

"Kellan seems happy enough, and Emily will be thrilled if I bring him home tired and ready for a long nap."

They started down the street, Rochelle and Piper exploring the stores, enabling Vanna to corner Aiden.

"Who's Michelle? She seemed familiar, but I can't place her."

"You've never met her." Aiden swung Kellan onto his shoulders. "Not sure you want to do this here and now."

"Why not? Who is she?" She narrowed her eyes. "It's to do with Tiffany, right?"

"Uh-huh." He stopped, turning toward her. "It's nothing bad, but ..." He shrugged. "I don't want you upset. Your three grandmothers are arriving tomorrow morning and your friends are here."

"If I promise I won't get upset?" Even as she said it, the pieces gelled in her mind. She'd seen pictures of the woman. "Michelle *Baxter*. That's why she didn't tell me her last name, and how she knew you and who I am. I thought she stared at me because I had Kellan, but it was because …" She frowned. "She's never seen me."

"Imagine my surprise at her chatting with you and bouncing Kellan on her knee."

"Sorry, I know I shouldn't have let her hold Kellan, but she knew who we were."

"Michelle would never harm you or your brother, but try not to hand him over to strangers. You need to be careful. Remember how you researched me online?" He squeezed her shoulder.

"I won't do it again." Savannah combed her fingers through her hair. "She sure likes you, but you seemed less than thrilled to see her."

"She's known me a long time." He had that wistful look on his face again, and his eyes conveyed sadness. "The minute she laid eyes on you, she knew who you were. The resemblance is unmistakable."

"Do we look that much alike? People say it, but do we? You didn't recognize me when we met."

"No, but I felt like we'd met before. It's not that unusual. Your mind sees what it wants to, and I never thought I'd ever meet you. You were from out of town, and I'd focused my attention on the casualties from the derailment. It didn't connect because I never expected it to be possible. It was an odd coincidence for you to appear in the middle of that mess."

His explanation made sense. She'd experienced the same phenomenon at lunchtime when Michelle appeared. Now she knew the woman's identity, the resemblance to Tiffany became obvious, but before that, she'd only had a vague sense of familiarity.

"What does she want?"

"To see you. Today presented her with an unexpected and irresistible opportunity, and she took it. Having her long-lost granddaughter sitting in the same room but not speaking to you was too much. Apparently, she's been biding her time and waiting for the moment to present itself."

"She's my grandmother." She pondered the thought. "I'll never have a grandfather. David Baxter doesn't want to see me."

"Count your blessings, Savannah." Aiden gave her an impenetrable look. "You have at least three unimaginable bastards in the family tree. I would never allow either James or David anywhere near you, and you've been spared the everlasting joy of meeting Thomas Hamilton. You have to promise you will never try to see them."

"I'm not scared." Savannah waved a hand. "They're stupid old men."

"This isn't a joke, Savannah, so wipe that smirk off of your face." Aiden grabbed her arm and forced her to look at him.

"That hurts." She brushed his hand off. "Don't try to scare me."

"You should be scared, little girl. You have no clue what they're capable of, and you can never, ever, go near either of them."

Savannah shivered at the harsh tone of his voice. She'd never seen Aiden like this before. "I'm their granddaughter."

"You think that means anything to them?" He stared into her eyes. "You're wrong if you believe they'd never hurt you. These are hard, ruthless men. They're unpredictable, and that means dangerous. James is in check, but I've never completely dismissed him."

"In check?" Savannah frowned. "How? Why do you think they'd hurt me?"

"Don't worry about it, but keep your distance." He tucked an arm around her. "I'm sorry. Enough about that. You have a family who loves you, Vanna, you don't need them."

"They don't want me anyway." Savannah's heart thumped in her chest. His abrupt mood change made her wonder what the men had said or done to put him on edge. "What about Michelle?"

"She would never hurt you. She's expressed an interest in seeing you, but …" He sighed.

"What?"

"She's married to David Baxter, that's what. I've kept Michelle away because I don't trust that man, and maybe it's not fair to either of you. But I don't know what else to do."

"It's okay, Dad." Savannah leaned into him, resting her head against his chest. "I don't need any of them."

CHAPTER 6

Tiffany

THIS WEEKEND HAD DISASTER WRITTEN all over it. She'd rather be holed up in her apartment, curled in front of a cozy fire watching *Titanic*. Instead, she hurried across frosty tarmac, casting furtive glances over her shoulder, a fugitive from conventional courtesy.

From the moment she'd boarded the plane, awkwardness set in. Should she pretend she hadn't seen Grace and Caroline Hamilton and their traveling companion? Should she say hello and introduce herself to the woman with the vibrant green eyes who could only be Emily's mother?

In the end, Tiffany slouched in her seat and hoped they hadn't noticed her cowering a scant three rows in front of them. Why would any of them want to see her anyway? Grace Hamilton was the only one of the three she'd spent any time with, and even that only amounted to a handful of dinner parties.

When she reached the terminal, she slipped through the doors, coming to an abrupt halt as she spotted her mother. There she was, chatting with a familiar dark-haired man. *My mother, the traitor, cozying up to Aiden.*

"Damn," she said under her breath, earning several askance looks from the other passengers as she ducked behind a pillar. Tiffany peered around it, hoping Aiden wouldn't linger. She should have anticipated he'd be here. After all, whom else would the three women be visiting, other than her ex-husband?

Relief rushed through Tiffany as her mother hugged Aiden, and he wandered toward the baggage carousel. She skirted the pillar as she caught sight of Grace, Caroline, and Nina entering the building, praying they would walk by without noticing her.

"I can't wait to hug mis hermosos nietos." Nina's voice carried to Tiffany as she hunkered in her hiding spot.

Caroline tucked her arm through Grace's. "I still can't get over the fact Savannah is in college."

Tiffany peeked around the corner, her gaze following as they approached Aiden, each taking their turn to embrace him, Grace with a gentle-but-reserved kiss to his cheek, followed by Caroline with a hesitant half-hug.

"Hijo mio! " Nina lit up with a lovely bright smile as she planted her hands on either side of her son-in-law's face and bestowed enthusiastic kisses on his cheeks. The rest of her words faded into the buzz of the airport, but she embraced her son-in-law, rocking on her feet as she clung to him.

Aiden's warm and genuine response sent a pang through Tiffany's chest, visions of Emily nestled against him overtaking her.

Aiden offered his arm to Gramma Grace and led them toward the carousel, happily collected the bags, and stacked them on a trolley before ushering the group toward the front entrance.

After a long deep breath, Tiffany approached her mother.

"There you are." Her mom hugged her. "How was the flight?"

"It was fine." Tiffany savored the lingering tang of Aiden's spicy aftershave on her mom's wool coat. The oh-so-familiar scent brought more memories and tears rushing to the surface. She turned away. "I need my bag."

They worked their way across the now almost deserted terminal.

"He left." Her mother emitted a deep sigh. "He won't bother you."

"Who?"

"Quit pretending. You hid from Aiden. You don't have to be so on edge or go to such lengths to avoid him. He doesn't bite."

"Huh. Sure, Mother." She scoffed. Her mother might reconsider that opinion if she heard a replay of the last conversation Tiffany had with her ex-husband.

After retrieving her bag, she followed Michelle to the parking lot and stowed her suitcase in the trunk before sinking into the leather seat. "When did you two get all cozy?"

"Oh, stop. It would have been rude not to say hello to my son-in-law. Besides, I like him. It's your dad who has issues."

"*Ex*-son-in-law." She rolled her eyes at her mother's insistence on bestowing the familiar title onto Aiden. "You didn't love him when I married him." *Or ever give him a loving and exuberant greeting that came even close to matching Nina's.*

The lukewarm reception she and Aiden received when they'd announced their marriage still burned. She had no illusions about her father's reaction, but her mother's coldness and lack of support stole Tiffany's joy during a time meant to be overflowing with happiness. That her mother loved the man now, almost ten years after their messy and chaotic divorce, seemed the epitome of craziness.

Tiffany twirled a strand of hair around her fingertip. "I never understood why Father hated Aiden. He's from a high-profile family and belongs to the right social circles."

"Perhaps David thought ..." Michelle sighed. "Ahh, what the hell. Your father considered Aiden to be too high up the social register. That appealed to him, but he figured Aiden would tire of you and toss you aside. Based on his grandfather and father's actions, that perspective could have been true. However, Aiden isn't like that, is he?"

"Classic." Tiffany bowed her head, hiding her tears from her mother. "My own father thought I wasn't good enough for the high and mighty Hamilton family?"

"That's not true. He didn't want you hurt when the inevitable happened, and Aiden's family put pressure on him to date someone they deemed more suitable. Then you ended up pregnant, you two hid it, and ran." Her lip curled. "Thomas Hamilton would never have consented for his precious grandson to marry you. He didn't count on you marrying the moment you turned eighteen."

"Even that never made my father happy."

"How could it? Thomas threw a fit and froze Aiden out. He put pressure on your father, but David did his best."

"Yeah, Father did a fantastic job of protecting me." Tiffany snorted, not bothering to hide the bitterness in her tone. "If he'd left it alone and let us have her, I'd be with Aiden. We'd have a family, and I'd have my daughter. Instead, he ruined my relationship and forced me into that farce of an engagement with Harrison, which was so much better. Clearly, that man is a real catch. If you're another man, that is," Tiffany muttered.

Her mother either didn't hear her words or chose to ignore them, but her lips set in a flat line. "Perhaps he'd have made different choices if he'd known how this would turn out." She drummed her fingers on the steering wheel.

"Quit justifying his actions, Mother." Tiffany glowered from behind her curtain of hair.

Michelle concentrated on negotiating the snowy roads, occasionally shooting her a sideways glance. "I have to tell you something."

"There's more fantastic news?" Tiffany wilted, too exhausted to hold herself upright. The constant loneliness and the feeling of isolation on top of today's revelations had worn her down. At the age of thirty-three, her life seemed over and done.

"I met Savannah. She's a lovely girl. Aiden is taking wonderful care of your daughter."

"Did I ever say he wouldn't be a good father?" She leaned her head against the window, fighting back the tears. "How did you manage to get within twenty feet of her? Aiden doesn't even want me in the same state."

"She visited town with her friends, so I seized the opportunity and talked to her until Aiden arrived."

"Then he told you to go to hell?" In her heart, she knew this couldn't be true, especially after witnessing the scene at the airport.

"He was sweet, not at all upset, which gives me hope." Her mother reached over and grasped her hand, giving a quick squeeze before returning hers to the steering wheel. "He's not keeping you from her out of vindication, or trying to exact revenge. In his mind, he's protecting his child."

"That's supposed to make me feel better? My daughter turns eighteen in January, and I've barely spoken three words to her." She brushed at the free-falling tears, wishing she'd stood up to her mother and refused the invitation. This weekend was supposed to be a getaway, not a chance for her mother to taunt her with what she could never have and make her feel even worse about herself.

Her mom pulled onto the shoulder of the road, turning in her seat. "Tiffany." Michelle rubbed her shoulder.

She shied away from her mother's touch. "Don't."

Her mother dropped her hand. "You're so prickly. I don't even know how to talk to you. Here."

Tiffany turned her tear-stained face toward her mother, who held out a box of tissues. She snatched one and dabbed her reddened cheeks.

"Inside, you are this loving and wonderful person, but on the outside, you're hard as nails." She held out her arms. "She's in there, you know. I see her peek out every once in a while."

Tiffany angled herself away, refusing to be touched. "It won't help me get my daughter back. Aiden hates me." The thought that her mother had crept into the protective circle Aiden maintained and visited Savannah burned deep inside.

"Don't be ridiculous. He simply reads you well. He has an incredible sense of people. This amazing gift of intuition. Maybe it's always been in the background, or perhaps it's his medical training, but it's there."

Tiffany gritted her teeth. "How would you know how he feels?"

"How did you get so far along in your pregnancy without anyone noticing? I've asked myself that a million times."

"You were oblivious. Admit it, you were relieved to be rid of me for the summer."

"I thought you'd have more fun with your friends rather than allowing your father to drag you along the campaign trail," Michelle said. "What's always disturbed me is how you never confided or asked for my help."

"You would have told Father, and he would've told Aiden's parents, and his grandparents. We were scared kids, so we kept it a secret. If we hadn't, Savannah wouldn't exist."

"You and Aiden discussed it? You thought that?"

"You never asked what we wanted or even cared. Now you're suddenly concerned?" She wrapped her arms around herself, shivering as a chill crept over her. "I'm a mother who has forever lost my daughter. End of story. Can we just get this weekend over with?"

"Giving birth to a child makes you a mother, but it's not the definition of *being* a mother. Being a mother is so much more."

"How would you know? Not like you'd ever win an award for mother-of-the-year," Tiffany muttered under her breath. "You let them take her. I never had a chance."

"Maybe we failed you." Michelle emitted a deep sigh. "Maybe you were denied the right to be her mother when they took her as a baby, but the second time was a choice. You want Aiden to make it all better, to rescue you like he did when you were eighteen, but you have to do that for yourself." Her mother put the car into gear, and they rode the rest of the way in silence.

⁓⤨

The rest of the day passed in a blur, and she pasted on a faux cheerful smile, pretending everything was okay. She played the expected role, glossing over the issues and hiding the cracks in her family relationships. An overwhelming urge to escape grew as the crowded house became cloying and claustrophobic.

She wrapped a scarf around her neck and pulled on her wool coat. Without a word to anyone, she slipped out the door, inhaling the crisp air as she headed for the deserted beach. She longed to feel something … anything … that would allow an escape from the emotional numbness that had plagued her since the ill-fated visit to Boston. The salty tang fill her nostrils as she stopped and closed her eyes, wishing the constant shushing of the waves lapping onto the beach could soothe her soul.

Then she walked. Bitterness welled up. *Maybe we failed you?* Those inadequate words made her want to scream. Useless words were all anyone offered. *Didn't anyone understand that nothing could ever compensate for what I endured? What I lost?* Patronizing words flowed from her mother in a never ending stream, like she repeated things by rote. *The woman pretended to listen, but did she ever really hear me?*

How could they not understand? She'd been told her daughter was better off, with people more capable of loving her. *But who better to love a child than her own mother? The one who carried that child within her own body, nurtured that tiny being, and mourned her when she'd been torn away?* That no one trusted in her had been hard to bear. *If everyone believed I didn't have the capacity to love my own child, then I must be unlovable too.*

Aiden didn't love her. *Had he ever loved me the way I loved him?* She'd given herself to him, heart and soul, and when things got rough, he'd abandoned her. He hadn't been hidden away, lectured, and shamed. In the hospital, the staff treated her like a pariah. Even her own mother couldn't be bothered.

Her steps carried her, time melding together, her cheeks numb and eyes burning as she stumbled to a halt. With closed eyes, she sank to her knees, picturing all the wonderful times on this beach and in this house. All they'd shared that had broken and faded.

Silent, scalding tears trickled down her face, and she bowed her head. The dampness from the sand seeped into her jeans, but still, she couldn't move. She rested her hands on her knees, dragging in breaths of air. *Why bother fighting?* Nothing was worthwhile. Everything had been taken. She fought her battles alone.

No one could ever know what it had been like to watch that nurse disappear down that stark, lifeless hallway, stealing her baby girl forever. The endless tears and grief as she lost not only her child, but the man she loved. It marked the beginning of the end, not only of her time with Aiden, but her entire life.

"Tiffany?" Hands on her shoulders accompanied the deep, gentle voice.

Her eyes snapped open. *Was he kneeling before me? Or did I simply wish he was?* "Sorry … I shouldn't be here." Her breath hitched, her cheeks flaming as she dropped her chin to her chest.

"What's wrong?" Aiden rubbed, his voice level.

"Everything," she whispered. "I don't know why I'm here, but … nothing's right, and it never will be."

"It could be."

Tiffany shook her head as sobs wracked her body. "N-no, i-it won't. It's over. All the wrong choices. I've lost everything. Everyone." She hauled oxygen into her lungs, her chest tightening, black spots dancing before her eyes. If only complete darkness would swallow her and end this misery. "S-stupid nonsense. Everyone patting me on the back, saying my life isn't a complete disaster. I'm a mess. I want it to be finished."

"No." Aiden voice sounded muffled and distant. He cupped her face, tipping her chin and forcing her to look into his eyes. "Never say that. Ever. You have more than you imagine, Tiffany. So much more."

Even his warm palms pressed against her cheeks couldn't penetrate the icy chill that gripped her. She clutched his hands, afraid he might pull away, even as dread seized her.

Looking him in the eye at this moment was excruciating. She'd fought so hard to keep it all hidden deep inside, but now it surfaced in an uncontrollable rush, every single feeling and emotion exposed. Laid bare to this man she'd loved for eternity.

They kneeled for the longest time, their gazes locked on each other, before she struggled to her feet. "This was stupid. I'm sorry. I'll go." She stumbled down the rough surface of the beach, tears blurring her vision. A raw bitterness seeped to her core.

Aiden caught up in a few strides. "Talk to me, Tiffany."

"What do you want to hear?" She wiped at her face, unable to stem the flow of the salty river.

"How you feel? You're here for a reason. Don't hide from it. Let it out." He grasped her arm, halting her progress and forcing her to turn.

"I'm sorry. For everything. You've got your own life. I get it. I'm trying, you know? But it hurt, what you said to me. Even if it's true." She blinked hard, desperate to quell the tears. "I ... want my daughter. Don't you understand? I've always wanted my baby girl, but they took her. I went through it alone. Hours of labor, with no one, while you were where?"

He closed his eyes for a moment before giving her a long look. "I wish I had been with you." He bowed his head, retaining a firm hold on her arm, remaining silent for the longest time.

Tiffany rested her hand over top of his, wondering at this change, this pain. Even though he'd denied hating her, she hadn't believed him ... until this moment. "Aiden?"

"I'm sorry, you know," he said. "You caught me by surprise, and ... I shouldn't have said that about you not being her mother. It wasn't a decision we made, but one forced on us. One that we live with. But"—he dragged in a rough breath before lifting his head—"it changes nothing. Savannah's fragile, and it breaks my heart every time she pretends she's not devastated by this whole situation."

Devastated. Unable to stand the torment so evident in his eyes, Tiffany closed her own, pressing her right hand over her heart. "I never meant to hurt her. I love our daughter."

"Yes," he whispered. "But it's not up to me, or you. It's her decision."

"I've lost her forever. Do you still think there's anything worthwhile in my life?"

"You never know what's around the next corner. Against all odds, our daughter found me when she needed me most. That's a true miracle." He rested his hands on her shoulders. "Don't surrender. You have so much to give, so much talent, and deep down, you know it. Figure out your life and things can be different."

"I've tried."

"Good. Now try harder. If you sort your life, I will help with Savannah. I can't do that until I'm certain it won't cause further damage." He contemplated her. "Saying she's fragile isn't an excuse to keep her from you. She's experienced devastating losses. She's dealing with her own issues. I refuse to pile yours on top of everything else, but I promise, here and now, if you make the effort and deal with your demons, I will do what I can."

"You'd help me?" Tiffany blinked, barely comprehending his words. "You'd let me see her?"

"The final say will always be hers, but don't give up. Remember, we never thought we'd ever see our daughter, yet we've been granted a second chance. Giving up would be the worst thing you could do for all of us. Promise you won't do anything stupid. If not for yourself, then stay strong for Savannah's sake. Don't put her through any further heartbreak or loss."

Tiffany drew in a deep breath. He'd seen it all. How far she'd fallen. That dark pit of hopelessness yawning below as she clung by her fingertips to the thin ledge above it. Everything. The way all of her hopes and dreams were slipping away, disappearing into the darkness. And not for the first time.

"Promise." He squeezed her shoulders. "Please, please, promise."

"I promise," she whispered, shuffling her feet. She focused on a shell that had washed up on the beach, squishing it into the sand with the toe of her shoe. "Is there anything that would make you believe in me again?"

He tipped up her chin, forcing her to look at him. "Hmm, there she is."

"Who?"

"This girl I used to know a long time ago." He dropped his hands to his sides. "It would be great if she stuck around. I hope someday you'll find her and let her out. When you do, that's the day your wishes and dreams will come true."

"Do you think so?" A tiny ray of hope peeked out at her.

"Yes. I believe it." He forced her into motion. "Let's get you home. It's freezing. Are you staying at Ruth's with your mom?"

Tiffany nodded, and for the first time in a long time, she embraced the emotions, allowed the pain squeezing her heart in its iron grip to remind her she was alive. The glimmer of hope his words brought gave her something to focus on, providing a sense that perhaps something was worth the struggle.

"This is it." Tiffany hung her head and hunched her shoulders as they reached the front door, unable to look at him. He'd spotted the demons stalking her, witnessed how weak and needy she truly was, and she felt humbled that he'd taken the time for her.

"Tiffany?" Aiden grasped her hand. "Remember your promise. Is there someone you can talk to if you need help?"

"I'll call my therapist." She stared at the bottom step. "I'm not planning to off myself. Anyway, I'm not your responsibility."

"I will always care." Aiden cradled her cheeks within his palms, lifting her gaze upward. "How are things with Michelle?"

"Tense, as usual. I can't talk to her. She never listens."

"It's tough, but it's time you open up. She doesn't know about the therapy, does she?"

"Why give her another reason to be disappointed?"

"Talk to her. She needs to hear it. Promise you'll at least try."

"I promise." Tiffany's breath caught as he pressed a light kiss to her forehead.

"Take care of yourself. I don't want anything to happen to you. Now, inside." He gave her a gentle push.

Tiffany took slow steps up to the door, turning the handle before she glanced over her shoulder, reassured he was still there. She slipped inside, pressing her back against the door as the warmth of the house enveloped her.

The man she'd encountered today had been her Aiden, but also not hers. He'd moved on and existed in a whole other time and space. The Aiden in the here and now, his heart belonged to someone else. She'd given it away, and she had to live without him. Even in that she drew comfort. Love truly did exist.

CHAPTER 7

Savannah

SAVANNAH PACED TO THE WINDOW, lifting the edge of the curtain to scan the beach for any sign of her dad. It had been over an hour since he'd disappeared. With every minute that ticked by, it became harder and harder to breathe.

She ran her trembling hands through her hair and dropped to her knees, dragging in long breaths, forcing herself to exhale each slowly while rubbing her hands up and down her thighs. This simple grounding exercise advised by her therapist, meant to calm her overwhelming anxiety, usually had good results.

"It's. Not. Working." She sprang to her feet and retraced her steps to continue her vigil at the window. After a long rough inhale, she grasped the heart pendant she wore daily, rubbing her thumb over the rough surface created by the diamonds. "Daddy will be back. Very soon."

It wasn't easy to block out the mirage that had appeared on the beach below. At first, Savannah had thought her overactive imagination was taking over, or it was the mist hanging in the air obscuring her vision.

The blonde woman in a dark gray coat dropping to her knees in the sand, head bowed.

A dark-haired man appeared and kneeled in front of the woman, lifting her face. Not a mirage, but two real people.

Her dad.

Tiffany.

"Why did she come here? To our beach?" Savannah curled up on the bed, her head swimming.

Tiffany had risen and wobbled away, Aiden only a few paces behind. Savannah spied on them until they disappeared into the mist.

"No, no, no." Tears spilled over, running hot and unchecked down her cheeks. He hadn't abandoned them, left them, for *her*.

Emily's retreat to the master bedroom, her eyes shiny with tears, and Aiden's exit, the way he'd snatched up his coat and stalked out the door, didn't mean he'd left for good. No. That could never happen. Losing Emily from her life would be unbearable. She couldn't say goodbye to another single person.

Hadn't anyone else noticed? Were they oblivious to the drama unfolding right under their noses? Savannah hadn't missed it, and the all too familiar sense of panic had risen. Embarrassed and worried she might meltdown in front of her new friends, she fled to her room. *They wouldn't understand.*

Don't be ridiculous. A hum rumbled low in her throat, and she wrapped her arms around herself, picturing Aiden returning and hugging Emily.

Aiden loved Emily.

Emily loved Aiden.

Even though Emily had been grouchy this morning and had snapped at Aiden, it didn't mean anything. They were happy. They loved each other. They were having another baby.

She concentrated on relaxing each part of her body, starting with her toes, working upward, repeating until the tension eased.

The faint creak of the stairs alerted her, and she sat, holding her breath and listening before rising from the bed. She stole across the floor, inching her door open enough to peer through the tiny crack.

Her breath caught as Emily appeared from the bedroom at the far end of the hall. Savannah remained riveted—a silent voyeur—examining the expression on Emily's face. It tugged at Savannah's heart, that mixture of sadness and hope, tears brimming Emily's reddened eyes as she gazed toward the stairs. Emily held out her arms, then ... her dad appeared in Vanna's frame of vision.

She couldn't see his face, but he slid into Emily's embrace, wrapping his arms around his wife, pulling her close.

His low and muffled voice prevented Savannah from catching the words as he murmured against her stepmother's hair and caressed her face with his fingers before he kissed her.

She'd seen him kiss Emily before, but never like this. The two assumed they were alone and unobserved. She couldn't tear her eyes away as Emily's hand wrapped around the back of his neck, pulling him closer.

Further intruding on their privacy was wrong. Savannah crept back to her bed. The pain and panic gripping her lifted, and the weight squeezing her chest eased. Everything would be okay.

She flopped onto her back, waiting several minutes before rising and peeking into the empty hallway. Their bedroom door had closed, the silence broken only by the faint murmur of voices and occasional burst of laughter drifting from downstairs.

Her mind traveled to the image of her dad on the beach with Tiffany. Would he tell Emily? What had happened? Why had she come? She pushed it aside and tiptoed down the stairs and into the kitchen.

"Gin." Rochelle grinned and sprang from her chair, waving her hands and swaying her hips.

"Again?" Abuela Nina said in a perky, happy tone. Her eyes brightened as she spotted her granddaughter lurking in the doorway. "Hija. There you are."

Savannah gave her a faint smile as people rose to refill their drinks and snack bowls.

"What's up with you?" Piper nudged her ribs, keeping her voice low.

"Nothing. I'm just tired. We stayed up too late last night."

"Uh-huh." Her friend examined her expression. "You're all tense, and you disappeared on us. Where'd you go?"

"Sorry, I went upstairs." She sighed, and drew Piper out of her grandmothers' hearing range. "My dad and Emily were at each other earlier, and it bothers me, you know?"

"Oh, that? Don't worry, Vanna. My dad and stepmonster fight all the time, then they kiss and make up and it's fine. At least yours don't have screaming matches. Mine go nuts and my stepmonster throws things. One time my dad had to go to the emergency room for stitches."

"Wow. That's crazy." She still couldn't banish the picture of her dad with Tiffany. "You think?"

"Cheer up. Married people argue. Believe me. Your dad and stepmom barely fight compared to most from what I've seen. So relax. Join us for the next round of cards."

"You're right." She retrieved a soda from the fridge before taking a seat beside her Abuela Nina at the otherwise vacant table.

"Cariño, I am glad you decided to join us." Her grandmother shot a glance toward the hive of activity in the kitchen and lowered her voice. "You stop worrying. My Emelia is a passionate woman." Her grandmother patted her knee. "She carries mi nieto."

"She told you about the baby?" Savannah kept her own voice low.

"She didn't need to say." Nina beamed. "I saw the signs. The mood will pass. They love each other, very much."

Savannah nodded, returning the smile her Abuela bestowed on her. It reassured her that the tension had not gone unnoticed, rather everyone had taken it in stride.

Even after Nina's reassurances, Savannah's gaze flitted toward the stairs. An excruciating amount of time passed before her dad appeared with a smiling Kellan on his hip. Emily followed soon afterward, cheerful as she stopped to peck Aiden on the lips. The storm had passed without leaving any lasting damage.

Emily busied herself in the kitchen, Grace, Caroline, and Nina joining her to assist with the final touches on dinner.

"Hey." Aiden slipped an arm around her waist after leaving Kellan to play with Piper and Rochelle. "You're awfully quiet. Anything wrong?"

She bit her lip, wondering if she should bring it up. "Can we talk?"

"Let's go somewhere quiet." He led her into the small office and shut the door. "What's up?"

"It's probably none of my business, but you and Emily were fighting. And you walked out."

"Oh, that? It's nothing, sweetie. Emily's struggling with morning sickness. She's exhausted, hormonal, and cooped up in a house with a bunch of other women, including her mother. She got grouchy, and I'm an easy target. I refuse to fight back, so she takes her frustration out on me." He sat on the arm of the couch. "Rather than letting it escalate and making something out of nothing, it's better to take a breather, calm things down, and then talk. I walked, she napped, and then we made up. That's a part of marriage. Or having any relationship, really."

"And Tiffany?" She crossed her arms. "I saw you on the beach with her, right after the fight with Emily."

"Ahhh, so that's what it's really about, isn't it?"

She nodded. "You and Emily argued and you left. With her. How could you do that?"

"That's an oversimplification of facts. I went for a walk after an insignificant disagreement with my wife and ran into Tiffany on the beach. She had something to say, and I walked her to their friend's house. So you commenting how could I *do that*? I haven't done anything to feel guilty about, so ..." He shrugged.

"Did you tell Emily that you'd seen Tiffany?"

"Wow, this is like the inquisition." His gaze remained steady and level. "I'm not hiding anything, Savannah. Especially not from my wife. We've all seen what secrets and lies do to a marriage."

She caught his meaning. Nobody within her family remained oblivious to the major upset in Joel and Alex's relationship over the past year. Not that anyone had bothered to explain it to her, at least not until Joel had barged into their home and attacked her dad. That hurricane had ripped through their lives, leaving major carnage.

"What did Tiffany say?" Vanna never wavered.

He gave her a long look, as if considering his words. "She'd like to see you, but she understands you're not ready, so she's backing off."

"Just like that? She's giving up on me?" She lifted her head at his drawn-out sigh.

"It's not nearly so simple." His terse tone confirmed his irritation, even if he kept it controlled. He motioned for her to sit beside him on the sofa. "I know you hate when I say this, but it's complicated," he said softly. "How do I even begin?"

Vanna shifted to face him. "You've never shared much about you and her, so start at the beginning. What did you like about her?"

"Hmm. You've seen such a small part of her, it must be tough to imagine. Being a teenage boy, I noticed right away that she was beautiful, but she had a sweetness about her, and she loved adventure." He pushed off the couch and dug in the small bar fridge, coming up with two cans of soda.

"Thanks." A grin spread across her face as she popped the tab. "Figures you'd notice her looks first. Typical guy."

"Smart ass." He swatted her arm as he dropped beside her. "It was more than that. At first she was so quiet, but underneath hides a different person. She had a wicked sense of humor, and she loved pranks and our night time escapes. We used to sneak out of the dorms. Lucky we never got caught, but we all became pros at scaling buildings."

"So you'd sneak out to meet her?"

"We all went. It cemented our friendships, and we become close, which you can see even to this day. The boarding school had acres of land close to the lake. Anyway ..."

"You were a badass. Sneaking out all the time." She observed him, contemplating how much he'd experienced at the age of thirty-three while she'd barely accomplished anything in her life.

"Uh-huh." He sipped his drink. "We did it all summer here too. The room you picked used to be mine, complete with the handy tree." He pointed a finger, wagging it. "I expect you to use the front door. No sneaking. And under no circumstances will you repeat any of this to your little brother. I'm sure he'll get himself in enough trouble as he grows up without your help."

"I won't, I promise. I'll save it in case I have a baby sister." She gave him an impish grin as he rolled his eyes. "When did you start dating Tiffany?"

"A couple of months before school ended, not long before we both turned fourteen. She stayed with Alex that summer. I don't know how to explain how easy it was to love her. Our group spent all summer hanging out, sailing, swimming and it was magical in its way." A faraway look appeared in his eyes.

"You truly loved her, didn't you?"

"Very much." He took her hand between his. "Maybe that's not what you want to hear, but it's true. By the time we went back to school that fall, we were inseparable. We'd been together for almost a year when you happened. On the surface, we were the same, but you can't imagine how hard we worked to keep it hidden. We spent less time with our friends, but then Michelle found out, and Tiffany changed. The experience closed her off, she was never the same. Our lives turned upside down, and we were powerless to control it." He rubbed a hand over his face. "Today, she seemed like a version of her old self. But still not." He stared at the can in his hands.

"Dad?" She rested her hand on his arm. "Are you okay?"

He shrugged. "Fine."

Something remained unsaid, an unresolved feeling or thought he hadn't shared.

"What did she really say today?"

"Hmm?" A lost look appeared in his eyes.

"You're so distracted. And sad. Why?"

"Sometimes …" Another long sigh issued from his lips. "You make decisions based on what you know or feel. Today, I started to wonder if—" He closed his eyes and sank further into the couch with his head tipped back.

"What?" She waited, hoping he would finish the thought. When he didn't respond, she prodded him again. "You can tell me, you know. I'm not a child. I can handle it. Please?"

He opened his eyes, focusing on her. "I'm aware of that. You grew up, and I wish I'd been there."

"You were."

"Not for nearly enough of it." He patted her knee. "This will be hard to hear, but maybe you should know. It might affect your future decisions."

"So tell me. I know you want to protect me, but I'm strong now." She rubbed her hands across her jeans, combating the sudden dampness of her palms as she took a deep breath to calm her jangling nerves. The way her dad contemplated her made her think he didn't quite believe it. Like he knew how she'd almost come undone only hours earlier.

Still, the questions burned in her mind. "How could you have loved her? She's cold and harsh, and she turned her back on both of us when we needed her. I don't believe she wanted me, and I have no idea why you think she ever did."

"I lived it with her. There are some things you can't fake." He turned, taking both of her hands in his. "She used to be the sweetest, most loving person in the world, but she endured so much. Alone."

She stared at him. Her dad, the strongest person she'd ever known, seemed about to cry. Over *her*, of all people.

He looked away. "She built a wall to protect herself, and she's never let that guard down. It's devastating to lose a child, and I couldn't be there. David kept everyone away, and we tried to escape it." He shook his head, his voice dropping to almost a whisper, "I wonder …"

"Tell me—"

The study door opened and Piper bounced in. "Dinner's ready. Tom and Jenna are here with Adrianna. She's adorable."

Aiden's demeanor changed in that split second. "Thanks. We'll be right out." He held his hand out to Savannah.

"Dad?"

He shook his head. "Now is not the time. Our guests are waiting."

Savannah cursed Piper's timing. That interruption had broken their moment, and maybe he'd think better of sharing whatever occupied his mind.

She took his hand and allowed him to lead her from the room, and they were soon immersed in the revelry of Thanksgiving dinner.

The next few weeks were busy with exams and Christmas preparations. Aiden became wrapped up in work, and they'd barely sat down for dinner as a family, let alone finish their discussion.

Rochelle accompanied her as they walked toward the dorms. They'd had lunch with Piper after their last final exam, and then their friend had left to gather her bags for her flight to Montana. "What are you up to now?"

"Delivering Gray's Christmas gift." She patted her bag. "He's on a plane tonight, so I won't see him for two weeks. I thought I'd surprise him. We haven't had much time together this week between work and exams."

"I'll leave you here. I haven't packed, and I have to be on the train in two hours. Have a great holiday." Rochelle hugged her, and they parted ways.

Savannah entered the building, stopping to examine her reflection in the mirror before she bounded up the stairs. Outside his door, she paused to extract the gift box. "Surprise." She sashayed through the door, halting abruptly at the moan and flash of movement. "Oh, I should've knocked, sorry Za—"

Vanna's mouth went dry and tears burned her eyes as she caught sight of blondish hair and glimpsed blue eyes … and pink manicured nails dug into the smooth flesh of his back.

"Unbelievable. You're such an asshole." Savannah's breath caught as he turned his head toward her. "Wow." She spun, heading straight out the door.

"Wait!" The thump of feet hitting the floor followed. His hand landed on her arm as he stumbled into the hallway behind her. "Vanna. It's not wha—"

"Seriously?" She slapped him away.

He planted himself in front of her, rubbing his fingers through his tousled hair, guilt written all over his face. "Don't overreact. It's nothing. She means nothing." He grasped her shoulders.

"Nothing?" She jammed her flattened palms against his bare chest, shoving hard. "You were the one who demanded we be exclusive. Do you even know what that means?"

"It just"—he hung his head—"happened."

"Are you kidding?" She snorted. "That's what they all say. Do me a favor and lose my number. I never want to see your lying, cheating ass ever again."

A heated flush rose in her face. Even though the dorms were emptying for the holidays, their altercation had drawn a crowd. People stopped and stared, and doors opened all along the corridor.

Gray wrapped his fingers around her wrist, dragging her toward his room. "We can't discuss this here."

"Let go." Savannah twisted, escaping from his grasp. "There's nothing to discuss." She dashed for the stairs, keeping her head down, rushing through the exit door only moments before the tears broke free. After ducking around the corner, she leaned against the cold stone of the building, sucking in deep breaths as she blotted at her eyes with her sleeve.

"Are you okay?" The deep melodic voice made her jump.

"Oh. Yeah, fine." Vanna kept her head bowed as she dug in her bag for her pack of tissues.

"You don't look fine."

Savannah lifted her chin only enough to peer through the blur of tears and register that a man stood only a foot in front of her. She shook her head and blew her nose on the tissue she'd managed to retrieve.

"Here." A water bottle came into view. "You need this more than I do."

She swallowed hard to release the lump in her throat. "I couldn't."

"Please, take it." He pressed it into her hand.

She looked up, and up some more. Savannah wasn't short at five foot eight, but this man towered above her, easily over six feet tall.

"I just bought it." A faint smile twitched at the corner of his lips as he ran fingers through his dark, wavy hair. "It's not poisoned or drugged, I promise."

His soulful gray eyes softened, and despite his imposing size and proximity, Savannah had the immediate impression he could be trusted. A rare good one.

"Thank you." She twisted the cap, the seal snapping as it broke, and she tipped the bottle against parched lips. The icy drink soothed her throat. "I'll repay you."

"No, no." He waved a hand. "You seem awfully upset."

"It's nothing."

He quirked a brow.

Heat rose in her cheeks. "Well, obviously it's something." She took another grateful gulp of the icy water. "Guys, you know?"

"Yeah, I do." He studied her. "He's not worth it. Any guy who'd cheat on a girl like you …" He shook his head. "He doesn't deserve you."

"How'd you know? That he …?"

"Call it a hunch." He glanced at his watch.

"You probably have somewhere to be. Thank you, I feel better."

"Good." He smiled, an adorable dimple appearing in his right cheek. "I have to pick someone up, but will you be all right? Do you need a ride? We could drop you on our way to the airport."

"Thank you, but it's not far." She met his gaze, her heart tapping a staccato beat as his smile widened.

"You take care, and remember that he's an idiot. Don't take him back."

"I won't." Despite her misery, her lips tugged upward.

He adjusted his bag and walked across the square. Once on the other side, he glanced over his shoulder and waved before he disappeared around the corner.

I'm sorry. It won't happen again. Promise.

Savannah swept her fingers across her screen, deleting yet another lame text. "No kidding it won't, asshole," she said under her breath and then scoffed. That he even dreamed she'd take him back shocked her.

One thing the kind stranger said resonated, creating an echo effect whenever she wavered.

He's not worth it.

Her phone landed on her bed and she turned her attention to folding another sweater, tucking it on top of the growing pile in her suitcase. Their flight left early in the morning, and the thought filled her with relief. It would give her two solid weeks with little chance of seeing anyone from Harvard.

Piper and Rochelle didn't yet know about the breakup, or the encounter with the tall, dark-haired man with the enticing dimple and warm gray eyes. *Man candy.* Smiles kept finding their way to the surface through the despair. Nothing wrong with enjoying the view, after all.

Gray. Her mood slid downhill as she remembered the scene from his dorm room. *No more men.*

Her phone buzzed, and she expected another lame apology from Gray, but it seemed her luck had changed. Justin.

I'm with Leanne, she says hi. Wish you were here.

Let me talk to her.

Moments later her phone rang.

"I've missed you," Leanne said.

"When are you coming to visit me in Boston? Justin stayed after our sailing trip. I wish you'd been able to come with us. Such an amazing summer."

"Sailing around the Greek Islands for three months? How could you go wrong? It sounds like you two had"—her friend giggled—"fun without me. I'd have been in the way."

Savannah heard Justin's muffled words in the background.

"He wants to talk to you," Leanne said in a singsong voice. "I'll text you later, and you can fill me in on your hot guy."

"Ha, no more hot guy. He's over and done."

"What?" Justin asked in a deep voice. "What happened?"

"Another girl, that's what." She combed her fingers though her hair. "I'm over it. And him."

"I'm sorry. Do you want me to come out there and beat him up?"

Savannah rolled her eyes. "Nah, he's not worth it, tough guy."

"You don't think I would? Do you want to talk about it?"

"Not right now. How about you? Anyone special?"

"Not at the moment," he said. "Are you sure you're okay?"

"I'm good. I have to finish packing, so can we talk later?"

"Sure."

"Love you." Savannah said goodbye and flopped on her bed, closing her eyes. Some days she really missed living near Leanne, but she especially wished Justin was closer.

Her ex-boyfriend tended to be the one to offer the best advice, and lately, they talked almost every day. Though the romance was gone, nothing could replace his friendship.

CHAPTER 8

Tiffany

THE CROWDED GALLERY BROUGHT JOY to Tiffany's heart. Her business remained a beacon, keeping her tethered to life while she struggled with the weight of her unkept promises.

Eventually, she would summon the courage, but for now, the effort to simply exist took every scrap of her limited energy. Even managing the rest of the Thanksgiving weekend, keeping the façade of normalcy in place, had been an excruciating task.

She smoothed her dress and glanced at her reflection before she stepped from her office, her bright smile covering the turmoil inside.

"Ms. Baxter."

She turned, coming face-to-face with the owner of the oh-so-sexy accent. Alluring hazel eyes captivated her. "Hello." A tiny frown knit her brow as she sought to connect a name to this familiar man. Her eyes lit up. "You're Stefan Cortes."

"And you're Tiffany Baxter." He smiled, enveloping her hand in a warm, firm grip.

"I love your work," she said in a breathless voice, heat rising in her cheeks. *Urgh. I sounded like a teenager girl meeting my favorite boy-band.* Tiffany swallowed hard. "Are you enjoying the show?"

"Very much. I met the artist in one of my workshops a few years back. I encouraged her to develop her skills, and it's paid off. You have a great eye."

"Thank you. What can I do for you?"

"Oh. Well," he said, "I thought perhaps we could get a drink sometime."

She froze. This man had been an idol of hers for years. Though not much older than her, his photography made him legendary in the art world. "That's very kind of you, Mr. Cortes, but I couldn't possibly."

"Stefan. And why couldn't you possibly?" A brow went up as he scrutinized her. "It's only a drink. I have some business to discuss with you." He still had a firm grip on her hand.

Maybe because I hadn't managed to let his go?

"Business?" She tugged, hoping to disengage from his warm grasp. *If only sinking into the floor and disappearing were an option.*

"Do you have time after the holidays?" He produced a business card and extended it toward her. "Maybe you could call to set up a time?"

"Of course." Her fingers trembled as she accepted it, the light brush of his fingers causing a frisson of anticipation.

"I'll see you again soon. It was a pleasure to meet you, Tiffany." Stefan nodded and drifted toward the next exhibit.

Tiffany tore her gaze away and moved to talk to a couple who were admiring one of the pieces.

Isla appeared at her side sometime later as the crowd thinned. "Did I see Stefan Cortes hand you his card?"

"He wants to discuss business." Tiffany snagged a glass of champagne and gulped it down. "I'm such an idiot," she whispered as heat crept up her neck. "I thought he was asking me on a damn date."

"He has been checking you out all evening." Isla surveyed the man, a wicked gleam appearing in her eyes. "Go for it. At worst he'd be a hot night in the sack."

"Stop it. I'm not going to ..." She huffed, fighting the urge to look his way. "It's business. You know how influential that man is. No way would he be interested in dating someone like me."

Despite her best efforts to avoid looking, Tiffany performed her own perusal. She'd always been drawn toward men with broad shoulders. Her imagination painted in the details, picturing the tight and toned curves of his ass under that tailored suit. Combined with thick dark-hair that would feel heavenly under her fingertips, beautiful hazel eyes, strong jawline with just the right amount of stubble ... Her mouth dried as her gaze locked onto his.

His brows rose the tiniest bit, a twinkle appearing in his eyes, followed by full lips twitching into a sexy smile. And then he winked.

She bowed her head, her hair falling forward to mercifully cover her flaming cheeks. The man would certainly avoid her calls after she'd brazenly ogled him.

"Not interested, huh?" Isla smirked. "Looks pretty damn interested to me."

"Get back to work," Tiffany muttered, her cheeks burning hotter than the kiln in the back room. "And quit drooling over the clientele."

Isla snickered. "You got it, Boss."

⌒≼

Tiffany set her purse on a stool and placed the large bag on the floor. "Father not around?"

"No." Her mom stirred the chili then set the lid on top with a clunk. "I told you it'd be just the two of us for dinner."

Tiffany sighed. She hadn't seen her father since the groveling session that earned her the extra funds for the art show in Boston. Disapproval had emanated from the man, making her wonder why he'd financed the gallery in the first place.

Michelle turned weary eyes her way. "How did the show turn out?"

"Great. We made several sales, and we're adding some pieces to the collection on consignment." She inhaled the familiar spicy tang complemented by the fresh biscuits baking the oven. "Dinner smells wonderful."

"Thanks." Her mother opened a bottle of wine.

Soon they were settled at the counter, each with a bowl of steaming chili.

Her mom pushed her dinner around with her spoon before taking a dainty bite.

"What's wrong?" Tiffany sighed.

Michelle set her spoon aside and reached for her daughter's hand. "Your father moved out. I've filed for divorce."

"What? Why?" Tiffany stared at Michelle. "The two of you have always seemed so ..." *Happy?* She couldn't help the tiniest twitch of her head to the side, negating that initial thought. *Miserable.* That fit. "A divorce?"

"At long last, yes." Michelle blinked, dry-eyed.

"That's big news. I don't even know what to say."

"You're not going to ask why?"

"It isn't my business." Tiffany wasn't sure she needed or wanted to know the disturbing details behind her parents' marriage. "Though it explains why he missed Thanksgiving."

"He spent it with his mistress."

Tiffany pushed her half-empty bowl away. "I'm sorry."

"Don't be. I've always known about his philandering. I should have left long ago, then maybe things would be different." Michelle drained the last of her wine before refilling both of their glasses. "Let's sit in the family room."

Tiffany quelled a derisive snort at the misnomer as she followed her mother. No room in this entire house had ever felt like a space where they'd been an actual family. She wandered to the mantel and ran a fingertip over the silver frame. "You put it out?"

68

"I don't know how you managed to get your hands on it, but I love looking at it every day. It makes me sad when I think of all I missed over the years." Michelle's eyes shimmered as she gazed at her daughter.

"I took the picture about a year ago. Stupid, but I saw them at the beach in the Vineyard. Aiden would freak if he knew."

"Sit, please?" Her mother extended her hands toward Tiffany. Michelle inhaled and then let out a long slow breath. "I've failed you. I can see you're miserable, that you're in pain, and I blame myself every single day. That Thanksgiving weekend, so much became clear to me, and I hoped we could talk. Or maybe you'll talk, and I'll listen."

Tiffany frowned and took a small step toward her mother. "Who are you?" *And what have you done with my mother?*

Michelle sighed. "I've done a poor job, and I have many regrets. Please. One honest conversation is all I ask." The corners of her mouth turned down. "Seeing my granddaughter and how you've struggled … I can no longer pretend," she said. "I choose you."

"You've never …" She sucked in a long breath.

"Why do you never talk to me? Why didn't you come to me when you needed help?" Her mother's voice was gentle.

"Because you never listened. I couldn't count on you to be there. And you weren't. You freaked out and told me how irresponsible I was. You didn't care what I thought, or what Aiden thought, or any of it. You packed me onto an airplane and sent me away. I didn't even have him, and I was terrified. You separated us, and it broke everything," she whispered as tears streamed down her face and her breath hitched in her chest. "No one cared. You hid me away like a horrible, shameful secret. They ripped my baby from my arms without giving a damn how I felt."

Her whole body shook, and her chest heaved as she tried to catch her breath. "I needed my mother, but you weren't there. I felt empty and shameful and dirty and unloved."

Michelle's eyes filled with tears as she stared at her. "Oh, my sweet girl."

Tiffany found herself wrapped in an embrace, neither of them able to speak through their tears.

"I'm sorry, so, so sorry we did that to you." Michelle pulled back, her eyes red and puffy.

"Are you?" Tiffany wiggled away. "Do you have any idea what you did? Why do you think we ran away? We wanted her, and there was no reason we couldn't have raised her, except for our fathers' political ambitions."

"Which is why I'm finished with my sad excuse of a marriage. And what he had done to that poor boy."

"What do you mean?" Tiffany narrowed her eyes.

Michelle stared at her hands. "In all these years, he's never told you?" She closed her eyes and shook her head.

"Mom," Tiffany whispered. "Tell me. Please."

Her mother heaved a sigh. "It's not pretty, honey. The hired muscle they sent was none too gentle with Aiden. David's doing, I'm sure. Exacting his pound of flesh and his retribution of sorts."

"They …" She wasn't sure she could bear hearing it. "They hurt Aiden?"

Her mom looked sad as she placed her hand over Tiffany's. "He came home in rough shape. They hid him away for a while so Grace didn't see."

"My father had my boyfriend beaten up?" A shiver twitched up her spine, her mouth watering. She swallowed hard to combat the queasiness.

"Are you surprised? It could have been worse, but Aiden Grayson stepped in and suggested they send Aiden overseas to keep the two of you apart. That man always had a soft spot for his namesake."

"Hiring grown men to beat the crap out of a teenage boy is having a soft spot?" Her stomach clenched and a sour taste rose in her throat. Lost in her own world of pain and grief, she hadn't thought it through. They'd made Aiden pay in far harsher terms than they'd exacted on her. "No wonder Father was so eager to help with financing the gallery and my apartment." Sadness enveloped her. "He figured he'd pay me off. Like anything could compensate for the loss of my child or how my marriage ended."

Her heart broke as truth washed over her. The only things David Baxter loved were power, control, and his damn job. She and her mother had always taken a distant second to his need to win and to protect appearances.

"I let him run my life, push me at Harrison, and so much else." She sniffled. "Parents are supposed to take care of their children, but all he did was steal mine."

"And I let him do it." Michelle took her hand. "I will regret it to the end of my days. I'm sorry I didn't stand up for you. I allowed him to take advantage of every situation, and to put himself above you and this family. Will you ever forgive me?"

Tiffany bowed her head. She'd wished forever that her mother would wake up and take notice. Now she wasn't sure how to handle it.

"It's okay, honey. Take all the time you need."

"I waited for you to take my side, just one single time. You're doing it now so you won't be alone. Who left who?" Tiffany tilted her head. "He left you?"

"I demanded he leave."

"Why the sudden epiphany?"

"I talked to Aiden."

"What?" Tiffany sprang to her feet. "What did he say?"

"You were right," Michelle said in a low voice. "Aiden wasn't pleased I approached Savannah, but he agreed to meet, and we had a long and eye-opening discussion." Michelle clasped her hands tight in her lap. "He forced me to see the truth. My husband is a bully. And … he told me you were devastated that I wasn't receptive to your marriage."

Tiffany clenched her fists, her nails digging into her palms as she fought the rising fury.

"I accept my part in destroying your marriage." Her mother bowed her head. "Aiden called me when you landed in the hospital in Philadelphia. Things had fallen apart, and he didn't know what to do or how to help you. Obviously, I didn't do any better. I've never done the right thing. I'm so terribly sorry."

"You think that sorry will ever be enough?"

"I can hope. I've made the choice to leave my marriage. If I don't, I'll lose you and Savannah forever."

An unsavory picture formed in her mind. "Aiden gave you an ultimatum."

That stunned look on her mother's face told the true story.

"It's not me you want. It's Savannah. The very granddaughter you forced me to give up. You think you'll never have another because I'm not good enough for anyone to love." Her entire body trembled. "Go back to David. I will never, ever, forgive you. I hate you." Tiffany stumbled into the kitchen and snatched up her handbag.

"Tiffany."

The pane of glass shook as Tiffany slammed the front door and fumbled blindly for her car keys. Once in her car, she didn't bother to fasten her seatbelt, intent on escaping. Her tires screeched against the pavement as she accelerated, speeding down the street.

She clenched her fingers around the icy steering wheel, dragging in breaths, fighting the dizzy, nauseous sensation. Finally, she pulled to the side of the road and flopped forward, draping her arms over the wheel, resting her forehead against them. After two hitching sobs, she burst into tears.

Tiffany curled up on her bed, her eyelids too heavy to lift. Her phone buzzed for the millionth time, dancing across the bedside table. It stopped, and then started again.

"Grrr. Go away, Mother." She slapped the offending device, sighing as the annoying vibration stopped, followed by the ding of a text, then it buzzed again. She hit the answer button.

"Where are you?"

She curled her lip, unable to stop her snarl. "Traitor."

"At least you're alive."

"You can deliver a message to my mother now that you two are so close and all. Tell her I never want to see her again."

"You'll have to tell her yourself," Aiden said. "You know she approached Savannah?"

"The Baxter family is to stay far, far away, but my mother manipulated her way in."

"I'm not blind. I saw what they did to you, but I hoped you and your mother could work out some of your issues."

"How dare you share my private feelings?"

"She needed to get her head out of the fucking sand."

"It wasn't your place."

"Damn it, Tiffany. I'm supposed to ignore that my ex-wife is scraping rock bottom? You want me to join the game of let's pretend and wait for the phone call? How exactly should I have that conversation with your daughter? How do I tell her she's lost yet another part of her family?"

"Your answer is to spill your guts to my mother? To pawn me off like you did in Philly?"

"What would you have had me do? You didn't want my help."

Heavy silence fell between them.

"I could barely take care of myself," he said under his breath.

She squeezed her eyes closed, biting down hard on her lip, remembering what her mother had told her about Vancouver.

"How can I watch you self destruct? You came to me for a reason."

A fresh flow of tears streamed down her cheeks. "You think ..." A sob choked off the words. That he'd seen into her mind so clearly scared her.

"Am I wrong?" he whispered.

Why deny anything? She'd given Aiden an intimate first-hand introduction to all of her demons. "You know you're not. You saw how it was in Philly. If it hadn't been for the baby ..."

What did I expect him to say? Ripping open old wounds from Philadelphia could only hurt him, and I'd done enough of that to last a lifetime. Me and my family.

"That day I walked without thinking, drawn to the only person I could count on." She dragged in a long breath. "I had no right to involve you."

"I'm glad you did." He emitted a deep sigh. "Michelle's on her way to your place."

"Why'd you do that?"

"She loves you, Tiff. She's not a bad person, but she has been controlled and kept in the dark by David for far too long. Surely you can relate to that."

She sniffled. "Thank you, Aiden. For caring enough ... for ..." She swallowed hard. "You saved me. Why?"

"I had no choice." He cleared his throat. "Talk to your mother. Call your friends. Start with Alex."

"Alex?" Tiffany wiped her eyes.

"She'll be in Chicago for Christmas. I'll text you her current mobile number in case you don't have it. And Tiff?"

"What?"

"Remember your promise. Think about your daughter."

"I will."

"Say 'I promise.'"

"I promise." She clutched the phone to her ear. "I'm sorry for what he did to you," she whispered. "Why'd you never tell me?"

Silence. Blank, dead air space.

"Aiden?"

"You never wanted to discuss it. Any of it. I'd hoped over time you'd let me in, but you never did, and then it was too late." His voice remained level, but she detected the tiniest edge, a minuscule quavering note that spoke volumes. Most would have missed the cue, that subtle hint at the magnitude of pain buried beneath the façade. "And maybe some things are better left unsaid."

She pressed the back of her hand to her mouth, stifling a sob. Every word that came to mind seemed inadequate in the face of what he'd endured, what had been said and done. *I'm so, so, sorry.*

Her phone buzzed as a call came through from the building's intercom. "She's here so you can stop talking me down from the ledge," she whispered.

"Take care of yourself."

She hung up and pressed the phone to her chest. "And it begins," she muttered and crawled from her bed.

"Can I come up?" Michelle asked.

Tiffany didn't answer, but hit the door release so her mother could access the elevator. She opened the door as soon as Michelle tapped to announce her arrival. "You called Aiden."

"Who else?" Her mother studied her. "Was I right?"

Tiffany nodded and motioned for Michelle to enter the apartment. "He saved me from my own dark thoughts that day at the Vineyard, but you already know that because he ratted me out."

"Please don't be angry with Aiden. He cares."

"I'm not angry with Aiden." Tiffany dropped onto the couch. "He's a better man than I ever deserved."

Michelle clasped her hands together. "I am sorry, honey. I wish I'd been more in tune, noticed more, and most of all, I regret I never stood up to your father. Can you try to forgive me? I love you. You're my daughter, and I haven't been there for you. Is there any way we can move forward, and help each other through this?"

A tear dribbled down Tiffany's cheek. "We can try." What else could she say? She owed it to both Aiden and Savannah to pull it all together.

CHAPTER 9

Savannah

ER BRIGHT SMILE FADED AS the new text popped up.

Still not talking to me? I miss you.

"Everything okay, sweetie? You've been quiet."

She peeked at her dad. Trust him to notice everything. "I broke up with Gray. You were right about him."

"Was I? What did he do?"

"He cheated." She wound a finger in her hair, tugging at the lock. "You can't imagine what it was like, walking in on him in bed with another woman."

Aiden drove in silence for a moment. "I'm sorry he did that to you." His voice remained gentle.

"Can't say you didn't warn me. Now I'm now sworn off guys." With a flourish, she swiped and hit the red delete button. "Can you believe he had the nerve to tell me it meant nothing? And it *just happened* like he couldn't help himself. Why do people say such ludicrous things when they're caught cheating?"

"I wish I knew." Aiden shook his head, clenching his hands around the steering wheel. "I hate that he hurt you, but not all men are like that."

"I'm beginning to wonder." Even as she said it, a vision of beautiful gray eyes floated through her mind. That guy had been sweet, offering consolation without all the platitudes. *Of course, I would never see him again. Besides, a sexy man like him would have a girlfriend.* He'd been meeting someone that day, on his way to the airport.

She shook off the thought. "Have you ever had to deal with it? Cheating, I mean?"

"Once or twice. It's never easy, but one day you'll find the right person."

She twirled her hair and peered at her dad. His response seemed nonchalant, but his knuckles whitened as he clenched the steering wheel, and he seemed riveted on the road in front of them. "Did Emily?" she whispered.

"Never." A startled look came her way. "Neither of us have been unfaithful, Savannah. There's no room in our relationship for bad behavior."

"Then who?" she asked, more to herself than to him.

"That's all you get. I'm not discussing past girlfriends with you, so don't expect details."

They pulled into the driveway of a massive white house. Savannah tipped up her chin, inspecting the large yard. Though nothing as grand as her Gramma Grace's mansion, it still presented an imposing sight. "This is it?"

"Yes. Tiffany grew up here." Aiden squeezed her hand. "Ready?"

"I am." She double-checked her reflection in the vanity mirror of the car.

"You look beautiful. Quit fussing." He slid out, coming around to open her door.

It felt like déjà vu, like the first time she'd gone to her Gramma Grace's house. "Don't you dare leave me." She worried she'd freeze up and not know what to say.

"I won't." He rang the bell.

"Merry Christmas," Michelle said as she ushered them inside. "Aiden." She hugged him before turning to Savannah, who'd taken a small step backwards. "Savannah. It's wonderful to see you." Michelle grasped Savannah's free hand, seeming to read the hesitancy.

"Hi." She felt tongue-tied and was thankful Aiden had come with her. "This is for you." Savannah extended the small gift bag she'd brought in from the car.

"Thank you. Come in, come in." Michelle led them into an ornate sitting room, complete with a small tree. Several presents sat beneath it, and she added the package from Savannah, along with two parcels from Aiden.

Savannah looked around, spotting the framed pictures arranged on the mantel. She wandered over to inspect them. There were several photos of a blonde teenage girl and a baby. *Tiffany?* And one of Savannah taken at the beach.

"Where did you get this?" She ran a finger over the delicate silver frame. "Oh."

Savannah almost missed the flash of guilt that crossed Michelle's face.

Aiden frowned as he took the photo from her hands and returned it to its place. "Must have been one I gave you, Michelle?" His eyes widened an almost imperceptible amount.

"Yes." Michelle nodded. "That's right."

Savannah pretended not to notice the silent communication between her dad and Michelle. She didn't know why Aiden had given Michelle this particular picture, which she didn't even remember him taking, but she let it pass and sat on the couch across from her grandmother.

It seemed strange to be sitting in the house where Tiffany had lived as a teenager. Savannah took a deep breath to relax, following along with the conversation between her grandmother and Aiden. Michelle kept asking questions, and Vanna forced herself to engage, but she was glad Aiden had stayed to smooth the tension.

"Can I use the bathroom?" Savannah asked after an hour.

"The downstairs one is being repainted, so you'll have to go upstairs. Second door on the right." Michelle motioned to the stairs.

Savannah stared up the staircase, taking a breath before mounting the steps. She found the bathroom, and took her time fixing her hair. As she left, an open door and a glimpse of pink enticed her in the opposite direction from the stairs.

She pushed the door ajar and slipped inside. The room was empty aside from a few boxes piled against the wall. A wisp of bright pink tissue paper showed through the tabs on the one on top.

Savannah crept across the carpet, lifted the cardboard tab, and peeked inside. The wrapped rectangle packed on top of a photo album caught her eye. She lifted the pink package and folded back the tissue paper.

Her eyes widened. The elegant silver frame, engraved across the bottom with names and a date, held a vibrant picture. *My dad with Tiffany.* She glanced at the door, straining to hear any sounds, but there was only silence.

After tucking the frame into its wrapping, she set it aside and brushed a hand over the photo book. On the front cover another photo, this one with Aiden's arm wrapped around Tiffany's slim waist against the backdrop of palm trees. He gazed at the blonde woman with complete adoration, his hand resting on her cheek, her arm looped around his back.

Aiden & Tiffany. Aruba, December 20. Savannah wrinkled her nose as she flipped through the pages, pausing only long enough to absorb the dates and signatures on the marriage certificate.

She snapped the book closed, feeling like an unwanted voyeur. Another glance toward the doorway told her she remained unobserved, but she placed it all back with care, hoping her snooping remained undiscovered.

She peered out the window and across the expanse of lawn. *Had Tiffany done this very thing as a girl?*

"Hey."

Savannah jumped. "Sorry." The flush rose as she stared at her dad. "I shouldn't be snooping."

"This was Tiffany's room." He joined her at the window.

"Stupid, right? It's only a bedroom, but it's weird being here." Savannah brushed back her hair, glancing around. "It feels like invading Tiffany's privacy or something." She tried not to focus on the half-opened box against the wall, hiding her expression by allowing her hair to fall across her face.

"I know what you mean." Aiden's gaze seemed drawn to the pile against the wall, but he rubbed her shoulder without commenting.

"We should get out of here before Michelle catches us."

"I doubt it would be an issue, but we can go if you're ready."

Savannah nodded and took his hand. "Yes, let's go home."

Savannah stared out the window, twirling the ribbon on the smallest box as they drove toward Gramma Grace's house. "Dad? One of these is from her, isn't it?"

He glanced at her and then returned his attention to the road. "The ones with the pink ribbons are from Tiffany."

She stared at the fancy parcels in her lap. "I'm not sure I should have accepted them."

"It's up to you." He tapped on the wheel. "If you feel uncomfortable, give them to me, and I'll deal with it."

Savannah fiddled with the radio, finding her favorite station before leaning back in the plush leather seat of the car they'd borrowed from Gramma Grace. "Remember Thanksgiving? What were you going to tell me?" She plucked at the ribbon.

He frowned and then flipped on the signal, turning into a parking lot. "Why don't we go for a walk before cooping ourselves up in the house again?"

She nodded, slipping the packages out of sight.

They started down the path, and she wrapped her scarf tighter around her neck, shivering as the icy breeze blew in from the water.

Aiden produced a black wooden hat from his pocket and placed it on her head, tucking her hair back. "Better?"

"Much." She patted it. "You always have one of these. I still have the one you gave me the first day we met. I can't imagine how many you go through if you give them to patients."

The corners of his mouth twitched. "I don't usually give them to random strangers, but you were freezing and more worried about Leanne than yourself." He grasped her hand as they walked along the pathway.

"Dad?"

"You're curious about what I was about to say."

She nodded.

He squeezed her hand and sighed. "I saw something in Tiffany that day on the beach, and I realized I've been too hard on her."

Savannah stopped in her tracks, a deep frown furrowing her brow. "She rejected me. Her own daughter. How can you even think you've been too hard on her?" Her voice rose to a high pitch. "She deserves everything she's gotten."

"Calm down." He made a downward motion with a flattened palm. "She may be a lot of things, but she never deserved the way her father treated her. You don't know David Baxter. He's an overbearing, pig-headed bastard."

"You've said that before."

"It's true," he said. "Tiffany has made mistakes, but so much of it I understand."

"It's okay that she said I ruined her life?" Tears sprang to her eyes. "How can you take her side, after all she's done to us?"

"Those were words. Careless, hurtful words, and I don't excuse them, but she doesn't believe you ruined her life." He shoved his hands in his pockets. "Maybe I shouldn't be telling you this, but if it helps you to understand, then you need to hear it."

Savannah dragged in a deep breath. "What?"

"She's struggling, and I have to help her. Her father has never been supportive, and her mother let it all happen without standing up for either of us. Tiffany's an only child, and it's been a tough and lonely time for her. I should have known, but I was too buried in my own problems to see it."

"You're an only child, and your parents weren't great." Savannah crossed her arms and took a step back. "Her crappy home life isn't any excuse. Anyway, she's not your responsibility."

"I'm simply stating facts. She's made serious mistakes, but at least she's trying. I'm cutting her some slack. This doesn't need to be so damn adversarial." He rubbed the back of his neck. "None of it means *you* have to accept her gifts or feel any sort of obligation. What she did wasn't right, and she knows it." He bowed his head. "She's well aware that *I'm sorry* isn't enough to fix what's been broken."

Thoughts whirled through her head as her hand crept under her scarf to grasp and rub the pendant. *Why did it feel like he'd traded sides and become a traitor?*

"How do you watch someone you shared so much with drown without even offering to help?"

"What about Emily?" Savannah's stomach twisted.

"There's a huge difference between loving someone you shared a life altering experience with and being *in love* with that one woman you can't live without." He grasped her hands. "Nothing's changed. Emily is the woman I want to be with every single day for the rest of my life. But that doesn't mean Tiffany doesn't occupy a space in my heart."

"How can you love two women at once?" Savannah swiped at her face.

"By now you must understand that there are different forms and levels of love. Tiffany and I were together for a long time. I've known her since I was a kid. It would be impossible not to feel something for her, don't you think? Especially considering what we went through, and that we have a child in common." His stare intensified. "She gave me you."

In her mind, she'd relegated Tiffany to a far corner and let her become an abstract idea. The enemy. A happiness stealing villain. But her dad—it had to be different for him. He'd loved Tiffany enough to protect her, to lie, to steal, and to run away, all in the name of saving their unborn child. *Me. They did all that to save me.*

She was their common enduring bond, proof their relationship and love had existed. Because of her, he would be forever reminded and feel obligated and indebted to Tiffany.

"Why now, though? You didn't want to be anywhere near her, and now you are all about how you need to rescue her."

"Before, she wasn't ready to be helped. She'd mired herself in misery." He met her gaze. "Now she's reaching out and asking. That's the difference."

"How do you know it's for real? She could be lying, trying to get you back."

He shook his head. "That's not what's happening. All she's asking for is a chance to earn forgiveness."

"For her ruining your life by having me?"

"I consider you the most wonderful gift she ever gave me." He grasped her shoulders. "Why can't you accept that we made our decision together? Give her some damn credit for ensuring you were healthy. Nothing about that was easy, trust me."

Savannah grasped her pendant again, struggling to ground herself. "Can we go back to Gramma's?"

Aiden held out his hand, but Savannah shoved her hands into her pockets, keeping her head down the entire way to the car.

Aiden opened her door, and then went around to slide into his seat. "Talk to me," he said softly.

She angled away, leaning her head against the window and allowing silent tears to fall as he sighed and started the engine.

"When you're ready, I'm here," he said.

Panic rose within, her thoughts becoming cloudy and unfocused, and she forced herself to breathe with deep, even inhalations. Concerned looks were coming her way, but she couldn't speak, so she cranked up the stereo and clutched her pendant.

The moment they pulled into the garage, she shoved the gifts at him. "I don't want these." She bounded through the front door and up the stairs. What she needed was time. Time to let his words settle. Time to think about what she wanted, and she hoped he'd have as much compassion for her as he did for Tiffany.

Chapter 10

Tiffany

TIFFANY PEEKED INTO THE OVEN to check on the roasting chicken before hurrying into her room to change. Her mother would arrive soon for Christmas dinner, and she wanted to be ready.

As she slipped on a light sweater and dress pants, the stack of boxes that had been delivered from her mother's house caught her attention. As much as she dreaded the task, it would be better to get the sorting over with while she waited for her mother to arrive.

The first three boxes were quick and easy. She sifted through the contents, sorting them for donation or to be tossed in the trash, which left only a few items that were true treasures.

The label on the next box written in her mother's familiar script made her pause. *Philadelphia apartment.* The thought of reopening that time, those blurry days after she landed in the hospital and Michelle had magically appeared at her side, caused a twinge.

Her mother had taken care of the details and packing the home she shared with Aiden, finally shipping Tiffany's belongings to Chicago. Seeing the mementos so many years into the future presented a reawakening of memories that should remain in the past. But she took a breath and stripped away the fresh tape.

The bundle of bright pink tissue on top turned out to be wrapping for the elegant frame containing their first picture as husband and wife. Underneath she found the wedding album she'd spent hours preparing before having it printed.

She hugged it against her chest for a moment before she opened the cover. The first picture brought tears to her eyes. *Aiden & Tiffany, Aruba, December 20.* Her honeymoon. Page after page of blissful memories followed, making her wish for the comparative simplicity of those early days of being married to Aiden.

The first page of the next album in the pile showed two teenagers playing in the surf on an expanse of golden sand. She hung over his shoulder, complete joy written across her face. It brought back memories of the summer she'd fallen in love with Aiden at the Vineyard. Back in a time when she smiled, happy and carefree, her final year of believing in the fallacy of her faux happy family.

She had few pictures of herself pregnant, but this album contained one of her favorites, taken by a kind soul when Aiden had escaped Chicago to visit her. His visits had eased the pain caused by her neglectful aunt. The bitter woman refused to take Tiffany anywhere, the sight of her pregnant fifteen-year-old niece clearly filling Aunt Harriet with shame.

Memories assaulted her. The look Aiden gave her that day in the clinic. The nurse relegating him to the waiting room like a naughty child as she spirited Tiffany into the back. The stern woman had bustled about, her mouth pinched in a disapproving moue as she shoved a mint-green gown into her hands before relaying terse instructions and pointing to the bathroom.

She sniffled and wiped away her tears as she had that day while laying on the frigid exam table, subjected to the indignity of being poked, prodded, and swabbed. *Why not just call me a dirty little tramp they assumed was sleeping with the entire football team?*

After enduring a lecture and the pamphlets all meant to convince her how wrong it was to bring unwanted and unplanned children into this world, Tiffany had resisted the doctor's attempts to coerce her into calling her parents to join her for a talk.

A shudder ran down her spine as she imagined the refined Michelle Baxter and the *great* David Baxter appearing in the shabby clinic. Aiden's idea to use an alias had been inspired. She'd dreaded anyone recognizing them, as it would have been all over the news with a bold headline.

Mayoral candidate David Baxter's slutty teenage daughter, knocked-up.

Maybe not in those exact words, but in headlines that meant the same thing. Not to mention the gossip, and rumors, and how she'd be under twenty-four-hour lockdown to prevent further embarrassment to her father. After a quick and quiet abortion, of course.

She'd been terrified and anxious, relieved to escape the hateful clinic into Aiden's welcoming arms, soaking up his promise to be there, always.

Tiffany placed each of the items into the box with care, unable to face the mix of beautiful but painful memories.

Tiffany tidied the last of the dinner dishes and emptied the dishwasher while her mom wrapped the leftover food and stowed it in the fridge.

"I'm glad it's over for another year." Tiffany admired the gleaming kitchen counters, still wondering why she'd spent so much time preparing a fancy meal for just the two of them. Neither had eaten more than a few bites.

"I declined most of the invitations this year. I haven't been in the mood to celebrate," her mother said.

Tiffany wrapped her into a hug, gratified when her mother hugged her back. *What could I say? That Mom was better off without him?* Even if it was the absolute truth.

"It's not quite done. We haven't opened our gifts." Michelle retrieved the few packages from under the small tree and handed three beautifully wrapped presents to Tiffany before settling on the couch with her own parcels.

Tiffany noted she'd received nothing from her father. All three gifts were only labeled *love mom*.

"You still have one." Tiffany pointed at the elegant package resting beside her mother once all the others were opened.

"I wasn't sure about giving it to you." Michelle hesitated before handing over the gift box.

Tiffany pressed two fingers to her lips, admiring the swirling script on the vellum envelope. "Why would you keep it from me?"

"I didn't want to upset you."

"Mother." Tiffany gave her a stern look. "You don't get to make those decisions." She held it in her lap and ran the ends of the fuchsia satin ribbon through her fingertips.

"I'm sorry." Her mother looked contrite. "I delivered your gift for Savannah. They're staying with Grace for the holidays and came for a visit."

"How did it go?"

"It was too short, but baby steps, I suppose. She's a sweet girl."

"Did she open them?"

"I didn't want to pressure her, so I gave them to her to take home. I'll ask Aiden when I see him."

Tiffany twirled a strand of hair around her finger. "So silly. I spent hours choosing gifts she'll never open."

"You don't know that." Michelle reached across and patted Tiffany's knee. "It's not silly to put extra care into selecting a gift for your daughter. I spend countless hours deciding on each present for you."

"Do you?" She studied her mother. Maybe she shouldn't be surprised. The gifts she'd received today were beautiful.

Michelle responded with a sad smile and almost imperceptible nod. "Thank you, Tiffany."

She gazed at her mother, perplexed.

"For not being upset that Aiden allowed me a visit with Savannah. I wish you could have been there."

Tiffany brushed her eyes, unable to admit to the resentment she harbored over the visit. "I've missed so much."

"We all have, honey." Her mother patted her knee. "Fate is a funny thing. It's always the way."

"What?" Tiffany frowned at her mother.

"The first time you were with a boy, you wound up pregnant. I wish I'd been more attentive, given you some guidance, and taught you to use protection." A faraway look appeared in Michelle's eyes. "Perhaps it was meant to be that way. It's impossible to wish my precious granddaughter away, especially ..."

Tiffany tucked her legs beneath her and flattened her palms against the pillow in her lap. The words left unsaid seemed obvious. *The only grandchild my mother expected to ever have.* "It wasn't our first time," she whispered.

"Why would you lie?" Michelle's eyes widened. "How long ...?"

"You dragged me into Father's office, and he called me a shameless, slutty, worthless, dirty whore. How would he have labeled me if I'd admitted we'd been having sex for months?"

"Months?" Michelle inhaled a long deep breath, clenching her hands in her lap. "When did it start?"

"The Fourth of July. His grandparents were out, and ..." Tiffany shrugged. "We weren't stupid. We used condoms, except for that one time."

"Oh, honey. You were so young. Was he your ...?" Her mother bit her lip. "No. I mean, why?"

"I loved him, and he loved me," she said, swiping at her cheeks, "when no one else did."

Tears brimmed her mother's eyes. "I always loved you."

"It never felt that way. Everything else was more important. Remember that party you threw the Easter weekend before Father was elected? You never even noticed I'd left."

"I'm sorry, honey. I did wonder where you'd gone, but I didn't worry. You were with Aiden."

"Maybe you should have worried. While you were downstairs with David, concerned about forming those precious political connections, Aiden and I were in my bedroom"—Tiffany leveled her gaze at her mother—"conceiving your first and only grandchild."

Her mother dropped her head into her hands. "Oh, Tiffany. In your bedroom, of all places? If David had caught you, he would have killed Aiden."

A shiver ran down Tiffany's spine, but she forged ahead. "He never did catch us, though."

"Never?" Michelle sucked in a breath. "What do you mean?"

"What do you think? David made such a huge deal of how we were running around the Vineyard unsupervised, yet he remained oblivious to what happened under his own roof." Tiffany threw her hands into the air. "That trellis was convenient, and neither of you had a clue." Now that the words were flowing, she was powerless to stop them. "It wasn't our first time—in any sense of the word."

"I failed you." Michelle's face crumpled as the tears streamed down her face. "Can you ever forgive me for not paying attention?"

Tiffany stared at her hands. "How can I judge you when I'm guilty of the same behavior with my own daughter? If I ever hope for Savannah to forgive me for my mistakes, then maybe I need to learn to forgive you for yours."

⁓

Tiffany snuggled under the down comforter, fighting complete exhaustion. Her mother had dissolved in a full meltdown, but Tiffany felt relieved. Confessing the secrets from her troubled teen years had shaken her mother out of that awful complacency, and they'd talked for hours. One by one, her burdens lifted, and she'd drawn enough courage to tell her mother about her therapy sessions with Liz.

She rolled onto her side, staring at the gift she'd placed on her bedside table. Despite her curiosity, she'd refrained from opening it. She craved privacy. Her mother had been supportive of late, but still, Tiffany didn't want to share the moment.

After propping herself up on her pillow, she smoothed her palms over the crisp, elegant paper, noting the precise corners. *He'd wrapped this himself.* She lifted the envelope and sniffed, then wrinkled her nose at the spicy, silky scent invading her nostrils. A change from the enticing, earthy tones of his usual brand.

She set the envelope aside. *Time for that later.* After a slow tug on the ribbon, she tucked a manicured nail underneath the edge of the wrapping, neatly severing the tape and revealing the flat box and the photo album resting inside.

Tiffany pressed a hand to her heart, blinking hard as she turned the pages, studying Savannah's happy smiles as she grew from baby, to toddler, to teenage girl. A small pang grew in her chest as she saw, for the first time, the people who'd raised her daughter. The magnitude of her loss—*our loss*—washed over her.

That Aiden had given her such a precious gift, that he'd take the time and trouble to prepare it, overwhelmed her. Her heart lightened at the thought her daughter had been so loved and well taken care of. Even though it was hard to see the people who'd become her baby girl's parents, she felt a sense of gratitude. Everything indicated that they'd been good and loving people.

Finally, she extracted the single sheet of paper from the envelope:

Dearest Tiffany,

There are so many things I wished I'd said and done long before now. I regret how things ended, that I couldn't be what you needed, and that you ever experienced unhappiness in our life together. I'm sorry for the angry words, for not taking the time to listen, and for not being there when our daughter came into this world. It remains a source of deep heartache and pain. To have missed so much of her life ... well, no explanation required, because you live it every single day.

Knowing you and having the chance to love you changed my entire world. You taught me the meaning of true love, Tiffany. That summer we spent together was one of the greatest times in my life. I wouldn't be who or where I am today without you.

Never doubt those feelings were real or that we shared something rare and precious during our life together. It's tempting for people to discount what we shared, to say that everyone reserves a place for their first love, that it means little.

I disagree. You own a piece of my heart, one that I will never get back, one I am now content to leave with you for safekeeping. I spent many years struggling to steal it away, but now realize all is as it should be. Anyone who truly touches and enriches your life must forever remain part of it.

You have so much to give, a beautiful and adventurous spirit that you've buried deep inside. I know it's there. I experienced it when we were together. Let your light shine, let people see you, and you will find the love you deserve, that one person who completes you and treasures you exactly as you are. Trust me, there is much to love about you.

Because of you, we have an amazing and wonderful daughter and she is someone I cherish and could never regret. Savannah is a wonderful gift, the greatest of everything you've given me, and I truly hope that soon you can learn that first hand.

One day, she will see you as you truly are, not through a veil of hurt and pain. One day, you will let go of all of your fear and doubts and open that big heart of yours, allowing her to be part of your life.

For everything that happened between us, I forgive you, and I hope you can do the same for me. I hope we have learned from our mistakes and how to not repeat them.

We have a daughter, a beautiful sweet soul we planned to raise together. Though our dream was stolen, we have a second chance to be her parents. I wish for us to find a way to make that work, despite our differences.

Keep moving forward and all of your hopes and dreams will come true.

Love always, Aiden

Tiffany pressed the letter to her heart, a fresh round of tears flowing down her cheeks. This man continued to surprise her, and she knew how hard these admissions must have been.

She too had struggled to reclaim that part of her owned by Aiden, but maybe she should surrender and accept that they were each powerless. That deep enduring love for him would forever be lodged in her heart, even if they could never recapture the magic they'd once shared.

After a glance at the clock, she dialed his number. "Sorry, I know it's late."

"Just a second." The voices in the background faded out. "How are you?"

"Good. I wanted to thank you for the album," she said. "It's amazing. I don't understand why you're so kind to me, but thank you."

"You're welcome. Though, it appears you don't need me to supply you with pictures."

"What does that mean?"

"The frame on the mantel at Michelle's house. You think I don't recognize your work?"

"I didn't take—"

"Don't bullshit me. You taught me photography. You took that picture at the Vineyard. I recognized the beach." His tone lightened. "Your mother looked extremely guilty at being in possession of such contraband."

"I'm sorry. I didn't mean to take them, but I saw her there, and I couldn't help myself. Are you angry?"

"No. But next time ask me for one instead of becoming a stalker." His admonishment remained light.

"Deal." She drew in a long breath. "I read your letter, and it means everything, Aiden. Truly, we had something, but now you have Emily. She's the one, isn't she? The woman who completes you?"

"She had me before I could even admit it to myself. I held back what I felt for her for the longest time, too scared to take the chance."

"It's good you did. Everyone could see the love when you two were together at Jenna's wedding. It drove me crazy, and I did some stupid things that week." She smiled even amongst the tears. "You deserve happiness, and I'm so thankful you found it. I promise to never interfere with what you have with Emily, ever again. Please tell her I'm sorry. And Aiden ... there's nothing to forgive. You were good to me always, and you can keep your piece of my heart too."

"We'll be okay, Tiff, even if it's taken ten years." He sighed "Michelle told me about David."

"The divorce. Yeah, shocker. I never thought she'd leave him, not in a million years."

"You hanging in there?"

"I am. And thank you for forcing my mother to open her eyes and see him for who he really is." She leaned back, staring at the ceiling. "Did Savannah open the gifts I sent?"

"Not yet, but give her time, Tiff. It was thoughtful, but don't force it and don't sneak gifts in through the back door. Vanna needs to build trust in her grandmother, and if you insist on that route, it might push her away from Michelle."

"I've never given her anything. She's my baby girl."

"The baby girl who's no longer a baby."

"Don't remind me." She twirled a lock of hair. This reminded her of how they used to talk long ago, before everything had become such a complicated mess. "I'm getting things together, like I promised. I thought I'd contact Alex."

"You should. She misses you."

"I'll be sure to call." A smile crept onto her face.

"Gramma Grace would like you to visit after Christmas, once we've left." She frowned. "Why?"

"She'd like to see you." Silence fell for a moment. "She doesn't bite, Tiffany. It'll be good for both of you, so promise you'll see her. She's been amazing over the past few years."

"I promise."

"I gave her your number, and you have the one at the house. Hey, I have to go. Emily needs some help with Kellan, but you take care, okay? Merry Christmas. Say hi to your mom for me."

"Aiden?" The words burned on the tip of her tongue.

"What?"

"Oh, just …" She couldn't force out the words. Not when things were finally turning around. Alienating him now would be devastating. "Wish everyone Merry Christmas from me."

"I will."

And then he was gone. Tiffany flicked off her lamp, wondering at the strange turn of events. *Grace Hamilton wants to see me?* That made her nervous, but hopeful at the same time. Aiden wouldn't set her up to be berated. She needed to trust him. If she'd placed more faith in him years ago, everything would be different.

Tiffany rose early the next morning, hitting the gym for a workout before fortifying herself with an extra-large coffee.

She unlocked the door of her gallery and stepped into the serene space. They were closed for a few days over the holidays, but she had loads to accomplish. Besides, she hated sitting around and found reviewing artwork brought her a sense of peace, body and soul. She needed the extra calming influence as she had promises to keep.

"Please don't hang up," she said as soon as Alex said hello. "I heard you were in town and hoped you'd have time for lunch." She bit her lip, tapping a pencil against the desk, worried at the silence on the other end of the line. "Please? A quick coffee?"

"Let me see if Sarah will watch Daniel. Joel's in the garage with his dad."

The sounds became muffled, and Tiffany shifted in her chair, the staccato of her tapping growing louder and faster.

"How about that little coffee shop down the street from your gallery?" Alex's voice carried down the line. "I can meet you there in an hour."

"Perfect."

The next forty-five minutes Tiffany spent sorting through proposals, and then she freshened up. Butterflies danced in her stomach. This could be the first step to mending the rift with her friends.

When she arrived at the coffee shop, she was surprised to see Alex already in a booth, huddled over a steaming cup.

"Alex." She slid onto the seat, noting the other woman made no move to stand or hug her. "It's been too long." Tiffany smiled as the server came by to take her drink order.

"I was surprised you called." Alex studied her. "Did Aiden tell you I was in town?"

Tiffany fidgeted with her spoon. "Don't be angry with him."

"I'm not. He told me he'd given you my number."

"I should have known. You two have always been tight."

"I consider him my best friend." Alex shrugged. "That hasn't always been popular with those around me, but it's true."

"Thanks for meeting me. I didn't know if you would," she said. "I need to apologize, for so much. You were always a good friend, and I acted like such a bitch. I'm working hard to get my life together, and I hope maybe someday you'll forgive me."

Alex regarded her for a moment. "What brought on the epiphany?"

"Do you need to ask?" She shifted on the bench.

"Ahhh. You two are on speaking terms again, apparently."

"We are. He's been amazing, but I guess I don't need to tell you that. I don't know how much he's told you about what's going on in my life."

"Not much." Alex sipped from her cup. "Though he did tell me about Michelle and David. Not that it's a secret, I suppose."

"It's not. David's living in some hotel, so the word was bound to get out. Whatever. I'm thrilled my mom finally booted his sorry ass. You know my mother and I can have an actual conversation now?"

"That is big news. She didn't give you much support with Savannah, or so Aiden said. And of course, I know you lost touch with her for what, two years after you married Aiden?"

"Yes, until the bitter end when she appeared to spirit me back to Chicago. Though we both know who made that happen."

Alex contemplated her. "You seem happier."

"Things aren't perfect, but I'm working on happy. Now that Aiden has forgiven me for being a horrible, devious bitch, maybe everyone else will too."

"Hmmm, perhaps." A grin appeared. "You've always been devious. Remember how you caught the man in the first place?"

"Hey. You helped, so I blame you for planting ideas in my head." Tiffany giggled. "Poor guy never had a chance."

"He sure didn't, but that had nothing to do with me inviting you to sneak out with us that night. You two were destined to be together. The big blue eyes, long blonde hair, and sweet smile had him captivated from day one, only you were too timid to see it."

"No." Tiffany frowned. "Do you really think so?"

Alex snorted and hooked her thumbs toward her chest. "Best friend? You think I'm blind, girl? The number of times I caught him staring at you, checking out your ass, not to mention the visible disappointment when you refused to talk to him told me all I needed to know. All I did was give you a little push in his direction. The rest"—she swept her palms against each other—"is history. Though I sure didn't expect you two getting busy the first time you had the beach house to yourself."

"I'm only human." Tiffany rolled her eyes. "The guy is sizzling hot, and he paraded around shirtless for hours that day. My hormones were raging, and damn, the way he kisses. Mmm-mmmm. I couldn't help myself. And I never regretted it, either. He's fantastic in bed."

"Urgh." Alex snickered and waved a hand. "Enough."

"You started it." Tiffany laughed. It felt good to be here with her friend, chatting like she didn't have a care in the world. It had been too long since she'd felt that kind of freedom and companionship. "Besides, we've talked about this before."

"Yes, but he's like my brother. I don't want to hear the down and dirty details about his sex life." Alex reached across to squeeze her hand. "I've missed you. It's amazing to have my dear friend back."

"It feels amazing to be back." Tiffany brushed her eyes. "How are Daniel and Joel?"

"They're both well. Joel and I had a few issues last year, but we worked through them, and our relationship is stronger than ever." Alex rubbed her belly. "We're expecting a new addition to the family this summer."

"That's amazing." Tiffany leaped from her seat and rounded the table to pull Alex into a hug. "I'm so sorry I wasn't there for you, Alex, but I promise I will be in the future. It's exciting that I get to be an aunt again."

"I'm sorry for my part. Aiden never wanted us to take sides, but it became so damn awkward." Alex sighed as Tiffany settled back into her seat. "How are things between you and Emily?"

"We haven't even begun that awkward discussion." She stared into the depths of her cup. "I don't know where I stand, if she knows what's going on, or what Aiden has told her. She's probably freaked out that he has a crazy-ass ex-wife who will never go away." Tiffany ducked her head. "Did Aiden tell you?"

Alex shook her head. "He'd never call you that."

"Obviously, he hasn't shared much with you." Tiffany twirled a lock of hair around her finger and tugged hard. "After our marriage collapsed, my mother brought me home. We kept my breakdown hidden. She even managed to hide it from Aiden for several months." She peered across the table at her friend.

Alex took hold of Tiffany's hand. "I'm sorry. Aiden never told me."

"I begged him not to tell anyone." Tiffany sniffled. "At Thanksgiving, my mother and I had another fight and it all came down around me. I felt so alone. For some stupid reason, I went to his house in the Vineyard." Her throat closed up and she sipped her water, the cool liquid soothing the burn.

"He saw how far I'd fallen, and he helped me. But he doesn't know that it's not just the second time I've been overwhelmed with this feeling of hopelessness. Losing Aiden and not knowing what happened to him, and then having them take Savannah away, sent me into severe postpartum depression. Neither of my parents ever acknowledged how devastated I was by the experience."

Alex's grip tightened on her hand.

"I really am the insane ex-wife. Breaking down twice is bad enough, if he knew it's at least the third …"

"Why did you never tell me any of this?" Alex's sadness reflected in her eyes.

"It's embarrassing to be so weak. To have people look at me like I'm unbalanced and totally nuts. Dealing with the horrified looks when I was fifteen and pregnant was hard enough, but adding in being …" She twirled a finger by her temple. "It leads me to make stupid decisions, like cheating on my husband and breaking his heart." She lifted her gaze to Alex's. "He told you, didn't he?"

"Not until two years ago, but he finally admitted the real reason you divorced."

"I screwed up. That he can even look at me is a miracle. Maybe sharing all of this is a mistake. You'll hate me even more, but I can't pretend anymore. This is who I am; a woman with serious issues."

"Oh, honey. I don't hate you, I never have. I've made mistakes of my own, and I want you to know I'm here. I'm sure this is hard, but we're your friends."

"It hasn't felt like it." She swiped at her tears. "I've missed all of you. Except for Emily, of course, but that's a whole other issue."

"Tiffany. She's a good person. I get it though. She's with Aiden, so that makes her hard for you to like."

"But I have to get over it. She makes him happy, and he deserves a little happiness in his life. I promise, I'll be better behaved in the future."

"You tell him that?"

"Yup." She smiled sadly. "Time for me to move on. I'll always love him, but that just means I have to work extra hard to let him be, even if that means surrendering him to another woman. As long as she doesn't ever take him for granted or break his heart, it'll all be fine."

CHAPTER 11

Savannah

THE SMILING FACES OF HER friends, who were seated around the table, lightened Savannah's heart. They'd gathered to celebrate her eighteenth birthday by treating her to dinner. Minus Gray, of course. After she'd returned to Boston, Savannah confided in Rochelle, pouring out her heartbreak over the betrayal. After that, her new group of friends ousted the cheating ex-boyfriend, even banning him from their study group.

Piper nudged her as Pete held out a card. "For you."

She accepted the envelope and slid a fingertip under the seal, extracting a cute birthday card. "Oh," she whispered as she opened it. "My dad will kill me if I get caught." The ID looked real. "Zoe King, and I'm almost twenty-two." She smiled. "Good, you didn't name me Beatrice or something awful. Where did you get this?"

"Can't say." Pete winked. "It's good, right? We're gonna have some fun tonight, baby. You can come back to the dorms and sleep there." He wiggled his brows.

"You wish." Savannah fluttered her fingers at him.

"No, you wish." Pete snickered. "You'd like to turn me, but it ain't ever gonna happen."

"He meant my room, silly. Your dad will never know about the ID or the club." Piper grinned like an idiot. "Come on, Vanna. You have to go, please? I've never been to one, and it's your birthday. Live a little."

"You can let loose, Vanna. I'm on duty." Jackson leaned in, a huge smile on his handsome face. He held up a hand. "I hereby promise to stay sober all night to ensure our birthday girl stays safe and sound."

"Awww, really?" Savannah placed her palm over her heart. "You'd do that for me?"

"You know it." Jackson pressed a kiss to her temple.

A frisson of anticipation grew in her belly. "This is so exciting." She'd never been clubbing, and she longed to celebrate and get out of the funk she'd been immersed in since Thanksgiving. "Thanks for the best present ever." She bounced to her feet and threw her arms around each of them in turn.

Savannah's heart thumped as they approached the door, which was guarded by a hulk of a man. The doorman eyed them before holding out a meaty hand. "ID."

Rochelle sashayed up to the bouncer with a smile and presented her card.

The doorman checked it and scanned Rochelle from head to toe, lingering on her shapely legs before waving her inside.

Savannah presented hers next, receiving the same once-over but slipping through the door without an issue. Tonight she could let loose as she fully trusted Jackson at his word to watch out for her. But first, she needed to let Emily know she wouldn't be home tonight.

Staying with Piper at the dorms.

I'll tell your dad when he wakes up. Have fun. Happy Birthday, sweetie.

I will, thanks.

A small pang of guilt hit her, but she wasn't lying. She would stay at the dorms. She'd only omitted they'd be spending the evening at the club first.

"Drinks, ladies." Jackson appeared, balancing several glasses in his hands.

Savannah sucked up half of the fruity cocktail, peering around as she swayed to the heavy beat thumping throughout the dim and crowded club.

"Shots." Pete waved at one of the passing waitresses, claiming several of the small glasses from her tray. "Cheers." He clinked his glass against Vanna's before they both tipped them back.

"Urgh." Savannah grimaced as it burned its way down her throat.

"One more." Pete pressed a second shot into her hand. "Bottoms up."

A warm glow rose from Savannah's toes as she washed the second shot down with the remainder of her mixed drink.

Jackson presented his hand. "Let's get you out there." He led her into the mass of bodies already occupying the dance floor and soon the rest of her friends joined them.

Savannah closed her eyes and let the beat of the music wash over her as the alcohol coursed through her system.

"Celebrating without me?" The familiar voice said in her ear.

Her eyes snapped open. "Why are you here?"

"To wish you happy birthday." Gray wound an arm around her waist, pulling her close. "I've missed you, baby."

"Get off." Savannah pushed at his hands. When he didn't let go, she slapped him hard across the cheek. "I said to get off me."

"Wow, gettin' feisty." He moved closer again, grabbing her wrist and squeezing. "I love it."

"Ouch. That hurts, Gray." Savannah twisted her arm and he released her.

Jackson stepped between Savannah and Gray, creating a barrier. He placed his hands flat against the shorter guy's chest. "Get lost, man. She doesn't want you here." Jackson's push propelled Gray into another couple who were dancing behind to them.

This earned Gray another shove and a glare from the other club patron, who wrapped a protective arm around his date. "Get lost, drunken idiot."

Gray held up his hands before stumbling into the crowd.

"You okay, Vanna?" Jackson asked.

"I'm fine. Thank you." She threw her arms around her friend, giving him a long hug before she stepped back. "Did he leave?"

"Yup. He's gone." Jackson wound an arm around her waist. "Forget that loser. Let's have some fun."

⁓≼

Vanna rolled, colliding with the wall. "Oof." She struggled against the warm body beside her.

"Quit kicking me." Rochelle sat, rubbing her hands over her hair. "Answer your stupid phone. It's been going off every five seconds."

"I'm squished." Savannah wiggled off the end of the bed, surveying her wrinkled clothes. "Disgusting. Remind me to never drink that much again." Her mouth felt like cotton, and her head thumped in time to the beat of music echoing through the wall from the neighboring dorm room.

"Ah, you'll recover soon enough." Her friend glanced over her shoulder as she disappeared through the door, returning moments later with a bottle of tablets and a glass of water. "Take these, drink lots of water, and you'll be grand."

"Ha. It'll take more than a glass of water and a couple of pain relievers. And why am I here? I thought I was staying with Piper."

"She was in worse shape than you. Pete managed to get her to her room, but trust me, you would not have wanted to stay there." Rochelle snickered. "Jackson and I took charge of you. A better deal, I'd say."

Nausea rolled through Savannah. She lunged for the bathroom, barely making it in time before she heaved the contents of her stomach into the toilet.

"Here." Rochelle gathered Savannah's hair, pulling it back from her face. "Ick, colorful."

Savannah wiped at her mouth with a tissue. "You still think I'm the better deal?" She slumped with her back against the bathtub. "Maybe I can drink that water and take the pills now. Not sure there's anything left." She rested her head on her knees, a vague memory of Jackson supporting her for the ride home on the subway flashing before her eyes. "Did I puke on Jackson's shoes?"

"Talk about colorful." Rochelle smirked. "He wasn't thrilled, but he volunteered to be the designated guardian last night, so he did a fine job of getting you back here safely."

"I'm so embarrassed." She curled into a ball on the floor.

"Come on, let's get you back to bed. You are some hung over, sweetie pie." Rochelle tugged on her arm.

"I can't. Don't make me move." Savannah groaned before her eyes closed again.

⌒⌁

"Hey." A warm hand patted her face. "Wake up."

"Hmm?" Savannah dug further down into the blankets, so sleepy and cozy.

"Vanna."

She cracked an eye open, meeting Aiden's concerned gaze. "Dad?"

He inspected her as she sat and combed her fingers through the clumps in her blonde locks. "Need a little hair of the dog?"

"What?"

"You're hung over."

"How do you …?" She snapped her mouth shut.

"Doctor, remember? Seen it all, so don't even pretend." He patted her knee.

Savannah looked around, realizing she was still in Rochelle's dorm room. "Why are you here?"

"You were supposed to be home by now. We have dinner at Tom and Jenna's and you, my love, are the guest of honor. We need to go."

"I have puke in my hair." Savannah picked at her stringy locks.

He wrinkled his nose. "You do smell rather disgusting. Good thing someone invented a wonderful contraption called a shower." He took her hand and helped her off of the bed, handing her a bottle. "Drink this first."

She eyed the container, but accepted it and sipped gingerly, hoping she wouldn't have a repeat of her earlier bathroom trip. The cool liquid soothed her throat and settled her stomach somewhat. "That's not so bad. What is this stuff?"

"A secret hangover formula. I feel your pain." The corner of his mouth twitched. "Drink up and shower."

Savannah took the offered overnight bag and headed into the bathroom, her eyes widening. "Oh, man. It's worse than I thought," she muttered under her breath. Her hair hung in a lanky mess, and her eyes were red and puffy with black smudges of mascara and eyeliner smeared underneath.

She dug into the overnight bag, smothering a laugh as she lined up the toothbrush, deodorant, makeup kit, brush, eye drops, and full change of clothing. He really had thought of everything.

Forty-five minutes later, she stepped into the main room.

"Much better, but now we're late," Aiden said. "Have a good night, Rochelle."

Savannah followed him to the car, gulping in the fresh cold air. "How mad are you?"

"Ahh." He waved a hand. "You should know better than that by now." He opened her door.

She slid inside and lean her head against the leather headrest. "You have to be the coolest dad ever."

"If I gave you a hard time, what does that make me? I did my own share of partying in my time. My main concern is for you to stay safe. Rochelle assures me that you all took care of each other, even if you did end up with her instead of staying with Piper. Would I prefer you stayed away from the frat parties and didn't get drunk? Yes. Those parties get way out of hand."

"Spoken from first-hand experience from your younger years as a wild partier?" Savannah smirked.

"Spoken from my experience working in the ER of more than one major hospital." He pulled into their underground parking garage. "Several girls have come in over the past few months after being drugged and assaulted at various parties, and they haven't caught the guy yet. Be extra careful. It's not senseless worrying."

"I promise I'll be careful, Dad." She wrapped her arms around him. "Love you."

"I love you, Vanna." He kissed her cheek after a long squeeze. "We need to head straight to Tom and Jenna's place. Everyone's waiting to wish you a happy birthday."

For the second day in a row, Savannah found herself surrounded, this time by her family. Though she wasn't sure what had been in the drink Aiden had given her, she felt much better and managed to eat dinner. She would have hated to disappoint Jenna. Her aunt worked hard on preparing a special birthday feast and baked a chocolate cake, decorating it with ornate lavender flowers.

After dinner, everyone gathered in the family room.

"Here you go, sweetie." Tom planted a kiss on her cheek as he handed her a beautifully wrapped box.

"Oh, I'm so excited." She peeled off the paper, squealing as she spotted the label. "No way. Is this …? You bought me the boots. I can't believe it." She hugged the designer boots to her chest and then leaped to her feet, bestowing hugs and kisses on both Tom and Jenna.

"Glad you like them. Let's see them on."

The process continued as she opened her gift from Alex and Joel—a gorgeous new suede jacket–and then a rose gold watch from Ryan and his girlfriend, Kaari.

"Your gifts from the grandparents are at home, so we can open those later." Aiden produced an envelope. "This is from Emily, Kellan, and me."

Savannah stared at the envelope for a moment before she broke the seal. "Wow, Dad. Are you kidding?" She flipped through the papers, noting the itinerary and hotel bookings for an all-expense-paid trip to California.

"Tomorrow you're on a flight to San Francisco so you can celebrate your birthday with Leanne and Justin. They'll meet you at the hotel."

She hugged both Emily and Aiden, and then planted a kiss on her little brother's cheek. "This is amazing. Thank you."

⤛

"Thought you dropped out." Gray settled into the chair across from her. "Where'd you go?"

"That seat's taken." Savannah didn't bother to look up from her open text book. "Go find someone else to irritate."

"Doesn't look like there's anyone here." He folded his arms on the table, propping his chin on them so he looked up at her. "I've missed you, baby."

"Go away." She glared at him before bowing her head over her book. The cheating had been bad enough, but the subsequent never-ending stream of texts only served to fuel her rage at his behavior.

"Did you hear me, babe?" He reached across and flipped her page. "I miss you."

"You refuse to take a hint. Get"—she narrowed her eyes—"lost."

"Harsh, baby. I said I was sorry. It won't happen again."

"You got that right." She leaned back in her chair and crossed her arms. "You know why? Because we're done. Finished. Finito. Terminado. Adiós, pinche pendejo." Savannah fluttered her fingers at him.

"You heard her. Adiós." Jackson flopped into the chair beside Gray. "Move your ass. You don't belong to our study group." He turned and smiled at Savannah. "We missed you. How was your trip?"

"Amazing. I had a fabulous time with Justin." She controlled the twitch of lips for a moment before she let the grin creep across her face. "The hotel was incredible."

Gray shoved his chair back from the table. "Tramp," he muttered as he stalked away.

"Thanks, Jackson." She bumped her fist against his. "I thought he'd never leave."

"No problem. That kiss off deserved a standing ovation, but what did you call him?"

"Emily speaks fluent Spanish, so I've picked up a few choice words, especially while driving with her in Boston traffic. Let's just say it wasn't flattering."

"I believe he got the point." He winked and then snickered. "Making him think you hooked up with Justin was classic."

Savannah grinned.

"You didn't … did you?"

"Nah." She shrugged. "Justin and I are better as friends. I'll always love him, but I'm not sure it could work long term, and I don't want to ruin what we had. Does that make any sense?"

"Not really. If you love someone, shouldn't you do everything you can to make it work?"

"What if it's not enough?" Savannah leaned her cheek against her hand, idly tapping her pencil on the cover of her text book. "Love, I mean. My dad loved Tiffany, but they couldn't make it work, and I don't really understand why."

"Tiffany? Your mother?"

"Well, the woman who gave birth to me, anyway. Never mind that. She and my dad were married for about two years, but it didn't work, even though they loved each other. They were my age when they got married. Man, that's so weird now that I think about it." She twirled a lock of hair around her finger.

"Have you asked your dad why?"

"We've talked, but I can tell there is something he doesn't want to say. It's a feeling I get when he talks about being married to her, like something happened between them that he doesn't want me to know." A sick feeling grew in her stomach. "Oh." She dropped her head in her hands. "It can't be."

"What?"

"He knows what happened. I told my dad, because Gray kept texting me. We had a conversation, and …" She frowned as the pieces added up in her mind.

"What's wrong?"

"Nothing." She forced a smile. "I'm not ready for a serious relationship, and neither is Justin, and we made a decision."

"I still don't get why you don't at least try with him. The girls always comment on how hot he is, and he's at Stanford. Isn't he what most girls would consider a great catch?"

"There's more to being happy than finding a great catch. We're not fishing." Savannah scoffed while shaking her head.

"Glad you think so, but woman are so complicated. If you can't find happiness with a guy like that, then what is it you want? He's not so different from me, except for maybe the scorching hot part." Jackson snickered.

"Honestly, Jackson. Why are you even asking me this?" Savannah rolled her eyes.

"There's a girl I like," he muttered, "but she doesn't even notice me. She's all about these guys who treat her like crap."

"Ohhhhh. Do tell. Who is it?" Savannah smirked. "Do I know her?"

"Nope." Jackson's gaze wandered downwards.

"Liar." Savannah studied him, but spotting the red creep up his neck, she decided to back off. "Fine. What do you want to know?"

"I'm a nice guy, and not bad looking, right? I'm reasonably intelligent, and I'm working on a career in law, yet she's relegated me to the friend zone. For example, a girl like you won't even stay with a guy who she professes to love because it might not be enough? I don't get it. I mean, I get you dumping a dog like Gray, but you left Justin so you could date ass wipes? What the fuck is that about?"

She considered him. Jackson was definitely all that and more, even if she didn't feel that spark of attraction toward him. "It's about being eighteen and unable to imagine making that kind of commitment to a guy at this point in my life. I want to live, and travel, and experience the world before I tie myself to one man and settle down. I also believe when I find it, I'll know."

"Find what?"

"True love. It sounds stupid, right? But my dad loved my mother, yet now he's married to Emily, and I can see how they fit so perfectly. The way they are when they're together, like they'll love each other for ever and ever. I want that, Jackson. Don't get me wrong, Justin is an amazing guy, but he's not the one. I'm not his one, either."

"That's some insightful shit for someone who's eighteen." Jackson grinned. "You are a very strange girl. But you're sweet. I hope you find the perfect man some day."

"Sorry, I'm late." Rochelle hurried across the room, joining them at the table. "Vanna. Let's see those pictures from California."

CHAPTER 12

Tiffany

The sight of the tall handsome man striding through the restaurant made Tiffany smile. She brushed her skirt, smoothing it as she stood and held out her hand. "Mr. Cortes. So nice to see you again."

"It's Stefan." His return smile lit up his entire face and caused a small crinkle at the corners of his eyes.

The deep blue of his shirt made his eyes appear even more vivid tonight. Or was it simply the lighting? Either way, her pulse rate sped up as he held her hand for a moment longer than necessary and then motioned for her to sit.

She eyed him as the waitress filled their water glasses. "So, Stefan," she said as the woman left with their drink orders. "What can I help with?"

"Straight to business. I like that, Tiffany." He met her gaze. "As you know, I've provided classes over the years for aspiring photographers. I have one who has shown particular promise, and I'd like to arrange a showing for her work."

Her. What did I expect? "Do you have some of this artist's work?" Tiffany smiled as the server delivered her cocktail. The words came out easily, but from the rising heat in her face, she knew her cheeks had turned beet red. "Not that I don't trust your judgment … I mean …" She clutched her glass, taking a moment's reprieve to regain her composure.

"I'd never expect any gallery to show work without seeing it first."

She raised her head.

He held out a portfolio. "If you like what you see, I can arrange for you to view some original pieces."

Her fingers brushed his as she accepted the portfolio, her heartbeat accelerating again. After inspecting the first three, she knew. "These are wonderful. I would love to see more. Let me know when you'd like to come by the gallery."

"Isn't this where you tell me what you can do for the artist?" He lifted a brow.

The corners of her mouth twitched. "Is this where you tell me you *haven't* done your research on my gallery and what we've done for our artists before you even considered approaching me?"

"Touché." Stefan chuckled and he reached across the table to clasp her hand in his large one. "I may have done a tiny bit of research. I knew there was something about you, Tiffany Baxter."

Tiffany stared at him for a moment, not sure whether to pull away or allow him to continue holding on.

Stefan squeezed her fingers before withdrawing his hand. "Maybe I should tell you what I'm looking for?"

"Yes, please." Tiffany gulped a mouthful of her cocktail.

Stefan raised a brow, and tipped back his own drink, draining the last of it before he waved at the server, motioning between the two glasses. "You seem on edge. Why?"

Tiffany furrowed her brow. "Why does Stefan Cortes, world renowned photo journalist, want my insignificant little gallery to host a showing? I'd bet there are numerous gallery owners falling all over themselves to get your attention."

"Referring to your gallery as insignificant is bad for business." He accepted his fresh drink and took a sip, studying her over the rim of his glass. "That you're operating a small unpretentious gallery is what I like about the proposal. I can tell from your set up that you know art and have a solid eye for detail. Where did you go to school?"

"The Art Institute here in Chicago." She bent her head over the menu, not wanting to get into further discussion about her education. Why bring up the lost time in Philadelphia? Her life had been a complete mess, her time spent fighting with Aiden and destroying her marriage. "I grew up in Chicago."

"A hometown girl." He opened his menu. "I'd love to see some of your own work. I hear you're an amazing photographer with a natural talent."

"Who told you that?" Tiffany frowned.

"Uh-uh. I have to keep my sources secret." He winked. "We should order. I'm starving."

The next morning she worked alone in the gallery for several hours. Isla had promised to work the afternoon and evening, leaving Tiffany free to run her errands, one of which was her appointment with Liz.

The small bell on the door tinkled, and she looked up. "This is a surprise."

"Have to check on my investment." David Baxter looked around. "Quiet in here."

"It's early yet, but we have a show in a couple days." Tiffany drummed her fingers on the counter, contemplating the reason for his unexpected visit. "Can I get you anything?"

"No, I'm on my way to a meeting. They'll have decent coffee and food." He wandered through, hands in pockets as he inspected the paintings. "You haven't returned my calls."

"Sorry. It's been busy."

"Yes, I can see how incredibly overwhelmed you are." He raised a brow. "We need to talk."

"About what?"

"It's no secret your mother and I are apart, or what she's been up to over the holidays. I need your help." He squinted at her, daring her to argue, but that would spark a lecture. "Your mother and I are getting back together."

"Really?"

"Yes, we've been married for thirty years."

Thirty-five, actually. Tiffany crossed her arms.

"I refuse to let her go."

Tiffany frowned. "What do you want from me?"

"Your support. Maybe you could talk to her?"

She leaned against the counter, hoping he wouldn't notice her trembling knees. "About what?" She managed to keep her voice level.

David wandered to the window, staring out at the quiet street before he turned to his daughter. "She needs encouragement. A little incentive to allow me to return home, per se. Breaking up our family is detrimental to everyone."

"Mother hasn't asked you to come home?" Nausea rose. "It's not my place to have that discussion. Besides, what makes you think she'd even listen to me?"

"Honey, I need your assistance. I've done so much for you, maybe you could find it in your heart to help me. Do you want your parents to be divorced?"

Tiffany bowed her head, avoiding his steely gaze. *Typical.* In his eyes, she remained a little girl who could be forced to comply with his every wish. Anger flared within her, but she pushed it down and composed her face into a blank mask before she dared look at him. "Please don't ask me to do this." She shook her head. "Truly, you need to work this out with her."

"She refuses to discuss it or forgive me." David moved closer, taking her hands in his. "But for you, she might reconsider her position."

Tiffany suppressed a shudder. After what she had learned about his treatment of Aiden, the cheating, and all of the times he'd treated everyone around him as disposable, she couldn't help her growing revulsion. This man didn't deserve a thing.

"I can't be without her. You know how important it is to be a united family. After your rash decision to break off your engagement, I must avoid any hint of a scandal or divorce."

"Don't bring Harrison into this. He cheated on me, more than once. And if he did it before, what do you think he'd be doing during our marriage?" She yanked her hand free and stepped back, rubbing her hands against her skirt.

"I don't know why you think that, Tiffany." Her father narrowed his eyes. "How do you know he cheated?"

"I caught him." She bit her lip, hoping he wouldn't ask for more details. Her father learning Aiden's role in the demise of her relationship with Harrison could only fuel the fire.

"Careful, or you'll end up alone. Harrison would have been the perfect match, but you just had to mess that up."

"How could I marry him after that?" The thought of enduring years with a man who barely touched her made her want to weep. That her own father had pushed them together in the hopes of furthering their respective political careers made her ill.

David clicked his tongue. "Love is overrated, or haven't you learned that yet? What did marrying for so-called love get you? Dumped and divorced by the age of twenty-one."

Tiffany wrapped her arms around herself, wishing to sink into the floor and become invisible.

"You're barely getting by with this gallery. You should have stayed with Harrison. You'd be married and set financially for the rest of your life. Now, what do you have?" David folded his arms across his chest. "Talk to your mother."

Tiffany squeezed her eyes shut, dragging in a breath in an attempt to calm her pounding heart. Her palms grew damp.

"I need your help. Like you've needed mine."

She opened her eyes, not wanting to look at him, but also knowing he'd persist until he got what he wanted from her.

David cast a glance her way, a malicious smile appearing as he turned in a slow circle, extending his arms with his palms facing upward. "It would be such a shame for you to lose all of this. You've worked so hard, but I'll lose so much in the divorce. I doubt I'll be able to continue supporting your little venture."

Her eyes burned as she absorbed his thinly veiled threat. If she didn't comply and he demanded his investment back, she'd have to close shop. And she wouldn't be able to afford her apartment, either. She'd been stupid to accept his offer of financial assistance. It gave him complete control over her and everything she did.

She blinked hard, fighting the urge to burst into tears. Taking a deep breath, she looked into his smug face. "Please, don't do this," she whispered. A bead of perspiration trickled down her back and she dug her nails into her clammy palms. "I can't do it."

His eyes widened before they narrowed again, and he scowled. "That's gratitude for you. My own daughter, and you won't help after everything I've done for you? I've protected you since you were a teenager, helped you recover from your mistakes, and bailed you out whenever you've required it. I need this one tiny favor, yet you seem reluctant to even try."

Tiffany bowed her head, refusing to allow him to see the solitary tear trickle down her cheek.

David glanced at his watch. "It behooves both of us if you assist me in avoiding a messy divorce." With a nod in her direction, he exited the gallery.

Tiffany willed her feet to carry her across the tile floor, her entire body trembling as she flipped the sign to *closed* and locked the door. Nausea rose, and she rushed to the bathroom, barely making it in time. Her stomach heaved forever before she sank onto the cold tile, burying her head in her hands.

A multitude of memories and overwhelming emotions rushed in on her. *Has he ever done anything for me? It was always about him.* She couldn't bear to remember his harsh treatment when her pregnancy had been discovered. How he'd forced her onto the plane with no discussion. How he'd considered her love for Aiden shameful. How he'd ignored her pain, his lack of compassion making her feel sullied and unworthy of her father's love.

She burst into tears as her world tumbled in on her. After the disastrous end of her marriage to Aiden, her search for love led her straight into the arms of a man much like her own father. A man only interested in furthering his career. A man incapable of loving her the way she needed to be loved. A sham engagement, which would have ended in a loveless marriage. An endless game of pretend with her a mere adornment on his arm for social events. A cover for his true lifestyle.

Her desperate need for love and acceptance had convinced her, at first. Until the cracks began to show, to widen, threatening to suck her into the crevasse that gaped under her feet.

Tiffany pulled herself together and splashed cold water onto her face. Isla would be in soon, so Tiffany wrote a short note saying she felt ill. After locking the gallery door, she trudged home, crawling straight into her bed and burying herself under the covers, willing herself into sleep. Maybe, by some miracle, she could forget.

Her own shrieks tore her from the nightmare. "No! Don't hurt him."

Tiffany snapped her eyes open, her hand pressed to her chest as she whimpered and gasped for air. She swiveled her head back and forth, searching, expecting to be in a tiny motel room, ripped from sleep as the door crashed against the wall. Nothing. Silence surrounded her, the only sound the hammering of her heart and the heaving breaths she dragged into her oxygen-deprived lungs.

She brushed her damp cheeks and rose from her bed, stumbling down the dim hallway. The icy water trickled into the glass and she gulped back several mouthfuls before leaning against the cool granite counter.

How had I forgotten the brutality of that night until now?

Her jaw clenched as she squeezed her eyes shut. If only she could banish the images. The two burly men hauling a half-dressed Aiden from the room, another restraining her with rough, calloused fingers as she cried his name and beat her fists against her captor's chest.

A shudder ran through her. *Get dressed.* The man shoved her toward the bed, his words a guttural hiss. Sweat beaded on her cold flesh, the man's icy stare sending fear clawing through her. She scrambled to cover her half-naked body, afraid of what he might do to her. Then she recognized the disgust in his eyes, the way his gaze flicked across her pregnant belly, his lip curling into a sneer. *Trash.*

In the dim light of morning, they finally dragged her from the room, Aiden nowhere in sight. The two men forced her into the back seat of a nondescript black sedan and tossed her belongings into the trunk. Tiffany huddled, curling into a ball, arms wrapped over her rounded belly, too scared to utter a single word during the ominous ride to Portland. After one stop barely long enough for her to use the bathroom, she picked at soggy fries in a greasy fast food sack.

She imagined the worst. Nobody answered her pleas to reveal her boyfriend's fate. Sadness consumed her. The only thing keeping her from giving in to despair was her love for their baby.

The final weeks of her pregnancy were spent under strict surveillance. The long hours confined to the small house and yard drove her crazy. With the exception of shuttling back and forth to the doctor's office, and then at long last to the hospital to give birth to her daughter, she was quarantined.

Her aunt grudgingly kept her in Portland until summertime, enrolling her in classes so she could catch up on her studies. In September, she'd returned to boarding school on the condition she keep up the pretense that she'd attended an intense study program. The threat of being torn from her friends, yet again, kept her silent.

Tiffany curled up on the couch under a soft throw, staring at the gray, overcast skies through the wall of glass until the first rays of light crept in.

She crawled from the couch with a sigh, heading into the bathroom. Her gritty red-rimmed eyes and sallow skin made her flinch. Over the years, she'd become a pro at hiding the tell-tale signs, though, and she dug out her eye-drops. She tipped her head back, squeezing two into each eye, blinking at the sting.

After a steaming hot shower, she applied concealer and makeup to hide the dark circles and bring color to her ashen face.

⌒≼

"You're early." Isla looked up from her task of unpacking and cataloging the current shipment of sculptures from a stack of crates. "Are you okay?"

"Fine, why do you ask?"

"You look exhausted." Isla studied her with keen eyes. "If you lose any more weight, you'll disappear entirely."

"Don't worry about me." Tiffany brushed off her concern. "I have paperwork to take care of, but do you need any help?"

"I've got this. Do the office stuff."

Tiffany smiled faintly at her ever-efficient and cheerful assistant before she entered her office and closed the door. She worked her way through her filing cabinet, locating the past three years of financial records. The numbers weren't stellar, but she had to try.

She spent the next hour writing a business proposal, silently thanking her stubborn ex-husband for forcing her to enroll in business classes at the University of Pennsylvania. It was irritating how often he was right, but his insistence brought a warm glow to her heart. Aiden considered her worthy and intelligent even if nobody else ever had.

Isla tapped on her door and inched it open, sticking her head in. "Your appointment is here." Her grin widened as she twitched her head toward the front of the gallery.

"Show him in, please." Tiffany stood and stretched before stacking her paperwork in neat piles on the credenza behind her. She straightened and forced a smile as Isla escorted the man into her office. "Stefan. Nice to see you." Her hand was extended before she spotted the two cups and bag slung over one shoulder.

Isla smirked. "Stefan?" she mouthed behind his back before she exited and closed the door.

Stefan offered one of the cups. "An extra-hot chai latte with a generous sprinkle of cinnamon."

"Thank you." Tiffany accepted the chai as she scanned him, admitting he looked impossibly sexy in those dark-washed jeans. It almost made her forget that he somehow knew her favorite drink. "Please sit."

He set his cup on her desk and shrugged out of his coat, hanging it on the rack in the corner before he adjusted the sleeves of his dark blue shirt. A small frown crossed his face as he studied her from across the desk. "Is this a bad time?"

Tiffany shook her head. "Why don't you show me what you have?"

"I brought a few more examples, but I'd love to take you to the artist's workspace. We could spend a couple of hours there and perhaps choose some pieces to show if you're up for it?"

"Of course. Now?"

"Drink up first. I'm in no rush." His slow and easy smile caused a flutter in her chest.

She lifted her cup and took a sip. "Sounds perfect."

Chapter 13

Savannah

Savannah swayed to the music as they entered the club. She grinned at Rochelle. "Too bad Piper is missing this."

"She had the chance to go home for a few days, so …" Rochelle bobbed her head to the beat. "Darn, I have to visit the ladies room."

"What's new?" Savannah laughed and fluttered her hand toward the bathrooms. "Meet me at the bar."

Savannah wiggled her way through the crowd and found a tiny space at the long wooden bar.

The bartender leaned in close. "What can I get you?"

Savannah ordered a shot, which she downed while the bartender mixed drinks for her and Rochelle.

He winked as he set them in front of her, but turned away as another patron's wave caught his eye.

She leaned against the bar, sipping her cocktail and searching the mass of bodies for Rochelle. A heavy sigh escaped as she caught sight of familiar blond hair and a flash of blue eyes. "Will he ever take the hint?" she muttered. Despite her comments about Justin, Gray had continued to text until she'd blocked his number, and his hungry leers in class were ever more uncomfortable as time passed.

"Hey, Babe." Gray widened his eyes to give that puppy-dog look he obviously thought girls found irresistible. He waved at the bartender, motioning over her drink.

"What are you doing?"

Gray slid an arm around her waist. "Buying you a drink." He pressed against her side.

"No, thanks." Savannah tried to slip around him, but the solid mass of bodies trapped her between Gray and the solid top of the bar. She cast a desperate glance at the bartender who had his back turned as he uncapped beer bottles for two other patrons.

"Come on, baby. We're good together. I forgive you for hooking up with pretty boy." He gripped her wrists, locking them at her sides as he kissed her cheek.

Tears rushed to her eyes as she struggled to break his hold. "That hurts. Let me go." She turned her head to avoid his pungent beer breath, gagging as he loomed closer, his mouth bare inches from hers. Savannah's throat closed up and a tear trickled down her cheek. "You're hurting me. Stop it."

His grip tightened as he brought her hands together, locking the fingers of one of his large hands around her wrists. "You like it rough." He dug his fingers into her cheek, forcing her chin up. A manic smile appeared and he crushed her lips onto hers, pressing a knee against her legs, pinning her in place.

She choked as he pushed his tongue between her lips, clamping her teeth down hard.

He reared back but only smirked, his hold tightening. The pressure on her wrists increased as his lips mashed against hers, growing heavier and more possessive.

Savannah squeezed her eyes shut, wiggling in a futile attempt to break away, bringing her knee up, but meeting the side of his leg. She winced as the weight of his body pressed against her, the edge of the bar digging into her back.

She sagged as the crush lifted, the sudden release of her hands and waft of cool air an immediate relief.

The arm wrapped firmly around her ex-boyfriend's neck propelled him away, allowing Savannah to drag in a long, ragged breath. Gray's mouth hung open in a surprise, making him look almost comical.

The newcomer spun, planting himself between Savannah and Gray, towering over her attacker. "What the hell do you think you're doing?" The deep and vaguely familiar voice carried over the thump of the music. "Get lost, asshole." The dark-haired man shoved Gray. "I won't say it again. If you ever touch her …" The rest of the words were lost as the volume of the music increased, and the stranger forced her ex-boyfriend to retreat step by step.

Gray's lips moved, his face contorting as he lunged toward the interloper, who held up a hand to fend off the shorter man.

Savannah cringed as the man seized Gray by the throat and drove a fist into his face, a gush of red spurting from her ex-boyfriend's nose. She gasped in a breath and turned her head, catching a glimpse of Gray pitching backward, an arc of juice, soda, and beer spraying over the unfortunate crowd, accompanied by screams.

Two of the club's bouncers muscled through the mass of bodies and descended on the two men. One twisted Gray's arm behind his back and hauled him toward the exit, the other took hold of the man who had intervened and steered him through the crowd.

"No, no." Savannah lunged after them, clutching at the bouncer's massive arm. "That other guy attacked me and … and …" She gaped at her rescuer, at a complete loss for a name.

The bouncer halted as they reached the hallway. He lifted one of Savannah's hands, inspecting her wrist before his gaze traveled to her tear-stained face. "That guy did this to you?"

Savannah nodded as she focused on the reddish rings on her wrists. "Don't make my friend leave."

"You should get that looked at." The bouncer squinted at Savannah. "Let's see some ID. Both of you."

Savannah swallowed hard and dug into the tiny purse slung across her shoulders. She fought to control the trembling of her hands as she offered the ID to the bouncer.

He scanned both of their cards. "Zoe King of Boston. You're twenty-two? Brandon Reynolds of Philadelphia." After an extra-long look at Savannah, he handed them back. "You two stay out of trouble."

Rochelle appeared at the end of the hallway as the bouncer returned to the club. "Are you okay?" Her friend hurried toward Savannah, wrapping her in a hug. "Damn that jerk. Nice shot, by the way." She nodded toward Brandon.

"Let me look at your arms, Zoe." Brandon cradled Savannah's hands between his, peering at them in the dim lighting.

Rochelle eyed Savannah. "Zoe?" she mouthed, her brows rising as she rolled her eyes toward the man inspecting her friend's arms. Rochelle flicked her fingers, giving them a shake, but her grin faded as she pointed at the fingerprints embedded in her friend's skin. "Wow, Asshole did that?"

"He had quite a grip." Brandon gave her hands a gentle squeeze.

"There you are." A guy with blondish hair arrived and joined their group.

"Hey, Dylan." He focused on Savannah. "I'm a medical student, so I know how to treat this. Does it hurt?" He pressed along her wrists.

Savannah winced. "It does. Sorry, Ro. I don't feel like dancing."

"No problem. We should get you home." Her lips twitched as she cast a look at Brandon, who still had hold of Vanna's hands.

"Why don't I take you?" Brandon lifted his chin. "I promise to get you home safe and sound. We'll get some ice for your wrists."

Savannah peeked at Rochelle from the corner of her eye. "Yes, please."

"Can I get your coat?" Brandon pointed to the coat check.

Savannah handed him her ticket.

Rochelle pulled her aside and lowered her voice. "Are you sure? Who is this guy?"

"Long story, but I've met him before," she whispered. "I'll be fine, Ro. He rescued me, and he's a medical student."

"And he's delicious"—her friend smirked—"but he could be lying."

"I don't think so. He's sweet. I'll be okay with him." Savannah studied the two guys. "I'll text you. Why don't you stay? I bet Dylan would keep you company."

"He's a hottie." Rochelle grinned. "You'd better keep in touch so I know you're safe."

"You too." They returned to where the two men were leaning against the wall. "I'm ready. Ro's going to stay for a while."

"Do you feel like dancing?" Dylan lifted a brow.

"Yes." Rochelle took his offered hand, throwing a last glance over her shoulder before disappearing inside the club.

"We should stop meeting like this." Brandon helped her into her coat.

A flush rose in Savannah's cheeks, and she bowed her head. "You keep rescuing me from the same asshole."

"Wait. That's the guy you were dating before Christmas? The one who cheated on you?" He hesitated before opening the door for her. "Why were you here with him?"

"I wasn't. I never went back to him, but he's slow getting the message." She couldn't help the smirk that appeared. "Perhaps this time he'll believe me."

"He just showed up and crawled all over you?"

"Yeah." Her smile faded. "Such a creep. So aggressive. Nobody even noticed, which is even scarier. Well, except for you."

"I'm sorry." Brandon rubbed her arm, and they walked several paces in silence. "You're not seeing anyone?"

"Finding your boyfriend in bed with another girl tends to turn you off romance and relationships." She kept her head bowed as her cheeks reddened. "Sorry. TMI. You didn't need to know that. I keep embarrassing myself in front of you."

"Hey." He rested a warm hand on her arm. "That guy should be embarrassed, not you."

Savannah resisted the urge to take his hand as she peered up at him. "I didn't even say thank you. So, thank you, Brandon Reynolds, for saving me not once, but twice."

"My pleasure, Zoe King. Guys that treat girls like possessions piss me off."

"I never thought I'd see you again."

"Call it fate. I hoped I'd see you again. You made an impression."

"Ha." Savannah smothered a giggle. "I'm sure my red eyes and waterworks made a great first impression."

He opened his mouth, but then pressed it into a thin line and looked away. "What?"

"Nah, we're already too far into the clichés and one-liners." His lips twitched. "We should look at those wrists. Where do you live?"

"Across the river." Nausea rose. She couldn't take Brandon to the penthouse in Back Bay. "I don't really want to go home." She shrugged.

"I live two blocks from here. I have ice."

"Uh-huh." Savannah tilted her head. "What was that about clichés and pick-up lines?"

"One-liners. Close enough. I won't take advantage, I promise. I want to make sure he didn't hurt you." He halted. "Maybe the ER at Mass General would be better. It's not far."

Savannah's heart lurched. Both her dad and Emily were on shift, and at least half of the nurses and most of the doctors would recognize her on sight. And her dad would freak when he saw the bruises. "I don't think it's serious. Besides, who ever wants to wait three hours for ice? Your place is fine. Unless you plan on taking me to Philly?"

"Huh? Oh." He shook his head. "I'm here for a rotation at the children's hospital. Should we get a cab?"

"Driving anywhere in Boston is a nightmare. Let's walk."

"Where are you from?"

"Who says I'm not from here?"

"You sound more west coast than Boston, but what do I know?"

"Ha, you got me," she said. "Portland, originally. Oregon, not Maine."

"You're a long way from home. You moved to attend Harvard?"

"Sort of." Savannah shrugged. "It's a long story. I'm planning a career in law."

"Harvard law. Good for you." He dug into his pocket, coming up with a key. "This is it." Brandon held open the door, following her into the warmth of the hallway before leading her up two flights of stairs.

"This is cute and cozy." Savannah peered over her shoulder as Brandon ushered her inside the apartment and helped with her coat.

"I got lucky. We move a lot for rotations, and some of the rentals aren't that nice. Make yourself comfortable." He motioned to the living room before he stepped into the tiny kitchen, digging in the freezer and filling two towels with ice.

Savannah settled on the leather sofa, taking in her surroundings. Though small, aside from a laptop and an assortment of medical books scattered across the coffee table, the apartment was clean and tidy.

He took one of her hands, rotating her wrist, and then running his fingers over it before moving on to her other hand. "You're right. It's not so bad, at least from a medical standpoint. The bruises will fade in a few days." He studied her. "Can I just say that I'm glad I punched that guy in the face? It takes force to cause bruises like this." He lifted her wrists and kissed the one, and then the other.

A shiver ran down Savannah's spine at the brush of his lips on her skin, followed by his tender touch as he wrapped the ice-filled towels around her arms.

"We need to do this for fifteen minutes at a time. I'll find something for the pain." He moved to the cabinet, retrieved a bottle, and poured her a glass of water.

He showed her the label. "This isn't sealed, but it's just—"

"I trust you, Brandon." Savannah smiled. "It's cute you're worried that I'd think you'd drug me. Even with the bottle of water that day."

"It happens, Zoe. Be careful about accepting drinks or medication from strangers." Brandon snapped the lid open. "I would never do that to a girl. And I'd never hurt a woman like that guy. You're too good for assholes. Why did you date him?"

Savannah brushed at her eyes. "I have bad judgment when it comes to men. He's not the first guy to cheat." She sniffled. "You think I'm stupid. That I asked for it."

"No." Brandon lifted her chin with a finger. "Trusting isn't asking for abuse. I can't stand when men treat women like that, which is why I stepped in. You looked terrified." He frowned. "Has he ever done anything like this before? You should press charges."

"He's never hurt me." Savannah bowed her head. "Not physically. The cheating hurt, but I'm over it. I don't know about pressing charges. He was drunk. I doubt he'll bother me again."

"Being drunk is no excuse. Don't let him get away with that behavior." He stared into her eyes. "Enough said. Here." He shook two tablets into her hand.

Savannah washed them down with the water and set the glass on the coffee table.

"Do you want to watch a movie? We need to keep the ice on for a while."

"That would be good. I'm not much for company, am I?"

"You had a tough night." Brandon switched on the TV and they settled on a light romantic comedy.

Savannah tucked her legs underneath her, her eyelids drooping as they reached the half-way mark. Over time, she sagged closer and closer to Brandon, who'd been removing the ice and then putting it back on at regular intervals. Finally, he set the towels aside.

She fought her fatigue, but her eyelids drooped and she rested her head against his shoulder, cuddling closer as his arm slipped around her.

Savannah woke up in the dark room, feeling disoriented. She smoothed her hand over the soft sweater and inhaled the distinctly masculine scent. *Brandon.* She splayed her fingers, pressing her hand into the firm chest as a picture of his face formed in her mind.

"You're awake." His warm breath wafted across her cheek.

She struggled to focus. "Where are we?"

"In my bedroom. You were a pretzel by the time the movie finished, so I moved you to where you'd be more comfortable." He chuckled. "You wouldn't let go of my sweater, and you asked me to stay with you, but nothing happened."

"I forced you to … oh geez." She covered her face with her palm. "I didn't mean to hijack your bedroom. You should have woken me and told me to get the hell out."

"It's not a problem. You're awfully cute when you sleep." He tightened the arm draped around her. "What guy would complain about sharing his bed with you?"

She buried her face against his chest, hiding the blush that rose to her cheeks. "What time is it?"

"About one? Go back to sleep, and I'll move to the couch."

"No … I mean … it's okay. You can stay here. It's more comfortable than the couch, and I feel I can trust you. Can I use your bathroom?"

"Through there." Brandon pointed.

She took a few minutes to splash some water on her face and freshen up.

"Hey."

Savannah jumped at the voice followed by a light tap on the door.

"I left a t-shirt on the bed in case you want something more comfortable to sleep in. I'm getting water."

"Thanks." She waited for a moment, and then peeked into the empty room. The folded t-shirt lay on the end of the bed. Savannah cast a glance at the doorway before pressing the soft cotton to her face, inhaling the fresh laundry scent but wishing it smelled more like him. After a moment, she peeled off the silky black blouse, wincing as she lifted an arm to release the clasp of her matching lace bra. She slid his baggy shirt over her head.

A sharp inhale issued from behind her. "Your back. You have a massive bruise. Let me look." The heat radiated from him as he moved behind her and eased the shirt upward.

Savannah flinched involuntarily as Brandon stroked his fingers across the middle of her back.

"Sorry. I'll try to be gentle. How did that happen?"

"The bar, maybe? He pinned me against it."

"Damn. I wish I'd hit him harder. This should be reported and documented in the ER."

"No," she whispered. "I should go home."

"Don't be scared, Zoe. It would be best if—"

"I don't want to go to the hospital." Her voice quivered as she stared at the hand he rested lightly on her arm, her eyes drawn to the scrapes across his swollen knuckles.

"I won't force you to do anything, but I can't allow you to wander around Boston in the middle of the night. It's not safe. Lay down and rest, okay? Take the bed, and I'll sleep on the couch."

"I'm not the only one who got hurt." She caressed the raw red marks with her fingertips.

"That's nothing."

"Still, thank you for what you did." Tears trickled down her face.

"Shhh." He pulled her against his chest, rocking her and pressing a kiss to her hair. "Don't worry, sweetheart. You're safe."

They stood there for the longest time before he led her to the bed, lifting the covers for her to crawl underneath.

"Close your eyes." He smoothed the covers, tucking them around her in a way reminiscent of the days when her mom would do the same.

She almost expected a kiss to each cheek followed by the soft words; *sleep well, my angel.* A surge of loneliness rushed through her. "Stay?" She blinked at him, wondering how she felt so safe with this stranger.

"Are you sure?"

"Please?" She placed her hand over his.

"You win." He propped himself up on the pillows on his side. "How are your wrists?"

"Better, thanks to my brilliant doctor." She extended her arms for his inspection.

"Hmmm, you'll still have bruises." He rubbed a fingertip over top, causing another shiver to run down her spine and goosebumps to rise on her exposed skin. "Cold? Come here." He opened his arms, wrapping her in his secure and comforting embrace.

Savannah pressed her face against the soft cotton of his shirt, not bothering to tell him that his touch caused the reaction in her body. She curled against him, closing her eyes and enjoying being cradled in his muscular arms.

Soft breaths tickled her neck, and she snuggled closer, feeling safe and warm, despite the proximity of this virtual stranger. For the second time, she opened her eyes, blinking in the dim light filtering through the blinds.

She inhaled, her heartbeat accelerating at the musky, spicy masculine scent of the man who held her.

"Are you awake?" he whispered against her hair.

"Mmmhmm. What time is it?"

"About four."

"I'm keeping you awake, aren't I? I should go home."

A low chuckle sounded in his throat. "Mmm, it is hard to sleep with you in my bed, but don't leave. It's been a while since I had a sweet girl to cuddle."

She lifted her chin and slid her hand up his chest, brushing her fingers along his jawline. "No girlfriend?"

"Uh-uh. No time while I'm in medical school." Brandon covered her hand with his. "Maybe holding you this close is a bad idea," he murmured against her hair.

Maybe he was right. The tension between them was palpable. Should she make the first move? He hadn't invited her here for any reason other than to take care of her, had he? He hadn't even tried to kiss her. *Why hadn't he tried to kiss me?*

He pressed his lips to her temple. "I'll move to the couch."

"You don't have to."

"Holding you like this … the thoughts I'm having …" He sucked in a breath. "That's not why you're here."

Savannah trailed her fingertips down his arm, stroking the warm smooth skin. "It's okay, Brandon."

He inhaled a long breath as he tangled one hand in her hair, giving a gentle tug to bring her chin up. His mouth covered hers, his soft lips caressing hers as their contact became deeper and more urgent.

She sighed against his mouth, pressing the length of her body against him.

He tipped his forehead and rested it on hers, letting out a long slow breath. "I don't even live in Boston. Are you sure you want to do this? I'll be gone in a few days."

She reached down to grasp the bottom hem of her borrowed t-shirt, and lifted it. His fingers caressed hers as he helped her remove it.

"You're beautiful." The tender butterfly kisses he trailed down her neck sent a shiver down her spine. He lifted his head to look into her eyes. "Zoe?"

Savannah bit her lip and nodded. "I want this. I want you."

Light crept in through a crack in the blinds, a rare ray of sunshine peeking through the clouds in the middle of a deep Boston winter. A bright spot in the middle of a series of ups and downs. She burrowed deeper under the covers, luxuriating in the soft sheets and light weight of his arm draped over her, his hand resting against her bare navel.

With a sigh, Savannah opened her eyes, turning her head. A smile twitched her lips as her gaze met beautiful gray eyes.

"Good morning, gorgeous." He leaned in to claim a kiss.

"Morning." She accepted it with a self-conscious smile.

"Sleep well?" He swept her hair back from her face, kissing her again. "That was incredible. There is definitely something about you, Zoe King."

"I bet you say that to all the girls." A faint smile emerged.

"I don't." Brandon nuzzled against her neck. "I study, and I slave away at the hospital for endless hours. I don't have time to pick up girls. I'm not like that. I don't have a girl in every city."

Savannah wasn't sure she believed him. No question where this man rated on the adorability scale. *An unquestionably perfect ten.* The early hours of this morning did nothing to change her opinion in that regard. The complete tenderness and attentiveness with which he'd loved her caused a warm glow to lift straight from her toes.

She wasn't naïve enough to think the feelings rushing through her meant undying love or that their off-the-charts chemistry meant anything other than they shared an overwhelming sexual attraction.

If her history with men had taught her anything, it was that a man would profess undying love in one breath, yet seduce another woman without a second thought.

A frisson of fear hit her belly, followed by a twinge of guilt. *This time I played the game, instead of being played.* Not intentionally, but he'd seen her fake ID, and now she felt obligated to follow through and let him believe her name to be Zoe King.

Not that it mattered. By his own admission, he'd soon be off to his next rotation, wherever it might be. She'd never see him again.

His gaze intensified. "Having morning-after regrets?" He sighed and rolled onto his back.

"No." She wiggled closer and rested her head on his chest. "We have an undeniable chemistry. Last night was amazing, Brandon. How long are you in Boston?"

"I have to go back to Philly at the end of the week. My rotation is over, though it's possible I'll be back." He studied her with those devastating gray eyes. "That's why I hesitated last night. I can't promise you anything, and some girls …" He shrugged.

"Get clingy and needy, even when they say they won't?"

"Yeah. And then I come off like I'm an asshole because I don't want to have a long-distance relationship. I'm a medical student. I travel to different hospitals, and even different states. Fourth year sucks."

"I understand. I'm a law student with a heavy course load and a job. I'm not ready to settle down, and I promise I won't get all crazy. If you want it to be one night, then I accept that. You never have to see me again."

"Hmmm. It would be a shame to limit this to one night. What if we see how it goes and have fun as long as it lasts?" Brandon closed his eyes. "That came out all wrong. I don't mean to sound like a complete asshole."

"I understood." Savannah rubbed his arm. "Just so you know, I don't usually pick up guys in bars and have one night stands. It's a first for me."

His eyes widened. "That wasn't your—"

"Is that what you were hoping? Some little innocent to save from the big bad ex-boyfriend in the club? Is that how you pick up women?" She drew her brows together.

"No." The alarmed look deepened. "It's just that it would surprise me if it was …" He massaged his temple with his fingertips and peered at her from downcast eyes.

Savannah contained her laughter, raising her eyebrows high, but one corner of her mouth twitched.

A smile crept on to his face. "Stop it."

Savannah dodged his outstretched arms, but he lunged from the bed and caught her, snaking an arm around her waist. A stream of laughter escaped her as he tossed her onto the bed, tickling her ribs. "Ohh. Stop." Giggles escaped as he found the small sensitive spot on her side.

"You." His grin widened and his own low laughter joined hers. He buried his head into the crook of her neck, his warm breath causing a shiver of anticipation to flow through her. "You're very unexpected, Zoe King," he whispered against her ear before laying a tender kiss on her lips.

The lightest sigh to escaped her as she entwined the fingers of one hand in his hair, even as the others trailed down the smooth warm skin of his broad back.

Brandon lifted his head just enough to study her as he brushed her hair from her face. "Is this the end of our road?"

She caressed his cheek with a fingertip. "We could see each other again." Her heart rate accelerated at his appraising look.

"What are you doing later?" He wiggled his brows. "I have the day off."

"It sounds like I have a date with this amazing doctor." She smiled.

"We could get breakfast."

"I'm starving. Can I shower first?"

At his nod, she slid from the bed, retrieving Brandon's shirt from the floor. "I hear my phone." Savannah pulled the soft cotton over her head as she covered the few short steps into the living room. She followed the buzz, locating her small purse and digging out her phone. "Oh, oh," she whispered under her breath as she scanned the list of texts and missed calls.

Vanna, where are you?

She tapped in a reply.

I'm fine, stayed at the dorms after study session.

Please remember to text or call if you're not coming home.

I'm sorry to make you worry. Fell asleep.

Love you, sweetie.

Love you, Dad.

"There are fresh towels in the cabinet." Brandon wrapped his arms around her waist from behind, nuzzling against her neck.

Savannah jumped, almost dropping her phone. "Thanks." She tucked the device away before he could see it, feeling even worse now she'd lied to her dad.

"Are you sure you don't have a boyfriend?" He pressed his cheek against hers.

"Why would you think that?"

"You're nervous and jumpy." He lifted the diamond heart pendant around her neck. "Who was on the phone?"

Savannah shrugged. "Nobody."

"Don't lie to me." Brandon turned her. "Is there someone? This necklace is expensive. Whoever gave it to you must love you."

"It's from my dad." She dragged in a breath. "The texts were from my dad. He checks in to make sure I'm okay." Her cheeks grew hot. "I live at home," she mumbled, ducking her head. "I forgot to text him last night."

Brandon frowned. "You're acting weird because you didn't want me to know you live with your parents?"

Savannah peered at him. "You don't think it's strange?"

"What's the big deal? Harvard is expensive, and if I could live at home while I finish medical school, I would, even though I'm twenty-three," he said. "Did you let him know you're okay?"

Savannah nodded.

"We're good then."

⌒≺

After showering, Vanna borrowed a fresh t-shirt and they went for breakfast. Shortly after they arrived at the diner, Rochelle texted.

Want to study?

"It's Ro—" Savannah caught herself before she said the full name, unsure what her friend had told Dylan.

"Text her back. Let her know you're safe." Brandon sipped his coffee and motioned to her phone.

Vanna nodded.

Still with Brandon. What happened with Dylan?

Spent the night at his place, and that's it. He's a jerk. What happened with Brandon?

Savannah frowned as she responded.

Spent the night with him but he's not a jerk. Sorry, Rowan?

Yeah. Figures you got the good one, lucky girl. Have fun and call me later.

"What's that look for?" Brandon unwrapped his utensils from the napkin as the food arrived.

"Nothing."

"What happened with her and Dylan?" He lifted a brow, shaking his head at the expression on Vanna's face. "Right. I should've warned your friend Dylan's a player. I don't hang out with him often, but I don't know many people in Boston and we study together. We've been on some of the same rotations."

"So, you're not like him?"

"I promise I'm not." He contemplated her. "I've been honest about what's happening. I'm not playing you, but I'm not promising anything more than a casual relationship. I can't."

"You're right, we both know what this is. Anyway, no relationship has any guarantees. So, what do you want to do today?"

CHAPTER 14

Tiffany

TIFFANY GLANCED AT HER WATCH as she stepped back to view the arrangement of sculptures, resisting the urge to wind her hair around her fingers. Instead, she intertwined her fingers behind her back and squeezed while forcing herself to take a long and calming breath.

The past several days had tested her patience and cost her many nights of pacing in front of her large apartment windows. All the while, she ran scenarios through her mind and wished she'd made different choices. Better choices.

I can never go back. Dread curled in her stomach as she glanced toward the front door. Ever since her long and humbling meeting with one of the account managers at the bank, and her heartfelt pleas to approve her financing, she'd been waiting for her father to reappear. If she had to deal with his smug judgment of everything she'd taken pride in accomplishing, she might break. That simply couldn't happen.

David Baxter's absence caused a mixture of emotions. She hated the sight of him, but keeping the man close meant she'd see what was coming. Turning your back on David Baxter never boded well for anyone's future.

Tiffany sighed and stared at the clock on the wall near the front desk, tapping her foot on the tile floor.

"You need to calm down." Her assistant gave her a knowing look. "Waiting for Stefan?"

"Hmm?" Tiffany raised her brows as she forced her foot into stillness. "He's not due until tomorrow."

"You two have been getting close. All that running around town together."

"It's business, Isla."

"Keep telling yourself that." Her assistant smirked as she adjusted one the paintings and stood back. "Perfect."

The ring of the phone made Tiffany jump. "I'll get it." She dashed to her office, squeezing her eyes shut and steadying herself before she answered.

"Ms. Baxter." The man's voice was clipped and succinct. "Thank you for your patience while we reviewed your files."

"What's your decision?"

"I'm sorry, but we have to say no at this time unless you have someone who could provide a guarantee."

"Can you tell me why?" Her stomach clenched as she sank into her chair, her knuckles turning white as her fingers curled around the receiver.

The man's words washed over her in a blur, and all hope of escaping her father's influence drained from her heart.

"Thank you for your time," she whispered, cradling her head in her arms and collapsing forward onto her desk.

"Bad news?"

Tiffany bobbed her head, unable to summon the strength to look up. "They denied my financing. The gallery doesn't have the income levels to warrant it."

"I'm sorry, Tiffany." Isla reached across the desk to squeeze her hand.

"If I have someone who can guarantee, they'll be more than happy to take another look at it. Awesome." A frisson of anger grew in the pit of her stomach. She'd never had a chance.

"Ask your mother. Surely she owes you at least that."

"Can't. Even if she agreed, their assets are tied together and they're still duking it out over who gets what. Besides, trading my father's interference for my mother's? Kill me now." She forced herself upright but then slumped again, tipping her head back against the soft leather.

"I see your point." Isla slipped into the chair across from her. "There's nobody you know that has that kind of money?" Her eyebrows rose.

Tiffany shook her head.

"Really. You don't know any rich men who might help? Say ... a wealthy ex kicking around somewhere?"

"Noooooooo." Tiffany's eyes widened. "Have you completely lost your mind? I'm lucky he even talks to me after the past ten years, and you want me to waltz down to Boston and ask him for an obscene amount of money to finance my gallery?"

"He wouldn't even miss it."

"How would you ...?"

"Oh, come on. I don't live under a rock. Everyone knows the Hamilton family is one of the richest in Chicago. Your ex-husband's father is a damn New York billionaire. His grandmother lives in a multi-million dollar mansion, and he owns how many houses? The man can't spare a little pocket change for the woman he married?"

"He doesn't … never mind." She waved a hand. "No chance. End of discussion."

Isla slid an envelope across the table. "This just came registered mail."

"This is my father's firm." Tiffany sighed. "I can't even look." She closed her eyes, concentrating on stilling the shake of her hands before she broke the seal. The words taunted her, confirming her place at the bottom of David Baxter's list of priorities in his life. Not that it should be any surprise that the man simply didn't value anyone or anything, aside from his own delusions of grandeur.

⁓

"Tiffany." Her mother waved from her seat at one of the tables. A frown tugged Michelle's lips. "You look exhausted."

Tiffany barely lifted one shoulder, not having the energy to show surprise that her mother even noticed. "How are things?" She flagged down the server, requesting coffee.

"Same." Michelle sipped from her cup. "My lawyer is doing her best, but your father is determined to hold this up as long as possible."

The wave of disappointment washed over Tiffany, and she couldn't help the soft sigh that escaped. "He called my loans."

"I'm sorry, sweetie. Have you tried the bank?"

"They said no."

"I'd lend you the money, but I don't have enough. Your father has my hands tied." Her mother reached across and squeezed Tiffany's fingers. "It'll all work out."

"For who? For him? Sure it will, but in the meantime, I'll list my apartment and hope it sells." She drew in a shaky breath. "If it does, I have to pay him first, so how can I keep the gallery afloat? I'll have to liquidate, and there will be nothing left. I'll owe him tens of thousands that I'll never be able to repay."

"Oh, honey, I'm so sorry. This divorce has your father all out of sorts, and I hate that he's taking it out on you. But don't give up quite yet."

"It's not your fault. I should never have opened the gallery." She sniffled, swiping at her eyes. "The whole thing was too good to be true."

"But it is my fault. If I hadn't stirred things up, he wouldn't be pressuring you. I've told him to stop, but he's a stubborn man." Michelle stared at her hands. "If I stop the divorce proceedings, he'll leave you alone."

"If you even think about staying with him, I'll never speak to you again." The anger rose. "It's emotional blackmail. Don't submit to his nonsense."

"But Tiffany—"

"No." She shook her head. "Seeing you miserable only makes it worse. Besides, I'd rather lose my gallery than be financially beholden to someone who doesn't give a damn about me. I've had enough. He's done nothing but control me my entire life, and it's time I grow up and manage on my own."

"I wish there was something I could do."

"There is." Tiffany cringed at the distress in her mother's eyes. "Divorce that bastard. We've kowtowed to him for far too long. He's ruined our lives. I lost the man I loved and my daughter because I couldn't say no. Damned if I'll let him force you to stay. Do you really want to be married to him?"

Michelle shook her head.

"I'll start over. It's not the first time."

"I hate that he's taking this too."

"So be it." She took both of her mother's hands. "I'll be fine."

"You're nothing but skin and bones. I can tell you don't sleep. How can he do this?"

"Because he's heartless, and I will never speak to him again if he does this to us."

"He's your father, Tiffany."

"And I wish every single day that he wasn't. How can I ever forgive him for all he's done. For all he's taken away? Forgiveness can only go so far. He doesn't deserve it. He doesn't give a damn about me, and he never has."

⁓≺

"How did it go?" Isla looked up from her paperwork. A furrow appeared between her brows as she leaned on one arm. "Hmmm, that good, huh?"

"Yup. Fantastic." Tiffany flung her purse onto the counter and bowed her head. "I have no choice but to close the gallery." She inhaled and let out a long slow breath. "You'd better start looking for another job."

"I can't believe your own father rescinded financing." Isla shook her head. "That's harsh."

"I'm sorry, Isla. I've enjoyed working with you, and I'll give you a great reference. You'll land on your feet."

"What about you?"

"I've got my degree. I'm sure I'll find something." Tiffany looked around the gallery. Yet another dream had crumbled. Another fantasy had become a nightmare.

"What about Stefan and his show?"

Tiffany groaned. "Damn. My career will be over if I mess that up. One word from him and nobody will ever work with me again."

"Then we go ahead as planned. Most of the work is done."

"Even if I do the show, it will never make enough money to make even a tiny dent. I have maybe thirty days and I'm finished."

"I hate to say it, but you're out of options. You know what you have to do."

Tiffany closed her eyes, her stomach clenching. "Our relationship is precarious at best." Visions of his face flashed through her mind. The dark stormy looks, but most of all, the devastation written on his features those last few months. The intense pain and soul-crushing damage she'd caused to the one man she'd loved beyond measure. "He'll tell me to go to hell."

"What if he doesn't? This is years of hard work, gone for no good reason." Isla rested a hand on her arm. "You owe it to yourself to try everything."

"Ugh. Fine. What's a little more groveling?"

Her assistant gave a small nod. "I won't let you give up. And I won't abandon you in this hour of need. We'll make it the best show ever."

"Thank you." Tiffany held back a sniffle. "I appreciate it."

Isla peered over her shoulder as the bell over the door tinkled. "Now smile. Guess who just walked through that door?"

Tiffany brushed her fingers under her eyes and combed her fingers through her hair. "I can't let him see me like this."

"You look beautiful, even if you're a tiny bit pale."

"Liar." She pinched her cheeks. "Time to get my game face on. Stefan doesn't care about my tragic personal life." As she lifted her chin and pasted on a bright smile, she squared her shoulders. It wouldn't be so difficult to pretend it was all okay. She'd had years of practice.

CHAPTER 15

Savannah

RANDON BRUSHED THE BACK OF his hand across her cheek as they stood in line at the club. "I can't believe it's my last night in Boston. I'll miss you."

The familiar twist in her gut made her want to cry. This had gone on too long, and now she felt trapped. This guy didn't deserve the subterfuge. They took several steps forward, with only one couple now in front of them. "Brandon?"

"What, sweetheart?" One of his beautiful smiles lit his features as he entwined their fingers.

"I need to tell you something." They reached the door of the club, and Savannah pulled her ID from her wallet. Her heart fluttered as she looked at the tall, dark-haired man beside her. Even considering what he might have to say filled her with dread.

The doorman waved them through, and her senses were assaulted by the flashing lights and thumping beat.

Brandon checked their coats, returning moments later.

"Brandon, I need—"

"Later." He pointed at his ear and then motioned to the bar with a raised brow.

Vanna nodded and clung to his warm hand, staying close as Brandon drew the attention of the bartender. She bounced to the pounding bass, smiling at him as he handed her a glass. She sucked up the fruity liquid before pressing her lips to his ear. "Let's dance."

In moments, they were surrounded by the crowd on the massive dance floor.

An hour later, they took a break, propping themselves against one of the tables scattered throughout the club. Savannah jumped as an arm curled around her waist.

"Well, hello, darlin'."

"Uncle Ryan." She threw her arms around the man before she stepped back, a flush heating her cheeks. "What are you doing here?"

"The real question is … What the hell are you doing in a club?" He glanced over his shoulder. "You see that rectangular thing there?" Ryan pointed, all the while staring at Brandon with a deep frown on his face.

"The door?" She lifted a brow.

He leaned in close. "Your dad is five minutes behind me. I'd be exiting the premises."

Panic rose and she threw a look toward the front door.

"Go." Ryan picked the glass out of her hands.

"What is your problem?" Brandon watched the exchange with a confused expression. "That's my …"

Savannah grabbed his arm. "I'm not feeling great. Could you take me home?"

Brandon frowned but nodded. "I'll get your coat."

"Thanks." Savannah turned to Ryan as Brandon headed toward the coat check. "You won't tell Dad?"

Ryan gave her a look but linked his pinkie finger with hers. "I've got your back, sweetheart, but don't ever let me find you in here again. And that guy is too old for you. Get yourself home, and find someone your own age."

"He's my date. Guys my age are so immature." She rolled her eyes.

"Are you kidding?" Ryan squinted. "This is against my better judgment, so get your butt out of this place before Aiden busts you."

"Thank you." She planted a kiss on his cheek and then pushed her way through the crowd.

Brandon helped her with her coat and led her through the door. They walked to the train in silence. Once they stepped aboard the car, he slumped into a seat. "What was that about?"

"Nothing." She noted his dark expression. "Are you jealous?"

He looked away. "That guy's too old for you."

"Ryan's my uncle." Savannah snorted, thinking how ironic it was that Uncle Ryan had said the exact same thing about Brandon. "Besides, what happened to no strings attached?"

"How can you even …?" Brandon scrubbed a hand through his dark hair, leaving it sticking out at all angles in a way she found completely adorable. "Never mind." He clenched his jaw and stared at the floor.

Savannah reached for his hand. "Brandon."

He shook his head and pulled away. "Not here. Everyone is staring at us."

He remained silent and withdrawn for the short walk to his apartment. Once they were inside, he threw his keys onto the tray by the door. With a surly look in her direction, he dug into the fridge before cracking open a beer and leaning on the counter.

"You're mad because I said hi to someone?" She took the bottle from his hand and swallowed a mouthful. "Someone who really is my uncle, by the way."

"It's not that. We've spent every night together for a week. I don't want to go back to Philly. And I hate the way other guys look at you, and I hate that your ex-boyfriend hurt you, and you won't do anything about it."

"Can you let it go? Please? He hasn't texted or come near me all week."

"What happens when I leave?" He shifted to face her, setting his bottle on the counter. "When we started this, I never …" He tipped his forehead against hers. "You're unexpected, Zoe. This sucks, because on Saturday I'm back in Philly for two weeks, and then who knows where I'll be?"

Savannah slid a hand around to caress the back of his neck. "You didn't want a relationship."

"Neither did you."

"But it's become one, despite our agreement." She studied him, a quiver running down her spine at the intense way he stared back at her.

"I'm breaking my own rules," he whispered. "I like you, and now I wish we lived closer."

"Brandon, there's something I need to—"

"Later," he murmured. "Can we have tonight? We can face reality tomorrow." Brandon tipped her chin to capture her lips, tangling a hand into her hair and drawing her closer.

Savannah closed her eyes, enjoying his sweet kisses as she stroked the back of his neck, causing a noticeable shiver from Brandon.

"I love when you do that." His warm breath tickled her as he planted soft kisses on her neck before returning to her mouth.

One more night. That's all we have. Then he'll be gone.

Savannah slid her fingers under the back of his shirt, tugging it upward. Her heart pounded as he tucked his hands beneath her, lifting and cradling her against him as he carried her to the bedroom.

Brandon placed a tender kiss on her lips before he pressed his forehead against hers, drawing in a ragged breath. "I'm going to miss you, so much." He kissed her again as he brushed a stray strand of damp hair from her face.

"And I'll miss you." Savannah gazed into those soulful gray eyes as she stroked her fingers up and down the smooth skin of his bare back. "Brandon, there's still—"

"Surprise. I'm back from … ewww!"

Brandon's eyes widened and he froze for only a moment before he yanked the sheet over their naked bodies. "Piper. Don't you ever knock?"

"Oh. Crap. I …"

Savannah caught a flash of auburn hair, and her breath stuck in her throat as she ducked her head against Brandon, hiding her face.

"For fuck's sake." Brandon glared over his shoulder at the intruder.

"Sorry. Are you decent yet?"

"Get out of my bedroom."

"I'll be … out there … yeah … sorry." The bedroom door clicked shut.

Savannah pressed her face into the crook of Brandon's neck, struggling to breathe.

"You'd think my little sister would have learned some manners."

"Your sister?" Nausea rose.

"Well, stepsister. I never should have given her a key, but it's her first time being so far from home. She moved from Montana this fall to go to Harvard College." Brandon cupped her face, a wry grin forming on his lips. "Want to meet her?"

"She's seen enough of me." She clamped her teeth onto her bottom lip as she fought a bubble of hysterical laughter.

"Not as much as she saw of me." Brandon snorted. "I'll get rid of her." He pecked her lips before he rose and strolled into the bathroom.

Savannah bit her lip, drawing the sheet up to her chin. Should she run before this blew up?

Brandon reappeared and fished his jeans from the floor. "Are you okay?"

"Yeah, well …" She twirled a lock of her hair around her finger, tugging at it. "We should probably talk."

"Let me see what she wants first." He rolled his eyes. "I love her, but she's so immature. Eighteen is an adult, but not, if you know what I mean. She probably has a glass pressed up against the door, listening to every word." He ran his fingers through his hair before he stepped into the main room, pulling the door almost closed.

Savannah flopped back against the pillow and clenched her eyes shut, trying to distinguish individual words out of the low conversation happening in the living room. She contemplated how she would tell Brandon she was one of those immature eighteen-year-olds, and that she'd already met his sister.

She frowned. Silence had fallen in the other room.

The bedroom door flew open.

"Unbelievable." Piper stood only a few feet from the bed, hands on her hips. She jutted out her chin. "How could you?"

Savannah clung to the sheet as she sat.

"Imagine my surprise when I realized the little tramp with her legs wrapped around my brother is Zoe King?" Piper flung the ID across the room. "Except that's not who you are, is it, Savannah?"

"I didn't know—"

"Shut up, slutty bitch."

"What in the hell are you doing?" Brandon appeared behind her. "Leave you alone for a second, and you barge into my room and attack my girlfriend?" He frowned. "Who's Savannah?"

"That's Savannah." Piper pointed. "Great, Brandon. You don't even know her damn name, yet she's your girlfriend?" She held up Vanna's purse. "I saw your fancy ass Kate Spade and other designer crap and had to find out if it were true. Some friend you are, screwing my brother." She hurled the small bag at the bed, the contents spilling as it tumbled to the floor short of its mark.

"You know each other?" Brandon motioned between them. "You're not Zoe?" His gaze burned into Savannah.

"She's in my study group and most of my classes. Her real name is Savannah. That ID is fake, and she's a big fat liar. I'm out of here." Piper spun and stomped from the room. Moments later the apartment door slammed.

Savannah bowed her head as the tears dripped down her cheeks. She couldn't bear to look at him.

"Is that true? You've been lying the entire time? Why would you do that?"

"I wanted to tell you, but—"

"Save it." He folded his arms across his chest. "How old are you?"

"Eighteen. But everything else I told you is true."

"I'm a dead man." He sank onto the end of the bed with his back toward her and hung his head. "You should go."

"I'm sorry. I didn't mean for it to go this far. That's what I've been trying to tell you. I never meant for—"

"Get out, Zoe, or Savannah, or whatever the hell your name is," he said in a low voice. "Just leave. I'll be gone by the weekend and this can be over. I'm such an idiot." He pushed off the bed and stalked from the room.

Savannah wrapped the sheet around herself, sniffling as she donned her clothing and patted down the carpet for the contents of her purse. She kept her head down as she crept from the bedroom.

Brandon stood by the window, staring through the glass. A bottle hung from his fingers, but he didn't even glance her way.

Savannah slid on her coat and boots. "I'm sorry. I would give anything to take it back."

He scoffed, keeping his gazed focused outside. "Just get out."

She took a step toward him. "Brandon, I—"

"Get. The fuck. Out," he said in a firm but flat tone.

"Take care of yourself, Brandon. I really am sorry." She slunk out the door, swiping at her tears as it clicked shut behind her.

⤙

Savannah peered at her phone, which had remained eerily silent all morning, before she slid into a seat opposite Rochelle.

"Where's Piper?" Rochelle glanced over her shoulder. "She's supposed to be here. Damn, this study group is falling apart. First Gray the jackass and now she's MIA. Is she back from Montana?"

"Oh, yeah, she's back." Savannah looked around at the empty seats. "Where are the guys?"

"Grabbing pizza. What's up with you? You look like hell."

"I doubt Piper's coming. She's no longer speaking to me."

"Why? What did you ever do to her?"

"Brandon." Savannah leaned forward. "Turns out he's the infamous stepbrother."

"What?" Rochelle's eyes widened. "Your Brandon? The one you've been …" She pressed her palm over her mouth.

"He's not mine anymore." Savannah dropped her head onto her forearms. "He's pissed and won't talk to me or allow me to explain."

"How did she find out?"

"She walked in on us." Savannah peeked at her friend.

"While you two were …" Rochelle slapped a hand over her face and peered through her fingers.

"Yup. She freaked out and busted me." Savannah sighed.

"Wow, that's … I'm sorry." Rochelle drummed her fingers on the table. "It's an honest mistake on your part, though. Piper raved about him, but she's never shown us pictures. He doesn't even have the same last name."

"Nope, and she never mentioned he worked in Boston."

"She'll get over it."

"I won't. She called me a slutty bitch." Savannah dipped her head. "Maybe I am. I went home with him without a second thought."

"That takes two, so stop it. Don't you dare doubt yourself. Did she give him some nasty label?"

"I've no idea. She stormed out, and he told me to get the hell out of his apartment." She lifted her hand in an unconscious attempt to soothe herself with her pendant. She pressed a hand to her chest, pain blossoming in her heart. "I lost my necklace at Brandon's apartment. I'll never get it back."

"Can you replace it?"

She shook her head. "It was the first birthday present Aiden ever gave me. Now it's gone."

"Awww, honey. Ask Brandon to return it."

"How? He'll never speak to me again."

"You broke the rules of engagement." Rochelle contemplated her. "You fell in love."

"Doesn't matter. He went back to Philly."

"So we both struck out. At least you had more fun than I did. Dylan the creep keeps texting me late at night for a booty call."

"Sorry, Ro." Savannah rolled her eyes. "Asshole. Well, I guess it's back to my original plan. Men are out. Time to concentrate on classes. The way things are going, I might take Uncle Tom up on his offer and transfer to Yale."

"Take me with you."

"Deal." Savannah offered her friend a faint smile.

Familiar voices carried from the living room.

Savannah peeked in. "Uncle Ryan. What are you doing here?"

"I'm in town for business, and your dad is allowing me to crash here."

"The prodigal daughter returns. I thought you had made a permanent move to the dorms." Aiden pulled her in for a hug.

Savannah avoided her uncle's gaze.

"What the hell?" Her dad caught hold of her arm, pushing up her sleeve. "Who did this?"

"Nobody." She tugged free from his grasp. "It's nothing."

"Uh-uh, Savannah. You've barely been home for days, and when you show up, you have bruises like that?" He caught her other hand, sliding up the sleeve. "Who, Savannah?"

She dropped her chin to her chest.

Ryan cleared his throat. "I might know."

She lifted her head, throwing a panicked look at Ryan.

"Oh?" Aiden narrowed his eyes. "One of you better start talking."

Savannah widened her eyes, shaking her head furiously at Ryan.

"Sorry, darlin'. I can't keep it a secret when I see that." He motioned to her arms. "I thought she was out having harmless fun, Aiden. Remember last weekend when we went to the club? She was there with some dude, and I told her to evacuate before you showed up. I shouldn't have kept it from you."

"We'll have a talk about that later." He pointed a finger at his friend. "You know better, Ryan. Does this guy have a name?"

"Hmmmm." Ryan tilted his head. "Brian, Bryce? No. Brandon. About six feet tall, dark-brown hair, early twenties?"

"What's his last name?"

"I'm sorry." She hung her head. "You're angry."

"Hey." Aiden slid an arm around her shoulders. "I'm not mad at you. I'm concerned that you got hurt, and I need to know you're okay and that the creep who did this never gets another chance."

"He won't. I'm fine." She couldn't tell him about Gray, or Brandon, or any of it. Too many things were stacked against her. Aiden's disappointment in her misjudgment, both about Gray and attending the bar, topped the list. "Please don't make this into a big deal."

"Except that it is a big deal when someone abuses you." Aiden held her closer. "Did you fill out a report with the police?"

"No. And I'm not going to, so leave it alone." Savannah wiggled free, crossing her arms and setting her jaw. It would take determination, but she vowed not to let him find her out.

"It's not right, Savannah," Aiden said in a gentle voice. "This should be documented and reported, right away. Guys should never get away with abuse."

She shook her head.

Aiden sighed. "Will you at least go to the doctor? I won't push if you do that one thing. I don't have to be the one to take you. How about Emily? Would that be easier?"

Savannah peered at him, noting the sad expression and concern reflected in his eyes. This left her little choice but to give him at least that little peace of mind. She nodded. "Emily can take me."

"Thank you." He kissed her forehead, drawing her in for a hug. "I love you, Vanna. Nothing will ever change that."

CHAPTER 16

Tiffany

BOTH TIFFANY AND ISLA TURNED as the bell over the door tinkled.

"Mmm-mmm." Isla grinned as she took in the well-dressed man coming their way. "You gave that man up why?"

"Stop drooling, and because I'm an idiot," Tiffany said under her breath. "Go find something else to do." She waved her assistant away.

Aiden leaned in to kiss her cheek, and Tiffany couldn't help the genuine smile that spread across her features. So many mixed emotions flooded her at seeing him here in her gallery, this time under far different circumstances than the last.

"How was your visit with Gramma Grace?" she asked.

"Good, though I wish she'd move into something smaller. I'd love it if she sold the mausoleum."

Tiffany snickered as she pictured the massive mansion. "It's a lot of house for one person."

"I invited her to move to Boston, but not sure she'll take me up on that. She has her friends here, though it would be great for her to spend more time with the grandkids."

The conversation seemed so normal that the tension drained from her body, the fear lifting.

"You needed to talk?" Aiden raised a brow. "Here? Or did you want to go out?"

"My office? I made fresh coffee."

"Sounds good."

Tiffany led him to the small break room, preparing cups of the dark brew for each of them before they retired to her office with the door closed.

"How is Savannah?" Tiffany leaned back in her chair, cradling the red ceramic cup in both hands.

"She's," Aiden said, giving her a long look, "having some issues. Things seem level and good for a while, and then something inevitably sets her back."

"Will she be okay?"

"Don't worry, I'll take care of her."

"I trust that you will." Tiffany bowed her head. "I'm sorry if I've made things more difficult. I've stayed away."

"It's not you. This is stuff teenage girls go through." He sighed. "It's tough some days. She's growing up, and I try to give her freedom, but there are times when it's excruciating to watch her make mistakes and get hurt."

"What happened?"

"Mainly the wrong choices in boyfriends, but that's all I can say." Aiden shook his head. "I've worked hard to earn her trust."

Tiffany held up a hand. "You don't have to break confidences. Can I ask you something?"

"Sure."

"How is Emily with her?"

"Amazing." He contemplated her. "You don't like Emily and probably don't want to hear this, but they're close."

A small twinge hit. "It hurts that your wife has a close relationship with Savannah"—she lifted her chin and met his gaze—"but I'm grateful our daughter has a caring woman to talk to. Someone to listen and give her advice. I never had that growing up. So I do want to hear it. I want to know she has a family who loves her."

"She has everything we didn't. I'm making sure of that, Tiff."

Tiffany took in a long breath and released it. That simple statement made everything seem brighter. "Good." She cleared her throat and stared into her cup.

"Let's have it."

"What?" She looked up, startled.

"There's something huge brewing," he said. "A personal visit is for more than idle chit-chat."

Tiffany closed her eyes. This man read her so well it was frightening. "David pulled my financing." The words tumbled from her mouth. "The bank won't help me."

"I'm not surprised." He leaned back in his chair and took a leisurely sip of his coffee. "Why are you?"

She peered across the desk. "You knew he'd helped with the gallery?"

"It had to be either him or Harrison, but after you dumped Harrison ..." Aiden shrugged. "So. How much do you need to keep the gallery in operation?"

"That obvious, am I?" Her smile was a touch rueful.

"It's not rocket science. How many independently wealthy exes do you have who you still talk to?"

She rubbed her temple with her fingertips. "It's a big ask. It's not like we're best of friends."

"And yet, we're hardly strangers, are we?" He lifted one brow.

Tiffany frowned. She'd been through so much *life* with this man who'd been her best friend, her lover, her husband, her greatest supporter, but at times, her worst enemy.

"I'll do what I can."

"You don't know how much I owe. Yet you're confident you can magic a massive pile of cash out of thin air?"

"Thin air?" He smirked and shook his head before his expression grew serious. "What's the damage?"

Confusion clouded her mind as she stared into his eyes. "Why would you help me?"

His brows went up. "Interesting question, considering the circumstances, but okay. Let's play." His mouth set into a firm line. "How about because the man has lorded his power over you your entire life? You've gathered enough courage to stand up to him, so he's decided to take you down."

"Is that what you think?"

"Am I wrong?"

"How could you know?"

"David Baxter is a spoiled man-child, and he can't stand hearing the word *no*. That his own daughter would deny him anything makes him furious. His instinct is to punish you and put you in your place so you'll never challenge him again."

Tiffany closed her eyes and drew in a deep breath. "Wow. You nailed it. He demanded my mother stop the divorce proceedings. It almost worked."

"The art of manipulation one-oh-one. Our fathers took the same class. So. Are you planning to give David the satisfaction of taking it all away? Will you let him trample you? Or will you fight back?"

"By letting another man control of me?"

He scoffed. "You'd think considering how long you've known me, you'd know better. Whatever." He waved his hand. "Let that bastard steal your dreams just like he's taken every other damn thing that ever mattered."

Tears brimmed her eyes. "Then why?"

Aiden scrubbed a hand through his hair. "I have money from the sale of Hamilton Grayson. It's fitting to use my grandfather's ill-gotten gains to help you. That man owes you for what he did. Pretend it's compensation."

"What?" She froze. She'd known the firm had been sold, but it never occurred to her the proceeds had gone to Aiden. Tiffany's chest constricted as she realized what that meant.

Aiden's expression softened. "Let Thomas Hamilton make up for his part in all of this. It's sweet justice."

Tiffany considered this new information. "What about your wife?"

"My relationship with Emily isn't your concern."

"Except I don't want her to hate me any more than she does."

"Don't be a drama queen. We're all adults, so let's act like it." He sighed. "Look at it however you like, but let me do this for you."

"For me? Or for you?"

"Maybe it's both? I never did enough back then, but there wasn't much either of us *could* do. Two teenagers pitted against three grown men and their vicious pack of dogs while our mothers looked the other way and avoided involvement? Time for us to get over it and move on. You're not a helpless teenage girl now. Stand up and prove it."

"Thomas is rolling in his grave." Despite her sadness, she allowed a smile to appear.

"May he never rest in peace."

"It's an embarrassing amount of money."

"Show me, Tiff." He pointed at her desk. "There's a folder lurking all ready with numbers."

Tiffany retrieved the file from the side of her desk and slid it across, resting her fingertips on top.

Aiden tilted his chin, and she nodded, leaning back as he opened the file and scanned the documents.

His expression remained impassive as he ran a finger down the columns. "You put your business classes to good use. These figures are accurate?"

"I've been over them a million times and examined them from every angle." She gulped a mouthful of coffee. "I'll understand if you can't get involved."

He flipped the page. "You have some new artists lined up. Projections look decent. Your business is growing. And ... Stefan Cortes." His looked up. "Did you show this to your bank?"

"Yes." Her eyes widened. "You know who he is?"

"We've met at various charity functions over the years. His grandmother was a friend of Gramma Grace's."

Tiffany bit her tongue. She shouldn't be surprised that Aiden knew Stefan. They were both Chicago boys from the same social echelon.

"Savannah is a huge fan of his work."

"She is?"

"Mmm-hmm." He glanced at her before he flipped to the next page of paperwork. "Her natural talent for art reminds me of someone."

"What mediums?"

"Photography, painting, sketching, and writing are her preferences." He gave a soft laugh. "Her choice to study law came as a shock. I blame Tom for that. I thought I'd be sending her to art school, but I have no doubt she'll excel in anything she puts her mind to."

"She inherited that trait from you."

"There are days when I see you, and days when I see me. She is most definitely our daughter." He set the folder on the desk. "David's tied you up financially." Aiden ran his fingers through his hair. "From the legal agreement, it appears he has an interest in every asset you own."

"Stupid, right?" She bowed her head. "This is embarrassing."

"Tell me everything."

"He helps with expenses. I sink what little income we earn into the gallery. Reinvesting in the business, trying to build it. I've made some headway but it's a house of cards."

"Do you have a good accountant?"

"David's." She lifted her hands in a helpless gesture.

"You need to move your business to someone with no loyalties to David. I recommend the one Tom and I used for the Chicago law firm, but feel free to choose whoever you like."

"I trust you." This felt like a strange dream, the stress lifting as she savored the fact she didn't have to go through this alone. Finding this unexpected ally in her darkest hours seemed miraculous.

"And the bank you use. One David recommended or uses himself?"

She nodded.

"That explains why they didn't take your current contracts into consideration. Change banks. I don't trust David, and I refuse to deal with anyone who's an ally."

"Done. I don't owe them any loyalty."

"I'd like you to take your financials to the accountant and get his advice on the best way to set up your financing, and talk to your lawyer. But," he said and sighed, "let me guess. He's David's too, right?"

"Yup."

"Not anymore. How do you feel about working with Ben Landon?"

"Are you still in touch with him?" Tiffany frowned. "He won't want me as a client."

"What happened between us has nothing to do with Ben. You can trust him, and he won't gouge you with unnecessary legal fees. If you're not comfortable, we'll ask for a referral."

"I always liked Ben. He's perfect." She pictured the file of accounts payable hidden in her desk drawer. "How long will this take?"

"It could be up to a month, but it depends on what you decide. Why?"

"I have bills and no funds."

"How much?"

Tiffany scribbled on the pad of paper, added the numbers, and turned it.

"Are you okay to use my bank for your accounts?"

"Yes."

"I need to make some calls." He eyed the door.

Tiffany rose and closed the door as she left her office, joining Isla at the front counter.

"You've been in there a long time. How did it go?" Isla squinted at the office, and they both watched as Aiden talked on his phone, pacing and referencing the paperwork. "What is he doing?"

"Setting up appointments? Calling his contacts?" Tiffany closed her eyes, the swell of emotions rising and threatening to overwhelm her. "He didn't even flinch." She pressed a hand to her chest. "And he didn't make me feel stupid for trusting David."

Isla grinned. "We're staying open?"

"Don't celebrate yet, but we have a chance."

Twenty minutes later, Aiden emerged from the office carrying the thick folder containing her paperwork. "We have an appointment at the bank."

"Now?"

He nodded.

Tiffany hurried to her office to collect her coat and purse then followed Aiden onto the snowy street. "What's the rush?"

"My account manager agreed to meet right away to set up your business banking and an interim credit line for your immediate expenses, which I'll guarantee. If I miss my flight home, Emily will kill me."

"She wants you as far away from me as possible?"

"No. We have an appointment tomorrow morning."

"Must be important."

"It is." They walked for a few paces in silence. "You're going to hear this sooner or later. It's for an ultrasound."

Tiffany faltered, but then lengthened her strides to catch up. "You're having another baby?"

"Emily is due in June."

"Wow. Congratulations."

"Thanks." Aiden opened the heavy glass door and ushered her into the lobby.

Tiffany started toward the reception desk, but Aiden caught her arm and steered her toward the elevators.

"She's upstairs." He pushed the button.

"She?" Tiffany lifted a brow.

Aiden gave her a look as the elevator rose toward the fortieth floor.

The doors slid open, revealing a luxurious reception area.

"Private client services? Only you, Aiden."

"Yeah, they opened an entire department, just for me," he said under his breath as he smirked.

A stunning dark-haired woman approached and grasped Aiden's hand. "Aiden. Nice to see you. And you must be Tiffany. I'm Gia Bianchi, and I'll be your account manager. Let's head into the conference room and get started."

Four hours later, Tiffany let herself into her apartment. The afternoon had been a whirlwind of signatures at the bank to open accounts and put a credit line in place, and then Aiden left for the airport.

Tiffany opted for a long walk along the lakeshore to clear her mind. The thoughts jumbled together. Her worries about the gallery were set to rest, but the baby news sent her spinning.

Tiffany flopped onto the bed and pressed a hand to her belly, a sense of longing enveloping her. Not that she wasn't happy for him, but all of the things she didn't have, but thought she would have at this point in her life, hit her. No husband. No babies. Her family consisted of a strained relationship with her mother, an ex-husband she'd begged to bail out her failing business, and a daughter who wouldn't give her a second glance.

She dialed the number by heart.

"How are you?" Alex's soft voice filtered down the line.

"Better than I was." Tiffany couldn't hold back the sniffle.

"Are you crying? What's the matter?"

"I asked Aiden for help to fund my gallery. There's nobody else."

"And?"

"He saved my ass, but don't say anything, please?"

"About what?"

"I'm so happy for him, but Emily's pregnant."

"He told you."

"It's stupid, but I've missed so much. I want to have another baby, but even if I had a man in my life, what kind of mother would I be? I haven't even been there for my daughter and even thinking it makes me feel disloyal to her."

"It's not disloyal to love another child. Loving our new baby won't change how I feel about Daniel. I have room in my heart for both. And if you believe that Aiden loves Savannah any less because he has Kellan and a new baby on the way, then you're delusional. He's amazing with his kids."

"I've never doubted his parenting skills." Tiffany laughed through her tears. "Remember when I babysat Daniel, and I melted down because he wouldn't stop crying? Aiden walked in and handled it like it was second nature."

"That was priceless." Alex giggled. "You looked so damn guilty when we found the thermometer. But hey, don't worry about it. You should have seen how awkward Joel and I were at first with Daniel, but over time it got much easier."

"You were?"

"Most parents go through it. Aiden is the exception, not the rule, sweetie. You're talking about a doctor trained in emergency medicine. A crying baby is nothing compared to what he encounters at work. And I happen to know he did more than one rotation in pediatrics during his residency."

"I bet Emily is super mommy." She slid from the bed and wandered to stare out the window.

"She has her moments, but she's pretty damn great with kids."

"Good thing since she has such influence over my daughter."

"Is that what this little cry fest is about?" Alex's tone softened. "Emily is good to our Vanna."

"But how will Emily react when she finds out her husband is helping me?"

Silence hung on the line.

"Alex?"

"She already knows."

"How? Aiden only left like …" Tiffany closed her eyes and massaged her temple with her fingertips. "Damn it. He phoned her from my office."

"Yeah, I was with her when he phoned."

"So she knows what an idiot I am. And so does everybody else."

"She doesn't think that, but be fair. It's logical for Aiden to talk to his wife before arranging financing for his ex-wife."

"Have you ever met his account manager?"

"Nope, can't say that I have. Perhaps Joel has, but we don't generally run in those elite banking circles. Why? What about him?"

"Her. And not just any *her*. Her name is Gia, and she made me want to cram a bag over my head. Trust Aiden to find himself a ridiculously sexy Italian woman to handle his banking."

"A bag?" Alex laughed out loud. "Somehow I doubt she has much on you. You're fairly gorgeous yourself, sweetie. And why does this bother you?"

Tiffany's breath caught in her chest. *Why, indeed?* "No reason," she said, even as the name *Angelica* flitted through her mind. Gia sexy-Italian-banker Bianchi forced her to picture the stunning woman who'd become Aiden's girlfriend soon after their marriage had collapsed.

She could never admit it to Alex, though. Heat infused her cheeks as she remembered how she had once cyber-stalked Angelica Giannelli, which had turned into a trip to New York. Her initial plan had been to confront Angelica, to demand she back off, but envy had gripped Tiffany's soul the moment she set eyes on the exotic beauty.

Tiffany had lost her nerve, the sight of the confident woman striding down the street in Manhattan making her doubt everything she imagined she knew about her husband. "It's typical. He surrounds himself with beautiful women."

She clenched her eyes shut, blocking the image of the curvaceous Angelica with her olive skin and lustrous dark hair, impeccably dressed for the office in form-fitting skirt and drop-dead-sexy Louboutin stilettos. Everything about the thirty-something professional woman in her power-suit made Tiffany long to run, to crawl into the darkest corner and hide forever.

"They surround him, but maybe that's semantics." Alex snickered before her voice became serious. "Did he flirt with said sexy banker?"

"No."

"There you go. He's devoted to his wife, so the lovely Italian bombshell will have to look elsewhere."

Tiffany sighed and vowed to quit torturing herself with past failures.

⁓≼

The next afternoon, she let herself into the gallery. She had a lot to think about, but plans were forming in her mind on how to move forward. She'd spent most of the morning with the accountant, who'd asked her a million questions and taken copies of her paperwork. He'd made several suggestions and promised to have some numbers back to her soon.

Then she'd stopped to see Ben, her new lawyer.

"Stefan." She gazed up at the man who appeared before her. "I'm sorry. Did we have a meeting today?"

"No. I happened to be in the neighborhood and brought you a chai, but it's getting cold. You're usually in earlier."

"I had a business meeting this morning, so I'm running behind." She glanced over at Isla, who's mouth twitched into a smile as she looked away. "You know what? I have a couple quick things to take care of, and then maybe I could buy you a coffee?"

"Sounds great. I'll hang out while you take care of business."

"I won't be long." Beckoning to Isla, she headed to her office and shut the door behind them.

"Wow, you're going out with him? Good for you." Isla grinned.

"Don't get excited. Coffee is not a date, and I asked him." Tiffany glanced through the glass, admiring Stefan's long, lean form as he propped himself against the front desk.

"Someone better tell him." Isla smirked. "He comes in several times a week with convenient excuses for showing up, and you should see the way he looks at you when your back is turned."

"Do you think he's interested"—Tiffany squinted at Isla—"romantically?"

"It's not a ridiculous notion. You're a beautiful, intelligent, and personable woman who has a lot to offer any man. Don't you think it's time to find someone to share your life with?"

"I've tried. I'm not sure I'm ready to begin again."

"Pffft." She waved a hand. "With who? That idiot Harrison? Stefan is a much better option."

Tiffany bowed her head. "I messed up with Aiden."

"Ten years ago. You aren't that girl anymore. If Stefan asks you out, you should accept. I kid about how hot he is, but he seems a sweet and caring man. Give him a chance. It's only one date, Tiffany."

"He hasn't asked me out."

"Not yet. Give it time."

CHAPTER 17

Savannah

SAVANNAH GLANCED AROUND THE WAITING room. She shuddered as she thought about her last visit to this office. The day she fully understood where Aiden's concern stemmed from. The harsh reality of what he'd seen in his work as a doctor in the ER of a major city.

Her doctor had asked invasive questions, wanting to know every single detail of what had happened. Savannah couldn't stand the thought of what not only Emily and Aiden, but her Uncle Ryan, assumed.

She had to shake it off. Today would be a happy day, and she'd skipped class to come here.

"Vanna." Her dad stood and pulled her in for a hug. "You made it." He kissed her cheek.

"I wouldn't miss it. Where's Emily?"

"They took her to do some blood work, pee in a cup, the usual. I told her I'd wait for you. Ready?"

"Are we finding out?"

"Yes." He grinned. "Emily gave in this round, because last time—"

"Yeah, you knew and she didn't. Sneaky."

"Danger of being a doctor. You see things." He slung an arm around her shoulders. "Let's go in."

She followed him down the short hallway, waiting while he peeked into the room to make sure they were ready.

"Just in time." Emily held out her hand as the doctor adjusted her gown. "Come see."

Savannah stood at the head of the bed on one side, while Aiden situated himself on the other. She watched as the doctor squirted a small puddle of gel onto Emily's belly and moved the wand.

After a couple of minutes, the doctor nodded. "Looks fantastic. I'll turn the screen for you."

Vanna's eyes widened as the baby came into view and the whooshing sound of the baby's heartbeat filled the room. Even though she'd been allowed to come for Kellan's ultrasound too, she still found it fascinating.

"Ready to find out?"

Emily nodded, tears glistening in her eyes as she looked up at Aiden, then back to the screen.

"Looks like you'll be welcoming a daughter."

"A baby sister." Vanna clapped her hands.

Aiden leaned in to kiss Emily. "A beautiful, healthy baby girl."

"You can pick up the video and pictures at the front desk. Congratulations, and we will see you in two weeks." The doctor smiled and left the room.

"How about lunch?" Aiden glanced at his watch. "No point in rushing back to class when you've missed half of it."

"Sure. I'll wait outside so Emily can get dressed."

"I'll come with you and book the next appointment." Aiden gave his wife another kiss.

Savannah found an empty chair.

Aiden joined her a couple of minutes later. "You okay?"

"Yeah." She nodded. "Dad? I know you've been worried about me, but don't be, okay? What happened isn't as bad as what you must be imagining." She stared at her hands.

"What do you think I'm imagining?" He looped an arm around her shoulders.

"It was only a few bruises. The guy didn't ..." The words caught in her throat. "He grabbed me, but nothing else happened."

"I'm sorry you were hurt." Aiden pressed a kiss to her temple. "I worry you blame yourself or feel guilty about something. It's not your fault that some idiot guy can't control himself. And you can tell me anything. I love you, Savannah. Nothing could change that."

"I know, Daddy." She leaned against his shoulder, taking comfort in his quiet acceptance. "I love you too."

⌒≼

After lunch, Savannah slid into a seat next to Rochelle in the lecture hall. "Hi." She dropped her bag onto the floor.

"Hey, Vanna." Rochelle smiled.

Piper threw a disgruntled look Savannah's way and angled her body toward the lectern.

Savannah swallowed the painful lump in her throat. It hurt to lose her friend and endure the judgment that had come down on her after the fiasco with Brandon. She forced herself to focus on the professor during the lecture, but she also mused on the choices she now had to make.

At the end of the two hours, she dug into her bag to retrieve the stack of papers and handed them to Rochelle. "I did my part of the assignment. Can you give the copies to everyone in the group? I won't be coming today."

"Why not? We have a lot to do, and you missed the entire morning."

"I can't." She rolled her eyes toward Piper who had retreated several feet away to pack her bag. "I should drop out of the group. It won't work with everything that's happened. Tell everyone I'm sorry." Savannah zipped up her bag and headed for the exit. Once outside, she dabbed at her eyes.

"Vanna." Jackson hurried up behind her. "Where are you running off to?"

"I don't know." She shrugged. "It's been a rough couple of weeks, and I can't sit through another study session where Piper pretends I don't exist. One of us has to leave the group. I committed the offense, so it should be me."

"That girl needs to get over the fact that her stepbrother isn't an angel." Jackson snorted. "She's being a damn drama queen. You two need to get past this. Come on." He grabbed her hand and dragged her along. "You are not quitting our group because of something so ridiculous."

They arrived at the table where they'd planned to study, finding Piper flipping through her notes and munching on a ham and cheese sandwich.

"I'll keep Pete and Rochelle out of the way for a couple of minutes while you two sort out your crap."

Savannah puffed out a burst of air, and threw a dark look his way before she sat across from Piper. "We need to talk."

"Why? You knew how I felt, and you did it anyway. How could you?" Piper glowered. "You were all *don't get all gushy* and then you do it. With my brother. Wow, is all I can say."

"Except I didn't know that my Brandon was in fact your stepbrother Brandon. You've never shown me a picture, and you didn't tell us his last name. And why keep it a secret that he'd come to Boston? I didn't know he lived here."

"Because of girls like you."

Savannah's stomach rolled. "What's that supposed to mean?"

"You lied to him about your name." Piper crossed her arms. "And you kept it from me. You sure didn't share you were seeing someone."

"Excuse me for using the ID you gave me. I didn't mean to lie about my name, but the bouncer made me show my ID, and then what was I supposed to say?" Savannah threw her hands in the air. "Hey, guy I just met? I'm in a club using a fake ID and drinking illegally. You don't mind, right?"

"Yet that didn't stop you. How long were you seeing him?"

"A week. For the record, I planned to tell him—"

"Right, sure you did. After you screwed him for an entire week. You used him."

"You know nothing. You don't know what we talked about, or what happened between us. Do you want to know, Piper? We agreed to spend the week having fun, with no strings attached. Do you even know what that means?"

"No. I'm not a slut." Piper slammed her book closed. "That's what kind of girl you are, Savannah. You get every guy you want, and then you dump them just as fast. You had your fun with Justin over the summer, but he wasn't good enough. Nope. So you moved on to Gray, who was next on the dumped list. And then you picked up Brandon. In a week, you'll be over him." She cast a glance to where Rochelle, Pete, and Jackson were standing. "You're already reeling in the next sucker."

"That's what you think of me?" Tears rushed to Savannah's eyes. "You know what? Forget it. Go ahead and judge. Your precious stepbrother is back in Philly and safe from the likes of me." She grabbed her bag and hurried across the campus, away from the group she knew had been observing from across the square.

"Vanna." Jackson caught up with her. "What in the hell was that about?"

Savannah ducked her head, hiding her tears. "Just go back and study. I'm out." A sob tore from her chest.

"Hey." Jackson pulled her to a halt and wrapped her into an embrace. "Don't worry about Piper. You made a mistake. You've paid for it. Quit beating yourself up. And you know what? If you're out? I'm out too. This group involves too much drama."

Savannah burst into tears and buried her face against his chest.

"Shh. Don't worry, hon. It'll all work out."

"Will it? I finally meet a guy I really like, and now it's so messed up. Piper thinks I entrapped him or something. I guess it takes times like these to see who your true friends are. But I can't ask you to leave the group."

"You didn't. I decided to leave all on my own. Why don't we get a cold drink, and then we can get through this homework? Deal?"

"Thanks, Jackson. You've been a good friend."

⌁

The arrival of Saturday filled her with relief. She spent most of the day with Emily, helping her sort through Kellan's clothing to pick out the items he'd outgrown, while Aiden took Kellan to play at Tom and Jenna's.

Emily held up a pair of Kellan's overalls. "I'm so excited we're having a girl. Boys clothes can be cute, but dressing a little girl …"

Vanna grinned. "I can't wait to go shopping. And we get to decorate the baby's room."

"Hmmm." Emily gazed around. "We should move Kellan. The room next door is bigger, and once the baby is ready for her own space, it would be nice if she were closer to us."

"Ohhhh. You could repaint. This one could be a jungle theme or something elegant with flowers."

"I'll talk to Aiden, and see if we can book our painter. There are so many things we could do."

They spent the next hour packing clothes and discussing ideas, each of them getting more excited.

Savannah's phoned vibrated. "Oh, I should check that. It's probably Justin or Leanne."

"Go ahead, honey." Emily smiled. "We're about done, and Aiden is on his way home."

Vanna frowned at the text.

I found something you'll want back.

Savannah glanced over her shoulder before stepping into the hallway and tapping the call button. "It's me," she said in a low voice. "Please tell me you found my necklace."

"I can tell it's valuable. Those diamonds look real."

"I'll pay the shipping."

"No need." His heavy sigh came down the line. "I'm in Boston, but I don't have much free time. Could you pick it up?"

"Yes." Relief streaked through her at the thought of her pendant being returned, but sadness overtook her at the same time. She'd ruined something that might have been great. "When and where?"

"Could we meet at the coffee shop in an hour? You know the one?"

Our coffee shop. "I'll be there."

⤝

Savannah hurried down the street and stepped into the coffee shop, searching the lunch time crowd for his face.

"Hey."

She turned and met the gaze of his serious gray eyes. "How are you?"

He shrugged and stood with his head down, hands shoved into his pockets. "Let's not do this, Z—" He sighed. "Savannah. I don't want to talk. I just wanted to return this." He suspended her necklace from two fingers.

Savannah stared at it, reluctant to take it. The moment she did he'd be gone. "I know you'll never forgive me, but I'm sorry that I—"

"Don't. Please." Brandon extended his hand. "Take it. Then we're done."

Savannah nodded as she caught movement and the sight of familiar faces through the front window. She stepped to the side, using Brandon as a shield as Aiden and Emily walked through the door and headed for the front counter.

Brandon frowned and glanced over his shoulder, lifting his hand in a wave.

Savannah's mouth dried and she bowed her head, hoping that Brandon hadn't waved at her dad and Emily.

"Brandon. Did you get settled—" Aiden's gaze fell on Savannah, and then on the necklace that dangled from Brandon's fingers. "What's going on here? Why does he have …?"

"You know each other?" Brandon looked between the two.

"This"—Aiden narrowed his eyes—"is *the* Brandon?" A dark look spread across her dad's face.

"The—"

Aiden wrapped his fingers around Brandon's throat as he slammed the young man against wall.

Brandon's eyes widened and he stared at Aiden. "What …?"

"You're finished. You think you can get away with abusing women? I should—"

"Aiden." Emily grabbed Aiden's arm as he raised his clenched fist. She wiggled in between the two men, planting a flattened palms on each of their chests. "Stop."

Aiden released Brandon and stepped back, oblivious to the wide-eyed patrons around them. He inhaled a ragged breath, his eyes still blazing. "Don't think this is over. You'll pay for what you did."

Brandon seemed frozen in place, his eyes still wide and his mouth hanging half-open as he rubbed his throat.

"Aiden." Savannah brushed at her tears. "It wasn't him."

"What?" Aiden glowered at Brandon before looking her way.

Savannah's cheeks flamed. "Brandon didn't do it."

"Let's take this outside." Emily gave Aiden a firm push toward the door. "You too, Brandon." She pointed to the exit before wrapping an arm around Savannah's shoulders, guiding her toward the exit. "Come on, honey."

Savannah gulped in the fresh air, keeping her head down to hide her burning cheeks.

Aiden planted his feet, crossed his arms, and glared at Brandon who kept shooting looks between Savannah and Aiden.

"Stop it." Emily frowned at Aiden. "There is more going on here, and we should talk it out. Obviously not here, if we go back inside they'll call the police."

"Good." Aiden curled his lip.

"Hey. I don't know what you think I did, but I didn't hurt Savannah. I have two younger sisters, so I understand being a protective brother."

"She's not my sister." Aiden's mouth set into a grim line. "Savannah's my daughter. When someone hurts her, you can be damn sure they won't do it again."

Brandon tipped his head back. "Shit. Your daughter?" He drew in a long breath and squinted at Savannah. "I had no idea, but I promise you, I'd never do that to her."

"Dad." Savannah put a hand on his arm. "Brandon saved me. He saw what was happening and it ended with him punching the guy in the face. You can't be mad at him."

"No shit." A smile twitched at the corner of Aiden's lips. "You punched him?"

Brandon nodded.

"I'm sorry for assuming the worst. Sounds like I owe you a drink." Aiden held out his hand. "Forgive me for overreacting."

Brandon nodded and shook his hand. "I'd have reacted the same way, Dr. Hamilton. I wish I'd hit the guy harder."

"Aiden when we're not at work. But there's more to this. Why do you have Vanna's necklace?"

Brandon's smile disappeared as he peered at Vanna from the corner of his eye.

A fresh rush of heat moved up Savannah's neck and into her face.

"Yeah. Never mind." Aiden shared a look with Emily. "We have a huge problem."

Emily shuffled her feet and rubbed her belly. "Can we find a place to sit and discuss this?"

"Sorry, sweetie. You've probably had enough for today." He tucked an arm around his wife. "We live a couple of blocks away. Why don't you come over, and we'll figure this out?"

⌒≺

Savannah watched Brandon as the elevator rose and opened into the marble tiled foyer. She didn't miss the way the frown passed across his features as he gazed around. She related to what he must be feeling as she'd had a similar reaction the first time she'd been to Aiden's apartment in Chicago.

"This is a nice place," Brandon said.

"Thanks." Emily kissed Aiden's cheek. "I need to lie down." She disappeared down the hallway toward their bedroom.

Vanna wished she could disappear, but no such luck.

"I'll be right back." Aiden rubbed Savannah's back. "Maybe Brandon would like a drink. Can you pour one for me?"

"Sure." She retrieved both a bottle of beer and a can of soda from the fridge and held them up. "Sorry, Brandon. This is awkward."

He accepted the bottle and cracked it open before tipping it back and taking a long swig. "Not as awkward as it'll be working with him now he knows I had sex with his teenage daughter. I'm surprised he didn't hit me anyway."

"He doesn't know much aside from what he's surmised, so don't volunteer anything. He's clever and has ways of getting you to confess things you never wanted him to know." Savannah uncapped a beer for Aiden and opened her soda. She leaned back against the counter. "The less you say about us the better."

"I learned that lesson early. I worked a rotation with Aiden a few months back. Though, I've now seen a new side of him. Dr. Anderson has guts. I can't believe that tiny woman stepped in the middle."

Savannah eyed him. "Aiden doesn't have much tolerance for violence against women. And Emily"—she couldn't hide the smile—"is fierce, but she's not stupid. That move guaranteed Aiden would back down. My dad would have hit you, but he'd never hurt Emily."

"She showed confidence and took a risk. I thought he'd lost it."

"It wasn't as big of a risk as you think." Savannah shrugged. "But you can thank her later."

"He seems too young to have an eighteen-year-old daughter."

Savannah sighed, too tired to explain her family dynamics. "You don't want to hear excuses, but I'm truly sorry, Brandon. That entire thing with the ID got out of control, but I promise, that's not who I am."

"So why do it? Couldn't you tell when things changed between us?"

"We'd agreed to keep it light, and then it wasn't, but I didn't want to morph into one of those needy clingy girls you despise. And then you said girls my age were too immature. And then, when I tried, you said what I needed to tell you could wait. And then your sister showed up."

"Yeah, Piper's been impossible the last couple of weeks. She's barely spoken to me."

"At least she didn't call you a shameless slut," Savannah muttered as she turned away.

"Did she say that to you?" Brandon blew out a slow breath. "I'm sorry, Savannah. She had no right. I'll talk to her."

"Don't bother. She expressed her opinion, and it's not like you and I have any hope of getting back together. I'm too young, right? Too immature? Just some girl you picked up and had fun with for a week?"

"This is fucking ridiculous." Brandon scrubbed a hand through his hair. "I liked that girl I spent the week with, but there's no way it'll work. It's too complicated given my work situation, and yup, you're too young. Besides, your dad might take another shot. He's a scary dude when he's angry."

"Maybe, but he doesn't get angry for no reason. He thought you physically abused me."

"Exactly my point. If he caught me messing around with his little girl, he might take exception to it. Anyway, it's not just that, and you know it."

She bit her lip as she registered the *little girl* reference. *What had I expected?* He'd judged her too immature, and she had to accept it without allowing her feelings to show. She lifted her chin as she dug her nails into the palm of her hand, willing the tears away.

They stared at each other, an expression she might have mistaken as regret flashing across his face.

Brandon looked away first and dug in his pocket. "I didn't get to return this." He motioned for her to turn.

Savannah swept her hair to the side, enjoying the warmth of his breath against her skin as he draped the chain around her neck. She closed her eyes at the gentle brush of his fingertips as he fastened the clasp. A sense of longing filled her, and she tilted her head, wishing for more of those sensuous kisses he'd once placed at the nape of her neck.

His audible inhale and slight pause made her wonder if he felt it too. "Damn." He stepped away as Aiden reappeared.

"Let's sit in the living room." Once they were seated, Aiden sighed. "I called Will Kavanagh as you are under my supervision right now."

Savannah threw a look at Brandon.

"I think we can both agree that given the circumstances, it would be inappropriate to keep you on my mentoring team or for me to give you any formal evaluations."

"So my rotation is done?" Brandon stared at the bottle in his hands. "Should I withdraw from residency in Boston?"

"That's up to you." Aiden looked at Savannah, then back to Brandon. "Dr. Kavanagh and I arranged a trade to move you to his team for your ER rotation. He's aware of the quality of your work performance to date and from your previous rotation. As far as your application," Aiden said, rubbing the back of his neck, "Will told me you accepted your match in Boston. This situation won't affect your standing at the hospital."

"I'm not out of the program?" Brandon drew in a deep breath as his head came up.

"Dr. Kavanagh and I both hope you decide to stay. You have a promising career ahead of you. This is your personal decision, and I understand it leaves you in an awkward spot."

"If Boston drops me, I'm screwed." Brandon dropped his head into his hands.

"That won't happen. Your position is confirmed."

"You can promise that?" Brandon raised a brow.

"Kavanagh is in agreement. Your residency offer is solid if you do well with this rotation and pass your final exams, exactly the same as in any other program. If this situation changes how you feel about the program, then we will do our best to assist you in finding a position worthy of your talents. We have connections at most of the major hospitals, and we'll hear if something opens up."

"I appreciate how you're handling this." Brandon gave a brief nod. "I'll give it some consideration and let you know."

"Good." Aiden looked between Savannah and Brandon. "Anything else I need to be aware of that would affect your employment?"

Brandon shook his head.

"Enough said, then. Time to put it behind us and move on." He rose. "Again, Brandon. I'm sorry about what happened."

Brandon shook his head. "No need to apologize. If she were my daughter, I'd be tempted to do the same."

"Dr. Kavanagh will meet with you tomorrow at ten to set up your new schedule. Vanna, could you walk Brandon out? I need to send Iona home."

Savannah followed Brandon as he headed for the front entrance. "So this is goodbye."

"It's for the best. It's not like …" He inhaled a long deep breath and let out an equally long sigh. "Never mind. Take care of yourself, and I'll tell Piper to lay off."

He disappeared behind the elevator door as it slid shut.

CHAPTER 18

Tiffany

A NURSE BECKONED FROM BEHIND ONE of the desks. "Can I help you ma'am?"

"I'm looking for Dr. Hamilton," Tiffany said. "Is he in?"

"Your name?"

"Tiffany." She straightened and lifted her chin. "Hamilton."

The nurse scanned her screen. "I'll track someone down to escort you. Wait there, please." She pointed.

Tiffany stepped aside and checked her messages, glancing up every now and then.

"Are you here to see Aiden?"

The deep melodic voice caused her to turn and she looked up into soulful gray eyes.

"Sorry. I thought you were …" The handsome dark-haired young man wearing a white lab coat took a step backward, though his gaze remained riveted on Tiffany.

"Brandon?" The nurse behind the desk waved. "Could you escort Ms. Hamilton to see Dr. Hamilton?"

A frown fleeted across his face as he motioned toward the sliding glass doors.

Tiffany caught the continuous glances coming from the young doctor. "I'm Tiffany Hamilton. Aiden's ex-wife."

"Brandon Reynolds." A smile twitched at his lips. "Lowly medical student."

"Where did you go to medical school?"

"University of Pennsylvania."

A little twinge hit as she registered this young man had attended the same school as Aiden.

Brandon led her into the unit and looked around. "It appears he's in with a patient, but you can wait in the family room." He tilted his head. "I'll tell him you're here."

Tiffany sat and watched the ebb and flow of staff and the occasional flurry of activity when new patients were wheeled through the sliding glass doors. Her eyes widened when Aiden appeared, deep in conversation with another man in blue scrubs.

He stripped off bloody gloves and tossed them into one of the medical waste containers, offering a small smile as he entered the waiting room. "What are you doing in Boston?" He rubbed at the back of his neck and blinked red-rimmed, tired eyes.

"There's an art show, so I thought I'd drop off a copy of the paperwork. Do you have time for a coffee? You look beat."

"It's been a long and busy shift. Let me wash up and grab my wallet." Aiden disappeared into one of the other rooms.

Tiffany glanced toward the desk, meeting the eyes of Emily.

The woman frowned as Aiden approached and leaned in close to converse with his wife.

Emily tipped up her chin and brushed her hand along Aiden's cheek as he rested a hand on her rounded belly. She nodded, and then followed his progress with narrowed eyes as he crossed the floor, her cool gaze meeting Tiffany's.

"Ready?" he asked.

"I am." She smiled faintly.

They exited through the main doors and strolled down the sidewalk.

"How are the plans going for the gallery?" Aiden asked.

"Great. I wanted to thank you again for helping with financing and the operating line. It's made all the difference in the world, believe me."

"You're welcome. Thomas owed you something, Tiff. This is the least I could do."

"How is your wife taking the whole thing?" She placed a hand on his arm.

"Em and I discussed it, albeit briefly over the phone before I took you to the bank that day."

"I bet she's less than thrilled."

"She accepts the situation for what it is. It's not affecting our lifestyle, and you could have asked for more when we divorced." He lifted a shoulder.

"I thought she'd be ready to murder me. That look she gave me was a touch on the cool side." Not that she expected Emily to dash across the office with open arms.

"Oh, so she should give a warm welcome to the woman who went to great lengths to sabotage our relationship? You think she missed the fact you hung all over me during the wedding? I sure the hell didn't. Why did you play those fucking head games?"

Tiffany opened her mouth to reply, but not a single word came out. *What could I say when he was so right?* She'd misbehaved and deserved to be called out.

"Why can't you accept that Emily and I are together?" Aiden blew out a long breath. "People wonder why it took me so long to get serious about another woman after our divorce," he muttered. "Maybe because of bullshit like this. It's fucking ridiculous. You two need to sort this crap out. You seem to think she hates you. Well, guess what? She thinks you hate her. What is it with women?"

Tiffany glared, a small snort escaping. This rapid escalation reminded her of those hot raging battles that used to erupt between them, fights that were followed by scorching, passionate make-up sex. That continuous roller coaster of emotions she longed for, yet dreaded. "Having a man in the middle. That's the problem. She's territorial when I'm anywhere near you."

"Kill me now," he muttered as he rolled his eyes. He halted abruptly and spun toward her. "So the whole thing at Jenna's wedding doesn't count? Just admit your actions didn't help. Not communicating with her about using my apartment, neglecting to tell her about booking a room, the digs about visiting Boston?"

The shameless flirting with and sexual innuendos about my ex-husband, who happened to be the man Emily had fallen in love with? Tiffany silently added.

"You two fight like a couple of damn alley cats."

"Well, she found a room, didn't she?" Tiffany bristled as she remembered the animosity at his apartment the night of the bachelorette party. "I saw her leave with Ryan the next morning."

"Don't even." He held up a hand. "Why you stirred things up with insinuations about Ryan, I'll never understand." He shot a dark look at her as she opened her mouth. "Don't even deny it. Everybody knows where Emily spent that night. Drop it."

"I'm sorry for involving Ryan." Tiffany peered at him, gauging his level on the pissed-off scale as fifteen out of ten. "It seemed like she took you for granted. It was a game. I hated the way she acted at breakfast that morning. And why did you two keep breaking up if you're so damn perfect for each other?"

"That's not up for discussion. What happened between Emily and me is a private matter between me and my wife. It's completely inappropriate for me to confide those details."

"Why?"

"Because you're my ex-wife?" He scoffed. "I don't share the intimate details of our relationship with her, Tiffany. Nor does she ask. She knows the basics, but there's a limit to what should be shared. Don't you agree?"

"Fair." Tiffany shuddered at the thought of Aiden discussing her many faults and transgressions with the almost-too-good-to-be-true Emily. The thought of him comparing what they had together to his intimate relations with the exotic dark-haired beauty turned her stomach.

When they reached the coffee shop, he held open the door and ushered her inside with a curt wave of his hand.

"I didn't mean to mess up your life," she whispered. "It's what I do where you're concerned. Even when we were teenagers, I got you in a pile of trouble. It was my fault I even got pregnant."

"It takes two to make a baby," he said, his tone softening. Aiden's anger seemed to have abated as quickly as it flashed to the surface. "Anyway, it's impossible to regret our choice to have her."

"Do you think she'll ever change her mind about seeing me?"

"I don't know. The usual?" At her nod, he ordered his coffee and her chai latte, handing money to the cashier before heading toward an empty table. "I'm sorry for whatever that was that just happened."

"Don't apologize. I did some rotten things I'm not proud of."

"I'm not as over it as I wished, but I'm trying to be." He lifted a shoulder. "It's hypocritical to say I forgive you, then lose it over those same damn things."

"I'm trying not to interfere, but I keep causing you pain. I'm truly sorry for that." She lifted her gaze to meet his. "We can't go back, but it doesn't mean it's easy for me to see you having the life we should have had with someone else. Expecting for it to be all repaired overnight is probably asking too much."

"Perhaps, but we should keep working at it for Savannah's sake. When the time is right, I'll talk to her again. I haven't forgotten my promise."

"Thank you, Aiden." She picked at the lid of her cup. "That young doctor, Brandon. He spoke to me before he knew who I was and kept staring at me like he wanted to say something." She shrugged. "I seemed to remind him of someone, and there was a connection for him when he heard my name."

Aiden frowned. "I'm surprised that Baxter means anything, but I'd bet the resemblance between you and Vanna threw him." He sipped his coffee.

Tiffany twirled a lock of hair. "Not Baxter. I introduced myself as Tiffany Hamilton. Legally, that's my name, and it causes fewer questions."

"Then he connected that he just met his ex-girlfriend's long-lost mother." He tilted his head, the slightest smirk appearing. "You're a Hamilton, huh?"

"Are you angry? I just …" She feared he'd take the name thing the wrong way. "It's a symbol, a way of cutting the cord from David. Childish, perhaps, but I want him to know he no longer has power over me, that my allegiance is no longer with him." Tiffany held her breath, unsure how he'd react to knowing she now felt allied with him after all this time.

The slight nod as his smile faded confirmed he truly understood. "Whatever makes it easier, Tiff. If you want to use Hamilton, then you have the right. When you went back to Baxter right away after the divorce," he said as he picked at the lid of his cup, "it felt like a dismissal of everything we'd had. It's strange to find out after all of this time that you never did the paperwork to change to Baxter."

"David hated hearing the name Hamilton, so he refused to acknowledge we'd ever been married. I went along with it, but somehow I couldn't let my name go." She cleared her throat. "How old is Brandon?"

"Twenty-three."

"You let our daughter date older men?" Tiffany's brows rose. "Why isn't she dating boys her own age?"

"She's eighteen." Aiden emitted a soft laugh. "I hate to break it to you, but she's a grown woman who's capable of making her own decisions."

"You need to say something to her. That's a five-year difference."

"I can offer advice, but I sure the hell can't force her to take it. We've had the talks about being safe and all that. What else can I do?" He gave her a look. "Besides, she could do far worse than Brandon Reynolds and he's not her first boyfriend. Think about what we were doing when we were eighteen. Or even better, answer this question. How old were you when we first had—"

"Urgh." She raised her palm toward him, then grimaced and covered her eyes. "I don't want to think about it."

"Neither do I, but it's something to consider the next time you decide to get on my case about how I parent our daughter."

"I bet you're doing a great job." She kept her expression neutral. "I have one more favor to ask. I included an envelope for Savannah in the package of paperwork. I don't expect you to give it to her now, but maybe someday soon?"

Aiden met her steady gaze. "When she's ready, Tiff. I promise she'll get it."

⁓≼

Her visit with Aiden had given her something to think about. Right from the comment about criticizing his parenting skills down to how she viewed Emily. He'd always done his best and never wavered from his commitment to his daughter, where she'd run like a confused juvenile, leaving him to deal with the fallout.

She wandered through the Boston Commons, halting when she spotted the familiar dark-haired woman heading her way.

"Emily." Tiffany fell into step beside her.

"What do you want?" Emily sent a cool look in her direction and increased her pace.

"To talk. Five minutes, please?" The tapping of her heels increased tempo as she matched steps with the other woman.

Emily halted abruptly. "Okay, talk."

"Can we walk around the park? Or do you want to sit?" Tiffany motioned to the conspicuous belly. "Congratulations, by the way. You must be excited."

"We are." Emily eyed her from under lowered lids.

"You're not planning to make this easy for me, are you?"

"You haven't made my life easy." Emily rested her hands over her rounded belly. "Why should I bother to accommodate you?"

"I've done many things I'm not proud of. I'm sorry for getting in the middle. I'm sorry for my attitude and actions toward you. In another life, I'm sure we'd be friends."

"Ha. Friends? You've got to be kidding. You've hated me from the moment you laid eyes on me, and you've spent an extraordinary amount of energy attempting to break us up."

"You didn't need my help," she muttered. "You took him down with that crap at the Vineyard and broke up with him when he moved to Boston. That had nothing to do with me. As for the wedding, you spent the night with him. The next morning, the breakfast conversation was nauseating. You acted like it was a damn one-night stand."

"Like I'd show you my true feelings. You got in your shots, tossing around innuendos." Emily's eyes blazed. "You were wearing enough ice to sink a ship, yet you insinuated with that not-so-subtle dig that you'd slept with my boyfriend. You flirted at Tom's bachelor party, kissed him, and if Ryan hadn't intervened, you would've invited yourself back to his suite. And you sent Aiden pictures of me with Ryan, suggesting I was messing around with one of his closest friends."

They glowered at each, neither blinking or even twitching.

After several tense moments, Tiffany bowed her head, not even sure why she rebelled against admitting the truth to this woman. She'd only finished reassuring Aiden that she'd let him get on with his life. Guilt washed over her. "You're right. I'd have taken Aiden back if he'd shown the slightest inclination. Don't you want to know why?" Tiffany peered at the other woman.

Emily folded her arms across her chest. She gave the slightest of shrugs, a mere motion of her shoulder.

"He's the only man who's ever treated me like I'm worthwhile. I fell in love with him so hard and fast, and he changed my life. You can't possibly understand. Everyone considered me lucky to be the Mayor's daughter, and assumed my life must be so wonderful." After dragging in a deep breath, she said, "It wasn't. My parents were too busy playing politics to pay me much attention. I didn't have anyone. Aiden got me, you know? He and I aren't all that different."

"You admit it." Emily's voice shook. "You would have taken him to bed on any number of occasions, even when he and I were together."

"I'm not proud my actions. It's humiliating to stand here in front of *oh-so-perfect-Emily* and admit my failings. But I promise I will never again interfere in what you have with Aiden." Tiffany lifted her chin. "That's not what's been happening these past weeks."

"What's been happening?" Emily asked softly.

"Closure." Tiffany met her gaze. "We've managed to forgive each other and get past all the awful, hurtful things that tore us apart. It's freed us both, and I can move on instead of clinging to what used to be. I wish nothing but the best for him. You've given him the happiness he deserves."

Emily tilted her head. "Why now?"

Tiffany emitted a soft laugh. "He told me that you and I needed to sort out our differences, though his words were far less polite. It has to be hard having two women playing tug-o-war over you. And we have been, Emily. Us being at odds makes everything harder than it needs to be. How about a ceasefire?"

"You're calling a truce?" Emily gave her an uncertain look, an edge of suspicion in her tone.

"Unbelievable, right?" Tiffany sighed. "It's for the best. I'm not even asking you to pretend you like me. I'm asking for your cooperation in making life easier for Aiden and Savannah."

"Well, when you put it that way …" A faint smile graced Emily's face. "Do you think we can be civil?"

"I bet we could." Tiffany bobbed her head. "I'll admit, part of my resentment isn't even about Aiden."

Emily nodded. "I get it, Tiffany, but know that I've never tried to cause issues between you and Vanna. I'd always understood you made the choice not to be involved, and by the time you changed your mind, the damage had been done."

"It's true. Aiden told me he'd seen her, and I freaked." Tiffany sneaked a look at Emily. "It's my fault, but it doesn't make it any easier to watch another woman build the relationship I wish I had with my daughter."

"I'm sure it isn't." Emily rubbed her belly. "Do you really feel grateful for my presence?"

"Aiden told you."

"I suspected he said it to make me feel better."

"I'm truly grateful. It hurts, but I'm happy she has two amazing role models who love her. I never had that. My mother and I are repairing our relationship, but it'll never be how it should have been. To know my daughter has a strong supportive woman to guide her through the worst of the teenage years is amazing. Thank you for being that loving woman who can take on a stepdaughter and treat her like their own."

"She's easy to love. I believe if you're going to be with someone, you accept the entire package."

"Even when it includes a crazy stalkerish ex-wife?"

"He's worth it, or I wouldn't be here." Emily's expression became serious. "I don't see you that way, Tiffany. Being sad doesn't make you crazy."

"I don't love that he's shared my issues." Tiffany hung her head. "Admitting how close to the edge I've been can't make you feel any better about my presence. You'll never want me near your kids."

Emily rested a hand on Tiffany's arm. "It doesn't scare me. Quite the opposite, in fact. Today I'm seeing a glimpse of the woman Aiden loved. I always wondered, but," Emily said, and she smiled, "I'm beginning to understand."

Tiffany frowned, not quite knowing how to respond, but a feeling of hope rose within her.

"There's a huge difference between psychosis and mental instability and someone who is struggling with depression induced by traumatic events. You lost a child. Forced adoption often creates the same emotions as the death of a child. Loss is loss."

Tiffany's eyes widened as Emily's words struck her soul. "How do you know? People always told me to get over it, that my grief wasn't real because my daughter was alive and well. But it hurt unbearably, and you understand," she whispered.

"How can I not?" Emily grasped Tiffany's hand. "I live it with him. I see it, every single day. The moments of pain, the grieving, and the struggle to accept what he lost when they took her away. Those doubts and regrets that haunt him, and the difficulty in building a connection with someone lost and then found. A father can feel that as much as a mother."

"He doesn't ..." *Show it.* Tiffany couldn't speak the words, because in that moment, she knew there had been something held back. An unvoiced pain lingered between them during their marriage. A subject Aiden had often broached, and Tiffany declined to discuss, refused to relive, or to even admit the torment lodged in her heart.

Grief and loss tears marriages apart.

Understanding came into focus with startling clarity. *We never had a chance.* The unresolved grief over the loss of their daughter had doomed them long before they reconnected at the age of eighteen. A love that should have carried them through many happy years eroded under the strain of everything left unsaid.

Emily tilted her head, studying her with an intense expression. "Are you okay?"

The first tear trickled down Tiffany's cheek, a small sob hiccuping from her chest. Her instinct was to run, to hide before she embarrassed herself in front of this woman who had claimed Aiden's heart. This woman she'd subjected to the worst of her venomous attacks. Her feet refused to obey her orders, and she remained frozen.

Tiffany managed a shallow breath before the dam broke and she burst into tears. She stiffened as Emily wrapped her into a hug, but the tension released from her body along with the flood. How did this woman know that words were of no use against these overwhelming emotions she'd locked up tight for so long?

After an untold amount of time, Tiffany pulled away. She fumbled in her bag, desperate for a tissue. "I'm sorry, this is …"

Emily waved a hand as she pressed a tissue into Tiffany's. "You don't need to explain."

Even through the tears, Tiffany couldn't suppress the laugh. "Aiden is … I have no idea what he'll think of me crying all over his wife."

"Well," Emily said as she patted Tiffany's arm, "I'll let you tell him. Or not. It's up to you."

"Embarrassing." She blotted her flaming cheeks and then accepted a second tissue. "Just when I thought I had it all together. What you must think."

"You want to know?" Emily drew her to sit on a nearby bench. "This is as real as I've seen you. I can't imagine what it's been like walking through life wound up so tight. To be so afraid and to carry so much pain inside. Now you've dropped your guard. If you can do that with me, then it means something. It's time to put our differences behind us."

"Really?" Tiffany peered at her through puffy eyelids.

Emily held out her hand. "Dr. Emily Anderson. Nice to finally meet you."

Tiffany took it. "Tiffany Ha—" She reddened.

"You can say it. You're going by Hamilton instead of Baxter."

"He told you?"

"Two of the medical students were gossiping, and I happened to overhear. It's only a name, and it doesn't bother Aiden, so who am I to argue?"

"You're handling this awfully well."

"What choice do I have? I love them both, more than I can ever express. And I can't find fault in anything he's done or discount how difficult his choices have been. All I can do is trust and support him while he makes some very difficult personal decisions."

"Now you've proven me wrong about you." Tiffany blotted her eyes again. "It's been hard to see him move on, but it makes it easier to bear knowing he's happy. His choices have been good ones."

Emily blinked slowly, a tiny smile gracing her lips as she placed her hands on either side of her belly. "We're having a baby girl." She lifted her gaze to meet Tiffany's. "Let's see if we can't bring you one step closer to yours."

Chapter 19

Savannah

Savannah wandered into the living room and grinned as she perched on the arm of the couch.

Emily hummed along to her workout music while performing awkward squats. Aiden's baggy t-shirt dwarfed her frame, but her rounded belly stuck out.

"Don't you be smirking at me. You try doing this around an oversized watermelon." Emily laughed. "On second thought, don't."

"Don't you worry. I'm not planning on any little monsters for quite some time. Besides, I'm terminally single." Savannah tilted her head. "You have tons of workout wear, yet you steal Dad's clothes?"

"Your sister's too big to fit under my tops. Besides, Aiden smells so yummy."

"Ahhh." Savannah closed her eyes and drew in a slow breath, imagining the comfort the warm masculine scent provided, a picture of a certain dark-haired man with warm gray eyes forming in her mind.

"Ooof." Emily stopped and placed a hand on her belly. "Our baby girl has some kick."

"Let me feel." Vanna placed her hand beside her stepmother's. "That's so neat but so weird at the same time. There's a little person in there."

"Mmm, and she'll be out here before we know it." Emily slid an arm around Vanna. "How are you holding up?"

"Dad's been shooting those disappointed looks at me, Brandon never wants to see my face ever again, and my former friend hates my guts." She pasted on a cheerful smile. "It's all fabulous."

"He's not disappointed. He's worried." Emily lowered herself onto the couch, sipping from her water bottle as she motioned to the seat beside her. "Someone hurt his little girl, and he's powerless to do anything about it. He's trying not to push, but it's hard for him. Why won't you tell us who?"

"Because, as we both know from how he reacted to Brandon, he would hunt the guy down and beat the living crap out of him, ending up in jail, or worse."

"Well, there is that." Emily patted Vanna's knee. "Why didn't you report it?"

"I was in a club using a fake name and drinking." Savannah hung her head. "Don't worry, Rochelle and I are planning a ceremonial ID burning. It's been nothing but trouble."

"That's the danger with lies. They circle around and bite you in the ass."

"This one sure did. Dad's angry, Brandon called me a little girl, and Piper labeled me as trash and gives me continuous dirty looks."

"This too shall pass, sweetie. Just give it time." Emily wiggled to the edge of the sofa and pushed herself into a standing position. She held out her hand. "Don't make me do this alone."

Savannah stood as Emily ambled to the sound system and shut off her workout video, putting on an upbeat playlist instead. A smile broke out as her stepmother began to dance.

Emily beckoned. "It's fun." She grinned. "Get out here and join me."

They were both shimmying around the living room when Kellan appeared, bobbing along to the music with his awkward toddler moves. Emily scooped him up and planted kisses on his cheeks and tickled his belly, making him giggle and squirm before she set him loose.

"I guess Dad's home."

"I am." Aiden appeared, grabbing Vanna's hand and swinging her around.

It seemed a free for all, with their group of four all smiles and laughter as they held their own private dance party. Savannah felt breathless, and also the most carefree she had in months. These were the moments she treasured—the total love and acceptance that filled this room. She flopped onto the couch, watching as Aiden caught Emily in his arms, holding her as close as her belly allowed, swaying to the music.

Things never seemed easy, but one thing remained certain. The one constant in her life. Emily and Aiden were meant to be, and they formed the rock-solid base of their little family, holding it all together even when everything else spun out of control.

"Do you want to go sailing on the weekend?" Aiden asked. "It's supposed to warm up."

"I can spare a few hours." It would be the first sail of the season, and the thought of the crisp air and salty breeze brought a smile to Savannah's face.

"You're supposed to set up the baby's room." Emily frowned.

"I'll get it done."

"When?"

"Next week, on my days off." He scooped up Kellan. "Jenn will take Kellan if you need some time on the weekend. You could even come sailing with us."

"Hours on the water, bumping over the waves in that little boat? No thanks." She crossed her arms and narrowed her eyes. "Don't change the subject. You promised you'd do it this weekend so I could put the clothes away, and now it's next week."

"The painter is booked." Aiden handed Kellan to Savannah and he cuddled Emily in his arms, nuzzling against her neck.

Her expression softened as she laughed and shook her head. "You make it impossible be mad."

"It's not worth fighting over." He cupped her face between his palms and kissed her. "Don't you worry, my angel." He bent down to place a kiss on Emily's belly. "Or you either, sweet angel. I haven't forgotten."

⌒≺

Saturday morning Savannah rose just as the sun peeked over the horizon. She showered and dressed for a day on the water. After tucking her waterproof layers into her bag, along with a change of clothes, she bounded into the kitchen.

Aiden looked up as she arrived. "Buenos días, cariño." He sealed a container and consulted his list.

"Buenos días." She kissed his cheek. "You're getting pretty good at Spanish."

"Thankfully. I have to keep up with Kellan. He has a better vocabulary than I do, and he's not even two."

Savannah grinned as she peered into the cooler. "That's a serious amount of food."

"Can't have starving sailors. Did you invite anyone?"

"Nope. Piper's still ripped over Brandon, and the rest of the group is having a study session. I opted out." Vanna stole a warm muffin from the pan on the stove. "The level of drama is ridiculous."

"Ahh, dramatic overload."

"Something like that. Besides, if they come we'll end up talking about school and projects, and I'll lose my mind. Lately, it's more effective to study by myself."

Twenty minutes later they were in the car on their way to the marina.

"So, speaking of drama …" He tapped his fingers on the steering wheel. "Will ran a competition and offered a day of sailing as a reward for two medical students. They'll be joining us today."

"That's cool. As long as one of them isn't Brandon, I'm good."

He gave her a sideways look.

"Oh. Hell no. Stop the damn car. Let me out." She reached for the door handle. "He'll jump overboard when he sees me."

Aiden's eyes rolled skyward. "Can't you be a big girl and play nice?"

"Ha-ha, funny, Aiden." She squinted at him. "Do I have a choice?"

"Nope. I need your superb sailing skills. Tom called, and he had to rescue a client, so we're the crew." He smirked. "If it makes you feel any better, you can order the guys around all day. They have to listen, because they want to learn how to sail."

"Brandon doesn't know how to sail?"

"Guess not. I don't know that his family has the means or the desire to own a boat. They have two kids on this side of the country for expensive Ivy League educations and another one only a year or two out from university. That has to be tough."

"I thought he earned a scholarship."

"It's not a full ride. It offset expenses enough to allow the move for school, but he's tight on cash." He pulled into the lot.

"Hmmm, Piper never talks much about her home life, except that Brandon's mom is horrible to her. She calls her the step monster. Thank you for marrying Emily. She's the sweetest stepmother ever."

"You're welcome." The corner's of Aiden's mouth twitched as he handed her two bags from the back of the SUV. "Are you really okay being around Brandon for a few hours?"

"I'll deal with it, Dad." She pointed a finger at her chest, giving him a saucy smile. "Grown up, remember?"

"Ahh, sass. That's what I love about having children." He wrapped an arm around her shoulders and squeezed, planting a kiss on her temple. "I'm thrilled about having another daughter."

"You should be. And don't worry, Kellan and I will have you all broken in before she's old enough to cause you any trouble."

Aiden gave a low laugh and a small shake of his head as they headed down the dock.

"Let me help with that." Brandon appeared moments later, taking the bags from Vanna. "Where are we going?"

"There." Vanna pointed to the sailboat.

Will appeared with the other student, who he introduced as Nate.

Nate gave Savannah a long appraising look, but glanced away after Aiden narrowed his eyes, and he received a simultaneous nudge in the ribs with an elbow from Brandon.

"Ready, sweetie?" Aiden asked. "You want to steer us out of the harbor?"

Vanna took the wheel, concentrating on navigating through the busy harbor. Once they were in open water, she worked to get the boat underway as Will and Aiden gave some basic instruction to Nate and Brandon.

Once they were skimming across the waves, Aiden and Will sat back, leaving her at the helm.

"You look comfortable." Brandon moved to her side. "When did you learn to sail? About the same time you learned to walk?"

"I wish. I didn't learn until I turned fifteen." She brushed back the strand of hair that had come loose from her braid. "Do you want to take the wheel?"

"Can I?" Brandon grinned. "You can teach me to sail. I have to claim the rest of my reward."

Savannah moved aside, and spent the next half an hour answering his questions and explaining the different sails and sailing terms.

"You're full of information. Aiden taught you all of this?"

"Dad and Uncle Tom taught me the basics. Last summer I traveled overseas and spent three months sailing in the Mediterranean."

"That's amazing. How did you manage to score that trip?"

"I begged my dad to send me."

Brandon laughed. "Lounging on the deck in the sunshine and seeing the world. I can picture it."

"We didn't lounge." Savannah grinned. "We learned to crew a sailboat and earned accreditations based on our performance and testing. We worked hard. It isn't like staying in a hotel. We took turns on kitchen duty, cleaning, and sailing the boat. We always had something to do. I took a university level Marine Biology course, along with a history course on top of that."

Brandon gazed at her, the corners of his mouth twitching.

"What?" The heat crept up Savannah's neck. "Why are you looking at me like that?"

"You." A smile broke out. "Your face lit up while you talked about it. It's adorable."

Their eyes met and the rush rose straight from her toes. She couldn't look away, those deep gray orbs drawing her in and causing a shiver down her spine.

"Cold?" Brandon peeled off his sweatshirt and held it out to her. "Put this on."

Savannah hesitated for a moment, and then slid her arms into the sleeves and pulled it on, savoring the lingering warmth from his body. She closed her eyes and inhaled, relishing the soft scent of him clinging to the cotton.

"Savannah."

She peeked at him, sure she had guilt written all over her face. "What?"

"Sorry, I …" Brandon sighed. "The name suits you better than Zoe. What's your middle name?"

"Jayde. After my mom."

"Pretty. Savannah Jayde Hamilton."

"Phillips Hamilton." Savannah wrapped her arms around herself. "Savannah Jayde Phillips Hamilton. What's your full name?"

"Brandon Darien Reynolds." He tilted his head. "You love being out on the water."

"You should have seen me the first time Aiden took me sailing. I thought I'd gone to heaven. I had never been out before, and it was magical."

"You're an accomplished sailor." Brandon looked impressed. "But this is a big boat for you to manage by yourself."

"Both Dad and Tom can handle this one solo, but they've both sailed since they were kids. I wouldn't dream of taking this out alone." She smiled as she reached over to correct their course. "And this one is Tom's. My dad's boat is dry-docked in the Vineyard for the winter. It's smaller and much easier to handle."

He studied her. "Piper went with you to the beach house. She told her dad, and said she had fun, but she never shared much about the trip with me." Brandon glanced over his shoulder. "So your dad sails boats and flies airplanes. Annnnnd, he's got his eye on me. I'd better be good."

Savannah peeked toward the stern, meeting Aiden's gaze as he quirked a brow. "He's making sure I play nice." She wagged her index finger. "But you still better behave."

"I've seen him angry." Brandon snickered before his expression became serious. "We're good, aren't we? You seemed upset that day I returned your necklace."

"Just reliving that awkward and humiliating moment when my dad almost punched you in the face, followed by the added mortification when he realized I'd slept with one of his medical students. Top that off with your sister treating me like trailer trash and it all spilled into a touch of bitchiness." A rueful smile appeared. "I knew the score, and I get why you don't want to be involved. I'm over it, so let's pretend it never happened and move on."

"Over it, huh." A slight frown marred his features as he returned his attention to steering them through the choppy water. "Is Piper still on your case?"

"Mmmhmm. I've tried to talk to her." Savannah stared over the waves. "She hates me. The circumstances don't seem to matter, and I'm done with explanations."

"She's acting like she's two." Brandon tapped his fingers on the wheel. "I'm sorry, Savannah. She has no right to treat you that way. I'll deal with it."

"You will?"

He nodded. "What happened is between you and me, and not for her to judge. She's getting involved in something that's none of her damn business. It pisses me off that she would turn on a friend."

"Her friends should stay away from you. It breaks the code or something."

"Until now, I would have agreed. In Montana, Piper hung around with a posse of immature little girls. Typical high school overly dramatic bullshit. Mia's friends are worse. You're nothing like them. I totally believed you were twenty-two."

"Thanks?" Savannah pasted on a smile.

"That's a definite compliment." He rubbed her arm. "I'm not mad, Savannah. I'm stunned. I expected theatrics, because that's how my sisters react."

Savannah raised a brow. Sadly, she understood what he meant.

"Guess I don't have to tell you. Piper." He emitted a long, drawn-out sigh. "I wish my family was more like yours. Both your dad and Emily have been incredible. Aiden could make my life a living hell."

"How would he do that? He's not your supervisor anymore."

"But he's influential, and he's close friends with Will Kavanagh. Every single routine or messy procedure could be mine, and I could be banned from incoming traumas for the rest of my rotation."

"Right. Uncle Will."

Brandon gave her a sideways look. "How long have they known each other?"

"They met overseas when Aiden was fifteen and they attended both Oxford and Penn together."

"Good thing your dad's not vindictive." Brandon grinned. "I almost didn't come today. I worried I'd meet a convenient end due to an unfortunate sailing accident. His retribution for my trespasses against his daughter."

"Don't joke." Savannah closed her eyes. "It's not funny."

"Sorry." He rubbed her arm. "I didn't mean anything by it."

She dragged in a long breath. "No, I'm sorry." Savannah peered over her shoulder at the small group on the bench. "Nate sure is quiet. He hasn't said more than two words to me. Is he terrified of my dad?"

"Well, he did get that look when he checked you out. Hey, if I'd known who you were ..." Brandon shook his head. "There is no way that week would have happened."

"I never meant to trick you."

"We both made mistakes. It's not all on you." Brandon nudged her with an elbow. "Is it too nosy to ask why you don't live with your mom? You look just like her, and she seems nice, but what's the story there?"

"What?" Savannah jerked her head toward him. "How would you know what she looks like? My mother lives in Chicago."

"Tiffany Hamilton isn't your mother? She said she was Aiden's ex-wife, so I assumed." His eyes widened.

"No, she is." She swallowed hard to get rid of the lump in her throat. "She was in Boston?"

"Last week," Brandon said. "I didn't mean to upset you."

"You didn't know."

"No, but it must be difficult."

She kept her head bowed, willing herself not to cry. If her mother had visited Aiden, she had a right to know.

⌇

Savannah slumped into the seat beside Jackson. She hunched lower, wishing to sink into the floor and disappear. "I can't wait until we have exams."

"I thought you hated them." Jackson snickered as Rochelle appeared and slid into a seat beside him.

"Exams mean this year is over. I don't know which is worse. The weird puppy-dog looks coming from that direction"—she rolled her eyes toward the left where Gray sat—"or the evil death rays from over there." She inclined her head a touch to the right.

"Don't you worry about asshole. I've got your back. As far as the other one, she needs to grow up." Jackson directed a glare at Gray, then at Piper. "I thought big brother clued her in."

"Guess not." The weekend had been great, but now, only three days later, the familiar sense of dread settled over her. It disappointed her that Brandon hadn't followed through with Piper after their conversation on the boat. "He doesn't owe me anything."

"Don't say that. He owes you some damn respect. As does his sister. Like she's never gone home with a guy?"

"Don't give yourself a coronary." Rochelle patted his arm. "Even if Brandon talked to her, she might still be upset. Her visit home wasn't all that wonderful."

Jackson's eyebrows shot upward. "No need to take that crap out on our Vanna."

Rochelle lifted a shoulder. "She's insecure, and a long way from home. Brandon is her closest family."

Savannah leaned back in her chair, only half listening to the ensuing debate between Jackson and Rochelle. Even after the professor began the lecture, her attention wandered. The year after she'd lost her own mother had been painful, but her dad had been her anchor. And after Ross died, Aiden and Emily had stepped in and become her security. What would it be like to not have anyone?

"Ready?" Rochelle poked her arm, making her aware the class had ended.

"You two go ahead. I have something I need to do, but I'll meet you in our usual spot." Savannah lingered until Piper left the auditorium and jogged after her. "Piper."

"What do you want?" Piper glowered. "You want to rub it in my face that you and Brandon kissed and made up? He gave me hell on Sunday. Thanks a bunch. Now he's pissed off because he thinks I'm being immature."

"Why would I do that? Brandon and I talked, but we're not seeing each other. Even if we were, he's still your brother. Nothing will change that."

"Yes, it will." Piper stopped dead in her tracks, her eyes blazing as she swung toward Savannah. "It's always like that. My dad and I were close until he married the stepmonster, but now he has no time for me. Brandon gets all caught up with the girls he dates and pushes me aside like I'm an annoyance. He told me I'm juvenile and to grow up."

"I'm no threat. Brandon's your brother, and I would never try to take him away. I always wished I had a brother or sister when I was growing up. I think it's special to have siblings."

Piper folded her arms across her chest.

"It doesn't have to be all or nothing. Have you ever told Brandon that you're worried about losing him? He must know what goes on at home."

"How could he? He's not the odd man out. His mother is the problem. Brandon and Mia are her children, and she takes care of them, but she'd like nothing better than for me to disappear."

"Then tell him."

"He'll laugh and tell me I'm a stupid little girl." Piper dipped her head.

"No, he won't. He forgave me for what happened. You don't think he'll do the same for you? Tell him how you feel." Savannah motioned a nearby bench.

Piper sat, angling toward Vanna. "But how? I can't discuss anything with my brother, yet you have no problem talking to him after you two ..." Her faced flushed. "Isn't it awkward?"

"Because we slept together?"

Piper shuddered and hunched her shoulders. "I wish I could banish that awful image from my mind."

"I'm sorry." Savannah sighed. "I wouldn't have been involved if I'd known, but it was a consensual relationship between two adults. What else can I say? Talking to him should be easy as you've known him longer."

"But it isn't. He treats me like a baby. I don't understand how you and Rochelle can pick up guys and go home with them like it's no big deal."

"If that's your impression, then what can I say?" Savannah asked. "I don't go home with just anyone. Your brother saved me, Piper. And it wasn't the first time I met Brandon. The day I found Gray cheating, he stopped to ask if I was okay."

Piper's brow knitted into a frown.

"I know what you think of me," Savannah said as she lifted a shoulder, "but I refuse to apologize for being who I am. If you don't want to be friends, then I accept the consequences of my actions, but can you quit with the death stares?"

"Is it over with Brandon?"

"Does it matter? This is between you and me. Can we shoot for civility so we can get through finals?"

Piper gave her a faint smile. "I'll try not to bring it up again."

"Fair enough. Let's meet the rest of the group and get those assignments done."

"Sounds good."

CHAPTER 20

Tiffany scrunched her nose, bracing herself against the words zinging down the phone line, all meant for her.

"You went to Boston, and what?" The words tumbled out of Alex's mouth in a rush. "Girl. Are you kidding?"

"Every word is true. I apologized to Emily, and she accepted it. She didn't even try to stab me to death." Tiffany closed her eyes, still in shock at how gracious the woman had been, even after the torrent of tears on her shoulder. "I hate to admit it, but she's sweet. I understand why he loves her."

Dead silence hung over the line.

"Alex?"

"Did hell just freeze over?" Alex giggled. "After all the drama, you like his wife? Wow, I am so proud of you."

A small smile crept onto her face. "Crazy, right? He's happy, and I can't ruin that for him." She sank onto the bed, staring at the framed pictures of Savannah. "They're having a girl." Tiffany twirled her hair.

"Hey. How do you know that? They didn't tell me."

"Emily only told me so I'd feel better about turning into a blubbering idiot. But she'll help with Savannah now. She seemed sincere."

"She wouldn't lie about that. She's seen the toll this ridiculous feud takes on Aiden. You've taken a huge step in making things right with the world."

"Do you think Jenna would talk to me?"

"Yes. This has been hard for her. She's loyal to Aiden because of Tom, but she's always been your friend."

"Even after I ruined her wedding?"

"Her wedding was beautiful, and she never thought it ruined. Call her and get it done. Hey, you managed to get over the animosity with Emily. Jenna will be easy compared to that."

"How can I argue with that logic?"

"You can't," Alex said. "How is the battle with your parents?"

"My mother has been surprisingly supportive and is forging ahead with the divorce. David, well, what can I say?"

"On a first name basis now, are you?"

"Pretty much. The financing has come together, thanks to Ben and Aiden. I can cut David out of my life."

"That's amazing, but also sad." Alex sighed. "I'm sorry it's come to that."

"I'm not. The man is toxic, and always has been. Very soon I can say goodbye and then, what else can he do to make my life hell? Nothing."

Tiffany hummed under her breath as she readied the gallery for opening, keeping her focus on perfecting each individual task. Today would be a landmark day, but she hoped she could keep it together long enough to enjoy it.

An insistent rap on the glass broke her reverie, making her jump. Her father's face appeared at the glass, adorned with his usual sour expression. He tapped on the glass again, beckoning her and motioning to his watch.

After a long, deep breath, she unlocked the door.

"About time. I thought you'd be open, though they aren't exactly lining up, now are they?" David pushed past her.

"It's eight in the morning. I said nine." Tiffany fought the urge to roll her eyes. "Mornings are quiet and—" She snapped her mouth shut. Why would he care?

He drummed his fingers on the counter. "I'm surprised you're open to the public. You'll never raise enough in time to save this little hole in the wall."

Tiffany stepped behind the front counter to retrieve the envelope. "This is a copy of the pay out calculation." She slid it across the surface, leaving it within his reach. "If you sign off your interest in the gallery and in my apartment, you'll walk out of here with a nice fat check repaying every single penny you ever lent me. By this afternoon, another check will be on its way to the bank to retire the balance of the financing."

"Where would you get that kind of money? No one in their right mind would lend you a dime."

"My welfare is no longer your concern." She shot a glance his way. "It's good news. I'll no longer burden you with my troubles."

"And if I say no?" David smirked. "I could refuse to sign and prevent you from throwing good money after bad."

"It's inadvisable. Take the money."

"Ha." David chuckled. "Imagine. My penniless artist daughter giving me financial advice."

"I don't know why you'd turn it down." She crossed her arms, thankful they had the reception counter between them. Her knees trembled as she met his narrowed eyes. "You'll be free."

"How …?" Her father tilted his head. "I've seen your financial statements. They're dire."

"When?" She raised a brow. "Did that loans officer at your bank show you my application? Did you enjoy a good laugh at my expense while they stamped the big red *D* on my application? Or maybe your accountant shared?"

"I'd never interfere." He held up both hands, palms facing her.

"Then why did you call my financing? You've never supported me. I could have used a little love and compassion and caring when I was a kid, but you never gave a damn." Choking back a sob, she forced out the words. "I made a mistake, and you punished me, over and over."

"That boy ruined your life." His expression darkened, and his tone took on a lecturing quality. "Having a child when you were only a child yourself would have been the ultimate mistake. It would have destroyed everything I've ever worked for. If it had gotten out, my career would have been over. Instead of whining about your illegitimate brat, you should be thanking me for all I've done for you, little girl. Without me, you'd have amounted to nothing."

"She's …" *Your granddaughter.* Tiffany bit her lip. He didn't care. He never had. He never would.

A gentle knock at the door sent her dashing around the desk. She exhaled as she spotted the dark-haired man through the glass.

"You okay?" Ben eyed her as he slipped through the door and locked it behind him.

A small shake of her head and a shaky breath had him patting her arm.

"I see David's early. Not to worry, everything's ready, so we can have him sign for receipt of the check and shuffle him out the door." Ben winked and adjusted his tie before striding across the floor. "Mr. Baxter, how are you?" He set his briefcase on the counter and snapped it open. "I'm sure you'd like to get on with your day, so we won't keep you long."

"Benjamin Landon." David's brow rose. "Ahhh. Now I understand." A frown settled on his face as he crossed his arms. "He bailed you out?"

"Who's that?" Tiffany entwined her shaking fingers behind her back.

He tipped his head down as his eyebrows rose. "How is Aiden Hamilton?"

Ben cleared his throat. "The source of funds is irrelevant, Mr. Baxter. The paperwork is in order under the terms of your legal agreement. You will be paid in full, including interest owed, and all joint debt will be cleared."

"Well, he's finally done something useful for you." David smirked. "Maybe he did learn a lesson or two." His lip curled. "It'll be a pleasure taking Hamilton's money."

Tiffany bit back a retort.

"This gallery will fail. It's only a matter of time."

"Thank you for your confidence in my abilities." Tiffany squared her shoulders and forced her spine straight. "Sign the papers, and you're free to go. You've never wanted to be part of my life, so I don't expect you'll visit."

David's brows drew together into a dark frown and he towered over her. "Don't think you can dismiss me, little girl." He snatched the pen from Ben's hand and scanned each paper before signing at the bottom with a flourish. "No matter if you've managed to make a *trade* to obtain this money, I'm still your father."

Despite her resolve, the tears burned Tiffany's eyes and she dropped her head, the tightness in her chest making it difficult to breathe.

Ben held out an envelope and ushered David toward the door. "Goodbye, Mr. Baxter."

"Good riddance." David disappeared into the street.

Tiffany sank onto the stool and dropped her head onto her forearms, her entire body shaking uncontrollably.

"It's okay." Ben's warm hands descended to massage her shoulders. "He's gone, and without crossing legal boundaries, he has to leave you alone. You did great, and now you have financial freedom. Enjoy it."

"Thanks, Ben, but I caved like a chastised child." She peered at him. "Did you hear him? He couldn't believe someone would want to help me. He might as well have called me a cheap whore. I'm the shameful tramp who dishonored him, and that's all I'll ever be."

"That's not who you are, Tiffany. You're a talented, savvy artist and business woman who now has the tools at her disposal to become a phenomenal success." His smile reassured her, his words a soothing balm to her stinging ego. "He lost his leverage over you, so he's throwing a temper tantrum. Some men get so caught in their power trip they can't even see beyond the end of their nose. Ignore him. He's nothing but a bully."

"I hoped to keep Aiden out David's sights. Now my father knows how I obtained the money. And I don't want to tell my mother, either." She cringed as she pictured the smug look on her mother's face when she revealed Aiden as her savior. Her stomach bundled into a knot at the thought of the *I-told-you-so* words spilling from her mother's mouth.

"Does it matter? Aiden's a grown man, and he understands the implications of getting involved. After dealing with James, David presents no problem."

"His father?" Tiffany frowned.

"He's had several altercations with James in the past three years, but he's kept the man in his place. David isn't foolish enough to take on Aiden, especially considering who has his back."

"Ahh. He has a posse." Tiffany couldn't hide the grin.

"He has more than a posse." Ben laughed. "He's connected in ways David only dreams of, and Aiden doesn't use fear or bribery to accomplish it."

"Aiden's not afraid?"

"You'd have to ask him that yourself. It seems you two have buried the proverbial hatchet?"

"We have." She brushed at her eyes and took a deep breath. "I am forever grateful to him. He saved me. Again."

After Ben left, Tiffany freshened up and unlocked the gallery at exactly ten.

Stefan strode through the doors. "Good morning, lovely lady."

She accepted the coffee he held out to her, taking a small sip. "Yummy, vanilla today. Thank you."

"Yup, have to keep you guessing." He gazed at her for a moment. "Maybe we could go for dinner one night. It would give us more time to talk than just over coffee."

"Dinner?" Her heart pounded as she considered it. "That would be lovely. Saturday?"

His brows went up. "Seven?"

"Perfect." She wrote her address on the back of one of her business cards.

Despite her reservations, she felt a thrill of excitement deep in her belly. Maybe it was too soon. Or perhaps, the timing was just right.

CHAPTER 21

Savannah

SAVANNAH WATCHED FROM THE CORNER of her eye as Aiden added fresh beans to the coffee maker.

He hummed along with the music flowing through the speakers. "Don't you have something better to do?" His lips twitched as he lifted one brow.

Her cheeks flushed.

"What's with you?"

"Nothing. Just forming a plan of attack for studying for my finals."

"Why don't you head to the patio? I'll bring breakfast." He slapped a pan onto the stove. "Coffee or tea?"

"The amount of studying demands a liberal dose of caffeine." She grinned even as he gave her one of those knowing looks. In a way, it reminded her of how Ross used to look at her and comment that she spent too much time on Google. A pang hit her. The loss of her adoptive parents always caused an inescapable pain.

The reality of how close she came to losing Aiden in the sailing accident, and how she almost turned him away before getting a chance to know him created a deep empty cavern. His presence would have been missed, even if she wouldn't have known exactly the full effect of his absence from her world.

"Coffee it is."

Savannah slid from her perch on the stool and rounded the counter to wrap an arm around his waist. "I love you, Daddy," she whispered.

He barely hesitated before pulling her into a hug. "I love you too, sweetie."

Savannah snuggled against him, savoring the warmth and security of this simple moment, the gentle kiss he pressed against the top of her head. The closeness reminded her of every moment he'd comforted her, carrying her through some of the darkest moments of her life. "Thanks for being a great dad."

Aiden squeezed her extra tight and kissed her temple. "Thanks for being an amazing daughter," he said. "Is everything good?" He tipped her chin up, studying her.

She smiled and nodded.

After breakfast, they both settled on the patio, spending most of the day working in a comfortable silence.

"Ready for dinner?" She stretched, wandering to the edge of the patio, looking over the harbor. "When will Emily be back from shopping?"

"In the next couple of hours, probably."

"Is everything okay with you two?"

"Mmmhmm. Why?"

"You keep sharing strange looks." She sucked in a breath. "Is she mad because of Tiffany?"

"Ahhh, and there it is." Aiden flipped the top of his laptop closed. "I thought you were spacey because of spending Saturday with Brandon. Or is that part of it?"

"What?" She ducked her head to hide the smile.

He laughed as he leaned his forearms on the ledge beside her.

"He thinks I'm too young for him."

"Ha." Aiden snickered. "He *thinks* I'll beat the living crap out of him if he makes the wrong move with my sweet daughter. He never left your side. And let's not forget the flirting."

"He did not flirt." Heat rose in her cheeks. "Hey. You're sneaky." Vanna wagged a finger at him. "Is Emily mad about Tiffany?"

"Uh-uh. She's exhausted from carrying an extra human around 24/7. And irritated about the bedrooms for the baby and Kellan, which I'd better get done or I risk banishment to the guest room."

"About that." Savannah twirled her hair around a fingertip. "Can I do the rooms?"

"Do you have time?" Aiden lifted a brow.

"I write my final exams this coming week. It could be a surprise if you take Emily away for a few days."

"Emily would love it. She needs a break before the baby. I'll ask Jenna if she can take Kellan, and I'll transfer money to your account for supplies."

"Deal." Savannah narrowed her eyes. "Why did Tiffany come to the hospital?"

Aiden sighed and rubbed a hand through his hair. "She came to Boston for an art show."

"Why did she introduce herself to Brandon as Tiffany Hamilton?"

"It's her legal surname." Aiden lifted a shoulder. "She no longer wants to use Baxter."

"You're okay that she took your last name?"

"It's been hers all along, she just chose not to use it."

"What did Emily say? She's still Anderson."

"Remaining Anderson was Emily's personal choice, which I supported. It doesn't lessen our commitment." Aiden shot her a sideways look. "Why are you so upset?"

Savannah frowned, searching for the answer.

"What are you thinking, Vanna?"

"I don't trust her." Savannah bowed her head. "She'll ruin everything with Emily."

"Hey." Aiden pulled her into a hug. "Emily isn't going anywhere. We love each other."

"Even you said that love isn't always enough." She buried her head against his chest.

"Emily and I have more than love holding us together. There's trust, respect, solid communication. This may sound strange, but we genuinely like spending time together. We were friends before we became involved romantically. Don't discount the depth that connection adds to our relationship."

Savannah closed her eyes and nodded. "I wonder if I'll ever have that."

"I bet you will." Aiden smiled. "You don't need to worry. Our family is solid."

"Promise?"

"I absolutely promise you, Savannah. Emily and I are committed to us."

⁓≼

Savannah stood back and rubbed her cheek with the back of her hand as she inspected her work. She tilted her head before adding another touch of azure blue to the wall. A smile appeared as she pictured the reactions when everyone saw how Kellan's bedroom had come to life.

Her belly rumbled and she stretched. Once she'd sealed her painting supplies, she wandered into the living room to change the music to something more upbeat. She danced into the kitchen before scrubbing paint from her hands, and then she prepped the ingredients for dinner.

Her phone buzzed, the tone indicating it was the doorman.

"Brandon Reynolds, miss. He has an envelope for Dr. Anderson."

"Send him up." She lowered the heat under the pan and dashed toward the foyer as the elevator opened.

"Vanna." Brandon stared at her.

"Come in. I have something on the stove." She motioned him to follow as she headed into the kitchen and stirred the vegetables. "You have something for Emily?"

He nodded and looked around. "Where is everyone?"

"Aiden and Emily are out of town, and Kellan is staying overnight with Tom and Jenna." Savannah pulled out a strainer before giving the pan another stir. She scooped up a noodle. "Perfect."

Brandon set the envelope on the counter and moved into the kitchen as she reached for the hot mitts. "Let me do that."

Vanna peeked at him from the corner of her eye as he drained the noodles. "Thanks."

"Emily asked me to drop those papers on my way home today. Is everything okay?"

Savannah tossed the seafood into the pan. "They're in Maine having *alone* time."

"I see." Brandon moved to her side and leaned in, his warm breath tickling her neck. "That looks amazing. What's in there?"

"Seafood sauce for the fettucine." She dipped in a spoon and held it out. "Try."

He took a taste. "Mmmm."

"I made extra."

His eyes lit up.

"Help yourself to a beer, or you can open a bottle of wine." She pointed at the small built-in fridge. "White for me, please."

He raised an eyebrow. "Are you allowed to drink?"

She snickered. "You can't corrupt this juvenile delinquent."

"Wine it is." He grinned and checked the bottles. "Champagne?" Brandon waved it in the air and tilted his head.

"Nooooooo. If you drink that it's certain death. Aiden and Emily are saving it for their anniversary. That bottle is ridiculously expensive."

"How much?"

"Four, maybe five hundred?" Vanna tossed the pasta into the sauce.

Brandon tucked it away. "I don't even have that much per month for food." He held up another bottle, turning it to show Savannah the label.

"Perfect. Corkscrew is in the drawer."

She rolled the pasta and arranged it artfully on the plates before spooning the extra seafood and sauce over top. Then she pulled the garlic bread from the oven.

"You cook like a pro." Brandon selected glasses from the rack and poured the wine.

"I've always loved being in the kitchen." Savannah delivered the plates to the table and motioned for him to sit. "Aiden taught me this recipe."

"How does he find the time? Like that feast he prepared on the sailboat. Amazing." He rolled fettuccine around his fork and popped them into his mouth, chewing thoughtfully. "This is delicious."

"Thanks." She took a dainty bite as he scarfed down his pasta. "Do they never feed you?"

"Rarely," he said. "I look forward to meals that aren't greasy burgers or pizza."

Once they finished, Brandon helped her tidy the kitchen.

"So why do you call him Aiden?" Brandon leaned on the counter as Savannah started the dishwasher. "My mom would flip out if I called her Carol."

"Are you sure you want to hear the sad details of my messy life?"

"I do, oddly enough." He lifted one shoulder. "I am curious."

"This calls for more wine." Savannah selected a second bottle from the cooler and handed it to Brandon to open. "Let's move this party to the living room."

She changed the music while Brandon peered through the bank of floor to ceiling windows.

"I can't get over this place. The mortgage has to be killer even on two doctors' salaries. Boston is brutal for rent."

"I've never asked how much my dad makes." Savannah shrugged. "But I doubt he's ever had a mortgage."

"Ahh." Brandon frowned. "Tell me about this messy life of yours."

Savannah inclined her head. "I didn't meet Aiden until I was almost fifteen."

"So you lived with your mom? I never figured Aiden for that kind of guy."

"You mean the kind of guy who dumps his kid for fifteen years?" Savannah shook her head. "I didn't live with either of them. I grew up in Portland with my other mom and dad, Ross and Jayde Phillips."

Brandon's brows rose.

"When I turned eight, my parents told me I'd been adopted. It didn't surprise me much. Something never quite fit. My parents both had dark hair and blue eyes as did all the family in pictures."

"Adopted. Wow. So Aiden's your biological father?"

Savannah nodded. "My mom left me a picture of the people she thought were my mother and father. I found Aiden right before I turned fifteen."

"What about Tiffany?"

"She refused to see me and wouldn't let Aiden tell me anything about her. I almost …" She bowed her head and cleared her throat. "Aiden and I visited each other. He'd come to Portland or fly me to Chicago."

"How did you end up living with him?" Brandon lifted her hand and held it between his.

"My dad died." She drew in a long breath. "I'd just turned fifteen, so Aiden asked me to live with him. And that summer, I met the woman who gave birth to me." She gulped a mouthful of wine.

"I'm sorry, Savannah. I had no idea. You've known Aiden for less than four years?"

She nodded and swallowed hard. "I don't know what would have happened if I hadn't found Aiden. My mom and dad had no siblings and their parents passed before I was born."

Brandon tucked an arm around her shoulders. "Sometimes we find the exact person we need when we least expect it."

"Like our own miracle." Savannah leaned against him.

"Piper never said anything. Does she know?"

"She knows the basics. Brandon, do you two ever talk?"

"We do, but she talks like a kid. It's never about anything real."

She peered at him. "Did you know she's scared to talk to you?"

"She is?" His brows went up. "Why?"

"You treat her like an annoying little girl."

"Most of the time she is. Like what happened with you. I'm embarrassed by how she treated you, Savannah."

"She's scared." Savannah frowned. "You should talk to her about what's going on at home."

"What? Why is she scared? Because my mother is a little nuts?" Brandon looked thoughtful. "How do you know?"

"We talked. She's not happy we had a relationship, but I'm not sure her reaction is about me. She lost her mom. That's devastating for a teenage girl."

"You lost both of your parents. How did you manage?"

"When I lost my mom, I had my dad. When I lost my dad, I had Aiden. He dropped everything to be there for me. *Everything,* Brandon. He left his job in Chicago to stay with me in Portland. I finished the school year with my friends while he took care of the details. And then we spent the entire summer at the house in the Vineyard before we moved to Boston. Those months meant so much to me, and I will never forget them."

"My stepfather is nothing like Aiden. He's done his best, but … Wow, Piper told you this?"

"Yes and no. Some she told me, some of it I just understand. I have good days and bad. Sometimes it's hard, and I miss my parents. You have no idea what I've been through. Just like you might not appreciate what Piper is feeling."

Brandon frowned. "Is it that bad for Piper?"

"No offense, but she refers to your mother as her stepmonster, and she doesn't get along with Mia. She's terrified of talking to you. What do you think?"

"Damn." He scrubbed a hand through his hair.

Savannah squeezed his hand. "You know I wished for a sibling? It might have made things easier."

"You have one, and he's a cute kid." Brandon grinned.

"He's not even two." Savannah rolled her eyes.

"Mmm, fair point." He rubbed her cheek with his thumb. "You have a little something. It doesn't want to come off."

"Paint." She smiled. "I'm painting the new nursery and Kel's room."

"Can I see?"

Savannah set aside her glass and tugged his hand. "Come on." She led him down the hall to the room that would be Kellan's.

"Whoa." Brandon stood in the middle of the room and turned. "When you said paint, I thought you meant with a roller. This is amazing. I would have loved a room like this."

"Kellan is fascinated with boats and the ocean, so I figured this would be perfect. I need to finish the waves. Dad said the bed would go there." She pointed. "I might paint an anchor right above it. Or a compass."

"Anchor. That's my vote." He wrapped an arm around her shoulders. "You have some serious artistic talent."

"I guess I have one thing to thank Tiffany for." Savannah leaned into him, savoring the warmth of his body. "My dad says she's an amazing artist, but I've never seen any of her work."

"I could see that about her." Brandon gazed down at her.

Savannah stared at him, the pull of attraction taking her breath away. "I … Let me show you the nursery."

He followed her into the next room. "Can I just say, wow? Why are you becoming a lawyer?"

"You don't think I can?"

"Oh, no, it's not that. But this mural looks professional. It's perfect."

"I have more to do, but I think Aiden and Emily will love it."

"I should get out of your way so you can finish."

"You could stay and make sure the anchor turns out." Heat crept into her face. "Never mind. It wouldn't be exciting to watch me paint."

"Maybe we could talk. Would that disrupt the creative process?"

Savannah shook her head.

"If I'd brought my books, I could review while you work."

"You need a medical text?" Savannah laughed. "I think we have one or two of those in the office."

Savannah smiled at the sight of Brandon standing in front of the massive cherry-wood bookshelf, thumbing through the thick medical text.

"Find what you need?" Savannah tipped the book to survey the title. "Anatomy. That sounds like an exciting read." She perched on the arm of the couch.

"It's riveting. Will promised to let me do a couple of procedures whenever they come up, so I have to review them." Brandon selected another thick text and set them on the desk. "Impressive number of degrees." He studied the documents on the wall. "I had no idea Aiden went to Oxford."

"He spent three years overseas." Savannah twirled her hair. "When he turned eighteen, he came home and went to Penn."

"Eighteen? Damn. I feel like a total underachiever."

"Right? He had his undergrad done at my age. Aren't you attending Perelman?"

"Yes, but I barely managed to deal with medical school. He double majored?"

"His grandfather wanted him to be a lawyer. My grandparents paid for his education."

"Sweet to have a full ride through medical school." Brandon pointed at the row of pictures on the wall. "Those are cool shots. Who took them?"

"Don't know, but that's Aiden." Savannah shrugged. "He's very outdoorsy. He's traveled all over the world, and he loves to ski, surf, and sail, or basically anything else that involves being outdoors. That shot was taken in the Swiss Alps."

Brandon tilted his head. "I've never had the balls to ask. How old is Aiden?"

"Thirty-three." The corners of her lips twitched. "Which is why you assumed he was my big brother?"

"You will never let me live that down, will you? You have to admit he looks young. I never would have—"

"I'm teasing, Brandon. You're not the first person to make that assumption." Her breath caught as she met his intense gaze.

"I'm sorry for being so hard on you."

"You are?"

"Uh-huh." He moved one step closer. "Are you really over it?"

"I'm trying to be," she whispered.

The scent of his aftershave tickled her nostrils as he rested his hand on the back of the couch and leaned in. "Your dad would kick my ass if he could read my thoughts."

She swallowed hard and swiped her damp palms across her jeans. "What are you thinking?"

"About this." Brandon captured her lips in a demanding kiss.

Savannah twined her arms around his neck, her pulse racing as he lifted her to her feet. She sank against him, sighing as he kissed the sensitive spots on her neck. "Wait." She pressed her flattened palms against his chest, reluctant to give in to her desires. This man had the ability to pull her in, but to what end? To him, she was simply a juvenile playing games. Yet, letting him go seemed like an even tougher request.

"Sorry … I …" Brandon stepped back.

"Brandon, please don't—"

"This is crazy." His face crumpled into something resembling pain. Or regret? He spun and strode from the room, the sound of his footsteps retreating down the hallway.

Savannah dragged in a breath and sank to her knees, the first tear trickling down her cheek, followed by a salty river streaming down her face. She grasped her pendant and rubbed, struggling to ground herself as she gasped for air.

"Savannah?" Warm hands touched her arms. "Are you …?"

"Go." She choked out the single word between her sobs. Her shoulders trembled, his past comments returning to taunt her. "I'm just a little girl, remember?"

"I couldn't leave." He drew her against his chest, tangling his hand into her hair as he rocked her in his arms.

Savannah wound an arm around his neck and buried her face, unsure she could let him go. All at once, she longed to pull him closer, even while wanting to lash out and push him away. To make him feel the same burning pain.

"Shhh, honey. Don't cry." The warmth of his breath wafting over her cheek only made her sob harder.

When he scooped her into his arms, she could only cling to him, hoping he wouldn't abandon her to her misery.

～⤳

Savannah opened her gritty eyes, conscious of the soft cotton shirt against her cheek. The warm arms cradling her both comforted and alarmed her. *Brandon's arms.*

He held her like a fragile piece of glass about to shatter, but he'd calmed her until the panic receded and she drifted into sleep.

Confusion clouded her mind. His mixed signals spun her out of control, and now she refused to move. If she alerted him that she'd woken, he might leave her all over again.

Lips touched her hair, and a gentle hand brushed against her cheek. "You have me tied in knots." A soft sigh left him.

She curled her fingers into the soft fabric of his shirt.

"It's wrong for me to want you, or for me to even be here," he whispered. "You're a temptress." His hand grazed down her back, coming to rest on her hip. "And the beloved daughter of a man I respect and admire. But I just ..." He placed a tender kiss on her forehead.

She dared to open her eyes. "You called me a little girl."

"I meant to your dad, you're his little girl, which is ..." He sighed and stroked her hair as he rested his forehead against hers. "When we're together, I see this incredible and passionate woman. I'm so damn powerless to resist."

"Shhh." Savannah pressed a finger against his lips as she lifted her chin. She stared into his eyes, searching for answers, but only finding more confusion. She traced her fingertip along his upper lip, never breaking their eye contact as she slid her hand into the back of his hair and caressed the nape of his neck.

A shudder ran through him, the look in his eyes telling her she'd accomplished her mission. Found the truth and reignited that broken moment in the office. Her own body trembled as she pressed her mouth to his and pulled him closer, working at the buttons of his shirt with her free hand.

Brandon groaned, tangling his hand into her hair as she succeeded in opening his shirt. He nuzzled his face into the crook of her neck, planting butterfly kisses on each sensitive point as she undid his belt and released the button on his jeans.

Savannah looped a leg over his hip, splaying her hand against his smooth bare chest. Her heart pounded and her entire body trembled at his tender touch.

"We shouldn't," he murmured against her neck.

She cupped his face between her palms, silencing him with more kisses. Savannah broke their connection only long enough to tug her shirt over her head and press herself against his bare chest.

Brandon cradled her head in his hands and stared into her eyes for a moment before his mouth descended on hers.

⌒≼

Brandon brushed her lips with his. "Where did that come from?" He sighed and nestled her against him, combing his fingers through the ends of her long hair, which fanned across his chest.

The corners of her mouth twitched, and she lifted her shoulder the tiniest bit.

He brushed the back of his hand over her cheek, a deep laugh rumbling in his chest. "Ahh, woman. I am so screwed."

Her smile widened. "We've proven a point. I'm a grown woman who makes her own choices." Savannah burrowed against his chest as she tucked the duvet around them.

"You sure are, but we still have to tell Aiden. I have to work with the man." He smoothed her hair back and dropped another kiss on her lips. "What do you think?"

"About telling my dad?" She lifted her eyes to meet his. "Or being a couple?"

"Both."

"What about Piper? I don't want to cause issues in your family."

"I'll talk to her, but you get to tell Aiden. Preferably when I am nowhere near."

"Oh sure, make me do it." Savannah poked him in the ribs. "Before it was we, now it's me."

"It's fair, isn't it?"

"Are you …?" She smothered a giggle. "You're afraid of him."

Brandon tangled his hands into her hair and pressed his lips against her ear. "Only a little."

Savannah wiggled closer and whispered, "Do you think it was an accident you ended up here when they're out of town?"

"Emily?" His lips twitched. "Did you know?"

She shook her head.

"So she set this up?" Brandon's brow furrowed.

Savannah shrugged. "How important are those papers?"

"Clever." He rolled onto his back and swept a hand through his hair. "Emily's playing matchmaker?"

"I could see her coming up with something like this. She wouldn't have done it if she thought it would upset my dad."

His eyes widened. "He knows?"

"I doubt she shared her plan. We'll tell him together."

He trickled his fingers up and down her side. "Always take a chance on those you care about."

"Emily?" She lifted a brow. At his slight nod, her heart eased and she curled up against him. "Stay the night."

"You're sure?"

"Yes." She gazed at him, determined not to waste this precious second chance. "I want to take the chance. Do you?"

CHAPTER 22

Tiffany

TIFFANY SNAPPED A PICTURE IN the mirror before wiggling out of the black satin and tossing it across the bed. She held the red one against her chest, tilting her head as she considered the options, visualizing each dress paired with her new stilettos.

She wished one of her close friends still lived in Chicago. She remembered the days when they'd shop and plan outfits for their dates. A small knot formed in her stomach as she longed for everything they'd lost over the years. But at least she'd made some amends.

Jenna. She smiled as she thought about the call she'd made the previous night, and the relief she felt now she'd cleared the air with her friend. Maybe she'd gotten in her own way and overreacted. If only she'd realized it sooner. But perhaps things were as they were meant to be. She'd grown in ways she'd never imagined possible.

She picked up her phone and sent the texts with the pictures attached.

SOS. First dinner date with Stefan in 20 min. Red or black dress?

Little dots danced in the corner of her screen and moments later she had her answer from Jenna.

Red. Very sexy. He won't take his eyes off you.

She held the phone to her chest for a moment, and then the reply came from Alex.

Def that sexy red number. Have an amazing time, sweetie.

Tiffany slid the silky fabric over her head and combed her fingers through her hair to settle it into waves. After adding earrings and a heavy chain, she dabbed a touch of color onto her lips. She stared in the mirror for a moment before she tidied up the clothing scattered across the bed.

Her intercom buzzed, and she grabbed her favorite stilettos and her tiny purse before she hurried to open the door.

Her heart raced and she barely noticed his crisp dress shirt and tailored suit as she admired the golden flecks in his warm hazel eyes.

"You look beautiful." He leaned in and planted a kiss on her cheek. "Ready?"

After dinner, Stefan invited Tiffany to a club, where they spent several hours dancing. Things were now a touch fuzzy, her head swimming from the alcohol as he escorted her toward the car waiting at the curb.

She clutched at Stefan's arm as she wobbled and sank into the plush leather seat, smothering a giggle as she relaxed and gazed around the spacious interior. The music flowing through the speakers had her swaying to the beat. It had been a while since she'd let herself indulge. No doubt she'd be paying for it in the morning.

She noted Stefan's smirk. "Sorry." Tiffany wiped the grin from her face as a flush crept into her cheeks.

Stefan took her hand. "Don't be." He raised her fingers to his lips, pressing a kiss onto them. "It's refreshing." Their entwined fingers landed on his firm thigh.

Tiffany blinked, the buzz of the alcohol muddling her mind. "Is that code for juvenile and I never want to see you again?"

Stefan's lips twitched. "It's *refreshing* to date someone who isn't trying so damn hard." He sighed. "At the risk of sounding like an ass, first dates are often excruciating. This one was"—his grip on her hand tightened—"different."

Tiffany's fingers tingled, the warmth of his body drawing her in. "Do you want to know a secret?" she whispered.

"Tell me." He leaned toward her, the musky scent of his cologne causing a rush of warmth to speed upward from her toes.

She pressed her lips to his ear. "You make me so damn nervous. Now I'm soooooo drunk. I'm never this much fun."

"Not fun?" Stefan slid an arm around her, cuddling her against his firm chest. "Hmmmm. I find that hard to believe. It's a shame to see our evening end."

"It doesn't have to." Tiffany tilted her head up, grazing his jawline with her lips. "Where are we going?"

"I planned on taking you home." He tangled a hand into her hair.

"Your place or mine? Either is good with me." She pressed her lips to his.

Tiffany dragged her eyes open, staring at the empty space beside her before observing the unfamiliar room. She rubbed a hand across her face as she sat and glanced down at the half-buttoned dress shirt. Her mouth felt dry and pasty, and her head pounded.

She crawled to the edge of the bed and stumbled toward the bathroom. After splashing cold water on her face and wiping off the worst of last night's makeup, she rinsed her mouth. As she massaged her temples, she took in her red-eyes and pale skin. "Real attractive," she muttered, pinching at her cheeks to restore some color.

"Morning." Stefan set his coffee cup aside as she padded into the kitchen. He looked fresh and well-rested, already dressed in dark-washed jeans and casual steel-gray shirt.

Tiffany ran her fingers through her hair, wishing she could sink into the floor. "Morning, Stefan."

"You look like you could use coffee. And a few of these." He slid a bottle of acetaminophen tablets toward her as he skirted the counter and poured a steaming cup and filled a glass with ice water.

She tipped two into her hand and accepted the water he offered as he set her coffee on the island. "Thanks." Tiffany washed the tablets down, drinking half the glass before she set it aside.

As Tiffany sipped her coffee, she wandered through the open living space, examining the pictures on the wall. She peered through the bank of large windows, squinting against the bright light as she judged where they were from their position over the lake. "You only live a few blocks from me."

"It's a great area, and this little place is perfect as I travel so often." He moved behind her and wrapped an arm around her waist. The heat from his body warmed her back as he massaged her shoulder with one hand. "You seem tense."

She leaned into him, closing her eyes as he pressed his cheek against hers. "I'm sorry about last night."

"Don't be," he murmured against her ear.

"Did we ...?" She bowed her head. "I feel like an idiot. I drank way too much." Heat rose in her cheeks. "You'll think I'm the stupidest woman on the planet, but I can't remember," she whispered.

Stefan gave a low chuckle. "We kissed." He wiggled his brows. "We slept in the same bed. We may even have cuddled. But that's it."

"I'm wearing your shirt with nothing underneath."

"But I didn't take advantage of you."

"This is embarrassing." Tiffany ducked her head. "Not only did I get stupid drunk, but now I've insulted you. I'll go." She pulled from his embrace and hurried down the hallway into his bedroom, beginning a desperate search for her clothes.

Stefan appeared in the doorway and leaned against the frame with arms folded across his chest. "I enjoyed our evening."

Tiffany peered at him from behind her mop of hair. "Did I actually say your place or mine?"

His deep baritone laugh caused goosebumps to rise on her arms. "Perhaps."

She slumped onto the bed and slapped a hand over her face, peeking at him from between splayed fingers. "How can you be even remotely interested?"

The mattress sank as he sat beside her on the bed. "I assure you, I'm very interested." He tucked an arm around her shoulders. "Why are you so hard on yourself?"

"I make stupid choices." She shook her head. "Not that going out with you is … Damn, I need to shut up."

Stefan pressed his lips against her hair. "I understand what you mean."

"Do you?" Her bottom lip trembled. "I'm a relationship failure. I destroyed my marriage and then followed up with an engagement to the wrong man."

"So you made a few mistakes. We all have. It would seem they've moved on with their lives, so why shouldn't you?"

"You know my ex-husband, don't you?"

"As does half of Chicago. If you're looking for someone in this city who hasn't met him, you might be out of luck. His family isn't exactly low-profile." Stefan shrugged. "Nor is your ex-fiancé's, or even yours. It doesn't change anything. Let's explore where this"—he motioned between them—"goes. What do you say?"

Tiffany lifted her chin, the corners of her mouth turning up. She tilted her head, a warm glow rising from her toes as it did every time she looked at this man.

He opened his mouth to speak, but she crawled to her knees and pressed her lips against his. Stefan cupped one warm palm against her cheek, wrapping the other hand into her hair as they kissed.

He pressed his face into the crook of her neck, his warm breath tickling her sensitive skin. "Is that a yes?"

She nibbled on his ear lobe. "Shh." Tiffany slid her hands under his shirt as she straddled him. Allowing this moment to pass her by would be criminal. She pulled back enough to look into his eyes, searching their depths for a clue. The raw, naked, unadorned desire she saw caused a shiver to rush down her spine.

His large hands stroked down her sides and over her hips, bringing her against him. He caught her bottom lip, giving it a tender nip before he captured her mouth.

Now she knew for certain that she hadn't imagined the hunger reflected in his eyes. Tiffany tugged at his shirt, bringing it over his head, savoring the gleam in his eye before their mouths joined again. She dragged in a long breath as he cupped his hands underneath her and rolled them.

Her heart pounded and her pulse raced, her craving to be touched and loved taking over. It seemed forever since she'd desired a man as much as she wanted Stefan at this moment.

Tiffany splayed a hand across Stefan's firm chest, before walking her fingers downward, tracing a fingertip across his abdomen. "Now I know nothing happened last night." She smirked. "There's no way I would've forgotten *that*."

Stefan chuckled low in his throat. "I aim to please."

She propped up on one elbow. "No worries on that front."

"I'd say a very good start to my suggested plan of seeing where this goes." He brushed a finger down her nose. "If you're up for it, we could spend the day together."

"I'd like that, as long as Isla is willing to cover for me at the gallery."

"Why don't you call her, and then we can stop by your place so you can find something more casual than that slinky little red number from last night."

"Oh. You didn't like it?"

Another deep laugh broke free. "No straight man wouldn't like it. You were a complete knockout. Me and every other guy thought so, but you might feel more comfortable in jeans or something?"

"Where are we going?"

"You'll see." He winked as a smile crept across his face. "It's a surprise, but dress warm."

"I love surprises." She pressed a kiss to his soft lips. "I can't wait."

CHAPTER 23

Savannah

T HE SOUND IN THE DOORWAY caused Savannah to look up. The sight of a shirtless Brandon created a yearning within her. Her gaze wandered down his firm bare chest, lingering on the trail of fine hairs leading from his belly and disappearing into the top of his sexy, unbuttoned dark-washed jeans.

"Morning." He rubbed a hand through his hair as a sleepy grin appeared. "You didn't wake me."

Vanna rose in a single sinuous movement, allowing her hips to take on a saucy sway as she stepped toward him. Her keen eyes took in the way he tracked her progress, delight bringing a soft smile onto her face. She stretched on tiptoes, pausing ever so slightly, tempting him, sighing against his tantalizing lips as he captured hers.

She snuggled into his embrace, pressing her head against his chest. "You looked so peaceful, I didn't have the heart to disturb you. I figured you were tired."

"Exhausted is more like it. You can't imagine how the shift changes mess with your sleep patterns."

Savannah wrinkled her nose. "I live with two doctors and a toddler."

Brandon gave her a rueful smile. "Ahh, right." He looked around. "This turned out amazing. You truly have talent, Vanna."

"Thanks. Once it's dry, Aiden can set up the furniture." She took a moment to inspect the work one more time. "Let's have breakfast. I'm in dire need of caffeine."

"Hmm." He practically devoured her with his eyes, eyeing the skimpy satin shorts and tank top she'd slept in. "I'm in dire need of more than caffeine." Brandon scooped her smoothly into his arms, tossing her onto the bed the moment they reached her room.

His steamy gaze pinned her in place, her mouth going dry as he shucked his jeans, the heat of his body causing goosebumps to rise on her bare flesh as he lowered himself onto the bed. Savannah bit her lip, anticipation making her tremble as he brushed the back of one hand over her cheek.

"You drive me crazy," he murmured in a deep, sultry voice before brushing his lips over hers, teasing, tempting her as she'd tempted him. "You are my weakness."

Savannah caressed the back of his neck, causing a noticeable shiver to run through him. If only this man knew that he was quickly becoming hers as well.

⌒≼

An hour later, Savannah stepped from the shower and wrapped a towel around herself. She rubbed at the steam on the mirror, clearing a spot as she ran a brush through her damp hair.

Brandon turned off the water and peered at her through the misty air. "Towel, hon?"

She grinned and tossed one his way. It felt comfortable having him here, a return to that amazing week they'd spent together.

"It's sick you have your own bathroom." Brandon slung the towel around his hips. "I'm sharing with three other guys, including Dylan."

"That jackass?" Savannah wrinkled her nose. "Why?"

"Because it's all I can afford. Trust me, if I didn't have to live with that misogynistic slob, I wouldn't." He accepted the hairbrush as he inspected his teeth in the mirror. "I need to brush."

Savannah pointed at one of the drawers. "In there."

Brandon smiled and leaned in to plant a kiss on her lips.

She glanced over her shoulder as she sashayed through the bedroom and opened her drawer, searching for fresh clothing.

Brandon appeared five minutes later, rubbing his towel through his hair. He slung it into the hamper before he tugged on his jeans. He held up his shirt. "Mascara smears."

"Sorry. I'll wash it." She motioned for him to follow her down the hallway.

His eyes widened as they entered the master bedroom. "A fireplace?" He stared at the picture hung above the mantel. "That's incredible. It's sexy, and almost sassy. And eye-catching."

"It's a beautiful picture." Vanna leaned against his shoulder and stared at the black and white photo of the woman who appeared to be walking away, her head tipped as if she were about to cast an inviting glance over her shoulder.

You could almost see the saucy sway of her curvaceous hips. Dark, wild curls cascaded down her bare back, and she had one thumb hooked into the back of black satin panties, pulling them down at an angle to bare a glimpse of her buttocks.

"How is Aiden allowed to have that in the bedroom?"

"That's Emily."

"She's very understanding."

"No." Savannah shook her head as she smothered a laugh. "That," she said, pointing at the picture, "is Emily. She hired a professional photographer for one of those boudoir sessions. Some amazing guy named Paulo who lives in Chicago, apparently."

"Paulo?" Brandon shot her a glance. "Now I feel like a voyeur."

"It's artistic. Why do you feel weird? Because you know her?" She pointed to the collection of frames on the mantel. "They had those done when she was pregnant with Kellan."

"They're attending physicians in the ER." Brandon stepped closer as his lips twitched. "A whole new side of Aiden and Emily."

"They're full of surprises." Savannah smirked as she wandered into the walk-in closet. She'd been stunned when she saw the photos so openly displayed, but she had to admit they were amazing. "You're about the same size as my dad."

"I can't wear his clothes." Brandon rubbed at his jaw as he trailed behind her.

Savannah snorted. "Yeah, he'll really miss a shirt." She ran a finger down the row of clothes lining the massive closet. "Sweater? T-shirt? Pick something."

"He'll freak."

"Uh-uh." She scooped a sweater from the shelf. "Blue's a good color for you. Or," she said, allowing her gaze to wander over his firm chest, lingering a moment before she ran a fingertip down his tight six-pack, "I'm good with shirtless."

Brandon lifted his brow, but slid the luxurious cashmere over his head, brushing his hands over the sleeves to straighten them.

Savannah smiled. "Perfect. And it's soft." She trickled her fingers down his arm. "Are you going to stay for a while? I have to finish painting the room."

"If you don't mind me studying while you work."

"Not at all. Let's have some breakfast first."

Savannah opened her eyes at the sound of a door closing down the hall. She frowned and glanced at the clock before turning onto her back and resting a hand over her eyes.

Brandon sprawled on his stomach beside her, his deep even breathing causing a flutter in her belly.

She slid from the bed and dressed in leggings and a t-shirt before tiptoeing into the kitchen, finding Emily leaning against the counter, still in her pajamas.

"I didn't hear you come in. Where's Dad?"

"Still in bed. The only reason I'm up is because your little sister refuses to stop squirming." Emily rubbed her belly. "Sleep is a precious commodity these days." She flicked on the kettle.

"How was the trip?" Vanna grabbed a lock of hair, twining it around her finger.

"Fantastic. I love our baby boy, but he's so busy and I craved the alone time with Aiden. We've only got a couple of months before this little girl arrives." A grin appeared as she placed her hands on either side of her belly.

"How do you manage the pressure? You have me, with all the crap I've put you through, and Kellan. Not to mention Tiffany, who reappears at the most inconvenient moments."

"I love that you're with us, Savannah. And I can deal with your mother."

"How? She drops in and out of our lives. Don't you wish she'd stay away from him?"

Emily slid onto the stool beside Vanna's. "I won't pretend it's easy, but she'll forever be part of Aiden's life. I understand why, but do you?"

"Yes … and no …" She lifted one shoulder. "I feel awful, but sometimes I hate her. She turned me away, but now she wants … what?" Savannah took a long breath to settle the swirl of emotions. "You act more like my mother than she does."

Emily slipped an arm around her. "Maybe you should see her, at least once."

"It wouldn't upset you?"

Her stepmother shook her head. "I love being here for you, but she's your mother."

Savannah rested her head on Emily's shoulder and closed her eyes.

Emily rubbed her back. "Even if you only meet her one time to satisfy your own curiosity and hear her viewpoint, it's worth it."

"Dad once said it might only be one visit, and it may never become a true relationship. But it feels like everything has changed since then."

"It has. Your dad and Tiffany managed to resolve their differences, and I support that one hundred percent."

"Morning." Aiden appeared, placing his hands on Emily's belly as he kissed her. "You two look serious." He leaned in to kiss Vanna's temple.

"Just a little girl talk," Savannah said. "Now that Dad's up, I have a surprise for you both."

"I love surprises." Emily wiggled from her seat and followed Savannah down the hallway with Aiden right behind her.

Savannah opened the nursery door first and turned on the light.

Tears shone in Emily's eyes as she pressed her hand to her mouth. "This is beautiful."

"Incredible." Aiden wrapped his arms around her. "You've outdone yourself."

"You like it?" Savannah bounced on her toes, a grin breaking out as she gauged their reactions.

"I love it." Emily grasped Vanna's face between her hands and kissed each cheek before hugging her. "The whole room is set up. How did you manage that?"

"Ummm." Savannah ducked her head to hide the flush in her cheeks. She hoped Emily wouldn't say anything about Brandon and the paperwork. Not that it would matter with him still sleeping in her bed. The trick would be sneaking the guy out.

Emily smothered a laugh and winked at her behind Aiden's back. "The Japanese cherry blossoms are perfect."

"There's more." Savannah grabbed her stepmother's hand and pulled her into the hallway. "Wait until you see this." She opened Kellan's door.

Emily's dabbed at her eyes. "You did a nautical theme. He'll love it."

Aiden stood in the middle of the two, and wrapped an arm around each of them. "The bed's assembled and in place? And the shelves hung? Hmmmm." He looked at Emily. "I didn't know our Vanna was so handy around the house."

Savannah twirled a lock of hair around her finger as the flush in her face deepened. "Don't be mad."

Aiden's eyebrows rose.

"Brandon helped. He dropped off something for Emily, and he hung the shelves and helped with the furniture."

Emily laughed out loud. "And?"

"Daddy?"

"Oh boy, here it comes." Aiden scrubbed a hand over his face. "Now we know who belongs to the shoes."

Emily prodded him in the ribs with her elbow.

Savannah's eyes widened and her stomach clenched. "You knew?"

"Not that it was Brandon, but we figured someone was here." A furrow appeared in Aiden's brow.

"It's complicated, right?"

"Ha." Aiden snickered. "All the times I said that, and you rolled your eyes. Ouch." He rubbed his ribs where Emily had elbowed him again, harder this time. "Take it easy, Em."

"Aiden." She shook her head.

Savannah wrapped her fingers into her hair and tugged, wishing to sink into the floor.

"Sweetie. I'm only teasing." His expression became serious as he untangled her fingers from her hair. "Please don't do that. And don't cry." He slipped his arm around her, allowing her to lean against his chest. "I'm not angry."

She sniffled even as she clung to her dad.

"I like Brandon. And I'm no longer his supervisor."

"You don't think he's too old for me?"

"Maybe a little." Aiden rubbed her back. "But I figured this was coming."

Savannah tipped up her head. "You did?"

"There's something between you and Brandon. It's obvious, at least to me. I won't interfere, as long as he treats you right."

"Thank you, Dad."

"We planned to take Kellan to the aquarium today. If Brandon is on days off, he could join us." He planted a kiss on her hair. "If you don't have other plans."

"Emily?" Savannah glanced at her stepmother.

"I'm in, after breakfast and a shower." She stretched.

"I need coffee." Aiden ran a hand through his hair. "Did you two want breakfast, Vanna?"

Vanna nodded. "I'll just …" She spun and hurried down the hall, slipping in through her bedroom door, and leaning against it. That had gone better than she expected.

"You're back," Brandon whispered.

Savannah gasped as she pressed a hand to her chest. "I didn't know you were awake."

He kept a sheet over himself as he sat on the side of the bed and stared at her. "They're home? How do I leave without being seen? Your dad will kick my ass for being here."

She approached the bed and sank down beside him. "You're invited to come to the aquarium with us."

Brandon frowned. "You told him?"

"You left your shoes by the front door."

"So they know it's me?" He scrubbed at his jaw, his eyes widening. "That I spent the night here?"

"That was evident, given it's seven in the morning. You wanted me to tell him. Now he's been told." Vanna entwined their fingers and angled her body toward him. "You were serious about dating, weren't you?" Nausea rose at the thought he might have been just saying what she wanted to hear.

Brandon stroked her cheek with his thumb and nodded.

"We don't have to go with them. If you have to study or have other things planned, I understand." Savannah patted his knee. "My dad's making breakfast, if you're hungry."

"So it won't be weird if I join your family today?" Brandon asked as he tugged the sweater over his head.

"You should come."

"Get that awkward part over with, huh?" A smile teased at the corners of his mouth. "Give your dad a chance to get in his shots at me for corrupting his daughter?"

"Exactly. And we don't have to remain glued to their sides for the whole day."

"True." The tension seemed to drain from his body. "Let's do this."

Vanna took his hand, entwining their fingers as they entered the kitchen. His grip tightened as Aiden turned.

"Morning. Anyone interested in coffee?" A frown fleeted across Aiden's face as he studied Brandon, before turning to retrieve two cups.

"What was that look?" Brandon said under his breath.

Savannah bit her lip. "You're wearing his sweater," she muttered before the corners of her mouth twitched. Watching Brandon's discomfort was entertaining, but she also found it endearing that he was so nervous about making a good impression on her dad, even given the circumstances. "Don't worry about it. It's fine." She pressed a kiss to his cheek. "Now, you get to tell your sister."

⌁

By the end of the day, a happy glow had overtaken Savannah. Brandon's acceptance of her dad's invitation on the relaxed family outing calmed the undercurrent of tension. Aiden and Emily's quiet acceptance of the situation put everyone at ease.

"Your dad's amazing with Kellan," Brandon said as he opened the restaurant door later that evening.

"He adores kids. You should see Daniel and Adrianna around him. He's the fun uncle for them. I would have loved growing up with him." She squeezed his hand. "My parents were great, though."

Brandon nodded, a slightly wistful look on his face as he leaned in to give his name to the hostess. Moments later, they were on their way to the table he'd reserved for dinner.

"Piper texted and she'll be here in a few minutes. It went well today. Aiden and Emily were great."

"I knew they would be. You don't need to worry about my family, Brandon." She rubbed his hand and leaned in to accept his kiss, pausing to caress his cheek with her fingertips. As she drew back, she glanced toward the door, her gaze falling on his stepsister, who had halted partway across the room, pausing for a split second before proceeding to the table.

"Savannah. What a surprise to see you. Here. With my brother," Piper said in a flat tone accompanied by an edgy, sharp smile. She settled in her chair and focused on their linked fingers, which rested on the edge of the tabletop. "So."

"Savannah and I are seeing each other again." Brandon fixed his gaze on Piper. "Hopefully, you can be supportive of our relationship."

After a moment, a smile spread over Piper's face, not quite reflecting in her eyes. "If you're happy, I'm happy." She grasped her glass of water and took a small sip. "What ever will your dad say?" The slightest narrowing of her eyes challenged Vanna. "Dating one of the medical students from his ER."

"We went out with Aiden and Emily today. It's all good." Brandon grip tightened in a subtle show of support. "No sneaking around."

"Mmmhmmm." A slight smirk appeared on Piper's face as the server descended with menus.

Savannah opened hers, glancing over the top occasionally, trying to decipher Piper's expression. Though Brandon's stepsister seemed immersed in selecting her entrée, clearly their news hadn't been well received.

Her suspicions grew as the evening wore on and Piper avoided direct conversation with Vanna, responding to any attempts with short, curt replies. The whole of Piper's attentions centered on Brandon. By the time Brandon excused himself toward the end of the meal, Savannah was ready to scream.

"What's your problem?" The words flew from her mouth the moment Brandon was out of earshot.

"Really? You have to ask? You told me the two of you were over and done. Yet here you are, butting in on our family dinner." Piper fixed an icy stare on Vanna.

"Despite your whole "if you're happy, I'm happy" spiel, you in fact don't support our relationship?"

"Hell, no. But, whatever. In a month or so, he'll be bored. He never stays with any girl longer than a few weeks. His relationships are counted in hours, if you know what I mean. You should end it now so you don't get hurt." Piper's smile was saccharine and a little gleam appeared in her eyes. "He might keep you around a bit longer than usual. Take full advantage of the little princess and the rich daddy who can influence his career."

"So concerned for my welfare." Vanna scoffed. "I thought you were my friend."

"Friends don't make moves on my brother." Piper's expression morphed into a bright and cheerful smile as she focused on something over Savannah's shoulder. "If you tell Brandon, I'll deny everything. Who do you think he'll believe?"

Brandon slid into the chair next to Vanna's. "Anyone for dessert?"

Piper shook her head. "I have a ton of homework so I should get going. Thanks for dinner."

Brandon rose to give his stepsister a hug.

Piper held on for an inordinately long time before laying a kiss on his cheek. "Catch you later." She rubbed Brandon's arm and shot Savannah a look before she headed for the door.

"Did you want anything else?"

"No. I've had enough." Savannah waited while Brandon paid the bill and then followed him onto the street.

"That wasn't so bad."

"Were we at the same dinner?"

"What?"

Savannah considered each word before she spoke. "Piper seems unhappy about us being together."

"She'll get used to it." Brandon slipped his arm around her waist as they wandered toward his apartment. "What did she say?"

"You really want to get into this?" Savannah sighed at his brief nod. "She reminded me that you don't have a stellar track record with women."

"Did she?" He halted, grasping her shoulders. "It's true. I haven't had many long-term girlfriends. Does that scare you?"

Savannah studied him for a moment, pushing aside her reservations about Piper's words concerning Aiden and his position at the hospital. "No," she said in a gentle voice.

"Good. I like you, Savannah, or I wouldn't be here. And I'm sorry Piper is being so tough."

"We'll get past it, I'm sure." She forced a reassuring smile for his benefit, even though she wasn't so sure Piper would be in any hurry to get on board.

~⋖

During the next few weeks, they settled into a regular routine. To Savannah's relief, Piper found a position at another law firm for the summer, so she didn't have to deal with the disapproval and animosity.

Fortunately, Rochelle still texted her often, even though her friend had gone home for the summer. Her friend had initially been shocked at Piper's words, but had told her not to worry. She was sure it would blow over before they returned to classes in the fall.

Justin had a slightly different take on the matter when she'd broached the subject with him, but in the end, his advice was simple. "Decide how much this guy means to you, Vanna. If you can't trust that he's there for you, then cut bait now. You're amazing, and any guy would be lucky to date you."

Vanna decided to hang on tight and enjoy the ride and see where the relationship led them, even as the danger signs flashed red alert in her mind.

Handing her heart to yet another guy seemed crazy, but she still wanted to believe this time would be different.

On this lazy Saturday morning, she kicked back on the sofa, perusing a magazine and sipping a latte.

Brandon hunched over a medical text, one of many scattered across the table. He leaned down and dug through his bag, then heaved a sigh. "Do you have a notepad?"

Savannah rose smoothly from the sofa, stopping to wrap her arms around him and plant a kiss on his cheek. "Dad probably has one. I'll be right back." She trailed a hand over his shoulder before she headed into the office.

She checked the top drawer before sliding open the bottom drawer of Aiden's desk. "Nope," she muttered, but froze as the name on the tab of the blue folder caught her eye. *Tiffany.* After a moment, she sank into Aiden's chair and set the thick file on the desk. She ran her trembling fingertips over the name before she flipped the folder open.

Her eyes widened as she scanned the legal document, noting the name of the gallery and the astronomical dollar figures. Her breath caught when she reached the end, her attention drawn by the signatures. Her dad's. And *hers.* Tiffany Gabrielle Hamilton.

Hearing that name had been one thing, but seeing it made Vanna's stomach clench in a heavy knot. *Gabrielle.* If things had been different, that would have been her middle name.

Savannah absorbed the details of the agreement. This had been executed not long after Aiden had visited Chicago, but before Tiffany's most recent visit to Boston.

She closed the file, but as she picked it up, an envelope slid out and landed on the desk. Savannah frowned, and stared at the note clipped to the front:

> *Dear Aiden,*
> *Please give this to her when she's ready. Thank you, for everything.*
> *Love, Tiffany.*

Love? A flicker of resentment rose at that word. This woman just wouldn't leave them alone. Yet curiosity burned at what her mother might have to say. She smoothed the note with her fingertip, staring at her name written in the flowing script across the front of the card-sized white vellum envelope.

"Hey, did you get lost?"

Savannah jerked her head up and frowned as Brandon appeared in the doorway.

"What's wrong?"

"I found this." She tapped a fingertip on the note. "From *her.*"

He circled around the desk, resting one hand on her shoulder as he peered at it. "Open it."

"I don't know if I can." Her voice shook.

Brandon turned the chair toward him and crouched to her level. He drew her into a hug. "This is hard for you, isn't it?"

She rested against his shoulder and closed her eyes, inhaling even breaths to calm her pounding heart. "I want to, but what if …?"

"Take your time, honey." He pressed a kiss to her temple.

Her gaze wandered to the envelope. "Aiden didn't give it to me. He thinks I'm not ready."

"Only you can decide that."

Savannah bit her lip. "Can you give me a minute? Please?" She squeezed his hand and he kissed her again before exiting the room. She drummed her fingers on the desk. What would be the worst outcome if she opened it? Took the chance? Let Tiffany have her say, even if not in person?

Vanna slid a fingertip under the seal and extracted the card. The intricate design sketched on the front caught her eye. Despite the small water stains, like droplets of moisture had fallen across it, the swirling lines were well preserved and seemed incredibly familiar.

She traced the intricate pattern, closing her eyes, the picture of a similar one forming in her mind. Her fingertip traveled to her mouth, and she nibbled her nail as she opened the card and read the words written in the familiar flowing script:

> *My heart aches*
> *It will never recover*
> *I vowed to protect you*
> *To never let you down*
> *But I've failed*
> *You were wanted*
> *Always*
> *You are loved*
> *Forever*
> *I long to hold you*
> *But never can*
> *I wish to see you grow*
> *But never will*
> *You were stolen*
> *From my loving arms*
> *I long for you*
> *I weep for you*
> *Wherever you are*
> *May you be loved*
> *May you be treasured*

My darling daughter

She brushed her eyes with the back of her hand as she read it again. And then again.

Unexpected. Savannah had braced herself for an impassioned plea. A meaningless bundle of words as her mother begged for forgiveness. But never this sweet missive, straight from the heart of a confused teenage girl.

She tucked it inside the envelope before she rose and crossed the office to the storage closet. The box tucked toward the back on the middle shelf beckoned her. Savannah carried the box to the massive desk and stared at the pink ribbons peeking out the top.

Maybe the time had come? She weighed each gift in her hands as she transferred them onto the solid wood surface and lined them up. *Five.* Not so many.

The first gift contained a jeweler's box. She gazed at the deep red stones as the earrings glittered on the velvet padding, and then held them up against her ear and inspected her reflection. "Pretty."

The second package contained a palette of makeup with a set of luxurious brushes. Savannah had seen the brand in stores. Not only was it expensive, but the colors were perfect for her complexion.

She moved onto the next present, not stopping until she'd opened all five gifts.

Nothing earth shattering or momentous, but still, each gift suited her and felt like they'd been chosen with care.

She read the card one last time before she rejoined Brandon. She placed her hands on his shoulders. "When are your next days off?"

"I'm off Friday through to Monday. Why?"

"How would you like to go to away with me this weekend? My treat."

⌒⊸

Aiden carried her bag to the sedan waiting at the curb. "Are you sure you don't want me to come with you? Can call her?"

Savannah shook her head. "I need to do this without you, Daddy. Besides," she said as she smiled at the dark-haired man beside her, "I won't be alone."

Her dad gave the briefest of nods before opening the car door. He patted Brandon's shoulder before her boyfriend settled in beside her.

"I can't believe he's okay with this." Brandon shifted in his seat.

Savannah reached for his hand. "He'll worry, but he understands." She stared out the window as they neared the airport. "I can't set up expectations. What if I'm unable to do it?"

Brandon gave her fingers a reassuring squeeze, but allowed a comfortable silence to fall over them until they towed their small bags into the terminal.

"This one." Savannah pulled him into line.

Brandon pointed to the sign. "First class?"

"Always." She presented the confirmation number when they reached the front of the short queue. After checking their suitcases, they zipped through security, and Vanna led Brandon into the lounge. She ordered them drinks and appetizers to share while they waited.

"When you said you were paying for flights, I didn't expect this." He gazed around. "How are you paying for this?"

"My dad's travel account. Our agent has standing instructions to book first or business class."

Brandon's eyes widened. "Did you ask him first?"

"Relax." Savannah patted his hand. "I always charge my travel expenses to his account." She tipped her head, listening to the announcements. "That's our flight."

They arrived at the gate as the first class passengers were filing onto the plane.

Brandon sank into the large seat. "This is amazing, Vanna."

She reached for his hand. "Thanks for coming with me, Brandon. I appreciate your support."

CHAPTER 24

Tiffany

B Y THE TIME TIFFANY ARRIVED at the gallery on Saturday morning, things were already picking up. With the new financing in place, the shackles had been lifted, and she could invest in advertising, travel out of town, and set up shows on an unprecedented level.

She said yet another silent thank you to the man who'd made this possible. Without David looming over her shoulder, a new sense of confidence and freedom flowed through her.

Isla gave her a small wave before she turned her attention back to the group of ladies clustered in front of one of the paintings.

A smile twitched her lips as she headed toward her office. Her business wasn't the only thing taking off. After the first date with Stefan, her personal life had taken a new direction. He'd been appearing almost daily with her favorite chai or a coffee, and last night they'd spent a cozy evening at his apartment.

She tucked her bag into the office before she headed onto the floor to help Isla with the customers. It always surprised her how much she loved this part of owning a gallery. Helping people choose the right piece of art seemed like a small thing, but she appreciated the hours of enjoyment a beautiful piece could give. How it defined a space, adding life and color.

The bell over the front door chimed and she looked up, spotting Stefan. He held up the large cup with a grin, and she excused herself from the group.

"I wasn't sure you were coming in today." She accepted the cup, sniffing the subtle hazelnut tones. "Thank you. This smells divine."

"I'm on my way to a meeting. I had to tell you how much I'm looking forward to this evening." He winked. "Can't give you any reason to get away, now can I?"

"I'm not going anywhere." She patted his arm. "I'll be ready by eight."

The bell chimed again.

"It's busy today. I'll get out of your way, but see you tonight." He planted a kiss on her cheek.

Tiffany turned, opening her mouth to greet the newcomer. Her voice locked in her throat and her eyes widened. Her breath rushed out as she stared into familiar brown eyes.

"Tiffany?" Stefan's own eyes widened at the young woman standing inside the doorway.

"Savannah." Tiffany breathed out. "Oh …"

Savannah shifted, her hand rising to brush back a stray lock of hair, but her gaze remained riveted on her mother.

"What are you doing here?" Tiffany wished her stubborn limbs would obey so she could wrap the girl into a hug. Always, that inescapable dread lingered. What if Savannah pushed her away? What if she squandered that one final precious chance with her daughter?

"Sorry, I shouldn't have come." Savannah bowed her head, her hair falling forward to hide her expression. "I'll go."

"No. No, stay." Tiffany beckoned her daughter. "Come in. Please?"

Stefan cleared his throat. "Umm, call me?" His gaze swung toward Tiffany, and then to Savannah before returning to rest on Tiffany.

"Stefan, this is Savannah …" Tiffany floundered. *How could I not even know my own child's name?*

"Savannah Phillips Hamilton." Savannah supplied after a moment, extending her hand to Stefan. "I'm a fan of your work, Mr. Cortes."

Tiffany rubbed her hands across her skirt. "Savannah is my daughter."

"Lovely to meet you, Savannah." Stefan smiled and shook the girl's hand. "Sorry, but I have a meeting in a few minutes, so I should run." With a touch on Tiffany's arm, he exited through the door.

Run. That's what Tiffany feared he would do, now that she'd disclosed the existence of an unknown child. Her gaze followed him for an instant, but then she redirected her attention to Savannah. Silence fell as she struggled to find the right words.

"I thought we might go for coffee, but I see you already have one," Savannah said as she glanced toward the door. "Stefan Cortes. Wow. I adore his work. Sorry, I didn't mean to interrupt."

"I'm never too busy for you, Savannah." Tiffany sought Isla, giving a hopeful look at her assistant, who was still chatting with patrons. The subtle widening of the woman's eyes and slightest motion of her chin toward the door told Tiffany the gallery would be in good hands. "I'd love a break. I'll get my bag."

Tiffany's knees shook as she dashed for her office, almost frightened that when she returned this mirage might have disappeared. It all seemed unreal. She closed her eyes and took several long breaths before she walked through the gallery to the front.

Savannah was examining one of the displayed paintings, her head tilted as she studied it.

"What do you think?" Tiffany asked.

"It's beautiful." Savannah peered out of the corner of her eye at Tiffany. "But I'm no expert."

"Oh, I don't know. You have the talent—" Tiffany froze. She didn't want to remind the girl of the turbulent night when they'd crossed paths in Boston. Silly, really. Her daughter wouldn't have forgotten. Savannah owned an obvious intelligence. But perhaps the memory of their encounter had been dulled by time, losing the vibrancy and whittling away the sharp edges. After all, her precious daughter had found her way here.

If Tiffany was lucky, Savannah wanted to open that long-awaited discussion. Or maybe, and more importantly, her daughter had loosened the guard over her heart and mind enough to listen and hear. "Shall we?"

After a brief nod, her daughter turned toward the door.

Tiffany turned to the right as they exited onto the street. "There's a wonderful little shop just down the block." She struggled to keep the tremble from her voice as she lifted a hand, making a brief motion.

Savannah took in a long, audible breath. "I should've called."

"I'm happy you're here." Tiffany held the door and they entered the small coffee shop, choosing a booth toward the back. Once they were settled with steaming cups of latte in front of them, she cleared her throat and fixed her gaze on the young woman across the table. "I don't even know where to start."

"I'm not even sure why I came." Savannah frowned and picked at her nail. "It was impulsive. Dad wanted to call, but I told him no."

Tiffany longed to comfort the girl, but she feared her touch would drive her daughter away. *Patience, patience.* She drew in a long breath, fighting the urge to give in to the mix of emotions. So many feelings threatened to bury her under the onslaught, she couldn't discern between them. "Aiden knows you're here?"

"I thought it would be easier if I came alone." Savannah dipped her chin. "Dragging him into the middle of this ... well, maybe that's inevitable. He's already there, isn't he?"

Tiffany gazed at this astute girl, this small part of her who was also a part of *him*. His words came back to her—how he often saw each of them in this young woman. At this moment, she could sense it. It almost felt like Aiden was right in front of her. She bit back the confessions and apologies for every sin she'd committed against him.

How would that help? Careless words could only damage what little she'd gained. The many disastrous actions and poorly considered choices had already destroyed too much of that which had been precious. *When would the pain end? When would I cease to torment those I loved?*

"I'm sorry, Savannah. I never meant to get in the middle of his marriage, but what is between me and Aiden, we can't let it ..." She blinked hard and sipped from her cup, hoping to loosen the lump lodged in her throat. "Please." The rest of the words seemed stuck, but she hoped her daughter could see the truth in her eyes.

Savannah contemplated her with those deep brown eyes in a way that made her connection to Aiden even more palpable. A harsh reminder of how he'd so often looked at Tiffany herself with cool detachment after their relationship had faltered, striving not to give anything away. He'd become skilled in the art of the blank mask, which fooled many. Yet, underneath, Tiffany had seen more; a subtle undercurrent of thought and emotion that was as obvious in her ex-husband as it was now with her daughter.

"He'd have come if I'd asked, but it wouldn't be fair to him, or to Emily," Savannah said. "Dad's supported every one of my personal decisions. It's been my choice to not see you until now."

"I understand." Tiffany nodded. "I don't know what he's told you about us, but I'm so sorry for everything."

"It's not that he volunteers information." Savannah sighed. "But he's never lied to me, either. I've seen and heard things."

Tiffany's stomach lurched, heat creeping into her cheeks. "I'm not proud of—"

"Don't." Savannah held up one hand, the other rising to wrap around a sparkling heart pendant. The girl exhaled a long breath, her tone softening. "Dad and I have already discussed it. I'm not ready to get into it with you."

Tiffany bit her lip, searching for a neutral subject that wouldn't cause this girl to bolt. "He's been good to you?"

"Dad?" Savannah's watery smile tore at Tiffany's heart. "He's the best. Without him, I don't know how I would have gotten through any of it."

Tiffany twirled a lock of hair around her finger. "He's an amazing man, and I've been unfair to him. But my biggest regret is that I've been unfair to you."

"Why did you turn me away? When I found Aiden, he gave you the opportunity to see me." She lifted tear-filled eyes. "I've never understood."

"I was scared and confused." Tiffany blinked to quell her own tears. "I've thought about it often, and it's difficult to explain, even to myself. Everyone had expectations, and I'd closed that door to my past. Opening it and facing it again terrified me."

Savannah ducked her head, her curtain of long hair hiding her expression. "You're ashamed."

"My failings have nothing to do with my feelings about you." Tiffany dragged in a breath. How could she explain the turmoil, the confusion? How her own family fed on her vulnerability and made her feel worthless? "When we made the decision to keep you, we acted on instinct. I never considered any other option. Then reality caught up to me. How could two fifteen-year-old kids provide a stable home for a baby? Everyone around me confirmed it daily and convinced me I wasn't equal to the task."

The girl lifted her chin.

"Aiden supported me, but imagine being powerless," Tiffany whispered. "They separated us and left me with no one on my side. I regret not being stronger, not fighting harder. How I wish we'd managed to disappear." Tiffany clutched the napkin in her hand, dabbing at the corners of her eyes. "So many stupid mistakes. Why do we always hurt the people we love the most?"

The slow blink of those shimmering brown eyes tore at Tiffany's heart.

"I'm not oblivious to what I've done to you. To Aiden. To everyone around me. All I ask is one chance to make it right. Please, Savannah, it would mean everything. I can never be the mother I should have been. The mother you deserved, but ..." *Please forgive me for not having the strength.*

"How either of you had the courage to do what you did, I don't know," Savannah said softly. "I don't blame either of you for what happened when you were fifteen. It's only now that matters. Having you look at me that way, knowing I ruined your entire life, hurt."

"You didn't. And you must know Aiden never felt that way. I've never forgotten how much we wanted you, Savannah." Oh, so much to say. An overwhelming litany of words, and feelings, and regrets, and longing. A deluge of emotions that would certainly crush this tentative and fragile conversation.

"From the day I learned I was adopted, I imagined what my parents were like, especially my mother."

Tiffany managed a faint smile, her head bobbing. "I often imagined what you looked like, and how you took your first steps, and ... just everything." She closed her eyes.

The fall Savannah turned five she'd envisioned a petite girl with blonde ringlets and a tiny pink backpack on the way to her first day of school, trudging through the colorful fall leaves, turning and waving, offering an uncertain, but precious smile that warmed a mother's soul. Tiffany reopened her eyes.

"I dreamed about everything I'd never see. The places I'd never take you. The holidays we'd never have."

"I couldn't believe I'd found my father. I spent hours staring at that picture, dreaming about how wonderful it would be to meet my mother." Savannah's tone flattened. "Then he told me it would never happen."

Those words shot straight into Tiffany's heart. The dream world building in her mind shattered.

"He flew to Portland. I expected him to bring you. But he didn't."

Nausea rose, and Tiffany forced herself to take several breaths. The girl's words resonated, echoing through her mind. When Aiden had approached her, it had been tough to accept her daughter as a real person. Over the years, as the memories faded and she buried it all deeper in her mind, the girl seemed like someone Tiffany had dreamed. An imaginary being, rather than a living, breathing person with her own thoughts and feelings.

"Do you know what that was like?" Savannah didn't blink, those piercing and accusing eyes so reminiscent of Aiden in another time and place.

"I'm sorry. So, so, sorry. I never meant to hurt you, Savannah."

"What about Dad? That moment hurt him as much as it hurt me. I punished him for it. Did he tell you *that?*"

Tiffany thought she knew what shame was, that her father had mastered the art of making her feel insignificant and worthless. She'd been mistaken. This time, she had no choice but to accept it. This time, the blame fell directly onto her. This time, she couldn't deny it as truth.

"There is so much I regret. So much pain, all caused by me. I hope you'll give me a chance to make it up to you." Even with the guilt written across her face, she forced herself to look at her daughter. "I promise, I will find a way to make it up to Aiden."

"How?" An almost silent scoff issued from her daughter. "You can't *unhurt* someone. Some wounds never heal. Some things you can never take back. Some words can never be *unsaid.*"

The hope Tiffany harbored at Savannah's appearance faded. She had to accept this might be the one and only opportunity to express everything locked inside. She may never have another. But still, she couldn't form the words. She could only wish she'd possessed as much wisdom at such a young age. Perhaps then, she wouldn't have fallen so far.

"I can't take it back, but I can wish for a miracle, can't I?" She reached across to squeeze her daughter's hand, but found herself grasping at empty air as Savannah tucked her hands into her lap. Tiffany closed her eyes as she withdrew and entwined her fingers. "I can beg for forgiveness and hope someone hears and grants my wish, however undeserved it may be."

Silence met her statement, and she peered across the table, thankful her daughter still sat there.

"Please don't lose touch, Savannah. I'll give you as much space and time as you need, but I'll always be here. Waiting for you."

Tiffany tossed her keys into the tray on the side table as she stepped into her apartment. She set her phone on the counter, ignoring the line of texts and missed calls. She simply couldn't bring herself to respond, no matter how unworthy that made her of his affections.

And she had to admit, there was an ever-growing emotional attachment between her and Stefan Cortes, which only served to make her feel worse about not returning the phone calls and messages. But she simply didn't know what to say.

If he broached the subject of her coffee date with Savannah, could she admit how her daughter's brooding silence had sealed her fate? How did she deserve someone so incredible when she'd treated everyone around her with such disdain for so long, including the man who would always be in her heart?

She fought the urge to contact Aiden. Who, besides Aiden, truly understood? Who else had gone through the same trials and tribulations? However, she'd made a promise she considered sacred; to quit interfering in the relationship that healed his pain and made him complete.

Her phone buzzed again. She owed it to the man to at least give him some clue as to what she was thinking. After all, they were supposed to meet for dinner, even though sitting through a meal in a busy restaurant was the last thing she wanted to endure.

She stared at the screen for the longest time before she hit dial.

"I thought you'd never call me back." His deep low voice greeted her.

"Sorry," she whispered. "Can I have a raincheck for tonight? I wouldn't be very good company."

"You still have to eat."

"I'm not terribly hungry. I might just crawl into bed."

"I could join you." His chuckle was deep and low, but his voice turned serious. "I'd love to see you, but I understand if you aren't up for company tonight. How about an early dinner tomorrow?"

Despite her misery, she allowed a faint smile. "That sounds nice. You're on."

"Perfect. I'll pick you up at five," he said. "You have a lovely sleep, sweetheart, and I will see you tomorrow."

"Night, Stefan." She flopped onto the couch, holding the phone to her chest, thinking about how the sound of his voice had made her feel better. She tipped back her head, catching sight of her art table, which had been a birthday gift from Aiden in happier times. One of the things that had attracted her to this cozy apartment had been the bright space where this precious piece fit perfectly.

She dragged the throw from the back of the couch, tucking it around her and flicking off the light, staring through the large windows, searching the cloudy sky for some sign. She burrowed her head into the pillow, allowing her eyelids to fall shut as exhaustion overtook her.

Her eyes snapped open, her heart pounding before she realized she was safe and sound on her couch. The dream had disoriented her, the final visions of the bright butterfly vanishing before she could reach it with her outstretched fingers, the futile chase down the beach vivid in her mind. The heartbreak threatened to overwhelm her senses, but a small thought niggled in the corner, prompting her into action.

A few steps through the dim apartment, and she stood before her closet. She dug through the pile of boxes from her mother's house, locating the one she'd hadn't finished sorting at Christmas. Tiffany settled herself cross-legged on the bed, with the box beside her. As she unpacked each item, she set them out in an orderly line.

She revisited them one-by-one, stowing the precious memories in her mind as she viewed the treasures from the happiest of her days with Aiden. When she came to a small velvet box, she closed her eyes and held it over her heart before opening the lid. She lifted out the engagement ring first, holding it delicately between her fingertips as she turned the ring, admiring how the diamonds winked and sparkled, still beautiful even after all these years in storage. Once she'd slipped it onto the end of her index finger, she inspected the matching wedding band.

These belonged to Aiden. They'd been his great-grandmother's rings, bestowed upon Tiffany when he asked her to marry him. Yet, despite how valuable they were, in both monetary and sentimental terms, he'd never demanded their return, even in the thick of their acrimonious divorce. And she'd never had the heart to part with them.

She nestled them on the velvet cushion and tucked the jeweler's box into the bottom of her dresser drawer. Tiffany located a smaller packing box and fitted the selected items inside like a jigsaw puzzle, padding them with extra tissue. With a faint smile, she carried it into the living room.

Her fingers itched, and her table beckoned, the plan hatching in her mind. Seating herself in front of the art table with two sheets of fresh paper, she closed her eyes, picturing Savannah, the beautiful butterfly who'd flitted out of her life, maybe for the last time.

And then she started, allowing her fingers to glide over the paper as she sketched, crafting each line with exquisite detail and utmost care. Two hours later, she lifted her head and stretched, holding up the finished piece with a satisfied smile. She selected a portfolio from one of the drawers and tucked the finished sketch inside. On the second piece of paper, she wrote a few simple words before folding it in thirds and sliding it into an envelope.

Once she'd wrapped and sealed the parcel with packing tape, she wandered to her room, stripping her clothes from her body as she progressed across the floor. She crawled under the covers and drifted into a dreamless sleep.

Chapter 25

Savannah

Savannah's vision adjusted to the dim room as she blinked, clearing the sleep from her eyes. A sliver of light infiltrated from the hallway along with the low sounds from the television.

Complete exhaustion had overwhelmed her when she returned to the apartment, but a perceptive Brandon had read her confusion. The man had cradled her in a warm embrace, causing a burst of tears and helpless sobs as she relived that painful hour.

As she closed her eyes and cuddled against Brandon's chest, his gently murmured words soothed and his light kisses against her hair comforted. She'd allowed him to tuck her into bed, nestling in his arms as she drifted to sleep, all the while her subconscious mind processing a bevy of conflicting emotions.

Her own barbed words had stunned her, released pent-up emotions buried in the many months … *years* … since that day Aiden had visited in Portland. The numerous counseling sessions hadn't uncovered the root of her frustration and discontent, or even her own guilt at how she'd treated Aiden. Her apologies were inadequate and pale when she contemplated the past. Yet, he persevered, remaining a spring of unwavering support, forgiving the words and actions he had every right to hold against her.

Now she crawled from the bed and padded down the hall into the living room, leaning over the back of the couch to wrap her arms around Brandon.

"You're awake." He tilted his head up and rubbed her hands, leaving his warm ones resting over hers. "Feeling better?"

"Much." She kissed his cheek. "I've neglected you."

"No worries. I watched the game on this amazing big screen."

"Guys and their sports." Her tummy rumbled. "Maybe I can entice you away for dinner."

"Sounds like you could eat." He grinned and turned to pat her belly with his familiar and comforting touch. "Are you up to eating out?"

Savannah nodded. "Let me change, and then we can go." The sound of the TV abated as she made her way down the hallway to her room, peeling the sweater over her head as she went. After splashing water on her face, and redoing the makeup ravaged by tears and sleep, she deemed herself presentable to the world.

"How did it go with Tiffany?" Brandon asked as they made their way onto the street a few minutes later.

"Awkward. Can you believe I've never said more than five words to my mother? Like ever?"

Brandon shook his head. "I can't imagine how that must feel. Did it help sort things out?"

She shrugged. "I expected someone different." Vanna gave him a sideways glance. "I had this vivid picture of how it would be when I met her, but it didn't happen anything like that. Even now, I can't reconcile who I thought she was with who she truly is. I have no idea how to feel about her or what she told me today."

Brandon ushered her inside the restaurant, throwing the occasional glance her way until they were seated. "Have you called your dad?"

"Not yet. I bet she did, though." Savannah ran a hand through her hair. "It's strange. For the longest time they barely tolerated each other, yet now they're friends and allies. And Emily is totally fine with it, which makes zero sense."

Brandon studied her, a slight frown creasing his brow.

"Why are you looking at me like that?"

"I wish my parents had made an effort. Our family dynamic is a mess, and now it's too late."

"We're so perfect for each other. We both have screwed up families." Vanna sighed. "I'm forbidden to go near either of my grandfathers. Aiden made me promise. He practically forced me to sign in blood."

"He worries, and he wants to protect you. That's not a bad thing. And if your mother and Aiden have learned to coexist, that's even better."

"Maybe it's too late for that."

"Or maybe not. At least they're trying, which is more than I can say for my parents."

She took his hand. "Do you ever see your dad?"

Brandon shook his head. "He bowed out of our lives even before the divorce. The last time I remember him spending any time with me was"—his lips twisted—"when I was eight. He took me to a ballgame."

"I'm sorry. What about your little sister?"

"Mia was a baby when he left, so she doesn't remember him. Maybe she's not even his kid. That time is a blur in my mind, but there was no shortage of guys parading through my mother's life. She may have cheated on my father. Hell, maybe he cheated on her."

Savannah closed her eyes, wondering if the same might be true of her own mother. *Is that what went wrong? Did my mother do that?*

"My mother used to pile sympathy onto Mia."

"What does she do for you?"

"Not a whole hell of a lot." Brandon scoffed. "Jeremy—Piper's dad—is okay, but I'll never be his son." He rubbed his jaw.

Savannah squeezed his hand. "I'm sorry for being harsh about how you relate to Piper. You haven't had it easy, growing up without your father."

"Could be worse. But you're a lucky one. Emily seems sweet and your dad spends a ton of time with you."

"I didn't have either of them for most of my life." Savannah tugged at a chunk of her hair. "Maybe Aiden's learned not to take our time together for granted."

He caught her fingers and untangled them from her long wavy locks. "You'll have lots of time with Aiden."

"You can't know that. One of my worst fears is losing my dad." Tears pricked her eyes. "Both of my adoptive parents are gone, and there are no guarantees. You work in an ER, so you must understand that."

"Well, sure. But I try not to let it get to me."

"I wish I could shut it all out, but I've come close to losing him, more than once. It's not so easy to forget."

"Because he gave you up for adoption?"

"That's its own unique experience, but I mean he nearly died. That happened only a couple of summers ago."

A furrow appeared in Brandon's brow. "How?"

"We were sailing off the coast of the Vineyard and he was knocked overboard. We were moving fast and the waves were pretty high, so it's a true miracle we found him in time."

"That had to be scary."

"It was. That's why I find it difficult to joke about sailing accidents. He didn't do anything wrong, and he still ended up in freezing water, with a dislocated shoulder, treading water for at least an hour. I still have nightmares about it."

He answered with silent nod and a squeeze of her hand. "You have a great family, Vanna. I love hanging around your place, and I'm sure Emily and Aiden are sick of seeing me, but they're like the family I wish I had but never did," Brandon said.

"Ah, so the truth come out. You're dating my family."

He smiled faintly. "That's not why I'm interested in you."

Even if her family were part of her appeal, Savannah wouldn't make an issue of it. She'd never trade her dad, Emily, or even her little brother for anyone and understood why people enjoyed being included in the happy and loving atmosphere that blessed her home. "It would be difficult for me to be with someone who didn't get along with my dad."

"But no pressure, right?" A grin spread across his face and his eyes sparkled. "Don't worry, he and I talked and established rules about me dating you, so—"

"*Rules?* You and my dad came up with rules?" Vanna's cheeks flushed as her anger flashed. "That's just so wrong."

"It wasn't like that."

"How could you talk about me with my dad?"

"Why are you freaking out? We agreed on how things are dealt with at work. Like keeping our personal business out of the ER. We've already been through that awkwardness once. Go for a second time and he'd fire my ass."

She frowned. "You promise work's all you talked about?"

He placed his warm hand over hers. "This is my career, Vanna. I've worked hard, and I can't screw it up. Punching your idiot ex-boyfriend will only go so far in redeeming me to your dad."

She lifted her head. "Oh, crap. You didn't tell him who it was, did you?"

"Well, pretty hard for me to do that since I don't actually know the loser's name." Brandon narrowed his eyes. "You haven't told your dad?"

"You saw how he reacted. What do you think he'd do if he knew it was Gray?" She bit her lip as a steely look appeared in Brandon's eyes. "Please, please don't say anything," Vanna whispered.

"Damn, Vanna. Piper wouldn't shut up about Gray last time we were home. That jerk is in your class?" He gasped both of her hands. "You need to tell someone."

"I can't." She pulled away. "I wasn't even supposed to be there."

Brandon slid out of the booth, and moved to sit beside her, curling an arm around her waist. "Do you want to talk about it?"

Savannah leaned into him. "Can we just enjoy our dinner? It's been a long day."

"I wish—"

She pressed two fingers against his lips. "Please let it go. It's too late to report it, and if you tell my dad who it was, I will never forgive you."

"I hate keeping this to myself, but okay. For you."

"Thank you." She planted a kiss on his lips. "Tomorrow I'll introduce you to my Gramma Grace. She wants us to join her for lunch, but you have to promise not to say anything at work."

"Ahh, okay." A furrow appeared in his brow. "Why?"

"You'll see."

The black sedan eased through the wrought iron gates and turned toward the airport.

Brandon threw a final glance over his shoulder before he angled toward her. "That was interesting."

She smothered a laugh. "Why?"

"That place. It's insane that Aiden grew up there."

"He mostly lived at boarding school. Summers until he turned fifteen were spent in the Vineyard or traveling." Savannah settled deeper into the plush leather seat. "When I first met him, it seemed strange that my dad's family is so wealthy, but he acts like a normal guy most of the time."

"You'd never know his family had money unless you deciphered the little clues. Penthouse apartment. House in the Vineyard. Sailboat. Expensive vehicles and designer clothes in that massive closet. Not to mention the jet."

"The law firm owns the plane."

"Right." Brandon snickered. "And who owns the law firm?"

Savannah rolled her eyes. "Now, remember your promise about work. Don't say anything to your big-mouthed roommate. There's a reason Aiden doesn't talk about his family at the hospital." She extended her pinkie.

He gave a low laugh, but he linked his finger with hers. "I swear. And now I feel like a chick for doing this pinkie thing."

She wrinkled her nose and smothered a giggle.

"Did I pass the test? It's hard to know what your grandmother thought of me."

"She invited you to call her Grace, and she said you should visit again. That's a positive endorsement." She entwined their fingers. "If Gramma didn't like you, you'd know it."

CHAPTER 26

Tiffany

TIFFANY SLID HER ARMS INTO the light coat and tucked in the pashmina as Stefan donned his own jacket.

Sitting through dinner with the heavy uneasy feeling flitting around her stomach while she awaited Stefan's reaction to yesterday's revelation had been unbearable.

She liked this guy and had allowed him to break through the barrier, but when he learned her truths, her realities, he'd run. If she discovered similar facts about a man she'd only started dating, she'd surely be out the door. People didn't change, did they?

"Are we going to talk about it?" Stefan slid a warm hand around her waist as they negotiated the sidewalk, dodging the crowds drawn outdoors by the mild spring weather. "You barely ate anything, and you've been quiet." Stefan sighed. "I can't pretend forever, Tiffany."

She peered at him. "Pretend?"

"That I'm not curious about yesterday. I'd hoped you'd open up, but it seems I'll have to pry it out of you."

Tiffany gave him a rueful smile. She'd been holding it all in, assuming his silence meant he had no interest. Or worse, he'd been contemplating how to break up with her.

"How old is your daughter?" Stefan maneuvered them around the queue of people waiting to enter a popular hangout, steering them toward the lake.

"Eighteen."

"Savannah is a beautiful young woman. She looks like her mother." He frowned. "Why didn't you tell me?"

"The relationship is complicated." Tiffany captured her wind-swept locks and arranged them in a neat ponytail with one of the hair bands she kept in her bag. She smoothed her hand over her head, tucking in the stray wisps that tried to escape. "I never see her. She lives with her father in Boston."

"Her father being Aiden Hamilton." Stefan raised a brow at her brief nod. "How did that one fly under the radar?"

"Savannah was placed with adoptive parents at birth." She shot him a sideways look, judging his reaction. "Our families buried her existence until she found Aiden four years ago. So," she said with a shrug, "I'll understand if this is too complicated. I didn't mean to withhold information."

"We've only been seeing each other a short time. I couldn't expect you to tell me your whole life story when you hardly know me. You were young, so I understand why you'd give up a child."

"It's not nearly so simple."

"It never is," he said as he enclosed her hand in his. "You must want to have a relationship with her."

"I do." She nodded. "It's been difficult, and I've made mistakes. Her showing up was a huge shock. It's sad, but yesterday we had our first actual conversation. Ever. And I doubt she'll agree to see me again. That hour might be all I ever get."

"I'm sorry."

"Ah, well." She waved a hand. "I won't bore you with the details."

"Don't do that."

"Do what?"

"Discount your feelings. Don't pretend. You had a difficult day. I'd like to hear about it."

Tiffany's grip on his hand tightened. Rarely did anyone take the time to ask how she felt about anything. Most of her existence had been spent on a rogue wave, forever struggling to regain her footing, weighing each word before she spoke. "Do you really? It's a classic faux pas to talk about the ex-husband and past marital issues this early in a relationship."

"Don't be like that. I'm asking you to divulge a few details about your daughter. You're not talking endlessly about the situation, and I'm interested. Is it too early for you to trust me, if only a little?"

"I'm not sure you'd understand." She bit back the words she longed to say, but couldn't.

"Give me a little credit." A dark look appeared. "Even though I haven't been through what you so obviously have, it doesn't mean I can't listen and understand how you feel."

She closed her eyes and nodded. "Don't blame me when you're ready to get as far away as fast as humanly possible."

Stefan sighed. "Why would you assume that of me?"

"In my experience, most men don't want to deal with my messy past." Harrison never had. She'd never discussed Savannah or her marriage to Aiden until toward the end. The revelations about her daughter, along with the infidelity on Harrison's part, had torn them apart. She'd feared him leaving, but in the end, his exit from her life hadn't been what she'd expected. Instead of the desolation and pain she'd braced herself against, there had been nothing but relief. Maybe Harrison's lack of remorse played a part, but he'd also revealed his darker side.

The whole affair stood in stark contrast to the devastation in the wake of Aiden's departure so many years before. In that moment, she'd known that settling wasn't an option, but finding another man she could love like she loved Aiden seemed an impossibility.

"I'm not most men." Stefan's words pulled her back to the present, even as he brought them to a halt and turned toward her. "And I'm not ideal boyfriend material, either. I travel a lot, and it's taken a toll on every single relationship I've ever had."

"I'm less than the ideal woman for you."

"Because you're divorced with a teenage daughter?"

"It's the *why* part of the divorce that makes me less than ideal. And I haven't been a good mother to Savannah."

"How old were you when you married?"

"Eighteen." She pursed her lips, contemplating how much she should admit to him. "It barely lasted two years."

"So young." He shook his head. "You blame yourself for the divorce?"

She nodded. "I screwed up and ruined everything."

Stefan tilted his head a touch, his expression giving her no clue as to his thoughts. "Why do you say you've not been a good mother?"

"I refused to see Savannah when she found Aiden. It hurt her, and it hurt him. I've done more than my share of damage to the people around me."

"Do you regret what happened?"

"Every single damn day." She forced herself to meet his gaze. "The truth is, I'm a horrible woman who cheated on her husband, which destroyed a marriage that should have lasted forever. And then I turned away my own daughter when she needed me most. Why would you stick around?"

"You are more than the sum of your mistakes. Don't discount yourself, or be needlessly strong. Sometimes the best thing is to accept your human failings and let yourself fall apart. It's the only way you can rebuild."

Whatever she expected, this was not it. This man confused her with his odd proclamations, but he still stood before her, waiting expectantly. "You sound like—" *My therapist.* She caught the words before they escaped. Admitting she attended counseling would be the kiss of death on this budding relationship. Maybe after tonight he'd avoid her. Never call the crazy lady he'd almost made the grave error of getting involved with.

"Sound like who?"

She looked away, unable to add this new admission onto the pile of evidence mounting against her.

"Tell me. Do you talk to your ex-husband?"

"Frequently." At least she had been in the past few months, so it wasn't a complete lie. "Is that a problem?"

"Nope."

"That's all you have to say?"

"For now." He tugged her into motion, seeming to get lost in his own thoughts.

"This is insane," she said, after they'd walked some distance down the path. "How can you be so nonchalant about all of this?"

"I'm simply accepting the situation for what it is." He glanced her way. "Somehow I think your life experiences make you exactly the woman I should be with. You've dealt with all of these issues. You clearly regret your mistakes."

"Yes, but ..." She studied him, uncertain of how to frame the questions in her mind, unsure of what her questions actually were. "I don't understand why you're interested about the frequency of my conversations with Aiden."

"If he has forgiven your mistakes and supports you on the quest to know your daughter, then isn't that enough? How do I have the right to punish you or even judge your past? The woman you were back then no longer exists."

"I'm still her."

"No, you're not. Time and experiences have a way of changing us, whether for the good or the bad. After spending time with you, I truly believe you're stronger for the trials life's put you through."

"Well, that's a positive and rosy glow placed over my less than stellar behavior."

"I'm a positive person. I refuse to accept my journey through life involves a dark cloud over my head, and neither should you. The future is what we make of it. I'd like my time here to include you. Why chase after the illusion of a perfect, cardboard cut-out woman when I can have someone who has wrestled with the dark side of humanity?"

Tiffany furrowed her brow, emitting a nervous laugh. "Oh yeah, the super catch of messed up contradictions."

"I'm not a saint. Casting stones would be hypocritical. I've never married, but that doesn't mean I haven't had relationships or made my own mistakes, or even harbored my own self-doubts. On the bad days, a tiny little negative devil reminds me that no woman in her right mind would even entertain a relationship with me. Maybe you're the one who should run."

"Perhaps I should." But she wouldn't. This man had entangled her, intrigued her, given her a sense of anticipation. He'd pulled her from her melancholy over her daughter's keen observations of how spectacularly Tiffany had failed everyone and reminded her she wasn't alone. Tiffany forced them to a halt, noting the amusement reflected in his expression. "Maybe you'll have to persuade me."

"I love a challenge." He caught a lock of her hair, leaning in close so the waft of his musky cologne washed over her. "You have a fire and passion burning within you," he said in a deep, husky voice that caused a shiver down her spine. "A sensual, sexy woman inside longing to escape and revel in a wonderful adventure after being locked away for so many years."

This unexpected turn sparked her imagination. Funny how the two men in her life cut right through the charade. Unsurprising that Aiden sensed her secret desires, but that Stefan had glimpsed them, perceived her deepest longings, and seen her as she truly was, shocked her.

"Now you're opening up to danger. Maybe I love my own kind of challenge. Taming the wandering soul of Stefan Cortes."

"Why tame me?" He lifted a brow. "Why not join my trek on the wild side? Next trip I take, you should come and experience life first hand. Enough hiding, Tiffany." A wicked grin crept across his face as he tugged at the band that forced her hair to submit and remain in its tidy, orderly place. He caught her fingers as she made a half-hearted attempt to stay his hand. A subtle shake of his head silenced her protests.

Tiffany remained rooted in place, staring into his dark and serious eyes as he loosened her hair, permitting it to billow over her shoulders in an unruly, wild cascade.

"Set her free, love," he whispered against her ear. "Let it all go, and set her free."

Chapter 27

Savannah

M ONDAY MORNING ARRIVED AND VANNA crawled from bed, still tired from the trip to Chicago, but too keyed up to sleep. She had the day off work to recover, but she could hear movement in the hallway, and figured her dad was already up.

"Vanna." Aiden kissed her cheek as she appeared in the kitchen. "You got in late."

"Hi, Dad." She hugged him tight. "Thank you."

"For what?" He rocked her against his chest, pressing a cheek to her hair.

"Everything." The rush of emotions swamped her along with a sudden urge to cry, but she willed away the tears. No matter what she did, he was always there with supportive words and love. "Want some company on your walk to work?"

"That would be great."

They rode down the elevator and headed onto the street.

Savannah tipped her face toward the sky, smiling as the morning sun warmed her cheeks. Spring was one of her favorite times of the year. She reached for her dad's hand, slipping her small fingers into his. Time to get it over with. "I have a confession." She caught the swift look her way. "I saw the papers on the gallery."

Aiden halted and turned toward her with a frown. "As in …?"

"Tiffany's gallery in Chicago. You gave her money. A lot of money. Why?" Her breath caught at his intense scrutiny. She searched for a clue as to what he was thinking. "I didn't mean to snoop, but I was searching for a pad of paper. When I saw her name on the file, I had to look."

"I'm not thrilled you went through my desk, Savannah." He pulled her onto one of the benches nearby.

She bit her lip and stared at her hands clutched in her lap.

"David yanked her funding without warning. She'd have lost everything."

"You bailed her out?" She lifted her chin. "Why?"

"She asked for help, and I knew she'd run out of options."

"How?"

Aiden's brow lifted. "Do you think she'd ask for my assistance if she had any other viable choices?"

She tilted her head, giving the slightest nod to acknowledge his point. "I suppose not. It's an amazing place. She's talented, isn't she?"

"That she is, and she's worked hard. Allowing David to rob her of her dreams for his own petty reasons seemed unfair."

"But still, why would you give her so much money?"

"It's not a gift. I guaranteed her business loans. She'd never take money from me."

"You would never give it to her anyway."

Aiden slung an arm over the back of the bench as he angled toward her. "Actually, I would. Without hesitation."

Savannah lifted her brow, her mind spinning at that declaration.

"You're dying to know why, right?"

"Well, yeah. You've barely tolerated each other for years. She was about to marry that Harrison guy. She seems very high-maintenance."

Aiden shook his head. "Whatever else you might say about your mother, she's not a gold-digger, and I guarantee she's not a high-maintenance princess or a brainless idiot. I damn sure wouldn't have married her if she was any of those things."

Savannah gazed at him steadily, willing him to continue.

"It's compensation for what my family did. Or maybe it's revenge. Watching as David loses the iron grip over his daughter is satisfying." He lifted a shoulder. "However you look at it, she's free. She can rebuild and live her dream."

Savannah took his hands. "What do you get out of it?"

"Good karma?" The corners of his lips twitched.

"It must be more than that."

"I loved her, Vanna. She was a huge part of my life for a long time." His expression grew serious. "I'll always care, despite everything we've been through. She's fought many battles alone, and maybe having someone on her side will make the difference. Seeing her find happiness would be amazing."

"She has Grandma Michelle."

"That relationship is strained. Her parents weren't any better than mine in many ways."

"Right, they dumped her in boarding school. Didn't they?"

"True, but she always stayed with them over the holidays. I rarely visited my parents in New York and usually ended up at my grandparents' house. Anyway, Michelle doesn't have access to that kind of money. This is something only I could do, and it made sense for me to help."

"Does Emily know?"

He nodded. "Remember what I said about trust? Our family is solid, Vanna."

She squeezed his hand. "Thank you for not freaking out on me."

"I'd never do that." He sighed. "Why do you feel the need to know about every interaction I have with Tiffany? It feels like you're watching every move I make."

Savannah furrowed her brow. "I'm not."

"Yes, you are. Even her visit to the hospital put you into a tailspin." Her dad linked her fingers with his and leaned back on the bench. "Is it simple curiosity about your mother? Or something else?"

She tipped her head against his shoulder, snuggling closer as his arm slid around her. "I don't know, Daddy. Maybe it's the same reason I can't bring myself to move out, even when my friends tell me how amazing it is to live in the dorms."

"Hmmm. I didn't know it was something you'd considered."

"I never did until they mentioned it. I love being home with you and Emily, and Kellan. If I move, I'll miss too much of everything." Tears pricked her eyes. "Being with you, and having Emily, and a little brother, and knowing my little sister will be born soon …" She sniffled. "I'm not ready to leave our family."

He pressed a kiss to her hair. "It feels like making up for lost time. All the things we missed over those years. I'm not in any hurry for you to move out."

A small smile emerged. Her dad understood.

"Do you feel like Tiffany being in the picture threatens what we have with our family? You're tense even talking about it."

"What if she's the one you were meant to be with? What if one day you wake up and decide you made a mistake?"

"I don't believe that will ever happen."

"How can you be sure?"

Aiden turned to look at her. "Nothing in life is guaranteed, Savannah. But this I know. What I had with Tiffany was the polar opposite of what I have with Emily. Yes, I loved her, but our relationship was volatile and unsettled. We were so young, and everything took far too much effort."

"You and Emily fight."

"Every married couple argues, but with Emily it feels very different. I can't say it's easy as we have our moments, but it's right."

"I don't understand how you know it's Emily and not Tiffany."

"Maybe it's not for you to understand. Some things are better left unsaid, and some relationships are not meant to be. Tiffany's great, and I encourage you to get to know her, but there's too much baggage between us. We had many opportunities to get back together, but we didn't. Even if something happened between me and Emily, it would never work with your mother. It's not an option, and you need to quit thinking that it ever could be."

"Because she cheated?"

Something flickered in his eyes, but his expression remained impassive. "Who told you that?" he asked in a level voice.

Sadness enveloped her. She sensed she'd hit on the truth, even if her dad was doing his best to keep his emotions under wraps. "You," she whispered. "When I told you about Gray cheating, I could tell whoever had done that to you meant something. If it wasn't Emily, it had to be her." She dug her nails into her palms.

"Whatever you're thinking, please don't hold it against your mother or let it affect your decisions about seeing her. Anything that happened in the past is between her and me. Our mistakes have already been paid for and forgiven."

"How can you have forgiven her?"

"I'm not blameless in the end of our marriage, Savannah. Can you let it go? Please?"

Savannah hated that she'd been right about Tiffany. It made her regret her visit to Chicago, yet the tiny curious part inside wanted to know more. More about her mother, and more about her dad.

Every time she had him figured out, he revealed another tiny piece of himself and made her realize she hadn't solved the puzzle of Aiden Hamilton. Not even close. "I'll try. I love you." She leaned in to hug him, wishing she hadn't brought up a conversation that caused him pain.

"I love you, baby girl." He squeezed her tight. "I have to go to my meeting." Aiden sounded regretful. "Are you going to be okay? You didn't tell me how it went in Chicago."

"She didn't call you? Or you didn't call her?"

"Nope. You told me to butt out, so as hard as that was, I decided it was best that I did. The two of you need to figure this out without my interference."

She gave him a faint smile. "Thank you."

Savannah wandered home, stopping for a coffee along the way and sitting a while in the Commons. The sun was high in the sky when she let herself into the still and silent apartment.

She found a note on the counter:

Gone to the park with Kellan. Back in a couple of hours. Package on the desk for you.
Love Emily

She hurried over to the small workspace at the side of the kitchen. A medium size box awaited with her name and address on the top. It appeared to be have been posted by overnight courier from Chicago, though she couldn't find any clue as to who had sent it.

She hefted it, feeling the solid weight before grabbing a letter opener and running the edge along the packing tape, breaking the seal.

On top was an envelope with that familiar flowing script, and just underneath, a folder rested on top of photo albums and other small items.

She tapped a finger against pursed lips, contemplating her next move. Her first instinct was to drop the package onto her dad's desk and let him deal with it. He'd become a skilled blocker, intercepting whenever she called upon him to create space between her and the Baxter family.

Savannah paced in front of the small workspace, back and forth while eyeing the package with suspicion. The problem was, she'd insisted on handling this round of communication with Tiffany herself and had been the instigator of said contact. Laying the responsibility onto Aiden to *handle* anything regarding his ex-wife seemed like the coward's way out, especially considering how she constantly reminded her dad that she was now a grown-up.

No way around it. Curiosity was edging out her irritation, making her twitch. The opportunity to get a sanctioned view into Tiffany's life was too good to pass up.

Savannah scooped up the box and carried it to her room, pushing the door shut with her foot before placing her package on the bed. She settled cross-legged with it in front of her before she began the process of unpacking, laying each item in an orderly row.

She scanned the items before rubbing her palms across her black leggings, gathering the courage to look at the framed picture for the second time in her life.

This time, instead of a brief glance, she held it in her lap, taking in each and every detail. Tiffany in Aiden's arms, cradled like he was ready to carry her from the sunny tropical beach over the threshold of a first home, the skirt of her white dress trailing toward the sand, the diaphanous chiffon fluttering in a feathery breeze.

Savannah tilted her head as she stared at Tiffany's face. A visage reflecting overflowing devotion and joy as the woman twined her arms around Aiden's neck. His gaze conveyed a look of tenderness akin to that she'd seen directed to those he loved most. Her, Kellan, and Emily. Her dad never hid his love for Tiffany. Lately, he'd stressed the connection he'd once had to the woman who'd given birth to her.

Next was the album. The pages inside told a story she wasn't sure she wanted to know, but there had to be a reason Tiffany sent these. She took her time, viewing each snapshot of two people on a blissful though distant honeymoon. Multiple photos led her through the pages filled with vibrant and vivid color.

Palpable warm breezes flowing in from the ocean, rich cuisine, and bright sunlight on palm trees. Happy smiles, all telling of a fairy tale love. One she knew had ended in deep pain, confirming that there could be no happily ever after in the real world.

This album wasn't a tale of two strangers. The intimate portraits contained within the pages were of her father and her mother. *My parents.* She hugged the album to her chest, for the first time feeling a tiny thread linking her to the woman who'd given her life.

"My mother," she whispered, squeezing her eyes closed and reclining against the pile of pillows at the head of her bed. Visions of how her life could have been flitted through her mind. Not that she regretted growing up with her wonderful Mom and Dad, but what if Aiden and Tiffany had raised her? What if she'd been encircled in the love her mother and father once possessed for each other? Would she have been the foundation that kept them together and allowed them to flourish as a family?

Now she seemed an unwitting participant in the destruction of their happiness. The key ingredient in a blend of misery and torment that tore Tiffany down and ripped her parents' marriage into shreds.

She opened her eyes, staring at the swirling pattern of her ceiling, an indefinable sense of mourning overtaking her.

Every moment of happiness and joy her adoptive parents had experienced in watching her grow had been a piece of joy stripped away from Aiden and Tiffany. Moments they'd never regain. Moments that changed the trajectories of their lives, creating a whole new journey for every single one of them.

She flopped out a hand, her fingers landing on the cool smoothness of paper. The letter and folder still awaited, along with several other albums and small boxes. She clasped the two items in her fingers, setting the letter across her chest with the album before flipping open the portfolio.

What?

In one swift movement she rose to a sitting position, her eyes widening. She inspected each line in turn, taking in the exquisite details, the smooth arcs, the fine embellishments. She held it away, relaxing her focus to consider the whole, her breath catching as she spotted the letters intricately woven into the design.

"*D-e-o-i-m-o-c-h-r-o-i,*" she whispered as she traced each intricate swirl with her fingertip, noting the odd the dot hung above the final *i.*

The whole sketch seemed familiar.

Slightly symbolic.

An echo of the pattern tattooed on her dad's shoulder.

She crawled from her bed and opened the drawer where she'd tucked the card with the poem. A single glance told her exactly what she needed to know.

Savannah pulled out her laptop and typed in the letters, forming them into words based on how they'd been arranged in the design.

Deo i mo chroí. Forever in my heart.

As much as Savannah longed to share her discoveries with Brandon, he'd been called in for a shift. Which in retrospect, might not be such a tragedy, considering the situation. It gifted her valuable time to ponder and finish her perusal of all the items and albums included in her package.

She tucked them safely away, not sure how to open the discussion with her dad. And in the end, it would be her decision whether or not to continue building a relationship with Tiffany.

Tuesday morning arrived too soon, heralding her own return to work. The moment she arrived, Tom called Savannah into his office.

"We received a pile of information on our case." Tom motioned for her to sit. "We need to dig into those witness statements and compare findings."

"No problem." She glanced at the pile on the small conference table. "Those?"

"I've booked the entire day so we can work uninterrupted."

Savannah grinned. To her, this was an exciting part of the job. Watching Tom prepare for a trial was incredible. Being allowed to work with him, to learn his process, and to hear the thoughts of a top lawyer seemed like a treat. Besides that, she loved investigating and analyzing and playing detective.

They each took a stack, and made themselves comfortable on the plush couches. Savannah commented when she found something interesting, and Tom did the same, their notepads filling with questions and observations as they examined each and every file.

A sharp rap on the door broke their concentration. Vanna realized they'd been at it for hours.

"Tom?" Joel said as he poked his head in. "Can I see you for a minute?"

"Tell me." Tom waved as he flipped to the next page of his file. "Vanna is sworn to secrecy."

"Tom." Joel's firm tone made the other man look up. "It's urgent, and ..."

Savannah didn't miss the significant look thrown her way.

Tom nodded and followed Joel into the hall.

It piqued her interest but she refocused on her file. It could be her imagination.

Moments later Tom returned, rubbing his jaw and looking serious. "I need to take you home."

"What's wrong?" She bounced off the couch. Her breathing grew shallow and spots danced before her eyes.

Tom took her by the shoulders. "Your family is fine, but Aiden needs me to bring you home." He gazed into her face. "Breathe, sweetie."

Savannah inhaled and let it out slowly. "What's wrong?"

Tom studied her. "I know you're not close to your grandfather, James Hamilton."

"He never wanted to know me." Savannah shrugged.

"This is about him." Tom gave her a long assessing look. "James Hamilton has been shot. Aiden asked that we escort you home. I'm sorry, sweetheart."

Tom and Joel flanked her as she rode the elevator to the garage level of the office building. The moment they were out the door, they were ushered into black SUV's, Joel in the first, and her with Tom in the second.

She clutched Tom's hand and cast nervous glances at the men in sharp dark suits sitting up the front.

"You're not in trouble. They're taking precautions." Tom's low voice reassured her. "Relax."

Spots danced in front of her eyes again. Even with Tom's reassurances, she worried about her family.

"Gramma Grace?" She choked out the words.

"Safe. Don't worry, everyone is safe, but you're needed at home." Tom slid his arm around her, letting her lean against his shoulder.

Minutes later they were in the garage at their apartment being ushered into the elevator. Savannah bounced on her toes, anxious to see everyone for herself.

The door opened, and they were met by a burly man in a suit and earpiece. He scanned them and then nodded to the agent in the elevator.

"It's okay," Tom murmured as he led her out of the elevator and through to the living room.

"Vanna." Emily wrapped her into a hug, holding her tight.

"Where's Dad?" She viewed the room, tears blurring her eyes.

"In the office." Emily rubbed her back. "Tom, he asked for you to go in as soon as you arrived."

"What's happening?" Savannah tried to breathe.

"Tom didn't tell you?"

"He said James Hamilton was shot? Is my dad in danger? Or in trouble?" Savannah whispered, panic running through her.

"They have questions. They're trying to find who did it, and all of this is a precaution until they have more information. I'm sure none of us are a target, Vanna. Aiden had little to do with James." Emily's phone buzzed and she glanced at it before hitting dial. "Hi, Brandon. What?" She raised a brow at Savannah. "Do you have your phone? Brandon has been trying to reach you."

She patted her pockets. "I left it in Tom's office."

"Here." Emily held out her phone. "I'll get someone to find it and bring your things home. It'll be a while before you go back to work."

Chapter 28

Tiffany

AFTER RUNNING THE NUMBERS ONE final time, Tiffany gave a satisfied nod. "Thanks, Isla. This is amazing."

"You're welcome." Her assistant smiled. "It's all coming together. I can't believe how much progress we've made in such a short time."

Tiffany sent another silent round of thanks to the universe for the upswing in her business and for freeing her from her father's iron grasp.

It didn't hurt that Stefan showed up daily with her coffee and they spent at least twenty minutes, and often much longer, chatting. It bolstered her confidence, and she looked forward to another date with him over the coming weekend.

"Thank you for sticking it out. I appreciate your work more than you can know."

"My pleasure," Isla said. "This place will be a major success. You have the most amazing eye for art."

"I love it so much. And Aiden has been amazing."

"I told you he wouldn't miss that little drop in the bucket." Isla sipped her coffee. "Your daughter is lovely, by the way. Stefan seems to have taken the news well."

"I felt like an impostor, pretending to be something I'm not, but he accepts my past."

"Why shouldn't he? We all have one. You're a wonderful person, and I enjoy working with you. You should let more people see this side."

"Thank you, but I don't feel wonderful most of the time."

"Why not?"

Tiffany stared at the list on her desk. "I've done many things I'm not proud of. Take Aiden. He has no reason to be so kind and supportive. I've been downright nasty to him countless times, yet he bailed me out, no strings attached."

"So what does that say? If you were a horrible person, would Aiden do all of these things for you?"

"I'm sure he sees a sad charity case. He's like a saint or something."

"Perhaps he is, I don't know the man well enough to say." Isla tapped a finger against pursed lips. "I understand it wasn't a small amount of money. I don't need to know," she said, holding up a hand, "but don't sell yourself short. Don't assume yourself unworthy. Even if Aiden is vying for sainthood, he must feel you deserve redemption. You've said he knows you better than anyone, so he must be right. And Stefan isn't shying away from spending time with you. The man is in here like clockwork every single day, even after you've spent the night with him."

"How do you know that?" A flush rose in her cheeks.

"Damn, woman. You look so content after a night with that fine man. Someone's falling in love."

She opened her mouth to reply, but a noise in the doorway interrupted her. "Mom?" Tiffany noted the puffy red eyes and drawn look on her mother's face. "What's wrong?"

Isla assisted Tiffany in seating Michelle on the office couch and dashed off for water.

"Mom, talk to me." Panic rose within Tiffany.

Her mother emitted a series of ragged sobs, followed by the floodgate of tears opening. She seemed to shrink, curling into herself and trembling uncontrollably.

"Here." Isla offered the glass.

Tiffany pressed it into her mother's hand, encouraging her to sip it. "You're scaring me."

"Your father." Michelle sobbed. "He's gone."

"Gone?" Tiffany's breath caught in her chest. "What do you mean?"

"He cleaned out the bank accounts. Cashed it all in and disappeared."

"When? Why? How?" Tiffany pressed a hand to her chest. "He took all your money? What about the house?"

"He drew all the credit lines and credit cards to the maximum. After the commissions and legal fees, there's barely anything left. I got the statement from the lawyer this morning." Michelle's entire body shook as she sank against her daughter. "It's all gone. He stole it before the lawyers collected what he agreed to pay me. Who knows where he went."

"Can we find him?"

"I don't know." Her mother's tearful gaze met hers. "The police are looking for him. James Hamilton …"

"What does that man have to do with this?"

"Somebody murdered him. Shot him on the street in New York this morning. I don't know if David knew it would happen and colluded to have him killed, or if he's scared about who's coming after him, but he's gone. I don't even know if he's alive."

"James Hamilton is dead? Does Aiden know? Is he okay?"

"If I got a visit, I'm sure they're all over him, considering what James did for a living." Her mother's chin quivered. "They think both James and David had ties to organized crime," she whispered. "It may have been a paid hit."

"Or it could have been someone he prosecuted." Tiffany pulled back. "Organized crime? So my father was involved with criminals?"

"The police believe so. It makes me ill thinking about it."

The bile rose as Tiffany thought about Harrison, and Aiden's comments about her former fiancé. Did he know? Is that what he'd been alluding to all this time?

Tiffany bolted from the office, barely making it to the bathroom. Tears streamed down her face as she dropped to the cold floor, heaving into the porcelain bowl. She dragged a hand over her mouth and slumped onto the icy tiles, wrapping her arms around her legs and curling into a ball.

A tap sounded on the door. "Tiffany?" Isla opened it a crack. "Phone call."

"Take a message," she muttered.

"You should take it." Isla kneeled in front of her. "I locked the doors. I checked the calendar, and we don't have any appointments this afternoon."

Tiffany sucked in a breath and allowed Isla to help her to her feet. A glance in the mirror reflected back her ashen face and red-rimmed eyes. She felt clammy and chilled to the bone, and her knees trembled. All she wanted to do was crawl under her covers and hide from the world.

"Tiffany? Your call?"

"I don't want to talk to anyone."

"It's Aiden. I think you should—"

Tiffany dashed through the bathroom door, snatching up the receiver of the nearest phone. "Aiden. Are you okay? Gramma Grace?"

"We're fine. Mostly, anyhow," Aiden said. "How are you?"

"Mom is flipping out. That bastard took everything. She'll be on the street." Now the initial shock had worn off, Tiffany seethed with anger. "I don't know what to do."

"It's a tough set of circumstances, but stay calm. Ben's aware of the situation, and he'll manage everything for you and for Michelle," he said. "Tiff? They're asking me questions about the gallery, and the money we paid David. We called Ben."

"We?"

"Tom's acting as my counsel. Does Michelle know about the financing?"

"I never had a chance to discuss it with her. She knows nothing, and I don't want her to know. She's intolerable when she thinks she's right."

"Yeah, I understand your sentiments. I'd keep it to yourself unless you're forced to tell her. I'm sure nothing will come of it."

"Okay." She clutched the receiver. "I feel like a horrible person. I don't even feel bad about James."

"Huh, try being his son and being unable to shed a single tear. I don't even know what to feel aside from stressed out. Gramma is having a hard time with it, and Caroline is in shock, but I feel nothing."

"Let me know if there's anything I can do for you."

"Thanks. I need to get back, but you know what to do, Tiff."

The call from Ben came only minutes after she'd said goodbye to Aiden, and after his assurances that he was on top of the issues, she returned to her mother. Isla had settled her on the small sofa with a light blanket over her.

Michelle bolted upright the moment Tiffany walked through the door. "What are we going to do? They locked me out of the house. The credit cards are frozen, as are the joint accounts."

She studied her mother's pale face. *We* stretched the truth. Tiffany had her cozy apartment to return to and her business had been severed from David's, though her mother didn't know that. All her mom knew was that her husband had split with their substantial savings and left her life in shambles. *The bastard.* After all the years her mother had devoted to that man, he'd left her penniless, homeless, and hopeless.

Michelle's normally perfect hair stuck out at all angles and she sported dark circles under her red eyes, both from lack of sleep and residual mascara. Her cheeks were mottled and blotchy.

Tiffany's heart softened and she sank onto the sofa, curling an arm around her mother's waist. "My place isn't big, but you can stay with me for a few days. Ben Landon will advise us on next steps."

"A lawyer? That means legal fees? I can't aff—" Her mother dropped her head into her hands. "And the gallery. You'll go under." Her head came up. "The gallery. He didn't take everything from me." Michelle sagged, dabbing at her eyes.

Isla sent Tiffany an inquiring look over the top of Michelle's head.

Tiffany widened her eyes and twitch her head, hoping Isla would remain silent about the financing. Her mother appeared so distraught, Tiffany didn't have the heart to break the news that she'd paid David out weeks ago. "My gallery won't go under."

A sick feeling curled in Tiffany's stomach. Had David planned this all along? Was it orchestrated to get every penny he could before he breezed out of their lives?

"My entire life is ruined." Michelle huddled into a ball, looking pitiful.

"I'm sorry, Mom. We'll work something out." She pulled her mother closer. Despite all the pain and differences they'd endured, Tiffany didn't have the heart to abandon the woman. That would make her no better than her parents had been when she'd needed them and they'd failed to show her compassion.

Someone rapped on the glass of the door, and Isla jumped to her feet and hurried across to unlock it.

Stefan strode across the floor, gathering Tiffany into his arms. "It's all over the news. Are you okay?"

"I'm a little in shock." She pressed her cheek against his chest, letting the steady beat of his heart lull her. It hit her how much she'd missed having the love and support of a man. It had been forever, aside from the recent compassion from her ex-husband, but she wasn't sure that counted.

They held each other for a minute longer.

"There's sure to be a service for Aiden's father in New York." She peered at him. "Would you come with me?" She blinked hard. "Oh, no, you have your photo shoot in New Zealand."

"I'll reschedule." He cupped her cheeks and placed a gentle kiss on her nose. "Being here for you is more important right now."

~≺

The funeral service for James was held graveside in the early afternoon, the spring sunshine casting an odd cheer onto the proceedings. A light breeze carried the fragrance of the multitude of flowers surrounding the coffin over the mass of people.

Tiffany eyed the photo of the man, shifting to avoid the gaze of those piercing eyes as she refocused on the Hamilton family. Grace moved slowly, supported by her grandson for a few feet before she straightened and placed a white rose on the top of the coffin, followed by Aiden, and then by Caroline who added their own roses.

She allowed a bitter smile. This should be a solemn occasion, not a cause for celebration, but she'd never rue the loss of James Hamilton from the earth. Not even the tiniest bit. Deep inside a twinge of guilt nagged at her. *How awful of me for thinking that way.* She dug her nails into her palms, reminding herself that James was Grace's son. Losing your child was devastating. That level of excruciating and soul-shattering grief she could relate to.

Her mother's eyes were on her even as Stefan slid his arm around her waist. *Was the conflict within showing?*

Her gaze wandered to the willowy young woman standing close to Gramma Grace. A tall, well-dressed young man wrapped his arm around Savannah's slim waist.

The minister stepped aside as a gray-haired man took his place, his eulogy washing over her in a meaningless wave.

Aiden shook his head when the man invited him to say a few words in memory of his father, which marked the end. People shuffled toward the family to offer their condolences, and then the crowd began to disburse.

"We'll see them at the reception." Her mother tugged at Tiffany's arm. "Grace looks ready to collapse."

Tiffany allowed Stefan to escort them to their own limo, even as the Hamilton family disappeared into theirs.

The ride to the hotel was silent, everyone deep in their own thoughts.

Tiffany reached for Stefan's hand as they entered the reception room. "Maybe this was a mistake. I didn't even ..." *Like the man.*

"This is about supporting the Hamilton family during a loss, no matter what the circumstances." Her mother looked around the room. "That's why these people are here. For Grace, and Aiden, and for Caroline, despite the divorce."

"I don't want to upset Savannah. Let's just do this, and we can get out of here." She wove her way through the crowd to Grace.

The woman looked frail, her arm linked through Aiden's. Her grandson had barely left her side through the whole service, and Emily hovered nearby as the main support for Caroline.

"Tiffany, my dear. Michelle." Grace accepted hugs from each woman "Thank you for coming."

"I'm sorry for your loss." Tiffany felt like a fraud as she forced the words out.

Michelle expressed her condolences to Grace, and then moved on to Aiden.

"Michelle." Aiden gave her a long hug. "How are you holding up? Is there anything I can do for you?"

Tears came to Michelle's eyes. "I'm managing." She pressed a kiss to Aiden's cheek.

Tiffany froze. Emily stood only feet away. This would be the first time she'd seen the woman since that day in the park when she'd broken down. She didn't want to send the wrong message, even though she longed to express her condolences to her ex-husband.

"I'm sorry, Tiff." Aiden pulled her in for a hug without hesitation. "Things can't be easy right now."

Emily appeared at his side. "Michelle." She took the woman's hands in hers. "It's good to see you." Then she turned to Tiffany. "I'm glad you came."

Tiffany stiffened as Emily bestowed a warm embrace, but forced herself to relax. The woman's sympathy for their plight seemed genuine.

Emily stepped back but kept hold of Tiffany's hand. "I'm sorry about David. Please let us know if there is anything we can do for either of you."

"Thank you." She blinked back her tears. How did this woman have such warmth and compassion? Tiffany released Emily's hand.

Despite the solemn occasion, Emily's skin glowed and a small smile touched her lips as she rubbed the belly outlined under her maternity dress.

Tiffany steeled herself for the familiar pain, waiting for the twinge to her heart, but it didn't come. A sense of peace enveloped her. *He'd moved on, found his happiness. This sweet, caring woman deserved his love.*

Stefan exchanged a few words with Grace and Aiden, but as soon as he finished expressing his condolences, he wrapped her hand in his warm one.

Grace focused on them. "We're having a family dinner tomorrow evening. Please join us. Perhaps Emily could give you the details." Grace grasped Aiden's arm. "Could you escort me back to the suite?"

"Of course, Gramma. Excuse us." Aiden supported the elderly woman as they left the room.

Tiffany waved a hand. "We don't need to come."

"No, you should." The soft voice beside her made her turn.

"Savannah. It's …" She reached out and rubbed her daughter's arm as a lump formed in her throat.

"Lovely to see you, Savannah." Stefan grasped her hands.

"I should track down Caroline and make sure she's okay, but please come to dinner," Emily said, pulling Tiffany's attention away from the introductions between Brandon and Stefan. "Seven. Tomorrow evening in our suite."

"We'll be there. Thank you." Michelle hugged Emily before the woman left to find her mother-in-law.

Savannah and Brandon had been pulled away now by Tom, who ushered the rest of the family from the reception.

"Why did you agree?" Panic rose within Tiffany at the thought of sitting down to dinner with the Hamilton family.

"That wasn't just a polite invitation, my love. We're all in this together. James is dead and your father is missing. You'd be a fool to think the two aren't related. We don't have to stay all night, but we should attend."

Tiffany slid an arm around her mother. Michelle was right, whether she liked it or not.

CHAPTER 29

Savannah

$\mathcal{S}$AVANNAH MOVED AROUND THE ROOM, buried in her thoughts. It had been a long day, and the ending had been almost more than she could handle.

"You okay?" Brandon stepped behind her, wrapping his arms around her, holding her in place.

"Yeah, of course. It's just that …" She turned and cuddled against his chest. "I'm glad you're here. I don't know what I'd have done today without you."

"Mmm. What's going on in that brilliant mind of yours?"

"Everything." Savannah rubbed at the tears trickling down her face, peering up at Brandon. "It was excruciating to hear that man's litany of lies about how wonderful James Hamilton was, and then Tiffany barely said two words. Stefan was warmer than her."

"Oh, Vanna." Brandon brushed her cheeks, dropping a kiss on her nose. "I think she was nervous, and there was too much happening. You're her daughter and she loves you. I see it in her eyes every time she looks at you."

"Thank you, you're sweet." She tipped her head up, giving him a long kiss. "A liar, but still sweet."

Brandon squeezed her tight. "I am not a liar. She's trying. So give her the chance."

She burrowed closer, not wanting to break the contact, not wanting to lose this moment. It felt so right, being held in this man's arms. "I love you," she whispered.

"Vanna. I …" Brandon rested his head on her hair, the silence stretching for several excruciating moments.

Vanna's face flushed as she wiggled from his grasp and backed away. "I shouldn't have said that. It's too soon. I've ruined everything." She dodged his outstretched hands and hurried into the bathroom, locking the door behind her before sinking down onto the tile and bursting into tears.

"Please don't cry." Brandon's low voice carried through the door as the handle wiggled and rattled. "Open the door."

"No," she muttered. "I'm stupid, thinking you could love me. I know what happens now." She tucked her legs up and curled her arms around them, resting her head on her knees, trying to smother her sobs. Brandon hadn't said it back.

"Please open the door. We need to talk about it."

"Leave me alone. Please." Heat rose to her cheeks. Not only had she blurted out those deadly words, but now she was crying like a baby. How could she face him again?

"Please come out."

The door handle wiggled again, and to her complete dismay, the door swung open.

"Go away." She hid her face, curling into a ball, then peeked up at him. "How did you get in?"

He waved the metal coat hanger.

Moron. Of course, there was a safety release on the bathroom privacy lock.

Brandon set it on top of the counter and sank down in front of her, resting his hands on her shoulders. "Look at me."

"You're going to break up with me."

"Why would you think that?" He sat on the tile floor and slid an arm around her. "I care about you."

"You don't love me."

He sighed. "It's not that simple." He held her closer. "It's just that I've never said it to anyone I've dated. I don't take it lightly, and I can't say it in the heat of the moment. I don't even know if you meant it, and for me, it's too early to know for sure."

She peered at him. "You've never said it?"

He shook his head. "There hasn't been anyone I've felt like that about. I've cared about girlfriends, but love, real true love, is precious. Sounds dumb, right?"

"No. But you don't feel it with me either, do you? You couldn't say it, so you don't love me."

"I have deep feelings for you. Don't ever think I don't." He stared into her eyes. "I'm not ready to label it as true undying love. We can measure our relationship by weeks, which is no time at all. We need to get to know each other better, to spend more time together, and to find out if we fit. Love at first sight isn't real or long lasting."

Savannah sniffled. "I feel like an idiot."

"Don't. I'm honored you feel that way. I'm not ready to say it back, but it's not that I don't see a future for us. I do, but when I say those three words to a woman, I want them to mean everything."

"You confuse me." Vanna blotted her eyes with a tissue.

"My mother is not the easiest woman to bond with." He handed her another tissue. "But she's an *I love you* slut when it comes to men. Did you know she's on her fifth marriage? She's had a slew of boyfriends. They came and went like we had a revolving door. Two weeks into a relationship, she'd be on about how much she loved this new guy, and he'd be the same, singing her praises, saying he loved her and couldn't live without her. A week, maybe two, and he'd be gone. Then she'd be on to the next guy. And it would be true love again. Over and over, and it never meant anything. Very few of them stayed and even her marriages were short."

"You can't say it because of your mother?"

"I vowed that I'd never be that guy who said it without meaning it. It would be so damn easy with you. You're incredible. I treasure the time we spend together." He took her hand in his. "What's the longest relationship you've had with a guy?"

"Six months."

"My longest was ten months. You're eighteen, Savannah, and I fear you're nowhere near ready to be saying those words to anyone or making that commitment. I'm a medical student. You're one year into undergrad."

"It comes back around. I'm too young for you."

He brought her hand to his lips, planting a kiss on the back of it. "If I'd known you were eighteen, I would've walked away."

"I should be sorry, but I'm not." Savannah leaned against his shoulder. "So now what? You want to break up? Find someone closer to your age?"

"Or we can go day by day and see what happens. It doesn't have to be all or nothing. I'm not ready to give us up, but I'm not ready to say those words either. Do you understand why?"

She gazed at him. He was one of the most honest guys she'd ever dated. Others would have said it to make her happy, whether they meant it or not. "Exclusively dating, right?"

"I don't want to change what we have or where we're going, but let's not rush it. Let's enjoy our time together, and if it's meant to be, it will be."

"Okay." She let a smile spread across her face. "You're right, it's too soon but I want us to stay together."

"Good." He tipped her chin up. "Your dad is pretty cool about me sharing your room. My mom would have trip wires strung down the hallway to make sure we stayed in our own beds if you were at my house. I'm surprised she lets my sister out of the house without a chaperone."

"I guess I'm lucky then." She ran her fingertips over his cheek. "Why don't we enjoy it? We should order room service and soak in the tub."

"Your dad will freak if we charge up the room bill."

"No, he won't. Trust me, I've stayed here before."

Brandon snorted. "Course you have."

"Stop the sass." Savannah rolled her eyes. "Aiden won't care if we order food, watch a movie or whatever. He'll be happy I have someone to lean on while he takes care of Gramma Grace and Grandma Caroline."

"If you're sure." Brandon looked wary. "If he gets mad—"

"I'll take the blame. He can't fire me." Savannah grinned, happy he'd given in.

⤛

Savannah awoke to insistent knocking on the door. "Hold on, I'm coming." She disentangled herself from Brandon and crawled out of bed, fumbling for one of the fluffy hotel robes.

She rubbed her eyes and opened the door. "Dad." She blinked at him sleepily. "What's the matter?"

"It's late and you're ignoring your phone. We have an appointment with the lawyer this afternoon so time to get dressed and have breakfast. Or brunch at this point in the day." His gaze seemed to be drawn toward the interior of the room.

"Oh." She shot a guilty glance over her shoulder, cringing at the clear view of Brandon sprawled face down and naked on the bed. Tiny bottles were scattered across every surface and clothing littered the floor. Heat rose in her face. "Umm, meet you downstairs in the dining room?"

"We ordered brunch. It'll be delivered to the suite as Gramma isn't up to sitting in the restaurant. Come over when you're both decent." Her dad raised a brow before turning to head down the hall. "Don't be long, we need to leave in an hour."

She leaned against the door, taking in the scene. At least they'd put the room service cart in the hall to be collected, but her dad must be appalled. She and Brandon had both been drunk by the time she'd performed a striptease. Neither of them had even considered cleaning up before they'd fallen asleep wrapped in each other's arms.

Maybe not something her dad needed to know, but then again, he'd seen worse, and she was an adult now. Not much she could do, he'd viewed the state of the room and could guess how they'd spent their night.

"Brandon." She crawled onto the bed, bouncing as she moved closer, hoping to wake him. "Wake up, sleepyhead." She nuzzled against his neck, shaking him.

He wrapped an arm around her, rolling, pinning her to the mattress. "Ha, got you."

"You were awake the whole time?"

"Sort of. Thanks for covering my bare ass before letting your dad in." He shook his head. "I bet he got a great eyeful. Now I have to face him over lunch. Classic."

"I was half asleep and not thinking or I would've thrown something over you." She laughed. "If it's any consolation, you have an amazing ass."

"Ha, right. I'm sure your dad thinks so too." Brandon wrapped his arm around her waist, kissing her. "I bet it's the highlight of his day, seeing me naked in his sweet daughter's bed."

"Let's not think about that." She gave a light laugh, not wanting to admit that Aiden had caught her in a far more compromising situation with her ex-boyfriend Chase. "Get up. We need to shower and dress if you want to eat. We're supposed to go to my grandparents' apartment and meet the lawyer."

"Lawyer? About what?"

"The will, I guess."

"Should I be coming?"

"Why not? Not sure I need to be in with the lawyer, but I'm curious to see the place. It has a view of Central Park and takes up an entire floor."

"A view like that one?" Brandon pointed to the window of their room.

"Exactly."

"This place blows my mind. I've never been to New York before, let alone stayed anywhere that compares to this hotel. My family is a little more motel and a lot less five star resort."

"Then enjoy it while you can."

"Planning on getting rid of me?" Brandon lifted his brow.

"I just meant, live a little. All too soon you'll be back to your shared hovel in Boston with your slovenly roommates."

"Don't remind me." Brandon hauled himself from the bed. "We'd better get moving. I call the shower first."

"No chance. You have to share."

Thirty minutes later she and Brandon let themselves into the suite. Tom and Aiden were at the table, drinking coffee.

Savannah fought back the grin as she squeezed Brandon's hand.

"Oh good, you're here. Help yourself to something to eat." Aiden motioned to the buffet set up to the side. "Everyone else has eaten and are getting ready to leave."

Brandon lifted the lid of one of the warmers, grinning as he loaded a plate.

"Wow, think you'd been starved." Vanna eyed his heap of food as she selected a few items for herself.

"I'm a medical student. I have to take full advantage," he muttered before digging in. "Besides, I worked up an appetite last night," he said under his breath.

Her lips twitched as she sneaked a look at her dad, but he seemed immersed in reviewing paperwork with Tom. "By all means, keep your strength up," she whispered. "Dig in, my ravenous wolf." She smirked. Perhaps she didn't need to remind him to live a little. Her boyfriend devoted a load of passion to many activities besides eating.

Savannah eyed Brandon as she ate. She'd learned many things about her boyfriend this trip. His home life was nothing like hers. Even her life in Portland had been different from how he'd grown up. It was scary how she'd gotten used to having money and thought nothing of luxury hotels, room service, and gourmet meals.

Emily wandered in, balancing Kellan on her hip. "Good morning. Everyone ready to go?"

Aiden rose. "Let me take him, Em." He scooped Kellan out of her arms, planting a kiss on her lips. "The cars should be here. Gramma isn't up to walking it."

⌁

It wasn't long and they were on their way up the elevator to the penthouse suite.

Savannah expected far worse, but though in disarray, it didn't appear there was much actual damage caused by the search.

"You okay, Caroline?" Emily asked. "Can I get you anything?"

"It's fine, Emily." The woman wandered off.

"Are you kidding me?" Brandon looked around then pulled Savannah toward the windows. "Check this out. This is where your grandfather lived?"

"I've never been here before. It's kind of amazing, though. It's the entire floor. Come on." She grabbed his hand and they walked through each room. They surveyed the exercise room, the massive office, and the large kitchen before touring the many bedrooms and examining the terrace.

"Vanna, I need you to come in with me. Brandon, can you keep yourself busy for a few minutes?"

"Sure, can I use the pool table?"

"Go ahead. There are drinks in the fridge. Help yourself."

Savannah followed her dad into the office, and Aiden shut the door. Everyone was seated around a small conference table, and she took the empty seat beside Emily.

"Now that you're all here, we'll go over the will." The lawyer cleared his throat. "There are some small bequests for Grace, and other than that there are two main beneficiaries. James recently redid his will, and left the bulk of the estate to Aiden, with a small trust designated for Kellan Hamilton."

"That's it?" Caroline stared at the attorney. "He left everything to Aiden?"

Savannah followed the conversation but detached as the words flowed around the room. Tears burned her eyes. Even in death James rejected her. It wasn't an oversight, because he'd left something for Kellan, but not for her.

She squeezed the arm of the chair, fighting the urge to run from the room.

Emily's brow knit in concentration, but the woman slid a hand over to cover Savannah's, rubbing before taking hold even as the conversation continued around them.

"As your divorce is finalized, you only have rights to the payout funds. I know you and James were having differences over those, and with his death and the structure of your divorce agreement, it could be tied up for some time."

"Wait." Aiden held up a hand. "James never paid the divorce settlement?"

"No. Why he held it up, I'm not sure."

"Pay Caroline the funds he owed her and be done with it." Tom looked at Aiden. "Agreed?"

"Absolutely. I won't dispute the agreement. What else is in there for bequests?" Aiden accepted the document, running a fingertip down the page as he absorbed the information. "Items for Grace, a trust fund for Kellan, and the rest to me. Nothing else?"

"Were you expecting something else?" The lawyer frowned.

"Nope, pretty typical of James." Aiden rubbed his temples before looking toward Savannah.

Something about the way Aiden looked at Savannah eased her disappointment. He'd noticed and seemed upset on her behalf. She wasn't the invisible girl as she feared, and he got it without being told.

The sting of rejection faded, even as Emily slid an arm around her and rubbed her back.

"Well." Aiden leaned back in his chair, rubbing his jaw. "No surprise, I suppose. Send a copy to Tom, and provide us with the statements of what the estate entails? I'm thinking we should sell this place and maybe send the furniture to auction? Caroline? Gramma? Is there anything you want or any feelings about that plan?"

Caroline shook her head. "I only need the funds he promised me in the divorce, but I took the belongings I wanted when I left the bastard."

Grace patted his hand. "Dispose of everything as you see fit, aside from the Hamilton heirlooms. I would appreciate viewing any jewelry before you make decisions. I don't want or need anything else." Gramma's gaze strayed toward Savannah. The elderly woman's shoulders sagged, her eyes growing misty.

"Done." He gazed at the assembled group, lingering on Grace. "Emily, you look tired, maybe you and Gramma want to take the car back to the hotel?"

"Please. These past few days have been exhausting." Emily patted her belly, and leveraged out of the chair. "Grace, I'd love the company. Are you ready to go?"

"Thank you, dear, I could use some fresh air and then a nap."

"Can I join you? I'll watch Kellan while you two rest." Caroline rose as well, following the other two from the room.

Savannah longed to escape the dark and dreary office and pushed out of her chair.

"Vanna." Aiden hugged her. "Please don't be sad," he murmured against her hair. "It's another one of his head games, don't let it bring you down. I love you."

"I know, Daddy." She buried her face against his shoulder. "I don't need or want his money. I'm fine, I promise, but thank you." After kissing his cheek, she turned and left the room, heading onto the patio and staring out over the city.

"Hey." Brandon wrapped his arms around her waist, letting her lean back against his chest. "You look sad. What happened?"

"He …" Savannah closed her eyes. "Never mind, it's not important."

"Yeah, sweetie, it is. Something must be wrong. Nobody looks happy, least of all your dad."

"It'll sound stupid."

"Tell me anyway." He linked fingers with hers and guided her to the couch.

"They lived here for twenty years. They dumped my dad in boarding school in Chicago and moved. Gramma Grace raised him, he went there for holidays, and no one offered to help when I was born. They made them give me away, and then they sent my dad overseas for three years."

"I didn't know, but Aiden doesn't talk about stuff like that at work."

"My grandfather never wanted me to be part of the family." She leaned into him. "They made me disappear so they could pretend I never existed. He left something in his will to my little brother, but nothing for me. I never wanted his money, but it hurts. I'll always be the shameful secret." The tears spilled over, and she brushed her fingers underneath her eyes. "It sounds dumb."

"It doesn't. Your grandfather should have loved and cherished you, but he didn't. No one should feel like that. Your dad loves you, he'd do anything for you. And Emily, you'd think you were her daughter, she's so proud of you. I wish my mom would talk about Piper like that, but she never does."

"I'm sorry."

"No, I'm sorry." He sighed. "James Hamilton is gone. He couldn't even manage to support his own son, let alone anyone else. Forget him. He's not worth your time or effort. You have an amazing family who loves you, focus on that, and leave the rest behind. It's all you can do."

Savannah rested her head against his chest, both of them staring out over the city. She took his hand, bringing it to her lips. "You get it."

"Yeah, I do. Nobody's life is perfect. Thanks for trusting me enough to share."

"Thanks for listening," she said. "Want to blow this joint and do some sightseeing?"

Brandon rose and stretched, holding his hand out. "For such an amazing place, it's depressing."

Savannah led Brandon through the heavy, oppressive apartment. "Dad?"

"In the office, sweetie."

Savannah arrived in the doorway just as Tom swung the heavy safe door open. Her breath caught at the sight.

"Holy crap." Brandon almost ran into her. "Is that real?"

Stack upon stack of bills filled every inch of space up to the second shelf, which contained a stack of velvet boxes in varying sizes.

Aiden picked up a bundle, fanning the edges. He peeled the band off and held a bill up to the light. "I doubt James would possess counterfeit currency."

"So that's what a million dollars looks like." Savannah giggled.

"You can fit a million dollars into a small paper bag when you have bills wrapped in bands like this. Assuming they're all hundreds …" Tom ran a finger down the stacks. "Looks like they go back several rows. Damn, Aiden." Tom finished his count. "That's millions of dinero."

"Why did he have so much cash stashed?" Aiden scrubbed a hand through his hair. "Any legal concerns? Do I need to report this?"

"They've concluded the investigation, and the assets have been released for distribution under the terms of the will." Tom rubbed the back of his neck. "Given the statements the accountant gave me today, James had been cashing out for a while. Which is why he named you in the will. Crafty, and more than a little disturbing."

"Sneaky bastard. Guess his plan to make me pay backfired."

"Dad? Do you mind if Brandon and I see some of New York? He's never been."

"Not at all. Do you have your card with you?" Aiden asked.

"I didn't think to bring it, but we can find stuff to do."

"Here." He pulled out his wallet and slid a wad of cash into her hand. "Have some fun, okay? Call the car service if you need a ride back to the hotel later."

"Thanks, Dad." She embraced him before she and Brandon left. Her heart lightened with every step away from that depressing atmosphere. It didn't matter anymore. The man could never interfere in her family again.

Time to put James Hamilton behind her. The man was gone, forever out of their lives.

Chapter 30

Tiffany

At five minutes before seven, they arrived at the door of the Hamilton's suite.

Tears came to Tiffany's eyes. "I can't do this."

Stefan squeezed her fingers, giving her a reassuring smile.

"You most certainly can. Grace wants us here." Michelle tapped on the door as Stefan slid an arm around Tiffany's waist. "Like it or not, you are part of this family. Your daughter is in there."

Aiden answered their knock. "Come in." He beckoned them inside.

Tiffany gazed around the luxurious suite. She'd stayed in similar places and knew the bedrooms would be located down the short hallway. The table in the dining area had been set and there were some trays of appetizers on the sideboard.

"This is lovely." Michelle kissed Aiden's cheek.

"We did our best to make it as comfortable as possible for Gramma. We have to be here several days as the apartment has just been released." He rubbed his jaw. "Not that I would have wanted to stay there."

Michelle nodded. "They kicked me out of the house in Chicago. I've moved in with Tiffany until it's sorted."

"I'm sorry, Michelle. Let me know if there's anything you need." Aiden wrapped an arm around her.

"Thank you, Aiden. If you know of somewhere I can rent, that would be helpful. I can't afford the lease I had lined up, and Tiffany's place is too small for both of us. The house is in escrow for the buyers, so I have to move out once I have access."

"Is Ben on that for you?" Aiden guided them into the main area.

"He is."

Savannah appeared, followed by Brandon.

"Grandma." Savannah hugged Michelle.

"Sweetie, how are you?" Michelle returned the embrace before greeting Brandon. "I should say hello to Grace and Caroline." With a small smile, her mother headed across the room.

"Can I get you a drink?" Stefan asked.

"Red wine?" Tiffany clutched Stefan's hand, not wanting him to go, but needing the fortification.

He nodded and disengaged his fingers, heading toward the bar with Aiden.

"I'm sorry about your father," Savannah said.

"Thank you." Tiffany resisted the urge to hug her daughter, turning instead to the handsome young man beside her daughter. "Brandon."

"Good to see you again." Brandon smiled and extended his hand.

Tiffany took a deep breath and forced the tension from her body. She could get through this, even with the absence of her friends. Most of their friends had returned home, aside from Tom who'd remained to help Aiden with the estate.

Not long after they arrived, dinner was served, providing her a respite. Tiffany pasted on a smile and responded when needed, but she couldn't shake her initial discomfort. She hadn't spent much time around Aiden and Emily as a couple, and the scene seemed so domestic.

Kellan squawked and kicked his feet, tired of being confined to the highchair. Aiden rose and freed the toddler, tucking the boy onto his lap and feeding him bites of dinner from his own plate until Caroline claimed her grandson.

Tiffany remembered the tales of how dinnertime had been as Aiden grew up. He'd been shuffled off to eat with the nanny until he was old enough to sit through an entire meal with proper etiquette. But tonight, even Gramma Grace made no comment about hosting a squirming toddler at the table, beaming at her great-grandson. It seemed that Aiden had won a battle and broken the chain now that both James and Thomas were permanently out of the picture.

How much had changed. She gazed around at the happy family, her gaze meeting Emily's. The woman offered a faint smile and a slight nod, an oddly soothing gesture, an acknowledgment that no matter how awkward, Tiffany belonged in this group surrounding the table. A family, which included her daughter.

Tiffany noted that Brandon seemed as attentive to her daughter now as he had been at the funeral service and reception. She couldn't find fault with the young man, even though she worried the young doctor was too old her daughter.

"Are you okay?" Stefan said in a low voice.

"Fine." She graced him with a soft smile, taking his hand under the table and squeezing.

Not long after the main course was finished, Aiden escorted Gramma Grace down the hallway, reappearing a short time afterward. "Gramma's settled in for the night, but everyone is welcome to stay for coffee and dessert."

"Perhaps we should go," Tiffany whispered to her mother, glancing to where Stefan sat chatting to Savannah and Brandon.

"Aiden made a point of welcoming us to stay. Perhaps you should take the opportunity to visit with your daughter."

Brandon leaned in to speak with Savannah, then rose from the couch, moving across the room, leaving her daughter with Stefan.

"You've been lost in your own little world all night. She doesn't bite." Her mother pushed her gently.

Tiffany approached, smiling at the sight of Kellan, his head resting on Savannah's shoulder. She lowered herself onto the couch.

Stefan caught her eye and motioned to the small bar in the far corner. "I was about to get another drink. Can I get either of you anything?"

Savannah shook her head.

"I'm good for now. Thanks, Stefan." Tiffany inhaled a long breath as Stefan winked and rose from the couch.

Savannah's gaze followed Stefan as he headed across the room. "I can't believe you're dating Stefan Cortes."

"Now you've had a chance to talk to him, what do you think?"

"He's great. A keeper." She tilted her head. "What do you think of Brandon?"

Tiffany swept her hair to the side, clasping her hands in her lap. "He seems nice." *Even if he's too old for you.*

Savannah gave her a knowing look. "Brandon is twenty-three. Did Dad tell you that?"

"Mmmhmm." Tiffany lifted one shoulder in a tiny shrug. "I can't judge whether he's the right one. I barely know him."

Savannah tilted her head, a smile twitching at the corner of her mouth.

Tiffany relaxed, reaching out and brushing a hand over Kellan's soft hair. "He's sweet. He looks like Aiden as a little boy."

"It's exciting that I get a baby sister." Savannah bit her lip. "Sorry, is that strange for you? Dad having more kids?"

Tiffany smiled and shook her head. "Believe me, he's had enough hardship and rough times. He deserves some happiness."

Kellan squirmed, wiggling from his sister's arms and toddling toward his dad. Aiden scooped up his son, cuddling him against his chest as he continued his discussion with Michelle.

"Grandma Michelle looks sad," Savannah said. "Will she be okay?"

"She will. She's moved in with me until we can get things straightened out."

Savannah took her hand. "You wrote a poem."

"You read it?" Tiffany's breath caught in her chest, not only because of the contact but the watch linked around her daughter's wrist. She forced herself not to react to the sight of the sparkling gold face surrounded by diamonds. "I wrote it not long after you were born. Aiden had been sent overseas, though I didn't know it at the time."

"Those words." Savannah pressed her free hand over her heart. "It's funny, you know? You've been apologizing for months. You even won Emily over to your side. It all seemed like noise." Her deep brown eyes, so much like Aiden's, reflected sadness. "That poem was the reason I came to see you in Chicago."

"It was?"

Her daughter bobbed her head. "And then you sent that package."

Tiffany tightened her grip on her daughter's fingers.

"Why?"

"Maybe it was a whim, but it felt right." Tiffany drew her brows together, trying to form cohesive words that her daughter could hopefully relate to. "Our marriage may be over, but the memories are still precious. I have them all stored here"—she tapped over her heart—"and here." She touched a fingertip to her temple. "It was time to share them. Destroying any of it seemed wrong."

"You looked really happy. It makes me wonder." Savannah gazed at Tiffany, her expression that of one searching to make sense of things that maybe could never be explained.

"All the what if's?" Tiffany lifted a shoulder. "I've been victim to allowing my thoughts to wander down that path."

"Have you?" A glimmer appeared in her daughter's eyes. "You designed the tattoo on Aiden's shoulder. I knew it the moment I saw that sketch. Dad promised me a tattoo. I thought that design might be fitting."

"You'd want to do that?" A warm glow built around her heart.

"*Deo i mo chroí.*"

"How did you see that?" Tiffany straightened, staring at her daughter, but then gave her head a small shake. Savannah had inherited the artist's eye, a gift from her. Or perhaps a curse. Having the temperament of an artist had never been easy.

"I just saw it. Like I knew about the word in Aiden's tattoo the very first time I saw it. Are there words in your tattoo?"

"Nothing gets by you." Tiffany angled her body and pulled her hair over her shoulder to expose the open back of her dress.

"Amazing." Savannah traced a finger over the design. "It's got some of the same elements as the one on the card, and some of Aiden's too." She hesitated, the next words coming as no surprise to Tiffany. "*A. Stór. Mo. Chroí.* Did I say that right? What does it mean?"

"The treasure of my heart." She turned toward Savannah. "I almost chickened out, but your dad held my hand through the whole thing."

"You were together when you got them?"

"We'd just gotten married." Tiffany smiled softly. "I was in art school, and I couldn't afford to buy him an expensive present. He'd bugged me to design him a tattoo, so that was my gift to him. After the divorce, I thought he might have it removed, but he never did."

"You didn't remove yours."

Tiffany closed her eyes and drew in a long breath, glad she had fought her reservations about coming tonight. For once, her mother winning their battle of wills was a good thing.

"What are you thinking?" Savannah whispered.

A small smile broke through and she opened her eyes. "That you are so much like your father it hurts. But it's such a gift, Savannah. Your dad is one of the best people I know." She couldn't hold back any longer. Tiffany wrapped her arms around her daughter and drew her close. "I have wanted to do this for so long, I can't even tell you."

Savannah's arms crept around her, tightening ever so slightly as she rested her head on her mother's shoulder.

Tiffany never wanted to let go. She squeezed her eyes closed, wishing she'd had the courage to do this years ago.

Savannah pulled back, brushing her fingers under her eyes to sweep away the tears. "Maybe I could come visit you again in Chicago. Just for a weekend, maybe?"

Those words had hope leaping within Tiffany's heart. Even now when their lives had grown dark, complete joy blossomed. "I'd love that, Savannah. You are welcome anytime." Tiffany gave her daughter another hug.

As she sat back, her gaze met Aiden's. A hush fell over the room as she deciphered the expression written across his face. He seemed frozen until the corners of his mouth turned up the slightest bit. His eyes shimmered, the tiniest quiver of his lip giving him away.

And then she knew. Aiden didn't show his emotions easily, and for him to be this close to the edge could only mean one thing. He'd wished this for her and their daughter as much as she'd desired and needed it to save herself. For this moment, they became the only three people in this crowded room.

In this small intimate moment, they took a huge step forward, united. This moment meant everything. This single precious and unforgettable moment that marked the first time she'd held her precious daughter since the day she was born. The true treasure of her heart.

Tiffany awoke early the next morning, a feeling of something close to contentment settling over her. Last night had reached epic proportions in her mind. Having your child embrace you seemed a small thing, but to her it was everything. An ending that promised to blossom into a wonderful new beginning.

A second wave of happiness swept over her as she rubbed Stefan's arm. He hadn't wavered through any of the revelations over the past weeks. The man had become an indispensable part of her life in an incredibly short period of time.

Longing to be in motion, she slid from the bed, leaning over to brush his full lips with hers.

"I'm hitting the gym. I'll be back in an hour," she whispered against his ear.

Stefan tangled his fingers in her hair and brought her in for a longer kiss. "I have a better idea." His tugged her onto the bed, rolling them and pinning her to the mattress.

By the time she actually bundled her hair into a ponytail and grabbed her shaker bottle from the mini fridge an hour later, a glow surrounded her. Once in the gym, she set the time on the treadmill and began her run. She concentrated as the deck adjusted for a hard uphill climb.

"You're up early."

Tiffany popped her head up. "So are you."

"I needed to burn off some energy." Aiden set his bag to the side, and dabbed at his flushed face.

She slowed her pace as the cool down portion of her program started. "Looks like you already did."

"Thought I'd follow up my run with some heavy lifting." He selected two free weights. "It's been a crazy few days and it's not over yet. I have to deal with that damn apartment."

She nodded as she finished and then moved to leg extensions. They both remained silent as they completed their reps. Tiffany inhaled a deep breath and lay back to take a small break. She glanced at Aiden, who eyed her. "Why are you looking at me like that?"

"You have a certain glow this morning. Stefan is clearly good for you."

"Do you approve?" She sent a cheeky grin his way.

He rolled his eyes upward as he selected a new set of weights.

"It's only been a few weeks, but he's been amazing, even with all the messy truths about my life."

"He's a great guy."

They fell silent as they each completed another set.

Once finished, she sat on a weight bench and drank from her water bottle. "I didn't thank you for last night."

"No thanks required, Tiff. The invitation was Gramma Grace's. You did the rest all by yourself."

"It wouldn't have happened without your support." She adjusted her ponytail.

"Maybe, but you need to give yourself the majority of the credit."

"You really believe in me?"

"It doesn't matter whether I believe in you, Tiff. It matters whether you believe in you. You know who you are and what you can accomplish. Don't let anyone else decide that. Go and get what you want, because no one's giving it away for free. You have to fight for it."

A small frown marred her features as she lifted her chin and met his gaze. She contemplated him steadily for the longest time.

"I have something for you. I'd planned to drop it off this morning, but since you're here …" He rose to pull a package from his gym bag. Aiden placed it in her hands before he sat on the end of the bench beside her.

"We're giving each other presents now?" She lifted a brow as she opened the top. Her breath caught in her chest at the contents. Tiffany reached in, but Aiden stayed her hand.

"Don't pull that out here. There are cameras."

"Why would you give me this?"

"It's to help Michelle. I offered her my penthouse in Chicago for a few months until she gets back on her feet, but I know she won't accept my financial assistance. She'll look to you, Tiff, and she still doesn't know we paid out David, does she?"

Tiffany shook her head.

"Don't tell her. Just hide this away somewhere safe, and let her think you're giving her money from the gallery. That you're repaying her what you owed David."

"Where did you get this?" She folded the top with trembling hands. "That's a lot, Aiden."

"James tried to screw me over by leaving me an estate mired in debt, but his plans were foiled. He had a full safe at the apartment on top of all the funds we caught before the wire transfers were processed. Even after paying out the debt he incurred and settling the divorce with Caroline, the estate is substantial."

A shiver ran down her spine as she realized the extent of what Aiden had just inherited. "What are you going to do with it?"

"I don't want or need his money, so I plan to support worthy causes. Remember Matthias?"

Tiffany closed her eyes and nodded. She would never forget. Aiden had taken his friend's death hard and had wondered on more than one occasion how he'd missed the signs that caused his friend to take his own life.

"I've been working on a study focused on mental health in physicians, particularly during medical school and residency. I plan to set up a charitable foundation in Matthias' name that will supply resources for medical students and residents. People are more aware now, but more needs to be done to take care of the mental and physical well-being of those pursuing medicine as a career. And perhaps I'll lend some support to a few other worthy causes."

"Like starving artists and their destitute mothers?"

"Something like that. Please take it, and I want to pay off the loans on your gallery." He held up a hand. "You'll be a success without my help, but please, let me do this."

Tiffany opened her mouth to protest, but something about the way he looked at her told her an entirely new story. Or at least one that had been hidden from her view, one she hadn't wanted to see. This not-so-small act of kindness might be more for him than for her. A repayment? Long overdue closure on their story? Whatever the motive, she knew she couldn't refuse.

She gave a brief bob of her head along with a watery smile.

He rose to his feet and slung his bag over his shoulder.

She followed suit, unable to stop herself from wrapping her arms around him, not even minding they were both damp and sweaty from their respective workouts. That he hugged her back without hesitation, holding her tight, didn't surprise her in the least.

"Where do we go from here?" Tiffany whispered.

Aiden drew in a long breath, and cupped her face in his palms. "This is where I kiss you goodbye and tell you to have a happy life."

She let those words sink in. It was exactly right. Not that they wouldn't ever talk or see each other. Their daughter meant they would surely have contact, but this closeness they'd been sharing, reminiscent of the old days together, was fleeting. Letting the last of their feelings fade away and moving on, him with Emily and their family, and her making the most of this chance with Stefan. It was time to stop looking back and wishing for things that could never be, for a love that could never be rekindled.

Aiden pressed a kiss to her forehead. "Take care of yourself." The gym door closed softly behind him.

Tiffany let herself into the hotel room. She noted the carafe and two cups on the tray. The soft patter of the shower made her smile.

She tucked the package from Aiden into the bottom of her carry-on bag before she peeled off her sweaty gym clothes and slung them over top of her suitcase to be packed. Then she slipped into the bathroom, opening the glass shower door just enough to join Stefan.

He turned and gazed down at her as he ran a hand through his wet hair and then over his face to clear the water from his eyes. His warm smile made her smile in return. "That workout did you good. You look amazing."

"So do you." She placed a flattened palm against his firm chest, tipping her head up for a kiss. Her heart skipped a beat, and she knew. What she had with this man was real. She was truly ready, committed to permitting her own happiness. To embracing the future. "When do you have to leave?"

"Tomorrow morning. Maybe you'll consider joining me this trip. What do you think?"

She wound a hand around his neck, stretching on tiptoes to kiss him.

His palms cupped her cheeks as he responded, lingering, his lips conveying both passion and tenderness. He drew back only enough to tip his forehead against hers. "So that's a yes?" he whispered.

She nodded. "I'm ready for a little adventure."

Things weren't perfect, and maybe they never would be, but she had much to look forward to. Building a relationship with her daughter and learning about this wonderful man who'd so unexpectedly appeared in her life. She would accept her new realities and challenges head on. Embrace the possibilities. She was ready. Time to set herself free.

Enjoy an excerpt from The Hamilton Series *Everything We Dream*, Book 5.

CHAPTER 1

Brandon

Visiting his mother and stepfather was far from exciting or even pleasant. For Brandon, the boisterous group of guys surrounding him made the long flight from Boston worthwhile. Their friendships made life bearable over many years in the small Montana town he'd once called home.

"Congratulations, Dr. Reynolds." His best friend, Rory, lifted a glass. "Both on earning your MD and on the new job. When do you start?"

"July." He tapped his drink against his friend's, smiling at the memory of the day he'd accepted the hard-won honor of calling himself a doctor.

"This bum, living the good life." His friend, Jayce, elbowed him in the ribs. "You'll soon be rich."

"I wish," he said under his breath. The numerous zeros on his loan statement far exceeded the few pathetic zeros accompanying his new salary as an intern. Four long years of intense training were in store before he'd earn more than a minimal income.

"… can't wait to meet this girl of yours. When are you bringing her for a visit?" Jayce asked.

Brandon brought his gaze upward, forcing himself to re-engage in the conversation. He curled his lip, taking another swig from his beer. "I like her. Why subject her to my mother?"

A round of laughter erupted around the table. His mother was notorious among his friends. Brandon rarely introduced girlfriends or even mentioned the women he dated within the four walls of her house.

Jayce reached for Brandon's phone, which lay face down on the table. "I haven't seen a picture."

Brandon grabbed for the device a split second too late, kicking himself for leaving it out.

"Is this her?" His friend peered at the screen as a new text notification appeared at the top. "No wonder you decided on a little cradle robbing. Awww, sweet. She sent you a picture. And she's about to call." The guy turned the phone, showing Brandon the name Savannah displayed across the screen. "This must be her now."

"Give me that." Brandon snatched at the phone.

"Uh-uh." Jayce cleared his throat as he tapped the answer button. "Well, hello there. What's that, darling? You wish to speak with our boy, Brandon? Might cost ya."

"Don't be an ass." Brandon wrestled the phone from his friend's grasp. "Sorry. Ignore Jayce," he said, throwing his friend a dark look.

"Sounds like you're having fun."

He let out a sigh, relieved she sounded more amused than upset at being addressed as darling. "Just drinks with the guys. How about you?" He exited through the front doors, reveling in the light summer breeze and silence.

"We climbed three hundred and eighty-seven steps to the top of the Notre Dame bell tower. Our reward is a scoop of the première crème de glace in Paris," she said. "The gargoyles are amazing. Did you see the picture of me with the bell?"

"Not yet, 'cause Jayce hijacked my phone." He swept a hand through his hair. "What flavor?"

"Caramel au beurre salé. I've gained ten pounds from eating ice cream and gelato."

"I bet you look amazing." Brandon closed his eyes, picturing her sweet smile. "I miss you."

"Me too," she said softly. "I hear you've been busy saving lives."

"That was an intense day." The major pile-up he'd attended with Aiden had been a nightmare. "Your dad kept his cool."

"Not much phases him," she said. "Have I ever told you how I met my dad?"

Brandon frowned. "No, actually."

"I'll tell you someday."

"Deal. How are you and Tiffany getting along now you've spent more than two hours together?"

"Another thing to fill you in on," she said.

"She's right there, huh?"

"Sure. But it's all good. Hey, I have to go. We're meeting Stefan for dinner. Only ten more sleeps, and I'll be home."

"Can't wait to see you. Enjoy that amazing French cuisine. Bye, sweetie." Brandon hung up and leaned back against the building, propping the sole of one foot flat against the brickwork. He stared at the wisp of clouds floating across the bright summer sky, wishing he was there with her.

Their weeks apart had been more difficult than anticipated. Even his busy work schedule, hanging out with Nate, and multiple dinners with Aiden and Emily hadn't soothed the ache of missing her.

"There you are." Rory tipped his head back, squinting skyward before focusing on Brandon. "How's Savannah?"

"Having a grand time in Paris." He sighed, watching as the wisps changed shape. It reminded of him of when they were kids. The hot summer days filled with adventure, far from the worries of adulthood. Those distant times were simple and easy, at least compared to now.

"Man, you have it bad." His friend furrowed his brow. "You're never like this about a girl. When do I meet her?"

"When can you visit Boston?" Brandon lifted one shoulder. "Bad enough Piper's a complete bitch about the relationship. I don't need Carol or Jeremy adding their opinions," he said with a sideways look. "You know how they get."

"Enough said." Rory patted his shoulder. "Sorry about Piper."

"The girl's ridiculous. Why does she assume calling dibs on Vanna's friendship gives her the right to interfere in my relationship?"

"You've heard my opinion."

"She's my little sister." Brandon grimaced.

"Who isn't blood-related, dude. At least consider her ulterior motives."

"I seriously hope you're wrong." Brandon shuddered. "Piper's too close to being related. And too young."

"Says the man dating her friend of the same age."

"Savannah doesn't act eighteen. She's more mature than most women our age."

"How long have you been dating?"

Brandon squinted. "Define dating." He struggled to calculate their relationship timeline. It had started as a passionate, amazing week, followed by a hiatus after the revelations rolled in. That his Zoe was eighteen, not twenty-two. His stepsister's friend. Real name Savannah. Followed by the complete awkwardness of discovering her last name was Hamilton. The beloved daughter of his ER supervisor. Not his finest moment. Or hers.

"That right there is a big ole red flag." Rory's lips twisted. "When did you date for real? Not some no-strings-attached week of hot sex with a random chick you rescued from the big bad ex-boyfriend in a bar, Brandon. A real, honest relationship, where you called her by her actual name?"

"April?" He'd been entranced by Savannah by the end of their first week together. Those amazing days they'd spent in late January before things went to hell. Maybe that didn't count. His friend didn't seem to think so.

"Three months, bud. That's nothing, even if it's challenging your record. Autumn was only ten." Rory smirked. "Bet she'd love to see you."

"Not a chance." Brandon shook his index finger at his friend. "I'm with Vanna."

"Kidding."

"More like testing."

"I hope Savannah is committed to you." Rory tilted his head. "A month apart is a long time. That's a third of the relationship, and she's a long way from home."

"She's traveling with her mother. I doubt she's club-hopping and picking up French dudes." Brandon kicked at the thin layer of grit on the sidewalk.

Rory threw a light punch against Brandon's shoulder. "Watch out, or she'll have you picking curtains."

"Shut up, asshole." He shoved his friend even as the grin twitched at his lips.

Rory feinted another couple of punches, laughing as they roughhoused.

"I give." Brandon held up his hands.

"Getting soft, are you?" Rory asked. "Hey, there's a barbecue tomorrow afternoon. You should come. You don't even have to talk to Autumn."

"We'll see."

"No excuses. It'll be the last time we see you for months." Rory observed him steadily. "Sorry for not making your celebration. I'm super proud of you, man. You worked your butt off."

"It's a long and expensive flight." Brandon hadn't expected his friends to show, given the distance. "Savannah made the trip with her family."

"But not your mother or anyone else from that household." His friend shook his head.

"Story of my life." A vague edge of disappointment bit him at his family's lack of support, but it was for the best. "Carol's embarrassing. She would have gotten loaded or done something stupid. Though, I'd have loved to have seen Mia. But," he said, smiling, "I had a great time and a celebratory dinner with my ER supervisors. It's all good."

"Wish your residency was closer. Hey, let's play some pool and have a few more drinks."

"You're on." Brandon followed his friend inside, glad the inquisition was over.

"Up." The stern voice dragged Brandon from his peaceful dreams.

"Tired," he mumbled as he burrowed deeper into his pillow.

"You wouldn't be if you came home at a decent hour." Her shrill tone sliced into his brain.

Brandon winced as a waft of cool morning air hit his bare skin. "What the hell?" He grabbed a wisp of the sheet, tugging it free from her grasp.

"Put some clothes on. Get your ass out of bed." His mother loomed over him, hands on hips. "Later, you're on a plane to Boston. I've hardly seen you."

He smothered his scoff. The only thing she ever wanted to do was get drunk and enjoy using him as a convenient emotional punching bag. "I'm up. Just get out of my room. Don't know who's worse, you or Piper," he muttered, cringing at the memory of his immature stepsister barging in on him and Vanna.

Half an hour later, after a hot shower, he entered the kitchen and poured himself a cup of coffee. He grimaced at the bitterness biting his tongue. Had it always been this bad? Maybe he'd become spoiled in Boston.

"What's that face about?" Jeremy shifted in his seat at the shabby, pitted kitchen table.

"Nothing." He dumped in a liberal dose of sugar to disguise the taste. Critiquing anything would invite a lecture on gratefulness.

Jeremy peeked over his shoulder, clearly scouting for Carol. "I hear you have a new girlfriend," his stepfather said in a low voice.

Brandon rolled his eyes toward the ceiling. "What did Piper say?"

"That you got involved with someone you shouldn't." Jeremy leaned back, leveling his gaze at Brandon over the rim of his cup. "Your supervisor's daughter? That doesn't sound smart."

"Did she tell my mother?" Brandon sighed before he downed a slug of foul brew, hiding his disgust.

"No, and neither did I." Jeremy drummed his fingers. "Eighteen? That's dangerous territory. It could affect your career if your supervisor finds out."

"Give me some credit." Brandon frowned. "My supervisors are aware of the relationship. Besides, Savannah isn't a child."

"It's true?" His stepfather's eyebrows flew upward. "You're having sex with her?"

"She's a grown woman." Brandon quirked his own brow. "We're not ..." Teenagers. A half-truth. Though she acted mature, Savannah was five years younger than his age of twenty-three. "It's not an issue."

"So you're not?" Jeremy contemplated him. "Or you'd prefer I shut up about it?"

He eyed the man over the rim of his cup. He liked Jeremy, but on occasion, his stepfather crossed boundaries. By the time the man had come into his life, Brandon been an adult. Far too late to dish out fatherly advice or to be the role model Brandon wished he'd had during his tumultuous and wild teenage years. Anyway, he suspected his stepfather was too weak and easily domineered to be a good example for anyone.

"Right. Be careful, Brandon. She's a young impressionable girl, not a woman. I'd take exception to a man your age sleeping with my eighteen-year-old daughter." The man emitted a deep sigh. "When are you planning to tell your mother?"

Brandon scoffed. "Since when does a grown man report his relationships to his mother?"

"Coward." A low laugh rumbled from his chest. "Keep on Carol's good side if you expect continuing support for your career."

Brandon bit back the retort. Neither Carol nor Jeremy offered much encouragement. His accomplishments were his alone, earned through hard work and the burning desire to escape this oppressive house and backward small town. The barbecue looked more and more appealing, even with the high probability he'd run into his ex-girlfriend.

Two hours later, Rory arrived at his house, practically dragging him into the car and driving them to the park.

"Brandon." Nick charged across the grass, hopping up and down, waving a mitt in one hand. "Play ball with me."

"Hey, Nick. You have an extra one of those?" He pointed at the glove, ruffling the boy's sandy blond hair.

"Yup." A grin spread across his face as he produced one from behind his back.

"A regular Boy Scout." Brandon followed Nick to a clear spot in the park and spent the next hour fielding catches and coaching the preteen boy on his pitches.

A willowy dark-haired young woman intercepted a pass. "Time to pack it in, Nicky. They're serving burgers."

Nick cheered. "Are you coming, Brandon?"

"In a minute, buddy. Check out the selection and save me some of the good stuff."

The boy nodded and raced toward the food-laden tables.

Autumn's gaze trailed after her younger brother before she shifted her focus to Brandon. "You're great with him. You've been missed." She extended a frosty bottle. "Your reward for being ..." The woman lifted one shoulder.

"Thanks." Brandon swallowed a mouthful of icy beer, which soothed his throat after the exertion in the late-afternoon heat. "I love that kid. Next time I visit, he'll be a teenager, and far too busy chasing girls to play ball with me."

"Thirteen next month. I'm not sure about the girls. He's quiet." She tossed the ball into the air, catching it with ease. "How's Philly? Or is it Boston now?"

"Boston. It's good." Brandon offered a faint smile. "How are you?"

"Same as always. Nothing's changed around here," she said as they wandered toward the fire pit. "I hear you're seeing someone."

"Word travels fast."

"It's a small town."

"Mia tell you?" Though he hadn't gotten into the details with anyone but Rory, his sister knew he was dating. At one time, Mia and Autumn had been close.

"Mia never says much to me about your big life in the big city." Autumn caught her braid and twisted it around her finger, fidgeting with the hairband securing the end. "What's her name? And how long?"

"Savannah. I met her in January."

"Savannah," she said in a low melodic voice. The corners of Autumn's mouth quirked down. "A proper southern belle."

He smirked. "She's a West Coast girl from Oregon."

"But it's serious? Is that why you chose Boston for residency? Didn't you have an offer closer to home?"

"It's a wise career decision, and where I matched. Savannah has nothing to do with it." Brandon refused to discuss the convoluted situation brewing with his new girlfriend. Especially not with his ex-girlfriend, no matter how long they'd known each other. Besides, he'd set his sights on Mass General during medical school and had jumped at the offered opportunity to intern at a top hospital. "Anyway, there's nothing positive about living close to home, aside from seeing Mia."

Autumn's eyes grew shiny, and she looked away.

He sucked in a breath. "Sorry. I didn't mean …" He turned toward her. "We ended things before I left, and you know how it is being around my family."

"I get it, Brandon. I just thought … never mind." She shrugged as a tiny smile appeared. "You'll be amazing. Dr. Reynolds. That title's kind of trippy. You have a fantastic future ahead." Autumn motioned toward the buffet table. "Better get in there before it's all gone. You have a long flight home."

Leaving Montana once again came as a relief. He never managed more than three days in a row before he itched to leave. To return to his reinvented life, far, far away from the negative influences of small-town life.

After a flight delay and the crowded conditions in economy, Brandon couldn't be happier to arrive in Boston, or as happy as one could be, given his current living situation.

He entered the apartment, wrinkling his nose at the rank odor of garbage. The bedroom was even worse. Dylan's dirty clothing littered the floor, his unmade bed a tangled mess, and dirty dishes and discarded takeout containers formed a grimy layer over top.

Brandon used one foot to shove the piles to his roommate's side before opening the window. The books spread across his bed landed on the floor with a thump as he gave them an unceremonious push.

He eyed the disarray of his covers and groaned. His sheets needed washing. The unsavory thought Dylan had entertained some girl he'd picked up at the bar made him shudder. How the guy even managed to entice a girl home, he'd never understand. Any woman with a modicum of sense would run.

One of his dresser drawers hung open. The guy had stolen clothes. Again. As he closed it, a note tacked to the front of a glossy, medical journal on the top of the dresser caught his eye:

Another present for you, doctor's pet.

Dylan never tired of commenting. Even though Will Kavanagh acted as his supervisor, it only took one mention that he planned to earn chief resident, and he'd received valuable tips plus a stream of extra reading from Aiden and Emily.

After years of medical school, he'd become accustomed to exhaustion, so he tucked the journal under his arm and hauled the sheets and duvet off the mattress. He slogged downstairs and crammed them into washing machines, adding generous doses of detergent and cranking the dial to the hot setting. He glanced at his watch and headed into the street, intent on finding dinner.

The pizza joint a few doors down offered quick and decent fare, so he ordered two slices and opened the medical journal. He'd barely managed three bites before a clatter of plastic against tile made him look up.

A young woman offered him a smile and retrieved a tray from the floor before she continued cleaning the nearby table.

Brandon bit into his second slice of Hawaiian, focusing on the medical terminology, which wasn't easy. The occasional loud clatter, along with the growing feeling of being watched had him sending a covert glance toward the offender.

She looked away, but tipped her chin, a sideways look coming his way as her smile reappeared. After tucking a lock of dark auburn hair behind her ear, she turned to the soda machine. Moments later, she approached his table. "I thought you might need this." She set the drink in front of him with a napkin tucked underneath. "On the house," her voice dropped to a whisper, "but don't tell my boss."

"Thanks." Brandon looked into wide hazel eyes as another smile twitched at her rosebud pink lips. Definitely cute. And flirtatious.

"What are you reading?" Her eyebrows rose. "I'm Naomi."

"Just a medical journal."

"You're a doctor?" Her eyes widened further as she twirled a finger in her hair.

"A resident." He loved the way the title sounded, even if he hadn't officially changed roles at work. Brandon motioned to the drink. "I hope you don't get into trouble."

She shrugged before she hurried behind the counter as another customer arrived.

Brandon ate the last bite and sipped from the drink. A flash of red caught his eye. A name and phone number written in red ink on the napkin, complete with a tiny heart over the i in Naomi.

He glanced toward the counter, but she was busy filling her current order. After setting the cup on top of the napkin to hide the writing, he scooped up his journal and made a speedy exit. He didn't want to hurt the girl's feelings, but his days of collecting phone numbers had come to an end. All he could think about was Savannah.

Share the Love

Thank you for reading. If you enjoyed this book, please consider leaving a review on the retailer where you purchased this ebook, on Goodreads, or recommending The Hamilton Series to your friends and family. Authors depend on word of mouth and reviews to spread the word on their writing, which allows them to continue bringing you new stories to enjoy.

The Hamilton Series

Purchase links for these book may be found at: KateSmithAuthor.ca

Everything we Lost

Everything for Love

Never let you Fall

Everything left Unsaid

Everything we Dream

Everything we Promised

Thank you for reading!

I always love to hear from readers. I can be contacted at http://katesmithauthor.ca

Follow me on social media:

https://www.instagram.com/katesmithauthor/

https://twitter.com/KateSmithAuthor/

https://www.facebook.com/katesmithauthor/